Praise for Sarah Mussi's *The*

THE LAST OF THE
WARRIOR
KINGS

SARAH MUSSI

Hodder
Children's
Books

A division of Hachette Children's Books

*This book is dedicated to the late MP for Tottenham,
Bernie Grant, who campaigned for the return of the
Benin Bronzes.*

CROWN PROSECUTION SERVICE

R

V

MAXIMILLIAN WOLF

INDICTMENT

IN THE CROWN COURT AT INNER LONDON
THE QUEEN – V – MAXIMILLIAN WOLF
MAXIMILLIAN WOLF is charged as follows:

STATEMENT OF OFFENCE
BURGLARY, CONTRARY TO section 9(1)(b) of the
Theft Act 1968.

PARTICULARS OF OFFENCE
MAXIMILLIAN WOLF on the eighteenth day of
February having entered as a trespasser a building,
namely The British Museum at Bloomsbury, London,
stole therein a quantity of priceless items.

Officer of the Court

URN: 09 MM 4536 05

I

Record of Tape-recorded Interview

Person interviewed	**Maximillian Wolf**	POLICE exhibit No: UY/3T
Place of interview	Div. 5 Police Station	Number of pages 1
Date of interview	7th May	
Time commenced	2.59 p.m.	Signature of interviewing
Duration of interview	Tape ref no: T6754398A	officer producing exhibit:
		Julius K Blantyre
Interviewing officer(s)	DC Guillane PC Coode	
Other persons	Ms Cassius (Solicitor)	

Tape Counter Times	Person Speaking	Text

		Introductions. Cautioned, fully explained and understood.
5.09 p.m.	DC GUILLANE	A record is being made of this interview and can be played later. Whatever you say will be transcribed as future evidence. Do you understand that?
	WOLF	Yes. But I'll write it down myself thanks. I don't want your scribe to edit out the important bits.

| | [Statement sheet provided for **WOLF** to write on.] |
| DC GUILLANE | Reads out statement written by **WOLF** reproduced below. |

Statement

My name is Maximillian Wolf, currently of no fixed address. I have listened to the Cautions and understand that anything I say, here, may be used in evidence against me. On January the sixteenth I was with my brother, Angelo Wolf. We were going to a youth club—

	WOLF	Please stop the tape.
5.35 p.m.	DC GUILLANE	This is a police interview. I am not at liberty to stop recording.
	WOLF	Look, what happened is important and I want to tell it my own way. I can't just write it all down like that. Can I have some extra time? Please?
5.45 p.m.		SIR CONRAD BEAUMONT QC, Barrister for the defendant, WOLF, enters the room.
5.55 p.m.	DC GUILLANE	DC GUILLANE is stopping the tape at the request of BEAUMONT. A sworn affidavit will be filed later with the court for the minor, WOLF. This will give him sufficient time to state his case.

Interview adjourned.

Sworn Affidavit

Filed On Behalf of the Defendant.
In the Crown Court Case Number....4536 05.......
BETWEEN:

....MAXIMILLIAN WOLF....... PLAINTIFF

And

.....THE QUEEN......................DEFENDANT

I MAKE OATH and say as follows:

1) I AM the Defendant herein

2) THE written contents annexed hereto are true

3) I THEREFORE ask this Honourable Court
to grant my request for judgement
in the above case to be set aside.

SWORN at Chelsea this day
Before me, A solicitor empowered to administer oaths

Part One

CITIES OF BLOOD

SOUTH LONDON,
WHERE I GREW UP

'. . . as it is with most civilizations, the Edo believe that if the gods
are to intercede to save them from an impending calamity,
then blood must be spilt . . .'
Dr Remi Akowumi, Professor of African Studies, ASASIC

The fact that someone was following us didn't stop
Angelo and me. We didn't care. We didn't care about
much then. You see, we lived in a land where the good
die young and there was no time to lose.

It was early evening. We'd come out of our street
and were taking a short cut round the estate. Nobody
was hanging about, apart from that man. It was cold, so
we stuck our hands in our pockets and kept our hoodies
up. Then we walked the gangsta walk. We thought we
were so untouchable. Behind us, London was shadowy
with snow clouds. Ahead, the horizon was a smudge of
sulphur yellow. You know, when I think back now, there
was something volcanic about it even then, as if
something was waiting to happen.

Darkness was falling. I remember my breath hanging on the air like smoke. If I close my eyes now, I can still see it – as clear as anything. I can remember longing for excitement. And trying to trip Angelo up.

'See what you made me do?' he said (he's my twin – younger by seventeen minutes – but I'm the joker). 'I've walked over three manhole covers and that's bad luck.'

'For you.' I laughed. And leapt to dodge the last one.

The man behind us crossed over, by the old pub. He began catching up. The pub clock read 5.32 p.m. exactly.

'That brother's from the Bang Bang Gang,' said Angelo, almost as if he'd been expecting him. 'That's Mogul "Rapper" King.'

I was surprised. The Bang Bang Gang didn't cross into our neighbourhoods. Well a few did – but they went back in coffins. Mogul King had released the *Sez Me* album, and was the Bang Bang General. He had the kind of stardom every kid south of the river longed for. Actually he'd known our mum. That's Mrs Richenda Everard Wolf. We'd begged Mum to let us meet him, but the nearest we'd ever got was his voice on the answer phone. Mum and him had worked on something, before the accident. I mean the accident that killed my mum.

Six months ago.

'D'you think we should stop and say something?' I said. I half turned and squinted. Out of the corner of my eye, I got a good look. He was in bad shape, really thin, and tired-out looking.

Angelo said, 'Why no limo?'

Mum had told us about his vast mansion and diamond-studded teeth. So he must have had at least ten limos. I was about to say, 'Bruv, we should really stop . . .' when I noticed something.

He wasn't alone.

Behind Mogul King, shapes were slipping through the shadows, staying almost out of sight. They moved together like wolves out hunting. That's when I noticed the street was eerily quiet too. You know, right then I felt scared. There was going to be trouble.

'What's with him?' I hissed, 'Doesn't he know not to come to our ends?' I glanced nervously around, hoping those shapes might just be on their way to pick up a snack at the patty shop or something.

'He's going to get it now,' said Angelo, quickening his step. 'You know some guys drove into his streets and burnt his mansion?'

'Hold up,' I said. 'Which guys?'

Angelo speeded up. 'Let's get the hell out.'

I skipped after him. 'Angelo,' I said, 'is that some kind of posse out behind us?'

Angelo didn't answer.

I turned to look at Mogul again. The famous Mogul King. He raised an arm, as if to catch my attention. There was something desperate in the angle of his shoulder. And I suddenly felt panicky. You know, if it'd been daylight at the Under-Fives Day Care Centre, where my little cousins went – and last year – I might have asked him for his autograph. Not now.

That's when I noticed something swing on his wrist.

Mogul King was wearing multicoloured beads. That was scary. Only gangster Olders wear them. Guys who are involved in BIG DODGY STUFF.

Pretending multicoloured beads didn't worry me, I started stupidly rapping his last hit. It was called 'Rules of Survival' and was, I guess, his story. I broke into a bit of a jog. I realize now, I was trying to prove I wasn't scared. But back then; I thought it was kind of funny, you know, that someone as big as him wasn't following his own advice.

Don't look at gangstas funny cos they don't like this
Friends from the ends should be there in a crisis
Don't tag mark my streets cos you need a licence
Don't feel safe round my place cos I don't like your face

I bounced on and off the kerb as if I was dodging bullets.

Don't get involved in my gangsta business
Cos you know you can't live like this
Got my finger on the trigger and I'm gonna pull it
Rule Number One – is you can't outrun a bullet
What I'll do is no mystery; you'll just be history
I'll send you a wreath so you won't be pissed at me

Rules of survival
Take out your rival
Bang Bang

'Shut up,' said Angelo.

The street light glistened red on the pavements. Suddenly I wished we hadn't taken that shortcut. Again I glanced behind. Those dark shapes weren't looking for patties, you know. Instead one of them was sprinting ahead, trying to cut us off.

Then it dawned on me. They thought we were with Mogul!

Angelo turned, his face drenched in red light. He tugged at my arm and whispered, 'It's bad. Run.'

I was fast, but I was only fourteen. And Angelo couldn't race anyone. He had asthma.

'Go,' said Angelo.

No way. Instead I rushed him on to someone's front walkway. 'Come on,' I hissed. We ducked down between the blocks. We took the stairs. We raced through the estate. Then out on to the main road.

But it was no use. Mogul King followed. And so did the others.

Angelo's chest was sounding like a loose exhaust and I was running out of ideas. So in desperation, I jumped into the street and dodged towards the traffic. I waved my hands, yelling, 'Hey, you! Help!' I was thinking: *Stop the cars. Attract a police patrol. Scare them off.*

Brakes screeched. Lights went on in the windows of a nearby estate tower. Someone's wingmirror clipped my outstretched hand. Agony spiralled into my shoulder. Oh God, I thought, I've broken my wrist. I prayed someone would dial nine-nine-nine. I prayed those hooded brothers behind us would back off. I prayed we were anywhere except where we were, and all the time Angelo was coughing and coughing . . .

And then we *really* ran.

I held my injured hand against my chest. I stayed behind Angelo, ready if he fell. Mogul King ran too. I think he was shouting something. Behind him, the darkness thickened. From the sound of footfalls, I knew the others were sprinting as well. It was like some kind of horrible nightmare. Pools of red light shimmered on the tarmac. Mega doses of adrenalin flooded into my legs. My heart banged. My hand felt like it had burst open. Angelo couldn't take it. His breath came like gravel. I gasped out, 'We can do it, bruv . . .' The lights went off in the tower block. Cars pulled to the side, did three-point turns, and sped off in the opposite direction. I heard the doors to The William Tell pub slam shut. There was nowhere to go, so we ran.

And ran.

MOGUL KING

'When death embraces even a stranger it is a warning to yourself.'
Yoruba wisdom – Nigeria

By some miracle just as we got to the end of the road, a bus stopped at the traffic lights. It was one of the old style, a routemaster, with the open back tail board. I think it was a special to celebrate Martin Luther King Day or something. It had an advert for some car pasted on its side saying: *Welcome to the Ultimate Safety Zone.* I liked the words 'welcome', and 'safety' – you bet I did.

Shoving Angelo with my good hand and screaming at the bus to wait, we just made it on. As it pulled off, Mogul King reached the junction. He skidded round the corner and threw himself on the bus too. In the neon light beyond, I saw the others. More than ten hooded guys – and pretty close.

I pushed Angelo down on a seat. I stood over him, trying to catch my breath. Angelo pulled for his puffer. The bus started forward. 'Maxi,' wheezed Angelo. 'Thanks.'

'You owe me,' I panted.

He smiled.

'I'll take two chocolate bars and a bag of crisps,' I said.

Mogul King was poised on the running board, clinging to the handrail, his multicoloured beads dangling from his wrist. And behind us, following the bus like a pack of bloodhounds, were the other brothers. With a sinking feeling, I realized it was going to take more than a bar of chocolate to sort them out.

The bus chugged on a lot too slowly. And the hooded figures followed. Then the bus stopped.

The figures didn't.

You know, we just ran out of luck. There were two sets of traffic lights ahead. And they were both on red. Mogul King put his head in his hands. Angelo nudged me. 'He needs help, call him over.'

Much later, I realized why Angelo did that. But right then, I wasn't thinking. My hand throbbed, my chest throbbed, my brain throbbed, and anyway Angelo was the smart one, so I did what he wanted. Although I couldn't see how it could help anything. Anyway I nodded at Mogul King. I made the brotherhood fist with my good hand, held it to my chest. *Safe. One love.*

Instantly, I regretted it. You see, Mogul King hurried

over and from inside his jacket he took out a small parcel. He pushed it at me.

Hell, I didn't want to take it.

'Come on. Manz finished,' he said. At the sound of his voice I realized how unnaturally quiet it was. I looked around. Everyone was glancing away, in the direction of something they couldn't name or avoid.

Mogul King pressed it into my hand. And all around that silence was like an avalanche waiting to happen. 'You know what to do with it,' he said, his face grey beneath his dark skin. 'Man tried his best. Don't underestimate them.'

Those next hooded brothers on the street behind us had started catching up. One of them grabbed on to the handrail and was swinging behind the bus. I didn't want him to see me taking stuff off Mogul. And I didn't have a clue what Mogul was on about either. God, anything could be in that packet.

'Promise?' Mogul said. He dug his nails into my bad hand.

'*Promise.*'

I just wanted him to go away, so I said, 'All right.'

'May the blade find a true heart,' he whispered. 'May our enemies be overturned.' Then he took off his beads, his *multicoloured* beads, and let them drop into my hand.

I felt sick.

He hissed, 'You've promised.' Then he turned round – as cool as that – and went back to the running board. He stood there. With that next hoodie brother hanging on to the handrail beside him. You know, it wasn't very funny.

The bus barely picked up speed before it stopped at the second set of lights. Then, without another look at us, Mogul King stepped off the bus.

I hadn't expected that.

I wanted to scream: 'WHAT THE HELL YOU DOIN?' But instead I hunched my shoulders down and tried to look invisible. Then I prayed those next brothers wouldn't get on and drag me off.

The bus shunted forward a little. Mogul King stood perfectly still. The street lamps seemed to light up a halo around him. The gang were only paces away. One of them had something in a long black sock. He raised it. There was a dense *phutt*. Mogul King fell. Right there, just behind the bus. The one with the long black sock stooped over him. He put the end of the sock on Mogul's head. There were two muffled firecracker bangs, then a jerking on the ground. The gunman yanked off Mogul's jacket. He searched it.

There was some confusion, then a howl of rage. One of them pointed at the bus. Some of them darted forward. Some disappeared round the side. I couldn't think of anything. My heart was going so hard, I thought I'd pass out. Then the lights changed. The Martin Luther King Special coughed into gear.

I clutched that package and looked at Angelo. Those next crew were after it, weren't they? For a split second I felt like chucking it at them, hoping they'd go away. But the bus started forward and picked up speed. They dropped behind, grew smaller . . .

I began to shiver. 'It's cold,' I said to nobody in particular. I looked up. Everybody on the bus had their heads down. 'It's cold,' I said again, loudly. There was still no answer, only the tilt of faces down, away, anywhere except at us. It seemed then that the avalanche started to crash around me.

'It'll be OK,' said Angelo, struggling to smile.

But it wouldn't. Mogul King lay limp on the road. The sound of that gun wouldn't go away. And I'd taken that stupid package. Those hooded figures might come after me now. I felt sick. A horrible feeling crawled up my spine. Something had been started – and it was out of my control.

I picked up the beads and fastened them around my wrist. Trying to look cool, I suppose. As I finished hooking the clasp, the bus drew level with the Barricade Housing Estate, where 'The Rules' had been sprayed on the first block, decades ago by ancient Rastas.

I looked through the window at that faded writing.

YOU ARE ENTERING THE ZONE

NO DISRESPECT
NO KNIVES NO GUNS
WE PROTECT AND LOVE OUR NEIGHBOURHOODS
RESPECT OUR WAYS

I felt the weight of that package in my hand. I thought of all the other rules. The ones that the wind and rain had washed off the brickwork:

DON'T GET INVOLVED IN OTHER PEOPLE'S BUSINESS
BE ON GOOD TERMS WITH THE UNIVERSE

and the unwritten ones that nothing could wash away:

ONCE IN THE GRIP OF EVIL THERE IS NO WAY OUT
LEARN TO KILL OR BE KILLED
THE GOOD DIE YOUNG THE BAD LIVE LONG
TRUST NOBODY TRUST NOTHING

Oh yes, I'd entered the zone all right – and it wasn't the Ultimate Safety one. Nothing was ever going to be the same again.

GOING TO A MEETING OF THE B.L.A.C.K. A.R.M.Y.

(Benin Lost Arts, Culture & Kings Association & Reparation Movement for the Youth)

'. . . *we refuse to believe that the bank of justice is bankrupt.*'
Martin Luther King Jr, 28 August 1963

Even now I don't want to remember that bus journey. The way that killing kept flashing up into my brain. The way Angelo and me jumped off the bus between stops. The racing heartbeats. The clumsy attempts to laugh it off. Why was Mogul King in our neighbourhood? Why were those brothers so determined to fix him? Why had he forced himself on us? Why had I got involved? Was he dead, I mean *really* dead, or should I call an ambulance? What if he was still alive?

I did call an ambulance, even though Angelo said it was no use. I couldn't bear to think of him lying there squirming. I didn't give my name though. I just said, 'I'm on a bus and I saw someone get shot.' I gave the location as best I could. And I tried to stay hopeful.

Of course I looked at what he'd given me. I ripped the cover off the package and tore open the taped cardboard. Inside, wrapped in a piece of paper, was a weird dagger. A really old-fashioned one, with a short, dark, buckled blade and an ivory handle. At the end of the handle was a large round shining jewel. Along its hilt was pasted a tatty note, as if it had been shipped to Timbuktu and back again years ago.

Handle with care

Maybe the blade was sharper than it looked. I tested it with my finger. It was so blunt you'd have had problems cutting mashed potato with it. There was no other clue.

What had Mogul King said? Something like: 'You know what to do.' I'd promised to do something, hadn't I? I suddenly felt worried about that. Promises are kind of important and I usually try to wriggle out of them. But now Mogul King was gone, and there was no wriggling out of anything.

Anyway, Angelo and me jumped off the bus as soon as we could. Snowflakes whirled in from every angle. The world was beginning to turn white. 'Let's get lost,' said Angelo as the bus slowed in front of a tapas bar.

'Right,' I said. 'They could be following. The sooner Man gets off and disappears the better, u-get-me?'

But for some reason we still carried on towards the youth centre. I thought that was because of Sapphire. Now I realize it was because of other things too. Things I didn't know about.

We took back streets and left a trail of footprints behind us. That was pretty dumb, even for beginners. But sometimes you can't think of too many things at once. I was having trouble just thinking about that killing. That's funny. I could almost laugh. I thought that killing was bad. That's definitely funny when it was about to get so much worse.

We ran, you know, dodged round corners, rested in doorways, like this was all some kind of mad prank. And all around the snowflakes swirled thick and silent. I swept my hand along a wall and crushed clean white snow into a crisp snowball. I turned and paused, then hurled it behind me, straight at them, whoever they were. It crashed on the street and sprayed the air with a thousand sparking fragments. I can still see it now. That snowy night. That snowball.

I was still a kid then.

THE MARCUS GARVEY YOUTH
& COMMUNITY CENTRE

*'If death has power, then count on me in death . . . I may come in an
earthquake, or a cyclone, or a plague, or a pestilence . . .'*
Marcus Garvey, Atlanta Prison, 10 February 1925

Off the high street, in a cut-through, lay Gervase Street
East and the Marcus Garvey Centre. It's closed now.
The old brick building bulldozed and the street
demolished. They saw to that. Anyway that was where
we were headed. The B.L.A.C.K. A.R.M.Y. met there
every Monday. The meeting would be typical. Our
Community Worker – that's Leon Nicholas Ziggy
Braithwaite Brakespeare, thirty-something with a bald
patch – would have organized a guest speaker who'd be
chatting on about the Campaign. Then there'd be the
fun bit. Maybe. A game of pool or a five-a-side kick
about in the fenced bit at the back. Despite the weather,
I was ever hopeful.

The guest speaker on that fateful night was billed as
coming from the University of Enugu, Nigeria. At least

that's what Leon said. But we all knew he just got his fellow 'comrades' to come. That way, they earned a bit of money.

Leon was an old friend of our mum's. I mean 'had been' before she died. The two of them shared the same obsession. The Campaign. In fact, the stuff she'd done for Mogul King had been arranged through Leon (who was the kind of guy who knew everybody – and let you know it). That's how we'd started going to those dreary meetings. Anyway the lecture that night was called: 'The Curse of the Lost Benin Bronzes and the Task of African Prestige'. Sounds pretty boring if you miss out the curse bit, doesn't it? Believe me, despite Leon's endless attempts to try and cheer it up, The B.L.A.C.K. A.R.M.Y. *was* boring. The whole Campaign was boring. It began and ended with 'return the Benin Bronzes to Benin'. Fascinating, considering the Bronzes had been looted from Africa over a century ago and were still collecting dust in the British Museum. To date, Leon had tried petitions, concerts, lobbying, leaflets, lectures and letters, but none of that had moved those Bronzes a centimetre nearer home.

As we darted through the snow, I was thinking about Leon and his Campaign. I was trying to hang on to something. Anything. And I was checking the streets behind me. Then my phone rang.

'You shouldn't have got involved,' said a clipped voice.

I stopped. My mouth fell open. Had I heard right?

'You shouldn't have helped Mogul King.'

I *had* heard right.

'Mogul King?'

'How much do you know?' said the voice.

'I don't get-u,' I stammered.

'Well *we'll* get you, Maxi, so listen very carefully.'

Horrified, I sucked in air.

'Those who try to stop us, die.' Pause. 'Those who do what we tell them, live.' Pause. 'How hard is that?' Pause. 'So I suggest you do the sensible thing and give us back our dagger.'

'Hang on . . .' I said.

'You have one hour. Someone will meet you very soon. Just be a good little boy and give it back. Then we can forget about the whole thing.'

Forget the whole thing?

'Look,' I said pushing my shoulders back. 'I think you've got the wrong number...'

'No, you look. Look behind you. Look everywhere. Keep on looking, because you can run but you can't hide.'

'Wait—' I started.

'One hour.'

Then the line went dead. I turned to Angelo. I

27

started to sweat, an icy sweat under my T-shirt, my fleece. 'He says we've got his dagger,' I whispered. 'If we don't give it back he'll kill us . . .'

'Ha ha,' said Angelo. 'Nice try, Maxi.'

I looked at him, puzzled. I checked the number: WITHHELD. 'I'm not winding you up . . . He didn't sound like any local brother either . . .'

'Yeah, yeah, sure, sure.' He turned his back on me.

I skipped round in front of him. 'Seriously, Angelo, he sounded kinda mean and posh . . .' Ahead, a builders' ladder rested against a wall. 'He said, Manz got one hour. If you don't believe me, Man'll walk under that ladder and we'll be even. You know with the manhole covers, and—'

'I don't care about stupid ladders,' said Angelo. 'What happened just now was serious. You need to grow up, Maxi.' And with that he walked right ahead – right under the ladder.

'Angelo,' I pleaded, 'it *was* them . . .'

'Look,' he said, 'I'll give you the chocolate, but just drop the whole turning-everything-into-a-joke routine.'

'They knew Manz name. They called me "Maxi" – only you and maybe Leon do that.'

'If you're bothered, give me the dagger and go home,' said Angelo at last, his voice like vinegar.

I looked at him. His hand outstretched. His face set.

He didn't believe me. The red street light flickered across his chin. He looked older somehow, as if he'd left boyhood behind for ever. Then, for just a moment, I felt he did believe me. That he understood everything. That something was terribly wrong. Something I didn't understand. Something he wasn't going to tell me. My jaw dropped. My shoulders sagged. And I stopped trying to convince him.

But I didn't give him the dagger either.

That was a bad move.

The first of many.

But you see, everything that evening was leaning towards disaster. However much I wish it were different. So I decided those gangstas could have their pathetic, blunt, buckled dagger back. They already knew my number. And they'd got me right first time. So they'd get me sooner or later, wouldn't they? I mean, they could tell the difference between Angelo and me. And *nobody* – not even Mum, could really tell . . .

Can people really get your number just like that? And know who you are? I started wondering whether maybe they could . . . whether out there, there was some huge organization . . . who everybody worked for . . . who knew who everybody was . . . where everybody went . . .

SAPPHIRE

'The brightest jewel is the one you cannot have.'
Hausa wisdom - Nigeria

Still, once inside the youth club I relaxed. Sapphire was there. That's Sapphire Issa-Hilcote. Sapphire is very, very beautiful. Thick dark hair. Unbelievable eyelashes. Wide sweet smile. Body like a goddess. She's also very, very serious. Angelo told me she wanted to go to sixth form to study Philosophy, Sociology, Government and Politics, and Psychology. And then to university to study The Universe, I guess. Right then though, she was inclining her lovely cheek towards his lips.

Did I tell you Sapphire preferred Angelo? I know, totally mad. We both looked the same. We both sounded the same. So why Angelo? What was wrong with me? Anyway there we were and Angelo was telling her all about it.

We were standing near the pool table. Leon was making sure he overheard everything. He was doing the: I'm-all-concerned-because-of-your-mum thing. Then there was a newspaper reporter as well. He was doing something on the Benin Bronzes. Of course Leon's little shadow, Denetia Cowan, was there too. I made a few stupid jokes. Angelo carried on describing the bus and the snow in boring detail. He mentioned the beads. He missed out everything about the package, the dagger, the note and the phone call. Sapphire grew paler by the minute. She kept throwing her hands to her face saying, 'Oh God!' and trying to smile at him – all at the same time. She didn't look at me once. Then she sighed and clung to his arm, as if *he* was the one who'd taken all the risks.

'But why was Mogul King in your neighbourhood?' sighed Sapphire.

I saw Leon and Angelo exchange a look. 'The only reason he'd go there was if it was something very, very important,' said Leon. 'Make no mistake, these gangstas live a tough, brutal life. They don't waste time on house calls.'

I showed him my beads. 'Does that mean I'm a tough guy now?' I said.

'Put them away, Maxi,' said Leon. 'Better still, take them off and throw them away.'

Sapphire nodded her head, like Leon was suddenly a rocket scientist.

'Spoken like a true tough guy,' I sneered.

The newspaper guy tittered. I ignored him.

'But why did Mogul King force Maxi to take them?' asked Sapphire, all large soft eyes.

'Nobody forces me to do nothing,' I said.

'Beads are symbolic,' said Leon. 'In most gang groupings, beads show membership and rank according to colour.' He pushed back his locks, rubbed a hand across his bald patch and nodded his head. 'Maxi was ready to help Mogul King, so giving Maxi his beads when he knew he was about to be executed was a sign of great respect, but nevertheless –' Leon turned to me – 'seriously, you should get rid of them.'

'Just like Maxi,' said Angelo, 'rushing in where some of us fear to tread.'

Ha ha. Sometimes, you know, Angelo is a pain. He was doing his super-clever thing. Trying – and succeeding – in impressing Sapphire.

Fools rush in where angels fear to tread.

Angels = Angelo.

What a not-funny joke. Ha stupid ha.

It wouldn't be the first time he's put me down in front of others either. Good old Maxi. Totally impulsive. All action. No brains.

It stung me. I stepped back a little. I looked at him in surprise. After all *he'd* asked me to friend

Mogul King. Hadn't he?

'But does that mean Maxi is now in their gang?' asked Sapphire. She clung more tightly to Angelo's arm – as if suddenly by some weird form of infection she and Angelo might be at risk.

'Hey,' I said, 'Man can look after himself you know.' Sapphire's obvious preference upset me.

'Unfortunately,' interrupted Leon, 'according to gangsta rules, as Maxi has accepted the beads, which were given to him by a chief original gangsta member – indeed a gang general (sadly deceased) – he must take over that position. In short, Maxi is now a gang chief . . .'

That's Leon for you. Thirty-plus, balding, and a know-all. I mean, why use one word when forty-two will do?

'*And* bound to complete any business Mogul left unfinished.' Here Leon shot me a curious look, like he knew maybe there was more to this than a string of beads.

But I thought, OK. Gang General, I can handle that.

'However, Mogul King doesn't really have a gang left to be a general of,' he continued, as if that would be a great relief to poor old stupid me. 'The Bang Bang Gang are all banged up!'

Denetia clapped her fat pink hands at his

devastatingly witty remark. 'Oh Leon!' she said. She flashed her unremarkable eyelashes from her unremarkable eyes at him.

He ignored her.

'Oh,' I said. So no gang. I thought of Mogul King then – alone on that dark street. I thought of the desperate angle of his reaching arm. I thought of Mogul saying: 'Promise?' I thought of that sinister voice on the phone: '. . . *those who try to stop us die . . .*'

I thought of how every kid south of the river would die to have Mogul's fame . . . except they wouldn't, would they? Not when it came to it. And I sent up a prayer: 'Let it be some prank call. Let everything be a huge misunderstanding.'

But, you know, as the evening wore on, and Leon took the whole thing more and more seriously, a gloom descended; and, try as I might to crack a few jokes, I began to feel as if somehow I'd opened up a chasm and fallen right into it.

Maybe Angelo was right. Maybe I was a fool.

Anyway, the lecture started and the Enugu professor went into long details about the reign of the Warrior Kings of Benin. I shrugged off Leon, all his questions and worries. I had worries of my own. I looked at Sapphire. I despaired. I nudged Angelo. I whispered 'boyakasha' in his ear. Denetia came up to me, a bit too close, and said, 'Poor, poor you, Maxi. You must be feeling so upset. I so feel for you.' Then I sat down alone in a corner on a ripped, fake-leather chair and thought about the note: *Handle with care*, and tried to erase everything that had happened.

And failed.

So I got a chicken wrap and a can, and I imagined myself in a movie called *Don't Mess with the Best*. I like to do that. I mean imagine myself into a movie. In this one I had two guns and a fast car and a wikked gold chain, and there was this girl . . . That was until my phone rang – the second time.

It was just as the professor was saying, 'Indeed, what you must not forget is that the British Punitive Expedition in 1897 effectively brought to an end the rule of the Warrior Kings' that the ringtone sounded. My hand trembled. I picked my mobile out of my pocket and walked to the exit. I stood outside in the frozen air and took the call.

'You have half an hour left.'

It was that same clipped voice.

Snow was falling.

'We're sending someone to meet you. Make sure you've got the dagger, outside, alone.'

I said, 'You crazy?'

The person on the other end hung up. I stood there

shivering. That's when the reporter guy came out. He lit up a cigarette. 'Want one?' he said.

First off, I hate guys who offer underage kids cigarettes. Not because of the underage thing, but because it's so fake, like saying, 'Hey, I wanna be your friend – or something.'

'I don't,' I said.

'Right on, dude. Wikked,' he said.

I also hate guys who try to do the Black South London thing, when they are obviously white and from Doncaster.

'Taliesin Jones,' he said, with a thick Welsh accent.

OK, I was wrong. Cardiff.

'Taliesin Jones – like Indiana Jones,' he said.

Oh dear.

'Pretty cool, all that Warrior Kings stuff, innit, dude?' he said.

'If you call blasting a culture of over a thousand years into history and stealing their treasures, not to mention burning their palaces "cool",' I said.

You know I was unhappy about the direction the evening was taking. I was unhappy about those Warrior Kings. I was unhappy about a lot of things, particularly chatting to him.

'Nothing's changed,' he said. 'Pillage and Plunder. One of these days I'm going to write a book on it.'

'Wow,' I said.

He looked annoyed.

Then a slow smile spread across his face. 'So dude,' he said, 'the crew shot your Mogul King – eh?'

I didn't know what to say. Maybe I'm slow. I didn't understand. Which crew?

'The knights of the More Dread Crew got him. Is that it?'

What did he mean – the More Dread Crew? I backed away from him, my legs suddenly off balance. Did he know those brothers? My God, maybe this was the set up. Who was this guy? Maybe he was the one sent to get the dagger! I looked frantically around. I tried not to panic. 'I don't get you,' I said. And I didn't.

He leaned towards me. His smile all dry-lipped and pale. 'Pillage and Plunder,' he said again. 'That's all you need to know.'

All the little hairs down my spine stiffened. Quickly, I turned.

Taliesin took a step towards me. There was something nasty in the angle of his chin. He looked at me. Like he could look right into my mind. Like he knew just what was going on. 'Just a joke, dude,' he said, without any trace of amusement.

THE NINE CEREMONIAL
TREASURES OF ANCIENT BENIN

'The Queen Idia Ivory Chest Mask of Ancient Benin marks the height of artistic and cultural attainment in sub-Saharan civilization. It's elegant and classic visage is the most celebrated face of an African queen after the Egyptian Nefertiti. When the government of Nigeria chose it as the icon for the Second Black Festival of Arts and Culture it became immortalized. The importance of the mask was internationally confirmed when the British Museum, after demanding two million pounds surety, refused to release it on loan to Nigeria, for the festival, despite the government of Nigeria putting the money up.'
Ancient Benin and its Rightful Place in Black History, Issa Musa R.H.

Boy, was I glad to get back inside! The Enugu professor was still delivering his stuff about Benin. He might've been boring, but right then he sounded pretty good to me. He'd got his Powerpoint show going. He was still speaking in that low, slow, clever voice. But you know, you can get to like low, slow and clever.

He said: 'This brings us to the interesting bit of this lecture, the Prophecy of the Last Fetish Priest . . .' I looked at my watch. I wanted to tell Angelo about the second call and about that Taliesin Jones. 'When the British sacked Benin City they stole over a thousand bronze plaques.' So I slunk up next to Sapphire and him, trying not to trip over anyone.

'Each plaque told a story of heroism, and were the only form of recorded history that the Edo had . . .' My watch glowed green. Twenty minutes left. 'Amongst these stolen objects were the nine Ceremonial Treasures . . .' I really hoped Angelo was going to believe me.

The professor flicked the Powerpoint display to show: 'One Queen Mother Chest Mask.'

Click.

'Six bronze plaques.'

Click.

'One ceremonial sword.'

Click.

'One sacrificial dagger.'

Hello . . . Wasn't that my dagger? The professor clicked the screen again. The picture of the dagger disappeared. Random words sped in from the side and lined up to read:

- **These treasures are of huge cultural importance**
- **Without them many ceremonies cannot take place**

I wanted to see that picture again. I wanted to shout out: 'Hey! Hold up. Flick back.' But what kind of idiot would do that? The moment passed; the professor moved on.

More speeding words lined up against more bullet points.

I looked at my watch. Again.

'And now the curse . . . They say that the fetish priest, when he was due to be executed by the British, picked soil from the centre of the Oba's palace compound, pointed to the brass head of Ewuare, the first and the greatest of the Warrior Kings, and cursed the British in his native language saying . . .'

Click.

THE CURSE & THE PROPHECY OF THE LAST FETISH PRIEST OF ANCIENT BENIN

1 Ewuare watches everything, and will have his vengeance yet on you and yours!

2 One will come in the spirit of Ewuare. He will call himself 'The Warrior King', and he will overturn even you!

'Then in front of the six plaques and the bronze head, which embodied the spiritual rulers of the Edo, the fetish priest called on his gods:'

3 May the blade find a true heart!

'He slit himself open from his throat downwards. His blood splashed on to the boots of Sir Ralph Moor and he fell, arm outstretched, the dust of Africa clenched tight in his fist, pointing still at the bronze head of Ewuare . . .'

Hang on. *May the blade find a true heart* . . . I'd heard that somewhere before too – hadn't I? Wasn't that what Mogul had said – or was I really losing it?

Fifteen minutes.

How could Mogul King have anything to do with an Enugu professor? I ought to ask Leon. Show him the dagger. Tell him the full story.

Thirteen minutes.

I watched the second hand creep round. My heart started thumping. Should I tell Leon or give it back?

Twelve minutes.

Was giving it back safe? I started feeling terribly restless. Maybe they would kill me too. I remembered the smirk on Taliesin's face. What should I do? Maybe I shouldn't do anything. Maybe staying here was *not* such a good idea. We needed to get out then. Go.

Ten minutes.

Now.

I caught hold of Angelo's arm. 'Let's move,' I said.

'Got to tell you something weird about the dagger . . .'

He smiled, like he was back to his old self, and seemed about to say something.

'But they say that if you meet the gaze of Ewuare, the Curse will follow you . . .' droned on the professor, trying to keep the audience interested.

I tugged again at Angelo. 'Come on,' I said. My throat was drying up. We had to go. NOW.

'Just want to look at the Warrior King,' said Angelo. He moved forward to the Enugu professor's elbow and gazed down at the photo of the head of Ewuare.

'I see you don't believe in curses,' said the professor to Angelo.

Sapphire slipped her hand into Angelo's and led him back towards me. I heard her murmuring, 'I think Maxi needs you, Angelo. He's looking a bit upset.'

I put on my Really? Am I? look.

Five minutes.

But I wanted to shake Angelo. To shout in his ear: 'You FOOL, hurry up! They're going to kill us!'

'Hey dudes, mind if I interview you?' Taliesin was back!

I pushed open the youth centre door and got out. All that talk of curses and boot splashing and city streets running with blood. And that Taliesin giving me the creeps. And a dagger that might be some kind of ancient treasure. And coincidences that were mad – and scary. And what was I going to do? I wanted to get away. Far away. Somewhere quiet where I could think.

Three minutes.

Angelo and Sapphire sauntered out.

Two minutes.

Taliesin started calling, 'Cool, eh dudes?'

And then my phone rang.

NEW RULES

'May the blade find a true heart.'
Olusegun – Fetish Priest 1897

'So?' hissed the voice.

'Who are you?' I said.

'I ask the questions.'

I didn't know what to say. So I didn't.

A shot rang out. It sang through the cold air and hit the youth centre wall about five paces away from me.

'What the . . . !' shouted Angelo. Sapphire screamed. Taliesin pulled off his lens cap.

'Don't move!' I shrieked. 'Please . . .' I flicked the phone on to loudspeaker.

'A warning,' said the voice.

'But—' I said.

'Walk to the wall on your right. Place the dagger on it.'

I opened my mouth. Closed it again. I found my voice somewhere at the root of my throat. 'Sure. Right.

Hey, forget about the gun. I'm going for the wall.'

Angelo sprang forward, his hand closing on my arm. 'No,' he said, 'Maxi, don't . . . There's something you don't know . . .'

Ho! So now Angelo was ready to talk! Well, he was about one hour too late. 'Look bruv,' I said, 'I'm too young to die. I'm going to put this blade right there on that nice, friendly, likkle wall.'

Angelo tightened his grip. 'You don't understand, Maxi . . .'

'Yes, I do, bruv,' I said. '*Nothing* is worth dying for.'

Angelo tried to pull me back.

The voice hissed, 'If you don't put the dagger on the wall, you will get the same treatment as Mogul King.'

'You can't give it to them,' said Angelo. 'Maxi – don't!'

But I wasn't in the mood for taking any more orders from him, so I said, 'Yes, I can.' I pushed him aside. 'Try watching this!' I turned and said into my phone, 'I'm doing what you ask – right now, bruv.'

'Which brings us back to Mogul King . . .' came the voice

You know, I wasn't so keen on the way he kept banging on about Mogul King.

The voice on the phone laughed. 'But it doesn't bring Mogul King back to us – does it?'

'Hey—' I began. He cut me short.

'Joke's over. Put it on the wall. You have ten seconds.'

Angelo was reaching out to stop me.

I hesitated . . . Maybe there *was* something I didn't know. I saw Angelo's face. Deadly serious.

Another shot rang out centimetres from Sapphire. She froze. Angelo froze. Taliesin froze.

I looked wildly around, trying to see anyone with a gun.

The youth centre door burst open and somebody started screaming.

'Put it on the wall NOW or I'll shoot the girl.'

Sapphire caught her breath.

Her face was so pale.

What should I do? What did Angelo mean?

I had to do something.

Anything.

I leapt for the wall. I put the dagger down.

'Good,' said the voice.

Down the phone there was a muffled noise. A click, then a pause. I looked around hysterically. He must be here? He must be one of those people in the meeting . . . How else could he collect the dagger? He must have been at the lecture. I stared at Taliesin. My stomach pitched into my throat. I tasted vomit. He must have been listening, watching all the time . . .

Flakes of snow settled on my face.

What was he going to do?

I looked at Sapphire, too scared to tell her to run.

Then the phone crackled. 'So, Warrior King of The B.L.A.C.K. A.R.M.Y. Now you can back away.' There was a faint snort of laughter. The voice was heavy with sarcasm. 'You are free to go. Oh – but there's one more thing. *Never underestimate us.*'

That pause. That snort. That faint click.

Angelo was faster than me. He leapt and pushed me sideways. He grabbed the dagger back. I staggered and fell.

He stood in front of me. Blocking everything.

Another shot rang out.

There was no terrible scream. Just a curious dull thump. In slow motion I rolled. Angelo was lying on the snow. He looked small and crumpled.

I got up.

The phone went dead.

I looked at that dagger, clutched in his hand.

Beneath Angelo the snow turned dark. I tried to rip open his jacket. I tried to stop the bleeding. Taliesin was taking photos. People were streaming out of the centre. Someone was yelling, 'Yeah, a shooting. Think it's a drive-by. One boy's down . . .'

'Angelo,' I was saying. 'Angelo.'

'Think it's a gangland thing . . .'

Angelo seemed to smile. A horrible stretched grimace. He loosened his grip on the dagger. He seemed to push it at me, but it might have been a convulsion. I took it for the second time that evening and promised again. 'I won't give it to them, I promise . . . I . . .' I held on to that dagger then, as if I was holding Angelo's life tight in my grip.

There was the sound of shouting, of screaming, of commands, of car horns. Then the sound of a police siren far away.

Leon was there, pulling me up.

Angelo couldn't be dead. I saw the ambulance arrive. They would save him. Leon grabbed me, twisted my face until I was looking square at him. 'Go,' he said. 'Go now. Go far. Go fast. Take Sapphire. I'll do what I can for Angelo. They'll kill us all if you stay here! Just go . . . and . . . God – this is all my fault. I'm so sorry.'

Terrified, I grabbed Sapphire's wrist. She was shrieking and fighting. I dragged her back from Angelo's body, down the cut-through. I dragged her right to the end of Gervase Street East. 'Let's go,' I said, like some kind of robot. 'They know who we are. We can't get involved. Talk to no one. Tell the police nothing.'

She trembled. She pulled at my arm, her beautiful face shrunken and wild. 'You,' she shrieked, 'you did this.' She hit out at me with clenched fists.

I shook her. I grabbed her hands. I held them tight. 'Look I'm taking you home,' I said.

'And you?' Her mouth sliced out the words.

'I don't know,' I whispered. 'I just don't know.'

GRAVESEND

'The ceremonial sword of Ancient Benin in its coral bead scabbard still waits in the Pitt Rivers Museum for the spirit of Eruware to return and claim it.'
'Legends & Beliefs in Ancestor Worship' from *Essays on Western African Primitive Faith Systems*, Naa Salla

Sapphire wrenched herself free and ran off. I ran after her into a wall of whirling white. I didn't know what else to do. The snow span behind her and settled. The street became empty.

I stopped. What should I do? I tried her mobile. Nothing.

I couldn't think about Angelo, but I couldn't stop thinking about him. I tried his mobile too, willing him to answer. It went to voice mail.

I wanted to go back, to see him sitting up with the ambulance crew sorting him out. But I was terrified. I was so terrified my mind couldn't hold on to anything. I crept on to a stone step and crouched up in an alcove, by a doorway. I didn't feel the cold; I didn't hear the ambulance, the police sirens, the loud speakers hailing the streets, the overhead helicopters. I suppose I must have heard them to list them here. But I don't remember it. My brain had stopped working.

Perhaps I stayed there many hours. It didn't matter. Perhaps it was only half an hour. I can't remember. Time stopped behaving in the way it used to. I just sat there, staring at the snow coating the step, and shivering. My skin was icy, but I was sweating. Even the shivering seemed to belong to someone else.

Maybe something in me wanted to survive. If not, I might have frozen to death. Looking back now, that might have been better. Anyway, suddenly I found myself standing up and walking down the street. I didn't know where I was going.

I was thinking: Is Sapphire safe? I should take care of her. I tried her mobile again. Nobody answered. I was thinking: Is Angelo safe too? In hospital? I should try to find him. But every time I headed back towards the centre, it seemed that Leon's shadow grew dark across the road and shouted terrible warnings at me.

So I wandered around not knowing what to do. Once I thought I saw grey figures – and then I ran and dodged and hid. I sat down on the kerb and a tiredness spread into my legs. And then I seemed to hear another voice, Mr Gordon Macnab, my

Geography teacher, saying, 'One of the dangers of hypothermia is the need to fall asleep. It must be fought at all costs. Walking is the obvious solution . . .' I don't know why I remembered that. I can't imagine that I'd ever had a lesson on hypothermia. But even now if I close my eyes, I can still hear his voice encouraging me to keep walking.

So I did. That night, it seemed to me I could walk anywhere. That is, except to the homes of people I loved. People that the More Dread Crew might get to. So I turned away from town and started dodging and hiding and walking out towards Kent. I got to one place and turned back when I saw a sign saying: *Gravesend.*

It was the words 'grave' and 'end' and suddenly I was sitting on a kerb shivering again. I'd never been parted from Angelo. Not like this.

But Mr Gordon Macnab wouldn't let me stay there. It seemed that he yelled in my ears and shook my shoulders. He told me to get up and start thinking straight and find some shelter.

I found a car that someone hadn't locked. I got inside, out of the freezing wind. There was a rug on the back seat and a thick jacket. There was a tin of travel sweets in the front pocket. I put on the jacket. I wrapped the rug around me. I sucked the sweets. I lay down, out of sight. I kept thinking about Angelo and seeing his face and his hand on the dagger. And that strange scary smile. Not like his real smile at all. I wish you could've seen Angelo really smiling. You'd have liked him. Everybody liked Angelo. He was so smart. He was the kind of person who'd go the extra mile to help you out, and you'd end up feeling so great about it. And he could make you laugh. Not like me, I make people laugh cos I *am* the joke. He'd be just clever and funny, and God, you'd laugh. I know you'd have liked Angelo. Everybody did.

Anyway, Mr Gordon Macnab would have been very disappointed to find out that I did fall asleep. Luckily I didn't die. The rug was a heavy fleecy thing. I woke to find myself twisted inside it. When I opened my eyes – before realization flooded in – I wondered where I was.

Dawn came. The Thames looked cold and greasy. The road was dark with ice, the cars and rooftops white. I sat and waited, checking the street in every direction. I wasn't feeling too good. I kept thinking that something was missing and then I'd think about Angelo. And you know, I could hear his voice and I could see his face all creased up and laughing. And I'd smile and then that something that was missing made me double up on that back seat. And then I couldn't see anything except that grin stretched across his face as he clutched that dagger, and I hit out at that back window and for some stupid reason I tried to smash it.

Anyway, I got out of the car. I threw the jacket and rug back in. I crossed over the street. I hid behind a bus stop. Both my hands were messed up now. I couldn't think of anything to do, so I started dodging back towards London.

I tried to figure it out. But how can you figure out something like that? My thinking was all random. Here's how it went. *Angelo was trying to save me. Mogul King. Who are the More Dread Crew? How did they get my number? Who's that creep Taliesin? The Nine Treasures of the Warrior Kings. Why did they call me Warrior King? Why was it Leon's fault? What was that Denetia person about? Why did Angelo care so much about the dagger? How did they know about the youth centre? What did the Enugu professor have to do with it all? And then Angelo. I must reach him. None of this is true.*

It was all my fault. If I'd done as he said, he'd be here now. Walking right beside me. Joking and jumping manhole covers.

Where was I going? Not home. I couldn't go back to my auntie's place. That's Ms Ella Everard. She had four small children. She'd been taking care of us since Mum died. And she was kind of all right, but totally stressed out all the time. You see, Mum had been her big sister, her rock. Angelo and I couldn't match that. She wouldn't be able to cope with this. We just ate too much and were a poor example for our cousins. Yeah – our cousins, all under ten, all plump and cheeky and ripe for a More Dread bullet.

No, I couldn't go there.

With some amazement I realized I was hungry. I didn't think that people in the state I was in could feel hungry. I wanted a packet of prawn cocktail crisps and orange juice. So I found a newsagent's that was open. The billboard outside read: *TWO DIE IN GANGLAND HIT*.

I went inside and looked at the front page. And my hunger disappeared. I didn't stop to buy the crisps. I just turned and left. Beads of sweat bust out on my face. You see, on the front of that newspaper was a huge photograph of Sapphire and me. And I remembered what Leon had said: '*Go now. Go far. Go fast. Take Sapphire. They'll kill us all* . . .' The photo was so large and clear and so us. That slimy Taliesin Jones must have taken it. They could easily find out Sapphire's name and address now . . .

And they'd threatened to kill her.

I tried to relax. I told myself: Angelo may be alive, but he may be dead. Sapphire is alive. Definitely. You must get to her. You must warn her. Don't mess around with this gang. Tell her there's been a news report. She's on the front page. Tell her she'll be a target. Explain that the police will want her as a witness. Explain no witness protection scheme ever invented can save her. *You* must save her. That's what Angelo would want you to do.

So I started running. Slippery pavements. Thick slush. Pounding feet. I tried to push myself faster. God, why had I wasted so much time? Why had I let her disappear? I should have stuck to her like superglue. I'd been told what to do. I'd been told not to underestimate them. Those were very clear instructions.

I'd messed up.

And as I ran, I tried to come to terms with *everything* on that front page. You see – not only was there a huge photograph of Sapphire and me, but behind us, in the same picture, there was a shape on the road. It was blurred out in digital squares. Underneath it read a caption: *Second victim of the terrible gangland killings.*

RULE NO 1

Don't get involved in my gangsta business
Cos you know you can't live like this
Got my finger on the trigger and I'm gonna pull it
Rule Number One is – you can't outrun a bullet . . .
Mogul King – R.I.P.

As I ran, I prayed that the More Dread Crew slept late. I pulled out my mobile and punched Sapphire's number. No answer. I punched it again. Still no answer.

I caught the bus. I changed at the Green and caught another bus. I tried her mobile again and again and again. And there was still no answer. She must have got home OK. I left a voice mail. Maybe she didn't want to speak to me. Like a scene from some horror film, I raced from the bus stop to her street and hammered on her door.

Sapphire's mum appeared, sleepy-eyed in her pyjamas.

'Sapphire,' I blurted out.

'You better come in,' she said.

She led me into the kitchen at the back. It was warm and smelt of geraniums and last night's supper. It had funny Mexican wall tiles. I sank down on a seat. 'Sapphire?'

'She's OK, though no thanks to you,' said Sapphire's mum. 'She's very upset. I had to give her one of my pills.'

'I've got to see her,' I said.

'You've got to call the police,' said Sapphire's mum.

I thought about it. Should I call the police? Would they protect us? Would they get here in time? I thought of that voice and that click and that pause and I thought of that horrible stretched smile on Angelo's face. If I'd called the police yesterday, when I'd got the first threatening call, would they have stopped that?

Maybe I *should* call the police . . .

But Leon had said: '*Go now. Go far. Go fast. Take Sapphire . . .*'

'No,' I said. 'This is what I've got to do . . .'

My voice trailed away, but my decision didn't. I was going to do what Leon told me. We could try the police thing after, if I ran out of ideas, but we'd do it my way first. When it comes to your own skin, you know, it's safer in your own hands.

So I didn't tell her about the dagger, but I did tell her about the More Dread Crew and what Leon said. I tried to tell her about Angelo, but she shushed me. I couldn't bear to try again. She fixed me a bacon sandwich. I couldn't eat it.

She did not like my plan.

'You can't take Sapphire away,' she said. 'Where will you go? How will you live? It's ridiculous. I won't allow it.' She said a lot more too, which sounded like she thought *I* was the real problem. I could see she didn't understand. She thought that Sapphire should stay with her and continue going to school. As if all this hadn't happened. As if the police were still the only answer and that it would all blow over . . .

It was just as she was saying, 'Really, Maximillian, you talk as if there's another world out there that I know nothing about. As if some hoodlum gang is going to scare me into allowing my daughter to . . .' when my mobile rang.

I saw WITHHELD flash on the screen. I put it on loudspeaker. 'Listen to this please, Mrs Hilcote,' I said.

'Warrior King,' said the voice. 'We're not happy. We still haven't got our dagger back. We've seen the papers and we'll pay your girlfriend a visit. And then we will find you.' Then the phone went dead.

I put it very bluntly to her. 'If you want to identify Sapphire's body today, you just pick up your phone an' dial nine-nine-nine.'

You see, she hadn't thought it through. Like what were the police going to do? Were they going to take us to some safe house? Or give us twenty-four-hour protection? Or were they going to wait until we were some **bold** CAPS on an incident board before they took action? After all, Mum would say, 'The police can only solve a crime *after* it's been committed.'

And that was not going to be a whole lot of help to Sapphire and me.

I tried to explain better. I went over everything again and this time I told her the whole lot: the newspaper, the photo, Mogul King and the dagger. She got the point then.

I said, 'We've got to go. Somewhere they can't get us.'

At length, she seemed to get afraid. She started to panic. 'I'll sell up. We'll move away. She can go to my mother's in Yorkshire . . .'

'It's no use,' I said. 'It'll take too long. Your way of solving this right now just won't work, believe me. You have to trust me, at least till you've got a better plan.' I suppose it was kind of funny asking a nice middle-class mother to trust a kid not yet fifteen who was already mixed up in two murders and a gangsta mess. Maybe if Sapphire hadn't woken up and come downstairs, rubbing her cute dark eyes, she might never have given up her belief that the police could protect us.

'Mummy,' said Sapphire, 'I know since last night you've wanted me to call the police, but Maxi is right, these people are above the law; they probably have policemen in their crew anyway.'

I hadn't even thought of that point, and it scared the pants off me.

Her mother just sat there terrified. 'I don't believe it,' she said.

'But can you take the risk?' I squealed.

'Leon says it's a huge, organized, criminal world – Mummy, you can't fight them. I love you, but staying here is like being a sitting target. I've got a better chance if I go with Maxi straightaway.' She swung me a look which quite clearly said: *Don't get any clever ideas. I still blame you.*

'But what about school?' gasped her mother, almost as a last resort. 'Your exams . . . ?'

Sapphire bit her lip. 'I've got to stay alive to do that.'

We left by the back door. Mrs Hilcote's head was collapsed on the table. She didn't know what to say any more. I was in a hurry, but as I left, I turned and said, 'I'll do my best to look after Sapphire, I promise. Please phone my auntie and try to explain. Tell her never to try and contact me. Never. Ever. If the More Dread Crew believes she doesn't care, they won't use her kids. If they think she does, then she better emigrate to New

Zealand – yesterday – or get ready to bury everyone. That's not a joke, Mrs Hilcote. It's not even remotely funny.'

And so there I was; pledged to take care of Sapphire; promised to do something I didn't understand, running for my life and with no place to go.

ROLAND ARUNDEL PIGGOT BLUNTSTONE

'You know your true friend when you are in trouble.'
West African saying

No sooner had I turned out of Sapphire's road than I remembered Roland.

Let me fill you in. Rols was a posh kid from a posh home in a posh area of town. The one thing that stood in the way of Roland becoming a posh lord for somewhere or other in his posh future was *me*. He hero-worshipped me. Actually he idolized black kids. He kept a forbidden hoodie in his wardrobe and listened to forbidden hip-hop. I expect you've guessed his parents weren't so keen.

Unfortunately (like one night when I was round at his) he sometimes said forbidden things to his mother, Lady Bluntstone, in a strange manner, waving his arms up and down with his palms turned in. Like: 'Me an me nigga, Maxi, gonna get down with the crewz.'

Lady Bluntstone was horrified. She said she thought that 'crews' were those nice sailors on the *QEII* – which in its own way was a 'cruise' too. Haw haw, very punny! (Her joke.)

I stood there blank-faced.

She had only a vague understanding of 'getting down' with them. Still, she did understand the word 'nigger', which she considered was an 'outdated and offensive term for African peoples'. (Huge horsey smile at me.) And 'how on earth' had Roland not realized it was absolutely 'not acceptable'? But what 'worried' her most, 'terribly' – in fact 'APALLED!' her – was his frightful use of grammar!

Roland, I guess, was born into the wrong family and was living to regret it. But right then he was my answer. Now, as far as I knew, nobody was aware of my friendship with Roland. We'd met when Mum was doing her research in the House of Lords, and whether they opposed the Return the Benin Bronzes to Benin Campaign. We'd all gone to Roland's to interview his dad. Lady Bluntstone had given us tea with mini pork pies, boiled beetroot and homemade Madeira cake.

It was a weird friendship, anyway. Not something that I was likely to admit to. I remember how Angelo used to bait me about it. He'd do a really brilliant imitation of Roland's voice and have you creased up.

God, Angelo was funny. You'd really have enjoyed the way he could mimic people. I remember once him doing a take-off of this teacher who came from Australia. He was so funny. I think he might have been a bit jealous of me and Roland actually. Angelo liked to be everyone's main man.

Anyway, as soon as it occurred to me, that this might be just the sort of situation that Roland would love to get 'down with', I yanked Sapphire into a minicab shop front. I watched the street until I was really sure we were safe. Then we took a cab.

On the way there I kept a check. I told the driver to pull over on some excuse. A few cars and two buses passed. One old woman with a hairy dog. A solitary biker in the distance. Nothing suspicious. I thought we'd probably got clean away. So as we drew out of Sapphire's area, I allowed myself a huge sigh of relief.

I should have known better, of course. I'd been told not to underestimate them. But I was still thinking in terms of gangs and neighbourhoods. Local stuff. I was about to find out just how big the More Dread Crew were.

And much sooner than I wanted.

That morning was beautiful in a terrible way. I remember everything about it was sharp like a knife edge. Sunlight shafted across the street, flashed off windows. Cars slashed by. Sapphire and I sat in silence in the mini cab. We didn't look at each other. I clutched my throbbing hands inside my jacket. Sapphire clutched her little pullie. She had fifty quid her mum had given her. I had one pound seventy.

But we were in luck. Not only was Roland in, even his housekeeper, ferocious Mrs Peel, was out. Roland opened the door. 'Yo bruv,' I said, giving him the brotherhood fist. 'Manz in a tight spot. Need a little love still. U-get-me?'

'Absolutely,' said Roland. His face lit up like Bonfire Night. 'You just come right on in, Maximillian. My yard is your yard.'

'Right,' I said, and leaving Rols to settle the cab fee, I shoved Sapphire inside. I scanned the street. Then I made Roland lock the heavy oak door tight behind us.

Once inside, Roland led us through the wide hall, past the staring stags' heads. He showed Sapphire the ground floor with its fine reception rooms. Then we went up past the portraits of his great-grandfathers that stretched in procession up the stairs, past the first floor, right up to Roland's pad, which was the classiest place imaginable for a hideout. Yep, that morning we were in luck: Lord Bluntstone was out of the country, and Lady Bluntstone in the country (where she preferred their

66

'darling' seventeenth-century manor house).

Roland pushed open the double doors to his suite.
But before I flopped down on the wine-red sofas, I
moved to the bay window and checked the street. A
couple at the bus stop. A biker examining his tyres.
Looked OK. I turned to Roland. 'Manz a brother –
right?' I said. 'We don't want to bring you no beef, but
we've got a situation here. We need to spend some time
on your comfy futons.'

You could see that Roland thought Christmas had
come early. He got up, poured us juice, fetched his pen
and paper and glasses. 'So what exactly is the "beef"?'

Somehow in those pleasant suburbs of South
London it all seemed unbelievable. So when I started to
tell him what had happened, I just couldn't. So I started
saying how Angelo was such a great guy and made
me laugh and about how after Mum's death he'd sort
of looked out for me and how people like Angelo were
rare and . . . then Sapphire started crying. I hadn't
meant to upset her, and I said, 'Sorry.' But then she
couldn't stop sobbing.

I thought it might have somehow helped, I mean, to
remember the great things about him . . . because I
couldn't bear to remember him with his hand all tight
on that dagger, and that smile that was like his face was
shrinking back from his skull. And we *shouldn't*

remember him like that . . . and I'd been trying to tell Roland how it had happened. About Mogul King. About the dagger and the phone calls. And the gang. And the shootings. But I thought I should really tell him about Angelo first, because it was just so hard to tell about it. And then I went out into the kitchen and smashed something.

When I came back, Roland had gone pale and Sapphire was shuddering in huge shudders that shook her from her shoulders to everywhere.

And then there was silence.

At last Roland blinked several times. 'I'm . . . well . . . Maxi . . . clearly, I'm . . . dreadfully sorry . . .' He poured even more orange juice into an already overflowing glass. He held it out to me. His hand shook a little. The juice spilt on to the table and trickled over its edge. '. . . and you say they are called the More Dread Crew,' Roland said. The glass of orange juice wobbled.

I looked hard at him. Willing him not to start it again. I needed him to be strong and upper class and objective. My chest felt tight. I thought my skin might pop like shirt buttons. If he started it again, I didn't think even breaking things would help, and then everything would be so out of control. I clenched my teeth. I took the orange juice. I tightened my throat. My mouth was dry. I couldn't swallow. My phone rang. It was Denetia Cowan. 'Just calling because I know Leon will want to know you're safe. You are safe, aren't you?'

I put the phone down.

'I do so feel for you . . .'

Roland picked up my phone and got rid of her.

Later. Much, much later. Roland said, 'The More Dread Crew?'

You see, gangs were Roland's passion. He researched them and belonged to all the gangbangers' chat rooms on the web possible. In fact he knew more about gangs than gangs themselves. I guess his lifelong ambition was to belong to one.

'Yes. The More Dread Crew.'

'Very interesting,' he smiled a bright attempt at me, 'because in all my research on gangs, I have never heard of the More Dread Crew. Clearly, that's odd, isn't it?'

Odd? Never heard of them?

'Listen, bruv,' I said, 'they're out there all right. Look at this.' I placed the dagger still wrapped in its paper on the low marble table.

Roland let out a whistle.

A bit confused, I went to the window. I mean, I'd somehow expected Rols to know all about them. I suppose I'd hoped he might be able to figure out something. Anything really – but mostly why had Mogul King been carrying the dagger and why would a gang want it? And more than mostly – would they ever give up or would they still try and get me?

Anyway the couple had long gone. But the biker was still there. I gazed at the pavements, the parking bays, the trimmed hedges, the leafless trees. The More Dread Crew must be out there somewhere, whether Roland had heard of them or not.

'Maybe you're not up with the latest crews,' I said.

If Roland heard me he chose not to. Instead he bent his head over the dagger. 'You know, of course, all about sacrificial poniards?'

Of course I did. Not.

You see, I forgot to mention, Rols goes to a public school. A posh one for total boffins. One of those ones with endless cricket fields – and obviously endless lectures on poniards. Roland is a total boffin. (He's probably the biggest one outside Cambridge.)

'Sacrificial poniards and daggers like this,' he said, 'were clearly used (it is believed) in human sacrifice . . .'

'Oh,' I said.

'The Edo, the people of Benin, the original owners of the Bronzes your mother was so passionate about, were widely believed to be involved in human sacrifice, which was clearly one of the excuses used by the British in 1897 to justify the attack on the city . . .'

My days! Where did he get all that from?

Roland crossed his legs and pressed his fingertips together. 'Some claim that they were not sacrifices at all though, but just the public execution of violent criminals. Clearly that would put the Punitive Expedition in a very different light, wouldn't it?' he continued.

'Would it?' I tried to imagine what exactly a punitive expedition was in any kind of light. I also started vaguely wondering why I hadn't heard the sound of that biker firing up his engine yet.

'Clearly, it would be hypocritical! After all, we publicly executed criminals during the nineteenth century!'

'We did?' I said.

'Indeed!' said Roland. 'The practice of beheading and quartering executed traitors was only stopped in 1870. And the last public execution was that of Joseph Philip Le Brun, killed in Jersey on the eleventh of August 1875!'

I looked at him and blinked.

'Anyway, you'll want to know the background. The great palace of the Oba of Benin in the sixteenth and seventeenth centuries was as large as a European town. It had many courts surrounded by galleried buildings,

71

their pillars encased in bronze plaques. Roofs were shingled, and there were numerous high towers topped with bronze birds. Benin City was full of lawns and spice trees and ivory and wonderful carvings – and was entirely burnt by the British. So clearly, why they did that is crucial, isn't it?'

'How awful,' said Sapphire. 'I thought there was nothing but jungle and a few huts in Africa before the British got there . . . I mean . . .' Her voiced trailed away.

Ho! So there were some gaps in Sapphire's education! Even *moi*, the despair of every secondary school in South London, knew that huge civilizations had lived in Africa for centuries. I thought about letting her know that too, but now something had started worrying me.

Why hadn't I heard that bike?

'Anyway, in 1897 Sir Ralph Moor manipulated a subordinate of his, a Lieutenant Phillips, to take a small band of men through the jungle into Edo territory. He didn't actually tell Phillips that the Edo had a ban on all visitors during a particular festival – in fact that it was a capital offence. Clearly, he set them up – probably trying to provoke a situation, I'd say,' said Roland beaming at us.

You could see he was getting into his top-of-the-class mode. I could just imagine his pleased pink face as he handed in (clearly, ahead of time) his A* history essay for Mr Pemberton-Pickles on: 'The Causes of the Punitive Expedition of 1897'. I mean what was 'manipulated' and 'subordinate' and a 'capital offence' supposed to mean?

Anyway, I tried to wave my fingers at him to slow him down. How long does it take to check two tyres? Hang on a minute. Can you check tyres if you aren't at a garage near an air pump?

'So of course, the Phillips expedition was ambushed and almost all of them were killed,' Roland continued quite cheerfully. 'It went down in history as "The Phillips Massacre".'

Suddenly I wasn't feeling comfortable. We were back to blood and killings again, and I could feel that hot sticky feeling on my hands as I'd tried to lift Angelo . . . and the smell of blood like salt and metal on my fingers . . . So I got up and walked to the window. The biker was still there. Still checking his tyres.

'That was exactly the excuse that Sir Ralph Moor needed to persuade the Foreign Office to invade the city of Benin and crush the Warrior Kings.'

'That's disgusting,' said Sapphire.

'Just keep away from the windows,' I said, 'and don't answer the door.'

Roland shot me a puzzled look. Sapphire jumped up.

'Merely a precaution,' I shot out. Then I changed the subject. 'The Foreign Office?' I said.

'What's this?' asked Sapphire, stroking the large stone set at the top of the dagger's hilt.

'A diamond, of course,' said Rols 'As I said, the Edo were famed for their riches: gold, diamonds, ivory and bronze castings. Some claim that was the *real* reason for the Punitive Expedition, to seize the treasures of Benin and gain control over Southern Nigeria and all its riches in rubber and hard wood, before other European powers like Germany got there first . . .'

'Yo, it's *ice*, Sapph,' I said, like I'd known all along.

Sapphire picked up the dagger. 'A real diamond,' she breathed, 'I was named after diamonds.'

I checked the window *again*. The biker was now fiddling with his tax disc. So I turned. Life is short. I smiled at her. 'Have it,' I said, 'I don't know if it's worth much, but it cost Mogul King his life, and Angelo . . . I mean . . . I think Angelo would like you to have it too. You can be its keeper. Make sure I don't give it . . . well, make sure they don't get it. Anyway, it's yours – whatever,' I finished lamely.

I really did think Angelo would have liked it. And I wasn't very good at keeping promises anyway. Sapphire would be much better. And I'd always wanted to be the kind of brother who could give a girl he loves ice. I figured giving Sapphire the sacrificial knife (plus supersized diamond) of the Ancient Benin Warrior Kings, might be the first rung in my career in diamond-giving.

For a moment she looked at me as if I was someone else. Then she frowned.

'Anyway,' she breathed, 'diamonds *are* a girl's best friend.' She turned the dagger with its monster stone over in her hand and stroked it. 'I'll take care of it. I know it's really valuable. I can tell.' Then she turned her back on me as if she could also really tell that I wasn't.

'Actually, if you're interested in how the European powers carved up Africa, there's a terrifically exciting text on it called: *Colonial History and the Rise of Empire*. It's in three volumes and . . .' Roland beamed at us, bright eyed.

Actually I was interested in why a strange biker seemed to be watching what should have been a safe place. Why a mysterious gang killed, but didn't exist. How somebody had got my phone number and . . .

Roland nodded, a sort of apologetic nod as if he was saying, 'Sorry I'm such a know-all. Clearly it's not really cool to be a know-all, is it? Forgive?'

At that very moment the biker fired his engine. The sound blasted the calm of Roland's fourth floor like a bomb going off. I spun back to the window. There he was, astride his huge BMW, in the middle of the street, right outside our front door. He looked up at me. I froze, caught in the gaze through his darkened visor.

Over his leathers he had on a grey hoodie. I was too shocked to move. He raised his gloved hand. Clenched it into a huge fist. You see, that hoodie was the same one like those brothers yesterday had had on. He shook his fist and wrenched his bike round. Then he opened the throttle and the giant bike roared like a herd of tigers. Two herds actually. I heard that bike roaring all the way to the South Circular. And then some. There could be no doubt now about the existence of the More Dread Crew, or what all that fist waving meant.

He knew I was here and he was going for back up.

ENTER HUGH HARDY

THE SACKING OF BENIN

'The Edo used long-barrelled, muzzle-loading, Dane guns and some breech-loading rifles. Muzzle-loading guns had to be hauled in for loading. This made them difficult to use. They were also very wasteful. The shot left the muzzle before the full power of the powder explosion had been used up. Both types of guns were only accurate at close range. All the rest of the Edo warriors used bows and arrows.

The British used British Maxims: the world's first automatic portable machine-guns, which could fire five hundred rounds per minute. The fire they delivered could penetrate thick foliage and be effective at long range. They also used three seven-pound Howitzer light cannons.'

Small British Victorian Wars and Military Expeditions

For a while I was jittery. What the hell was this all about? I made Roland check the front door, the back door, the side door, the conservatory door, the French windows, the double garage doors, the fire escape doors, the balconies, the smoke alarms and all the windows. When we were alone on the fifth floor, I told him my worst fears. He took it pretty well.

'Please don't worry about it,' he said. 'You're my

guests and I – well – clearly, I can take care of it.'

I looked at him, wondering how he could take care of anything.

'My father has a security insurance and when I'm here alone, I've got the authority to call them out on twenty-four hour duty,' he said apologetically. 'They'll send security guards and I know it's horrid having to have them around, but I think, with your permission, it might be a good idea?'

Well, I was impressed. 'Call them up,' I said. 'Your dad thinks of everything, doesn't he?' Secretly I was glad. I didn't know what that biker had in mind. And I didn't want to find out either.

'It's only if I get scared, really,' Roland said, 'the guards, I mean, and because Mummy and Daddy are away so often.'

After Roland had called them out: two at the front, two at the back and Arnold inside; he warned them that this time he was scared of guns.

He told them he'd watched a really scary movie and couldn't get gangs and armed robbery out of his head. He even did a really neat trembling routine. To give the guards credit, they only rolled their eyes once and made him phone his dad to OK it. Lord Bluntstone sounded cool. 'Whatever,' he said. 'I'm in a meeting. Whatever Roland wants.'

After that, Roland said it was 'clearly imperative' to find out all we could about the sacrificial knives and sacrificial habits of the Warrior Kings. I said, 'OK' although I couldn't see how it would be of much use. Still, it might shed light on why the gang wanted the dagger.

Roland opened up his laptop.

I thought Sapphire might feel better if she was busy too. So I suggested she might like to fix something tasty in Roland's kitchen. I left whatever that tasty something might be up to her imagination. There were two huge fridge-freezers in the kitchen. They had loads of stuff in them. There was a spare room – what Roland called a pantry. It was crammed full of soups, spices, sauces, cereals, packets and cans. There was every kind of saucepan imaginable, and a huge central cooker with a huge hood and an extractor fan. A cook's paradise. But she still looked annoyed when I said, 'Root around – you're a girl, I'm sure you'll find something you can cook up,' as if it was going to be difficult.

Sometimes I don't know what her problem is.

After all I was only trying to help. Nobody was hungry. It was just that we had to do something. And I'd somehow ended up in charge. I had a horrible feeling that unless we tried to stay normal and have mealtimes and do stuff, we'd all go to pieces. She should have understood that.

Anyway once I'd got them sorted out, I lay down on the wine-red sofa. I watched the light sparkle off the chandelier and chase pale spots over the plaster ceiling rose. Then I closed my eyes. You see, a terrible tiredness had swept over me. Suddenly I longed to slip away into a black empty world.

It was well past suppertime when I surfaced. The sleep hadn't refreshed me. I had no new ideas about the More Dread Crew. I had even less on what to do next. I lay for a while with my eyes still closed, letting random thoughts drift through my head. *Mogul King, Angelo, Benin Bronzes, Leon, dagger. Gangs. Hoodies.* I was looking for a connection. Something that linked everything together in one logical pattern. But even though nothing came, I was sure that pattern existed. For one thing, Mogul King had given me an ancient Benin Bronze on the very evening I was going to a lecture on exactly the same topic. I mean – let's keep it real – how often do you get coincidences involving Benin Bronzes? But despite wracking my brains, I couldn't think of any reason (other than it was probably priceless) as to why the dagger could be so important, or why a famous rapper would be carrying it around. Also, why would a street gang even know about it, let alone care? Like, it wasn't drugs or hard cash, was it? And how come that linked up to Leon and his campaign? Angelo was right. There must be a lot more I didn't know.

There was only one thing that vaguely clicked. It was to do with the dagger. Something about it was familiar. But I couldn't remember what.

I went to the bathroom. I splashed water on my face. As I dried, I looked in the huge gold-framed mirror. I saw Angelo looking back. His tired eyes looking into mine. He seemed to be saying, 'I am not at peace, bruv. I'm out here lost . . .'

I shook my head until the drops of water sprang from my cheeks. 'I'll find out who did it,' I said. 'I will. I promise. And when I do – I'll . . . I'll . . .' I tried to smile. The face in the mirror did not smile back.

I wandered back into the living room. I saw Roland working on printouts at the dining table. I leant over his shoulder and said, 'Before Angelo was shot, this weird newspaper guy said something about the "More Dread Crew and *knights*", does that mean anything? Is there some next crew who call themselves that?'

Roland breathed in sharply. 'There is one organization . . . but it can't be . . .' He shook his head as if whatever had occurred to him had somehow got stuck between his ears. Then looking alarmed, he continued, '. . .but maybe it can be.' He got up from the table and stomped about. 'Max, "knights" is a term used by the secret service when they're referring to the teams they send out on missions. A bit like Spooks.' He stomped back to the table, scratching his head. 'Clearly, it's some kind of in-joke about "knights in shining armour". Please think,' he thumped down on his seat again, clearly not happy, 'did you ever hear anyone say anything about the government, MI5 or the Home Office being involved with these Bronzes, I mean, before all this?'

That was scary, you see, cos I sort of had. And not so long ago . . .

Mum and me and Angelo sprawled out on cushions in front of the telly. Watching Spooks. Mum pouring herself a glass of wine, saying, 'It's not really like that, I mean MI5 and the Home Office.'

I'd just shrugged. Who the hell were MI5 and the Home Office to Angelo and me? The show made them look like heroes, out there saving Britain from foreign terrorists, and I liked it. I wanted to be a hero in a film too.

'The truth is very different,' she said.

Angelo popped a fresh pack of crisps. I wasn't listening. I was trying to get a bottle of Coke to explode by seriously shaking it.

Mum sighed and stood up. '*They* are the real people to be afraid of,' she said. '*The men in grey suits. The new knights in shining armour.*'

At the time I'd thought that was funny. I mean, how could you be afraid of men in grey suits? Everything was funny back then . . .

I turned back to Roland. 'Mum said something about knights in shining armour, but that was when we were watching telly. Nothing about the Bronzes, actually . . .' My voice trailed off. Had Mum really been scared?

I sat down beside Roland and picked up a plate, admiring its gold rim.

He typed something into his computer and did a quick search. He seemed to draw a complete blank. He shrugged and scratched his head again. Then he looked round and saw me holding the plate. 'Royal Doulton. Only the best for you, Maximillian.' He proudly showed me the thingy bit on the underside.

You know, I was impressed. It wasn't just one off the wall either. The whole table was laid with them. 'Yo,' I said, 'Manz had a likkle rest and can appreciate the love you're showing, Rols.' I punched his shoulder. 'You're all right, you know.'

He beamed at me.

Sapphire sniffed from the direction of the kitchen.

'I've had some really good results too, actually,' he said. 'I've looked up various sites on Google and found out an extensive amount about sacrificial daggers. I'm absolutely convinced you've correctly identified yours. Definitely one of the Nine Ceremonial Treasures of Ancient Benin. You see the early visitors to Benin, in the 1600s, describe a dagger which was used in a rite-of-passage ceremony . . . Anyway, they particularly mention the dagger as having a large diamond!'

'You're amazing,' I said. 'If I asked you to conduct emergency brain surgery, do you think . . . ?'

'Ah! Now brain surgery . . .'

'Roland,' said Sapphire, frowning at me, 'Max is winding you up.'

Roland's face fell. He stammered, 'But the best news is, I've made a successful bid for a scrapbook on the internet, at least I thought it was a good idea . . .' Trembling, he held up a printout.

Genuine private journal, old photographs, detailed illustrations, Parliamentary papers, proverbs and unpublished memoirs . . . this eccentric scrapbook reveals the adventures of Gunner Hugh Hardy, junior officer and aspiring chronicler, aboard the *HMS Theseus* during the British Expedition against the West African Kingdom of Benin. 'Members of this expedition were appalled by the sights and smells of the fallen city – sacrificial victims lying where they had fallen, crucifixion trees outside the Oba's palace . . . blood-soaked altars . . .' Buy this now or Save to basket . . .

'Wow,' I said, 'well done.' I confess, I was a bit puzzled about the scrapbook thing being such good news. Anyway I took the printout. I looked at it. Old photos and drawings. I thought about the Benin Bronzes and Mum's obsession with returning them. I remembered her face lighting up as she described the fine lines of the plaques and the ivories: '. . . *so beautiful that nobody in the Western world would believe an African could have carved them.*' And her voice would swell with pride and dip with hurt that the African was so talented and yet held in such low esteem. And I would stop and listen and wish I were in Africa, hunting elephants and carving ivories under palm trees in steamy jungles far away . . .

'Are you hungry?' Sapphire plonked something large and hot down on the table.

My daydream cracked. The mist thinned. The rattle of seed pods faded. The Bronzes sank back into history. And Mum's voice with them.

Hungry? I didn't really care if I never ate again. There was such a huge lump in my throat that nothing could squeeze past it. But I didn't want to disappoint Sapphire, especially as I'd sort of forced her to cook. So I went to the table and stared at the food.

And so there we were at Roland's polished, walnut dining table, sitting on posh chairs, not eating spag bol, off the finest Royal Doulton, with solid silver cutlery. And Sapphire was trying not to cry any more. And Roland was trying to fill the void by giving us a PhD dissertation on 'The History of Sacrificial Practices amongst the Edo from 700BC to the Exile of Overami'.

Needless to say, it was fascinating.

I pushed spaghetti around with my fork. I couldn't swallow. The lump in my throat was much bigger. I twisted the serviette in my hands. I stared at all the empty chairs around the far end of the table. Angelo could have sat in any one of them . . . I closed my eyes and tried to imagine him there. But all I could think of was an endless cold hillside stretching ahead of me. And I was out there in that dismal landscape where there was no hope and no comfort.

The grandfather clock on the landing chimed. The meat sauce congealed into thick orange blobs. Night fell. The snow started again. Roland twitched. I turned on *BBC News* to see if the shootings were on. The presenters covered: petrol shortages and the rise in fuel prices, new oil deals hanging in the balance, the rise in street crime, fire bombings, numbers of illegal immigrants who were trafficked into the country every month, and the need for British Values to be taught in schools . . .

And outside it got colder. Mrs Peel came in. Roland

sorted that and checked Arnold and the guards. We turned up the radiators. Sapphire's shoulders shook as she huddled in an armchair. I paced about. We drew the curtains and sank into silence.

And between us there was a huge emptiness. A chair where Angelo should have sat. A plate that Angelo should have eaten off.

And out there the More Dread Crew sat and worked out how to get their dagger back. Worked out all our weakest points. Worked out how small and afraid we were. And perhaps they laughed as they worked out what they would do to us – when we made our first mistake.

LIMBO

Papers relating to the Massacre of British Officials near Benin,
and the consequent Punitive Expedition.

Presented to both Houses of Parliament by Command of Her Majesty.

August 1897

No. 44

Admiralty to Admiral Rawson. (Communicated by Admiralty,
24 January 1897)

Admiralty, 23 January 1897

Sir,

I am commanded by my Lords Commissioners of the
Admiralty to acquaint you with the news that an unarmed
party of Niger Coast Protectorate officers have been attacked,
and the greater number of them murdered, when on their way
to the city of Benin on a friendly mission to the King of that
country, that it has been decided by Her Majesty's Government
that an expedition shall be dispatched for the punishment of
the King for this outrage.

(signed)   EVAN MACGREGOR

And so my first day without Angelo passed. And my second. And my third. And after that, others. All passed, leaving little changed behind them. It didn't get any better. But maybe I learnt to push that last ghastly grin that stayed stretched across his face into a place in my brain where it couldn't get out. I did it by conjuring up the memory of him standing on the pavement outside the youth centre, and then I wouldn't go any further. I'd leave him still standing there on the tarmac. I learnt to pull a sort of armour over me, put on a smile and crack a joke just like old times, and sometimes I just stopped caring and that made it easier.

Of course we didn't go out. Roland reminded me that a calm always comes before a storm, and that just because the bikers hadn't come back, it didn't mean they'd gone. So he told the guards to stay till his mum came back. The scrapbook he'd bought over the internet arrived. Nobody really read it. Sapphire got snappy. Nobody knew how to break the tension. We ordered new clothes through a twenty-four/seven catalogue. Roland paid. Sapphire cried. I tried not to. Roland was very patient with both of us. We tried to figure out how long we'd have to stay in hiding, when the gang might give up, or the police might catch them. Roland got us some of those prepaid phone cards that are impossible to trace and Sapphire called her mum. There were a lot more tears and she very nearly went home, even though her mum didn't have a plan worth nuts. In fact if her mum hadn't asked her who her new friend on the bike was that seemed to be hanging around the place, I think she would have. That and how the police and Victim Support had called. Apparently they'd said they would look into a Witness Protection Scheme if she would like to make a statement, and if anything she said in an interview led to an arrest. Like afterwards.

That dried up Sapphire's tears. Although they soon started again when she heard her school friends were missing her, sending her flowers and telling her how her teachers understood she must be in terrible shock . . .

I didn't think my teachers would miss me or send me a 'we are thinking of you in your time of loss' card. At my school the staff have more days off than the kids. I didn't phone my auntie either. I wanted to but I didn't know what to say. And my auntie gets hysterical, you know, she might have gone totally off on one. I wanted to say something to my cousins, but I was too scared. I mean how do you talk to little kids about death?

Roland carried on as normal. He went into school, came home, chatted to the guards and convinced them he was still a wimp. He told Mrs Peel to take some of her holiday as he'd be fine with the guards. Nobody in the whole outside world knew we were there. Except they did, didn't they? They knew damn well we were there. They were watching and waiting. I mean just how long could we stay hidden?

And I wish I could say all those empty mornings and gloomy afternoons gave me the chance to grow strong. Gave me time to discover who the More Dread Crew were and why they needed the dagger back, and what we could do about it. But they didn't. Instead I lay on the futon and gazed at the ceiling rose, thinking of how Angelo had died instead of me. And my head ached. And a hard lump grew in my chest. It was bigger than the one in my throat. And sometimes I felt I couldn't even breathe.

I should have used that time better. I should have got into training for what was to come. I should have read that scrapbook. Because when the storm broke everything happened at once.

And I wasn't ready for it.

HURRICANE HITS

Papers relating to the Massacre of British Officials near Benin,
and the consequent Punitive Expedition.
Presented to both Houses of Parliament by Command of Her Majesty.
August 1897

No. 41
Admiralty to Foreign Office, 19 January 1897 – List of ships
ordered to proceed to Niger Coast Protectorate.

St George, (flag), Captain G. le C. Egerton

Theseus, Captain C. Campbell, C.B*

Forte, Captain R.F.O. Foote*

Philomel, Captain M. P. O'Callaghan

Phoebe, Captain T. MacGill

Barrosa, Commander J. Startin

Magpie, Lieutenant H.V.W. Elliott

Widgeon, Lieutenant J.H.S. Burder

Alecto, Lieutenant C.E. Pritchard

* * *

This was how it happened.

One afternoon, after Roland got home and Mrs Peel had gone downstairs to her basement to watch television, we sat tense around the walnut table. Sapphire was playing with the dagger. Roland was mumbling on about Ancient Benin. Suddenly, as if he'd cracked a crossword clue, he sat up. 'Tell me about the campaign and how your mum was involved?'

I told him as best I could. I mean what I remembered. She was interviewing people, collecting their signatures. Lobbying them. Annoying them really. I mean she'd just go and turn up at their offices and sit there and refuse to leave until she'd spoken to someone or other. She did that at the British Museum for a week. In the end they threw her off the premises. She said that she was researching into the history of the expedition that had got the Bronzes. She was preparing a case to take to some committee, a sort of warrant that she was going to serve on the museum, bit like a bailiff. You know, demanding their return. She was very hopeful, especially just before she died. She said there were definite grounds for proving that the Bronzes were taken illegally and therefore didn't fall under some legislation or other that museums have. There was something else too, some sort of wrong practice she'd discovered, which she said set a precedent and made nonsense of their arguments. Somewhere down the line the Nigerians were involved. I think. 'My grandma was born in Nigeria,' I ended.

'I know it's not very sensitive of me to ask,' said Roland, 'but have you ever considered that your mum's death . . . well . . . I mean . . . might not have been an accident?'

I stared at him.

'I don't get-u. She was doing political stuff, art history – nothing to do with gangs and guns. She drowned. She fell off a boat on a Black History tour going up the Thames. It was an accident, a wet deck, deep water . . .'

'I'm sure you're right. I'm sure it was,' he said.

'There were gales blowing . . . and the lifeboats were—'

Roland abruptly changed the subject. He ran his hand over his face.

I could see he was embarrassed. I wasn't mad or anything. He just didn't understand. My mum had drowned because in a gale she'd somehow slipped overboard. Nothing to do with the Bronzes.

Was it?

Sapphire had been listening and laying out everything to do with the dagger on the table. She was moving the pieces around like sections of some huge puzzle. 'Is this the same piece of paper the dagger was wrapped in?' she said, waving the empty sheet, trying maybe to break an awkward tension. 'Because if it is, there's something written on it.'

Trying to stop the panic that was rising up my throat, I took the sheet and looked at it. She was right. Although there was nothing actually on it. But if you looked hard, you could see the impression of writing. As if someone had rested a piece of paper on it and written on that.

'Can we read it?' said Roland.

'We could try,' said Sapphire. 'But how?'

'Graphite!' said Roland.

Sapphire and I both looked at him.

'I've seen it done on *Crime Scene Investigation*. You dust the paper with graphite.'

'And?' I said.

'You brush it gently with a paint brush so that the depressions show up white.'

'Yo!' I said. 'That's it then.'

So we did. We got pencils and split them and crushed up the lead. Roland got a paint brush and clean paper in sheets on the walnut table, and had others ready in case by some bizarre means we might need them. Sapphire had her gel pen set to transcribe the words on to a different sheet as they appeared. I sat there just hoping it was all going to work.

And this is what we read:

Dear Le (might have been Leon?)

If you are reading this it means I am dead, and we are in a desperate situation. I'm going to give this to Errol downstairs to post if he wakes up tomorrow to the news I'm gone. Firstly, trust nothing. Trust <u>nobody</u>. The organization will not hesitate to murder you. I have discovered, over this matter, they intend a complete clean up — they have informers in every branch of public life. Don't trust the police especially — ha — as if you would! Instead try to get the Ceremonial sword of Ewuare. Some notes of Richenda's state that concealed with it is a vital clue as to the name of the person who is the leak in the Campaign. At least that will be a great help. If you can get ... we might stand some chance of stopping them.

I write this in great haste, for I see them down there lurking at the corner of this street — the grey coats, gathering like wolves. I shall go now and try to get through them, to deliver the dagger with its precious evidence to you, before they burn this building — and me and this letter along with it. Wish me luck.

Mogul King

'They burn buildings down,' said Roland. And a new terror struck us.

'They hang out like wolves,' I said, remembering that night.

'The police are in their crew,' said Sapphire. And I remembered how she'd said that to her mum.

'I'll call Leon,' I said, 'and find out if this letter was meant for him – if he ever got it? I'll warn him. Maybe he can tell us what's so important about this Ewuare sword that Mogul mentions. And about this spy person.'

'Don't mention any spy yet,' said Sapphire. 'We don't know there is one. We don't know anything – and if the letter wasn't for Leon . . . be careful.'

'And ask him about the "precious evidence" too?' said Roland. 'It might throw light on why, apart from the diamond, this dagger's so important.'

I called. There was no need to be careful, because I only got the answer phone. I left a message, asking him to call back. He didn't.

So we just stared down at the paper. I don't know about the others, but I was pretty scared. 'Mogul knew they were on to him,' I whispered.

'Just like we know they're on to us . . .' said Sapphire.

'And this isn't like any normal gang,' I said. 'Normal gangs don't have "informers" in "public life". They just take you out or murk you, but they don't do "clean ups".'

'So who are they?' whispered Sapphire.

'And what do we do now?' Roland scratched his forehead.

We were in a desperate situation – for real. And desperate situations need desperate remedies.

'Looks like we'll just have to go and get that rude-boy sword for ourselves then,' I said. 'That's what Mogul wanted done.' I smiled at them encouragingly, as if I'd just suggested going for an ice cream. 'You know, the Sword of Ewuare that holds the vital clue to the name of whoever-it-is. So that we can stand a chance of stopping whoever-they-are!' I flapped the paper at them.

They both looked at me.

'So?' I said. 'Come on, hands up if you're coming.'

I picked up the dagger and I waved that at them too. But there was really no need.

Two hands had already shot up.

THE MOST STUPIDEST IDEA EVER

'Even if you are as thorny as the kapok tree, I shall meet you in battle.'
West African saying

It is amazing how once you know there is something to do (and you have decided to do it) that you cheer up! You could almost see the tension in the place evaporating. Sapphire stopped sniffing and did the washing up. I picked up the dagger and did a few karate moves with it, wondering how easy it might be to straighten the blade a bit. Roland flipped his laptop open, got up Google and typed in: *Where is the Ceremonial Sword of Ewuare, greatest of the Warrior Kings in the sixteenth century?* The answer sprung back at him: *Do you mean Ceremonial Sword of Ironware?*

Roland typed in something to bypass that question and looked like he was getting into Researcher Mode. I did a few press-ups. Sapphire actually made some coffee!

Then, boyakasha!

'The Ceremonial Sword of the Warrior Kings is currently displayed in the Ambulatory at St Theobald's College!' announced Roland.

Yo! My man Rols was getting somewhere! 'Keep chatting, bruv,' I said. 'Man likes the sound of your voice!'

'Absolutely, Maximillian, and I've had a bit of a brainwave about how we could, you know, obtain it.' He turned back to his computer and carried on searching sites in Google.

Sapphire hung over the back of his chair saying, 'Do you want a chockie bickie with your coff, Rols?'

Everybody was happy. Rols's glasses gleamed. I did a perfect series of left hooks into the cushions. Sapphire announced she was going to fix taco shells for supper. Even the chimes on the grandfather clock had a cheeky jingle to them. I could see a path now. We'd get the sword. We'd find out who the killers were. We'd get our evidence and nobody would stop us!

Then suddenly, just as if they'd been waiting for the right cue, the sound of bikes, BMW engines, ricocheted through the room like gunshot. At least two or more. One of them backfired. Instinctively Sapphire screamed. I ducked. Roland was left open-mouthed saying, 'I thought we could . . .'

Sapphire dropped her head into her hands. I sprang

to the nearest window. Nobody was there. Only the security guards standing by the front gate. Just letting us know, I thought. Slowly I returned to the others. 'False alarm,' I said mostly to comfort Sapphire. 'Just bikers.'

Sapphire was shaking with either anger or fright. 'And they're not "just bikers",' she said, 'they're going to kill us, aren't they?' She walked to the window and stood there. At last she turned. 'Let's do this, Max.' Her chin wobbled, but her voice was firm. 'Let's get this stupid sword and . . . and . . .'

I think she was going to say: '*then we can get back to normal*.' But you see, we couldn't. Angelo was dead. So instead she said, 'And I want to come with you.'

'Me too, please,' said Roland. 'I mean we could be a sort of gang all of our own actually, couldn't we? Clearly, you'd be the Boss, Maximillian, and I could be your side-kick – I mean, if you'll have me?'

'Consider yourself side-kicked in. Your new name will be Rollz Royce, bruv.'

'Oh thanks,' said Roland. 'I mean "Yo!" And your name can be Maxi – Mi££ion!'

I laughed.

Sapphire rolled her eyes. 'Just don't say it, Max. I am not going to answer to Ice Ice Baby.'

I smiled at her, my most disarming, Thaw-an-Iceberg, Defrost-a-Refrigerator, Would-I-Do-That?

But instead of melting, she shot Freeze-the-Atlantic back at me.

(Well you can't say I don't keep trying, can you?)

I turned to Roland. 'So Rollz, chat me about the brainwave?'

'Well, Million, I thought a really brilliant way of getting into St Theobald's and, you know, "acquiring" the sword – would be to go to their Sixth Form Evening and pretend we're prospective pupils. Clearly, it would be quite easy to . . .'

Sapphire started laughing. I don't know why. 'You'll have to smarten him up a bit,' she said.

'I'd lend you one of my suits!' said Roland.

'For real,' I said. 'Thanks bruv, your heart is in the right place – but your suits . . .'

'I'll lend you *any* of my suits,' said Roland anxiously.

'And make him act a bit more mature,' said Sapphire.

I ignored her.

'Even my Aquascutum jacket . . .' said Rollz.

You know, I couldn't see how anything of Rollz's was going to do. First off, I'm TALL and handsome. Next, I'm FIT and handsome. Last, I'm particular about my LABELS and handsome.

'I checked on the school's website and we're in luck, there's a sixth form open evening tomorrow!' Rollz beamed.

Madness.

I thought of Angelo, of daggers, of swords and revenge, of British expeditions and fire bombs and city streets running with blood. I thought of me in a borrowed suit at a posh public school. Completely insane. But I nodded like it was the best idea ever. After all, I'd told Angelo I'd find out who they were. I'd promised myself I'd die trying. Obviously this was the first sacrifice of the journey.

Roland looked so happy.

Yep, I'd get the sword and the clue we needed. Even if I had to do it in pyjamas.

'That's settled then?' said Roland biting his lip. 'You'll wear the suit?'

'Heavy,' I said. 'Manz just longing to go to that rude-boy evening.'

THE SCRAPBOOK

THIS IS THE CHRONICLE OF HUGH HARDY, BLUE COAT, GUNNER, ABOARD THE THESEUS, *IN THE YEAR OF OUR LORD EIGHTEEN HUNDRED AND NINETY-SEVEN.*

Warrigi, Benin River, the Bight of Benin and Biafra, Atlantic Ocean off-shore from the Niger Coast Protectorate of West Africa.

5 February 1897

If today be the judge of our future here in this strange and terrifying country, then I must conclude our future is bleak. It has already begun with a death – that of Private C. 'Collie' Mill, a poor lad from Lancashire. He died from sunstroke after standing all day throughout this torturous heat, in full uniform, on board ship, awaiting instructions. As I sit now, I hear the ship's chippie, Amos, nailing up his makeshift coffin. Amos is trying to fix it so that the stencilled lettering BUTTER TO BE STOWED AWAY FROM THE BOILERS does not show when we drape the

Union Jack over Colin and consign him into the waters of the creek.

Tomorrow we disembark and march six miles from Warrigi through the jungle to Ceri. They say the Edo are a bloodthirsty and terrible enemy, who decapitate you for the very fun of it. They say these savages creep up behind you as you march single file and slit your throat. There are whispers that they tortured the Phillips party last month before they beheaded them in some grisly sacrifice. I am bringing up the rear. May God bless and protect me, and keep this chronicle safe if none of us return.

Hugh Lloyd Hardy (of Ross-on-Wye, seventeen years and three months).

OFF TO GET THE SWORD
OF EWUARE

'It is he who enters the forest that finds the tusk.'
Edo proverb – Nigeria

The next day, Sapphire did my hair and I shaved off my nearly-there moustache. Roland went through his wardrobe, his dad's wardrobe, his mum's wardrobe, even Mrs Peel's wardrobe until he'd got Sapphire and me kitted out.

Boy, did we look stupid!

Just for a taster – get this – I was wearing fawn trousers creased down the middle and thing, and an off-white waistcoat over a white starched shirt! No gold chain, no huge diamond earring, no mobile around my neck (on its nice little celebrity cord), no gold coin ring, no dark designer sunglasses. In short nothing nice at all.

'I'm really, really sorry, Mi££ion,' said Roland, 'but clearly if you're going to commit a theft it's probably better to look as inconspicuous as possible.'

Inconspicuous! What about the golf bag we were going to trawl around? I mean couldn't we think of something less 'inconspicuous' to put the sword in after we got it?

'I know you're the boss, Mi££ion,' said Roland, 'but nobody will even notice a golf bag, and everybody will be in cream and white.'

'Yo, bruv,' was all I said. 'Manz gotta get used to the posh thing, innit.'

'I think you look nice,' said Sapphire.

Drop down dead in amazement.

So that was it. I went to my first-ever serious crime dressed like a complete idiot. And believe me the humiliation didn't stop there. All the way through the afternoon Roland was in despair. 'It's not every *F*ing, Mi££ion, you've got to pronounce the "th" – no not *V*ing either, it's *TH*ing.'

'OK, I tell you what,' I said, 'we'll go straight there, and then *you* do the talking. I'll just nod my handsome head and say, AB-SO-LUTE-LEE, whenever.'

So that was the plan.

The plan changed, however; just as soon as we got out the front door.

I could tell something was up. The street lay half in shadow and the sun was setting in a red wash. Patches of crimson snow melted and dripped into deep gutters. I saw a curtain twitch in an opposite room high above us. I heard a bike, maybe a BMW, splutter in the distance. A blackbird twittered once. Like the afternoon was gasping its last.

'Manz feeling something,' I said. My breath rose like a ghost in front of me.

'What?' said Sapphire, her eyes wide.

'I believe we should take a taxi,' said Roland.

I thought about it. *They were out there waiting for us to make a wrong move. How had they known my number? How had they managed to find Roland's place so quickly? Did they know we were on our way to get the sword? These brothers weren't any normal gang. I must not underestimate them. If I'd not been so stupid last time, Angelo would still be alive.*

'I wish they could come with us,' said Sapphire pointing at the guards.

How should we get to the school? What did they think we would do? They had bikes. Think about it. They had guns. Make a plan. But they don't know where we're going – or do they? Best plan: lose them. Keep moving. Keep dodging.

I laid my finger over my mouth. I scanned the entire length of the street inch by inch. About five parked cars in the *Residents Only* bay, a girl smoking a cigarette at the bus stop, one old lady walking a dog. Nothing too scary. But I was too wise, so I stayed scared. Think of what to do. A taxi was too obvious. It could be followed too easily. (As for the guards, *please* – when you're off to do a burglary?)

'What did you do with the dagger?' I hissed at Sapphire.

'It's OK, I've got it here.' She went to pull her hand out of her pocket.

'Go back in, just behind the hedge. Hide it.'

She looked like she was going to argue.

'Now.'

Sapphire gave me a sour little smile, but she ducked behind the hedge anyway.

I decided that going on foot would be best. Least likely. Too slow for long though. Then we'd take public transport. It would be harder for those bikers. Going in bus lanes, or down one-way systems. Also we had time. Some.

So we set out. We dodged from street to street. We took cut-throughs where bikes – if there were bikes – couldn't follow. At one point we walked across a park. The empty swings creaked ominously in the dusk. The branches from the trees rustled like restless fingers. After that we took any bus we could. We chopped and changed at random. We timed a bus stop, which had two or more buses pulled over at it. We jumped off the 436 and on to the 171. We doubled back towards central London. We took another out and doubled back again. Often in the distance I heard that BMW. I could have been wrong. I'm not an expert on bikes. There's a lot of traffic in London. It makes a lot of noise. At last I figured if we were being followed, they must be having a rough ride. That gave me some small satisfaction.

It didn't last long.

We were taking a short cut through a shopping centre when they jumped us. Three guys. Three bikes. We were going through the underpass. Typical. Suddenly there was the throb of that badly-tuned BMW engine. And coming towards us at full speed was a biker, dark visor well down. My heart cut and my chest crumpled in. We had only one choice. Flatten ourselves against the wall. Stop breathing. Pray for a miracle. We took it.

The guy on the BMW was the first of three. One from the front. One from the back. I never did figure out where the third came from. They lined up in front of us. First bike on me, second on Rollz Royce, third a centimetre away from Sapphire's slim waist.

'What d'you want?' I said, trying to pretend they'd got the wrong people.

There was no reply. Biker One revved his engine and looked like he was struggling to keep it from squashing me against the tunnel wall. I was thinking fast. *How do we get out? How did they get in? They must be good. Better than us. The must have radar or satellite links. No satellite could see us in an underpass . . .* I was scared. So scared, it felt like the whole of my intestines had melted. I looked longingly up the underpass, hoping that escape or rescue lay that way. I felt a golf club and the rim of the golf bag scrape against my backbone. I pushed myself hard against it. I used the pain to numb my fear.

'Where is it?' said the rider in a quiet voice. 'Give us the dagger.'

I smiled stupidly as if I didn't have a clue what he was on about. 'Search me!' I said.

He did. He searched me. He searched all of us, although there was nothing to find. I knew it. Rollz knew it. So did Sapphire. So we waited until the bikers knew it too. When that knowledge finally dawned on them, I can say with some pleasure that they were not as pleased about it as we were.

There was a nasty, disappointed, dangerous kind of silence. I tried to think of football in the park and birthday cakes. Time slowed down to nanoseconds. There was much threatening revving of the BMWs but, hey, if something isn't there, however much you rev up won't help. Will it?

Biker One shoved me aside and wrenched out the golf bag. He turned it upside down in disbelief. The printout about the open evening at St Theobald's fell out. I prayed they wouldn't pick it up. Biker Two bent down. He picked it up. He opened up the printout. He glanced at it and shoved it in his pocket.

How could I play for time? This was a public underpass. It was barely evening. Someone would have to come soon . . . ? I prayed for one small advantage. Sometimes that's all you need. One small advantage. I tried to shrink my fear into a tiny ball inside me and push it down into my little toe. I glanced at Sapphire and saw her eyes wide and scared.

Rollz swayed forward. 'I say, chaps, I think we can solve this with a bit of give and take . . .'

'Yes,' snarled Biker One, 'you give us what we want, fatty, and we take it . . .' He flexed his knife like he was going to take a large chunk off Rollz's stomach.

Rollz stood his ground. 'You wouldn't by any chance be from Farnham in Surrey would you?' he said. 'Only I noticed the way you pronounced "give us" . . . you don't actually mind me asking, I hope?'

Biker One looked a little bit surprised. 'What is with you?' he said. 'This is a stick up, not a garden party.'

I felt I ought to say something – *do* something – to save Roland from himself, but he didn't give me a chance.

'I say,' said Roland, 'I've never actually been, you know, "stuck up" before. Would it be beastly cheeky of me to ask you a few questions? I mean, do you just do it for the money, or do you find that it's something you're sort of forced into by peer pressure?'

Sometimes I just love Roland. You know! Those bikers didn't have a clue what to do with him. Luckily I didn't need to jump to his rescue. You see, from the corner of my eye I'd seen a group of Arsenal supporters winding their way into the underpass. And as Roland delivered his lines about peer pressure, I knew those three bikers would have more to think about than answers to Roland's question time.

So that was it. They had no choice but to revv off on their revving BMWs.

I sagged to my knees.

Sapphire started crying.

Roland stood there quite pleased with himself. 'It's called victim and persecutor psychodynamics,' he said. 'You have to draw them into conversation without revealing that you know they're about to kill you. The theory goes that once some common ground is established, clearly it becomes harder for the persecutor to reveal his intentions to the victim . . .'

'Rollz Royce,' I said. 'Common ground! You are the Man!'

And Sapphire kissed him.

Lucky devil.

By that time (of course) all thought of the Sixth Form Open Evening had vanished. Unfortunately, I soon remembered. I was about to become a badly dressed criminal. The whole evening was going to be filled with loud exclamations of AB-SO-LUTE-LEE. And I was probably going to get arrested.

We were late too. Dodging around South London had put our planning seriously behind schedule. And none of us was feeling too hot. So I reversed my decision about the taxi. That helped with the time and the stress levels, but not with my appearance.

As I settled back for the drive across London, I tried to think about the sword and whose name we were going to discover. What had Mogul written again? *Instead try to get the ceremonial sword of Ewuare. Concealed with it is a vital clue as to the name of the person who is the leak in the Campaign. At least that will be a great help. If you can get . . . we might stand some chance of stopping them . . .*

Of stopping who? From doing what?

And did the word 'Campaign' mean the Return the Benin Bronzes to Benin Campaign? I hoped when we got to the school and saw the sword it was all going to click into place.

Again I tried to slot together the pieces of the puzzle. *Me. Angelo. Mogul King. Leon. Taliesin. The Enugu professor. Hooded figures. BMW bikers. Not regular gangbangers. The Benin Bronzes. And the dagger . . .*

The dagger. A memory fluttered, half formed: *Mum – a room – a half-opened curtain – the smell of perfume . . .* Something about Mum. *Fingernails tapping on a desk . . .* I tried thinking hard. I tried thinking by association. I tried to trick my memory by concentrating on something else and then suddenly switching back. But it was no use. Whatever it was stayed hidden.

So I pressed my nose against the cab window. I looked for other hidden things. I searched the streets behind. Were they going to follow us? Would they read that printout and figure out our next move? The answer was obvious.

Of course they would.

LEMONADE AND LATIN

'Since I was a king I have always been a friend to the White man. But I will receive no more messages. If they want to come and fight, let them come. I will send more soldiers down to the waterside to kill the White men. If these [Edo] soldiers are killed. I will send more, until all soldiers are killed and then I will run away.'
Oba Overami, the Last Warrior King of Benin, 1897

An hour later, we swept up the grand drive of St Theobald's. That's St Theobald's College, practically the oldest, poshest public school in the world.

'Let me do the talking, remember?' Rollz said.

'Ab-so-lute-lee bruv,' I answered, clapping him on the shoulder in a fake cheery fashion. 'You're the chief now.' I sat bolt upright on the squeaky upholstery, chewing my lip. I was trying hard to stay positive. I was trying hard not dwell on my cream waistcoat.

Sapphire smoothed back her beautiful long hair. 'You look nervous, Max,' she said.

'Damn right,' I said, 'but if you'd consider giving me an all-over body massage, Man might relax . . .'

I won't repeat her answer.

(Give me my due, when it comes to Sapphire, I keep getting up and climbing back in the ring.)

But anyway, I *was* nervous. For a start, I was in some kind of deer park, out of my ends, and I didn't like it. Next I'd got to steal a massive sword without being noticed. And you know I'm not totally brilliant at everything. Take stealing massive swords for example. Not one of my best talents. So I wasn't super-confident I could do it. Then there was the whole school and teacher thing. I'm not the next discovery for *Mastermind*. I think the last time I actually did my homework was when Angelo bet me ten quid I wouldn't. And as for my skills at planning the Great School Robbery, this was about it:

- get there
- get in
- get it
- get out.

Sounds simple, doesn't it? I could easily see it on the big screen. Me striding through the antique halls of St Theobald's. My footsteps echoing on the ancient slabs. Me seizing the sword. Drawing it forth from the block of stone in which it was for ever fixed. The music swelling to crescendo. The voiceover saying: '*Behold the once and future king...'* Me charging into battle, shouting: *'One for all and all for one!'*

Sorry, I think I got two films mixed up.

Obviously not much good at that either.

No it wasn't going to be easy.

And the complications started just about as soon as we got there.

'Delighted,' said a tall lady in a white suit as she keyed in the door code (one, two, three, four – rather obvious). We entered the foyer of St T's. *'Smashing* to get a chance to really *use* the Elephant Door.' She waved her hand at the stone pillars of the entrance. Beyond them, a gravelled drive and immense lawns stretched away.

Down that drive, huge trees spread bare branches into the evening mist. Their ginormous trunks were big enough to hide skulking figures. I shivered as I examined their shadows. Dark shadows that stretched spookily over vast lawns.

The tall white wrinkly lady started shaking our hands. 'We want you to feel *completely* at home.' She beamed at me. 'We've got *piles* of different nationalities: Japanese, Korean, Indian, Sudanese – everyone, bar none. We've had *twenty* canonized saints pass through these doors! We've *even* got a world-famous ballerina here!'

I nodded and searched the shadows. I strained to catch the slightest hint of a BMW.

'Now the programme for tonight is a get yourself a drinkie. We've got orange squash, lemonade, tea, coffee. *Sorry*, no alcohol for you boys – *that's* for the grown-ups!' (Toothy smile.) 'And there're nibbles! Then in the Ambulatory you'll find *all* the departments have a stand. You can chat to your tutors and find out the things you need to know.' Her head, with its ridiculous blonde bob, jerked up and down as she punctuated each sentence with a weird waggle. '*Then* we'll go for prayers at seven-fifteen and after *that* the Head will be making a little *presentation* . . . Now if you'd like to tick your names *off* . . . yes?' She looked over her glasses at us.

'Ah!' said Rollz. 'I'm afraid we may not be on your list. I did inform the receptionist that I was unsure if we'd be able to make it. You see *we* –' he waved his hand at Sapphire '– were waiting for the prince –' he waved his other hand at me '– to arrive. In fact it's jolly good luck that we made it. Taxi all the way from Heathrow, y'know.'

Groan. I wonder where he'd just got that idea from.

'Oh *really*? Oh *good*,' she said. 'Then . . . um . . . just *pop* your names and schools on the *list* and . . .' She looked at me with renewed interest. 'A *prince*! Wonderful! From *where*?'

'Nigeria,' said Rollz. 'Benin City – actually, father's Paramount Chief of the Edo.'

'Wonderful, *wonderful* – you're going to *love* it at St T's. We've had simply *oodles* of Nigerians here.'

'Yes, Prince Wongaboulawoula,' added Rollz, getting carried away. 'Clearly, you may have heard of him . . .?' He looked at the woman.

'Quite so – how *wonderful*,' she repeated. 'So would it be *overseas* status you'd be looking at?'

'AB-SO-LUTE-LEE,' I said and reached for the list where I wrote WONGABOULAWOULA in capitals. Then accidentally-on-purpose trod hard on Rollz's foot.

While Rollz filled the rest of the details in on the list (and God knows what else he came up with), the lady in the white suit showed me into the Ambulatory. I cast one quick backward glance past her, past Roland and Sapphire, out through the open double doors, under the elephant arch, across the lawns, out to where the shadows stretched beneath the colossal trees. I tried for the last time to decide if those were figures crouched there, waiting . . .

'So which *subjects* would you be taking?' the tall weird lady asked.

'Ermmm,' I said.

'We allow up to *five* at AS level, but recommend *four* really.'

'Ermmm,' I said again.

'I suppose *English* would be one?' she hazarded.

'AB-SO-LUTE-LEE,' I said. Then (thank God) Rollz caught up.

'We'd like to see all the tutors in the Arts and Humanities areas,' he said. 'At least I would, but I think Prince Wongaboulawoula's father rather wants him to do something in Business Management and Government and Politics.'

'Well, I'll *leave* you here.' She nodded at the long line of displays down the Ambulatory. 'Grab a *nibble* – you'll find everything we *offer*. Just tick the registers on the *courses* you feel interest you most. It's not written in *stone*, but we do need to *plan*.' She beamed a scary smile at me and nothing at Sapphire.

The Ambulatory stretched in front of us, like the nave of a huge cathedral. Nearby were tables laden with strange bits of food – something that looked like pink fish, and little biscuits, balls of brown stuff on sticks which might have been meat, and other things that you could dip into sweet chilli sauce (or not), as you fancied. Beyond that were the stalls of the various departments. Each of them had exhibitions on display screens. Beside the screens, a line up of intense teachers peered out. I saw a wistful look come over Sapphire's face. And I remembered how keen she'd been on finishing her education.

But this was no time to go soft. Instead I scanned the stands. *Don't underestimate them. Remember. Stay alive.* When the tall lady had gone, I turned on Roland. 'Wongaboulawoula?' I hissed. 'Not only is that embarrassing, it's so racist. It's probably dangerous too. It probably means something insulting in Yoruba.' Roland gulped and turned pinker than the fish. 'Manz not happy, bruv, u-get-me?'

'Sorry, Mi££ion,' said Rollz, 'I'm just so, so sorry. Clearly, it was a spur of the moment thing. I didn't realize you had to book for these evenings. I don't know any proper Nigerian names. I was just thinking of money and the word "wonga" slipped out. Oh God! I just said it to confuse her – royalty does that to administrators. I read a whole article on social status and—'

'Well, just cool it on the prince thing, OK? And try never to mention Wongaboulawoula to any Nigerian we ever meet – if you value your front teeth.'

'I think you did fine,' said Sapphire. 'You actually do look a bit like a prince.'

Woo! Did you hear that?

Call out an ambulance!

I smiled, my best You-Are-The-Most-Loveliest-Girl-In-The-South-London-Area-Who-Knows?-Probably-The-World at her.

She shot me a look that would have sunk the British Navy.

Then suddenly I panicked. 'Look, bruv,' I said, tugging at Roland's tux. 'What does this sword look like anyway? I mean, how am I going to find it? How am I going to know it's the right sword? There might be hundreds of them. There might be a whole armoury of swords . . .'

'Good point, Mi££ion,' said Rollz. 'We don't want to steal the Fifth Duke of Fife's duelling rapier, do we?'

'The wot?' For some reason the thought of stealing the sword had triggered that memory about the dagger again. Yes! It was something to do with Mum! She'd said something about a dagger when she'd been doing her Return the Benin Bronzes Campaign. What was it?

'The Fifth Duke of . . .' Roland interrupted me.

'Really!' said a booming voice behind us. 'Duke of . . . ?'

The memory of Mum and the dagger vanished.

I turned round a bit too quickly and knocked Sapphire's lemonade sideways. 'Max!' she yelled. 'YOU IDIOT.'

'Ahh, the Duke of Manx,' said the man. 'Didn't know there was one actually – silly me! Definitely am an idiot.' He stuck his hand out. 'Very pleased to meet you – not really a wally, don't you know; name's Derby Walton: Classics.'

'Like the ice cream?' I said.

'Haw, haw, what a spunky little joke. Have to pinch it myself.'

'So not like the ice cream?' I said, very confused.

'Classics, you know: Latin, Greek, a little Aramaic. First term we'll be looking at Ovid, translating a tad of *Metamorphoses . . .*'

'Ahhh – AB-SO-LUTE-LEE,' I said.

'Really? I say! Do you mean it?' gurgled Derby Walton. 'Do you think you'd be interested?'

'No,' I said. I mean, I had to say something didn't I?

'Oh crumbs!' said Derby Walton, quite crestfallen. 'What a sausage!' He turned round and wrung my hand, wiped my jacket, pressed a glass of squash at me and said, 'Look old chap, I'm frightfully sorry. It's just that I thought, you know, you being a duke and all, well you might. Got to fill my quota, you see. If I get less than five students they'll lay me off!' He tugged at his chin sadly.

'Mr Walton,' I said. 'I've changed my mind. I'd AB-SO-LUTE-LEE love to do Classics.'

'Fantastic! Beastly terrific of you,' said Walton. 'Look why don't you just come and sign up, right now?'

I followed him past a wide-mouthed Roland and lemonade-wet Sapphire and a whole bunch of professors to his little stand. He handed me the sign up sheet. I noticed that I was the first one on it. I wrote: *Prince Wongaboulawoula, Duke of M'banza and Associated Chiefdoms, Benin State, Nigeria.*

'I say!' said Derby Walton. 'Really *am* an idiot. I thought you meant Duke of Manx. Double silly, eh?'

'Don't mention it,' I said. 'Glad to show a likkle love.'

'Bravo!' said Walton. 'Now I've got a titled student at the top of the list, that'll tickle them in. Oh thank you so very, very much, Prince Wongybouly!'

'Well,' I said (wincing), 'one good turn deserves another. How about you show me something. I believe the sword of my ancestors is displayed here. I'd like to have a likkle scope at it.'

'Umm, yes, we do have quite a few trophies. Donated, you know, by old boys back from their stint in the colonies. Totally fascinating period of history. All gung-ho, derring-do and bully boy stuff! Well you'd know all about that! Think you'll find most of it in those display cabinets at the end of the Ambulatory. But wait a min . . . um . . . Prince Wongy-Thingy – did I really say thank you properly? Look, jolly thank you, and we'll look forward to terrific times, eh?'

'*TH*anks,' I said, and struck out for the end of the Ambulatory.

Roland and Sapphire caught up.

'Now that *wasn't* my fault, Mi££ion,' said Rollz.

'Just a minute,' said Sapphire, 'I'd like to sign up for Psychology.'

We waited while Sapphire chatted to a bony-faced teacher.

'What did you say to him?' asked Rollz. 'Do you think he suspected anything?'

'Look, bruv,' I said. 'Man can talk proper, you know.'

'Yes, clearly,' said Rollz, but the worried frown stayed drawn across his brow.

At last Sapphire finished. We started again down the long hall.

'I wonder if Philosophy would've been a better choice,' said Sapphire. 'What do you think?'

I rolled my eyes at her. 'Sapphire?'

'But if I take Psychology *and* Philosophy, then I've got to choose between Spanish and Sociology . . .'

'*Look*, rude-girl, you ain't going to do no sixth form Addition or Spelling or Spanish, or first century Taxidermy or Nothing, u-get-me? All you're here to do is some instant Criminology.' I mean I wasn't trying to be harsh, but I ask you!

'Typical,' she said. 'You know something, Max, that's why I preferred Angelo. He *really* cared. He cared about me *and* my future.'

Wow, that hurt. And it wasn't fair. I cared more about Sapphire than anyone in the entire world. I think

I cared more about her than Angelo ever did. And she wasn't the only one who had a future. I needed someone to care about mine too. And I thought about Angelo. That old smile of his. And the way he made you feel so important. And a rush of longing swept over me.

I was still smarting when I saw him, standing there with his camera on one shoulder and the Headmaster on the other.

Taliesin Jones.

My heart sank.

They must have read that printout. I'd been right about those shadows under the trees.

He *must* be one of them.

I smiled with my teeth only.

HEADLINES

'Wherever there are soldiers there must be war, particularly if you have helpless people to slay in order to get your ends quickly. Moor is at his work again killing people in order to make them more humane and civilized . . . I consider that the punitive expeditions of South Nigeria since the establishment of our government in that district have been a disgrace to our country.'
John Holt, 1901

Sapphire went pale.

I froze mid-step.

What should I do now? He'd expose me. They'd call the police.

'Ah! Here are some prospective sixth formers,' said Taliesin. 'Just what I need.' There was not a flicker of recognition. Not a trace of any Welsh accent.

He stopped. The Headmaster stopped. Taliesin raised the camera. 'Well, hello there students, I'm Taliesin Jones of *Times Today – South London*, making a documentary on "Post-Sixteen Opportunity and What Kids See As Their Options". Don't suppose you'll mind answering a few questions?'

The sight of his round, pink, fuzzy face made the orange squash curdle in my veins.

'What brings you to St T's?' he crooned, pushing the mike towards us.

'Well not the lemonade,' said Sapphire, stretching a wet and now almost see-through lilac silk blouse over her upper body.

The Headmaster ducked his head down and said, 'Splendid, splendid.' But whether he was referring to Sapphire's chest or 'splendid', was some kind of fallback comment that he trotted out during embarrassing moments, I couldn't tell.

Just like before, Taliesin Jones was right where he wasn't wanted. I had to do something quick, so I stepped in close to him, and hissed, 'Whadda you up to?'

'You forget,' he returned icily. 'The Premise.'

'I don't forget anything,' I said. 'I don't forget you were there at the Marcus Garvey Centre, and I specially don't forget your front page picture and headlines.'

'Stick to the Premise,' he repeated.

'What premise?'

'Pillage and Plunder,' he said. 'And right now I've got a career to make. If you like headlines, try imagining tomorrow's: *FROM DA PITZ 2 THE RITZ – SOUTH LONDON'S KID GANGSTAS. Just weeks after his brother and Bang Bang Gang boss, Mogul King, were mown down in a gangland hit, gangsta teenager and new Bang Gang General, street name Warrior King, signs up for Latin in the oldest, most expensive public school in England.* Now that's a story I can sell, dude! Oh yes!'

I stood there, seriously shocked.

The Headmaster took a step towards us, as if he wanted to join in and make helpful remarks. Roland plucked at my sleeve.

'You know, don't you?' I stared at Taliesin Jones. 'You know all about this More Dread Crew . . .'

He held out the microphone.

What was I going to do?

I didn't need to do anything, as it happened. I was saved by the bell. Sort of.

A large tolling church bell.

Evening prayers.

I wasn't the only one who looked relieved. With more than a grateful roll of his eyes heavenwards, the Headmaster turned away from Sapphire's wet top and strode off down the Ambulatory.

This was my chance. With a sickly smile, I leant near enough so that only Taliesin could hear me and hissed, 'Go on then, but when all this is done, lock your doors and don't sleep easy, because remember, I don't forget.'

Then before he could react, I turned my back and walked up to the nearest stand. I said in my most politest stopped-by-the-police voice, "Scuse me, m'am, can you show me the way to the rest room?'

She pointed to a grey door at the opposite end of the Ambulatory. I said, 'Fanks, must dash. AB-SO-LUTE-LEE don't want to miss prayers,' and headed off fast.

As soon as I got out of sight, I stopped. I pulled out my mobile. I sent a text to Roland. GO IN 2 PRAYERS AND TRY 2 GIVE ME AS LONG AS POSS. MANZ GOIN 4 DA SWORD NOW. DEN MEET US BAC IN DA TAXI ASAP WEN U GET OUT OF MASS. Then I sent one to Sapphire. MAKE AN EXSE USE − YR WET TOP − GET 2 DA LOO. Then I walked as politely as I could away from everything else until I was standing alone in a stone-flagged high-ceilinged visitors' toilet.

Suddenly I felt ill. I felt cold. I felt hot. A slight sweat condensed on my face. I shivered. I crossed over to a huge radiator. I just wanted to comfort myself against it. It wasn't on. I looked to see if it had a thermostat knob. If it did, I must have missed it. Looked like that radiator was as old as the school, anyway. Probably had instructions to turn it on in Latin.

Keep it real, I told myself. *You're doing this because you have to. Manz got to stay alive because Man is too young to die. Just concentrate on staying alive. Get the sword. Find out all you can. Find out about the spy. Work out why they're spying. Why they want the dagger. Think of a way to fix*

Taliesin. Figure out what he's up to. Use your head. Grab a chance. Any chance. Don't lose guard. What a useless plan. I was shivering more violently now. Go to the police. Commit suicide. The Post-Sixteen Options got worse.

I crossed to the sinks, large square white stone basins, and turned on a hot tap. I ran it over my hands until it scalded me. Then I left it running. At last the door squealed open.

Sapphire stood there, her face tense. 'What's that creep Taliesin doing here?' Like it was my fault.

I had no answer.

'Seems like a bit too much of a coincidence, doesn't it?'

'Yep,' I said.

'So do we abandon?'

'Nope.' I didn't tell her about his Pillage and Plunder plan, and how he was about to plunder us. 'Taliesin's having a bubble bath if he thinks he can mess with me,' I said. 'This is the deal, Sapphire. You watch my back, cough, sing, yell, yodel, answer your mobile, do whatever you need to, to warn me if someone shows. I'm going out there to get the sword. Let's do this thing and find out that name.'

'OK,' she said.

'If alarms go off, or Superman shows up – get lost, you're not here. OK?'

'Understood.'

'Good. We haven't got long. They'll be in mass for maybe forty-five minutes. Maybe Roland can keep them a little longer if he chokes on his holy wafer. I'll go straight to the display cases. If Taliesin is there, I'll deal with him. You count to fifty, then come out. You wait in that alcovey thing under the stained glass, halfway up. Stay out of sight. I've scoped everywhere. There's a door near there, says *Laundry* on it or something. Door code is one-two-three-four. Watched that tall lady do it. Just get out if it goes wrong. Then emigrate. Join the foreign legion, but don't go home. OK?'

'Yes, Max.'

'Good,' I said, surprised. I turned. I shut down the tap. I laid my finger across my lips. I tiptoed to the door.

If Taliesin was still there, he was going to need plastic surgery.

Outside was empty. Taliesin had gone. Lucky for him.

In front of me, the Ambulatory stretched away, more than a hundred metres long and maybe twenty wide. Halfway down, the empty sixth form stands still advertised Maths and History and Science. Behind them hung a line of portraits. And right at the very end, just before the corridor which led to the chapel, the old colonial display cases waited. I stood balanced in the doorway. The mournful echo of hymns snaked down the pipework towards me. The worn stone flags dappled in the light from the high ceiling. The abandoned curriculum stands swayed, flimsy and strangely garish. I pulled my jacket over my face and set off at a sprint.

I was fast. I say it myself, because after I had sprinted to the wall socket there would be no one else to say it for me. People are stupid you know. They invest in high-tech security systems and then just plug them in as if they were a TV or something.

It took all of one second to disable the entire system. On / off.

After that I made it to the display cases in under fifteen seconds. I was not out of breath, although my heart was racing. What if the sword wasn't there? What if it was?

The first case was empty – well, didn't have colonial bric-a-brac or St Somebody's relics in it. It was filled with butterflies made from coloured paper. A square card announced: *St Jude's Junior School, Ms Eastham, 2B.*

I crossed to the other wall. There above me, a row of stern faces peered down. Each one had eyes that followed. *Just portraits*, I told myself. *This is not Hogwart's. They can't see you.* I gave them the victory V. They didn't blink. Typical. I thought about drawing a moustache on one, but decided that was juvenile. Pity.

I turned to examine the second display case with the

entire board of governors of St Theobald's for the last two hundred years watching me. Man, those Gs were there sitting up on the wall in oils unable to do a damn thing. They must have felt really stupid. But I was out of luck. Again.

No ceremonial sword.

Last try.

I crossed the Ambulatory to the final display case. My back to the jolly old portraits, I shut my eyes like I used to do when Mum gave me a present, back in the days before the accident. I crossed myself for good luck. I'm not religious, but I figured the school was. Every little helps, doesn't it?

And there it was. The Ceremonial Sword of the Warrior Kings lying beside bits of armour from medieval England and a few Roman coins. I knew it was the sword. No, not because of any warm and woolly feeling. I don't do warm and woolly. You see there was a little card next to it, which read:

This Ceremonial Ada Sword was carried in observance before the OBA by a naked page. It is associated with the Ancient Benin dynasty and signifies the right to take human life. It was donated to St Theobald's College by Lieutenant Cowan, Royal Marine of Portsmouth and old Theobaldian. It was given to him by Sir Ralph Moor in consideration of his brave and soldierly conduct on the Punitive Expedition of 1897 into enemy territory on the Niger River, Benin State, Nigeria. It was believed that this sword was the sword of Ewuare, the spiritual ruler of the Warrior Kings of the Edo. Lieutenant Cowan kindly donated it as a tribute to his Alma Mater.

Nice one, Lieutenant. Just take the equivalent of Excalibur off the natives, so that it can end up as another piece of junk. Never mind, so long as you can get a mention with the old boys! I looked at the display case, trying to figure out what to do next. It was one of those cases like a museum has to show off birds' eggs. Slightly sloping, wooden framed, a bit long, and as much wide, a bit deep, with a green felt background. One lock set in the centre of the lift-up lid. Pretty easy, even for a beginner.

Casting an anxious look to either side, I made sure there was no audience other than the portraits. I checked Sapphire was in position, gave her the thumbs up and slid the end of my handy all-purpose penknife under the wooden lid.

You gotta say it. I'm The Man.

THE PEN (KNIFE) IS MIGHTIER
THAN THE SWORD

*'The campfires were beginning to twinkle between the trunks of the huge
trees whose boughs were festooned with giant creepers and among whose
foliage little fireflies were flitting. On the still surface off the river the
lately arrived steamers lay noisily blowing off steam; but above all
the shrill scream of the cicadas rose high.'*
Lieutenant Haggard of the Forte at Warrigi, from his log
of the Benin Expedition, 1897

It took longer than I liked for the lock to give. I didn't
know if the case wasn't wired to some back-up security
system. So after about ten minutes of levering and
sweating, you can imagine how relieved I was to hear a
dull click and feel the lock pin snap back. After that, the
rest was simple(ish).

Lift up the lid. Take out the sword.

The next bit got harder.

I mean, should I look for the name I was supposed
to find and then put the sword back? Or should I take
the sword plus the name and get going with the whole

thing? I was spared that decision anyway, because I couldn't see any name anywhere. Looked like I'd have to take the whole thing. But how do you cart around a metre of wide bronze with a twenty-two centimetre handle? I suddenly regretted all my objections to the golf bag and wished we'd not left it in the taxi. I hadn't really thought that through, had I?

Anyway according to my schedule, prayers would last about another fifteen minutes, so I had a short window of time. But, hey, you never knew, some workaholic might have decided to leave mass early to add a few touches to his display stand. I might have to battle my way out. I really didn't want to stress out the night staff at the local A&E department, so I figured the sooner I got the sword out of the case and both of us out of the school the better. Looked like I'd just have to pick it up and carry it out and hope to hell that nobody was manning the front door. I could just imagine the conversation if there was!

PERSON: Hello! I say! Can I give you a hand? That looks terrifically heavy.

ME: Oh don't worry, it's actually made of Styrofoam – for the junior school drama, y'know.

PERSON: Jolly convincing – which play are you putting on?

ME: *Harry Potter and the Sword of Doom*.

PERSON: Sounds marvellous, haven't heard of that one.

ME: No you won't have; it was written by Grade 5C – could you get the door for me?

PERSON: Sure, there you go . . . HEY, COME BACK HERE! . . . WE DON'T HAVE A 5C . . .

I put my hand into the case and grasped the handle. Wow, it was a lot heavier than I'd expected. A weird sensation ran down my fingers and a tingling started in the palm of my hand. Boy, this was the Sword of King Ewuare! This was one of the treasures Mum had dreamed of returning to Nigeria!

The Sword of Ewuare!

Imagine.

I felt oddly insulted at it being dumped there amongst medieval tin cans and Roman coins probably worth less than a centimetre of its blade. I felt like writing another note and leaving it in place of the Lieutenant Cowan one.

STOLEN PROPERTY

The ceremonial sword that once lay here really belonged to the first of the Warrior Kings, the Lord Ewuare, whose strength and wisdom were legendary. In its shining blade lies the history of a lost people who rebelled against the British invasion into their

lands on the Niger River, Benin State, Nigeria.
Rather than be taken by the British, they fought
until death. The Punitive Expedition of 1897
massacred them all, plundered all their riches, and
burnt their palaces.

The brave soldiers of the Edo lived and died by
the sword.

No pen.

I forgot the idea of a note. I thought of something better. The big screen. I whirled round with the sword held high in my hand, my imagination whirring like a film projector . . .

The opening sequence shows a palace decorated with thousands of bronze images. The rays of the setting sun flash and sparkle off the polished metal. Behind everything, a dense steamy jungle stretches away. In the far distance, a silhouetted figure stands on top of a mountain with his sword raised. He is the Last of the Warrior Kings. Streams of golden light spurt from the blade as he swirls it above his head. A war cry breaks from his lips . . .

CUT TO:

A montage of pillage and plunder. Children scream, women run for their lives as the British army hack them to pieces.

CUT BACK AGAIN:

The Warrior King leaps on to the back of a monstrous stallion and charges down towards his kingdom . . .

Suddenly I heard a sharp hissing noise. 'Sssssssssssss.' Sapphire was leaning out of the alcove and pointing behind me. I brought the sword down and spun round. A light had snapped on in the corridor leading to the chapel. I heard a door open and the sound of choir voices floating towards me.

Time to get lost. It's odd how when you give your brain a problem to solve, it comes up with a solution. I dashed to the Geography stand and ripped a map off the side of it. I laid it on the floor and quickly rolled the sword up – diagonally – just as if it was a present I was wrapping for Christmas. Once that was done, I walked nonchalantly down past Sapphire. I indicated with a nod of my head and a flick of my eyebrow that she should follow me.

'Did you get the name?' she whispered.

I shook my head.

'Why not?'

Like did I know?

On the way out, I flipped the security cameras back on. Before the first white suit came out into the Ambulatory, the laundry door was clicking to behind a wide-eyed Sapphire and a five-hundred-year-old priceless Benin ceremonial sword.

'What on earth were you doing then?' snapped Sapphire, her face suddenly red after its intense pallor. 'You were just standing there holding it in the air for ages.'

I thought about explaining to her the sequence of jumping astride the monstrous shining stallion and charging to the rescue of a ravaged kingdom, but decided against it.

'Chillax,' I said. 'Boy thing.'

Sapphire scowled at me. I guess she still hadn't forgiven me for bursting her Further Education bubble. I weakened.

'I was just imagining the Warrior King holding his sword,' I explained with a disarming grin.

'Oh God preserve me!' she said.

The sound of heels on stone and voices echoed under the door. I nudged Sapphire forward. Together we crept down to the end of the service corridor, past *Laundry Bay One* and *Staff Only* to the thick grey outside door. Behind us, the heels on stone changed into the firm tread of shoes that seemed to know exactly where they were going. I heard the door to the laundry corridor open. I imagined Taliesin and the Headmaster shouldering their way past Bay One. I punched in the code to the exit door. *Code not needed.* Duh! I thrust it open. And then we were outside breathing in night air, scented by giant spruce and the sharpness of a winter's frost. I looked backwards to see if we'd been spotted. I hissed at Sapphire, 'RUN!'

Together we sprinted down the side of the college, round another wall until we were clear of the main building. We caught our breath beneath a giant fir tree set to the side on a triangle of frosty green.

St T's rose splendid beside us, huge gothic walls against which moon shadows flung eerie fingers of darkness. An owl hooted. Far away the roar of the M25 rolled across the hills and down the hedgerows of good old England.

It wasn't quite the same as the steamy jungle, but I felt my fingers itch to unravel the sword and once more brandish it into the night . . .

I checked behind us, screwing up my eyes into the gloom to see if those firm heels were still on our trail.

'What *is* that Taliesin about?' whispered Sapphire.

It was a good question. One I'd been avoiding. I turned to Sapphire. 'Forget Taliesin,' I said, 'we got other problems.'

We certainly did. Just as I was sure I could see someone stealing around the side wall of St Theobald's, the school alarm went off.

'Max!' shrieked Sapphire. 'They've discovered it's gone!'

'Nah,' I said, 'they're just doing a likkle fire drill to impress the visitors with their health and safety arrangements.'

Yes, it was a dark figure, rather fat – and probably on our trail.

Alarmed in more ways than one, Sapphire and I fled like shadows down behind the giant spruce to the staff car park. We dodged and swerved between a three deep line-up of expensive cars, until we gratefully climbed back into our own cab. The driver shot us a questioning look. I held up my hand and held back my breath. I motioned him to be patient. I'd give Roland a mental countdown from ten and then, with or without him, we'd go.

Ten.

At that point I started feeling very strange again. The shivering was back. I wasn't expecting it. I was surprised at my own reactions. I went hot, then cold.

Nine.

I remembered the weight of that sword in my hand and was overcome by a weird feeling. I don't know. Maybe for all those lost Warrior Kings. Or maybe it was about me and Sapphire, what was not and might never be . . .

Eight.

Maybe it was about Angelo. I'm not sure. I wasn't going to open up that place again. In my mind, you see, he was still standing on that patch of pavement outside the youth centre. And that was the only way I could deal with it.

Seven.

Anyway having feelings is something that Man doesn't allow Max to have. So I shrugged and sat back with attitude.

Six.

'Manz not feeling too hot,' I said. 'Text Rollz Royce and hurry him up. Tell him we're gone in five seconds – please.' I shifted against the squeaky seat and clutched the sword to me. The alarm sang into the night. I did not think: *Hello, how are we going to get out of this one?* To tell you the truth, as Roland might say, 'Clearly, you were not thinking with your usual perspicacity . . .'

Five.

Do you remember I told you a while back about my feelings for Sapphire? Well here's something you might need to know. It might explain why later on in this story I crack bad jokes even when they're not funny. Why I take risks. You can take risks when nobody cares what happens to you.

You see, as I was resting there, feeling a bit strange

after my first robbery, I did do a bit of thinking. I thought: *Well, I'm The Man. I've just done a successful robbery to try and save the girl I love from certain death. I've given her the biggest diamond ever set in a sacrificial dagger in the entire world. Might be a good time to capitalize on it. Might be a good time to ask Sapphire about 'us'.* So I said, 'Sapphire?' Then I cleared my throat.

That is as far as I got.

Four.

'No, Max,' she said. 'I know what you're going to say.'

I was a bit surprised at that, because even I hadn't been too sure.

'Look, I like you. And for Angelo's sake, I'd have loved to have you as a brother, sort of. But that's all. So it's *no*. Just NO. All. The. Way.'

I looked at her. 'But,' I started, 'I mean Angelo and me, we look exactly the same . . . so I don't see the difference . . .'

Three.

'You don't get it,' Sapphire snapped. 'It's just not about the looks.' She laughed in a bitter hurtful way. 'Well it *is* about the looks. The plate gold chain, the little cell phone, the fake diamond in your ear, the stupid coin ring, the pathetic dark designer glasses, the right brand name shoes. You're just so two-dimensional, Max. So yes, it *is* about the looks. But only because that's the way *you* think. And because you think like that, that's why I can never, *ever* love you.'

Two.

OK.

I paused, trying not to let that sink in. 'Please,' I said, 'Man can change. Man can be whatever you want . . .'

She sat up. 'No,' she said. 'Man can't.'

One.

I tried to put on a bit of a rude-boy smile. I tried to tuck my feelings right under my bow-tie. 'Start the car,' I said to the driver.

'And that's before I add the *fact* that *you* are to blame for Angelo's death,' she snapped.

There was no need to rub it in.

Zero.

Roland pulled open the taxi door. He threw himself inside. He lay panting on the floor rugs. The taxi picked up speed. The gravel crunched beneath its wheels. A plump shape blobbed into view, but was quickly left behind. I stuffed the sword into the golf bag. I sat back with my arms crossed and my bow-tie tight.

Good job feelings are something Man doesn't allow Max to have, eh?

THE SOUTH LONDON PUNITIVE EXPEDITION

NO SAFE HIDING PLACE

*THIS IS THE CHRONICLE OF HUGH HARDY, BLUE COAT,
GUNNER, ABOARD* THE THESEUS, *IN THE YEAR OF OUR
LORD EIGHTEEN HUNDRED AND NINETY-SEVEN.*

*Ceri, Benin River, the Bight of Benin and Biafra,
Atlantic Ocean, off-shore from the Niger Coast
Protectorate of West Africa.*

6 February 1897

*We are at Ceri, alive and as well as can be expected on
the rations we have. Dreadful flies swarm over everything.
Captain Rawson, however, is determined to press on with
the expedition despite a number of setbacks, the main one
being that the creek is far too swampy to cross to enable us to
attack Ologbo by land. He had thought we could string up a
sort of rope-bridge and I and a few other chaps thought
that would be great fun, but alas there were no firm uprights
to sling the bridge from, so we shall attack Ologbo by
boat instead. It's getting dark now (six-fifteen p.m.) and we are*

to rest, as we leave for our first encounter with the enemy at dawn tomorrow.

I do not think I will sleep well for this night may be my last.

Hugh Hardy

12 February, Ologbo

At last a moment to catch up with this chronicle. Two days ago as the dawn seeped through the canopy of the forest giants above us, we packed and left Ceri, our boats struggling against the current of the river. To either side of us on the riverbanks, trailing palm trees dabbled their fronds in the water, lilies opened creamy flowers, and around us the African morning blossomed. A quantity of dragonflies flitted over the water, and from time to time kingfishers darted in front of the boats showing iridescent-blue plumage. It was cool and the dew shone on every blade of grass.

As a precaution, at two hundred yard intervals we fired into the jungle with the Maxim, so as to kill any hidden enemies. At eight a.m. we arrived at Ologbo. There the enemy fired back. It was sudden and I was deeply shocked. In mid-stream our boats were easy targets and Captain Coe was hit. I could not reach him to help, and I could not see the enemy, as they were hidden in the bush. It was a confusion, but after a quarter of an hour we successfully landed on a river beach. There we set up the two Maxims and searched the bush with them. Some reinforcements arrived. I was tremendously glad to see them.

Together we advanced six hundred yards down a bush path and found six dead Edo warriors.

We camped at Ologbo last night. I do not really feel well enough to write much. During the night an overpowering smell kept me awake and in the morning I was sent out on a detail to search for the cause. Our detail found thirty-two more enemy bodies. I believe that was not all, for the smell still lingers. Even the meagre rations I am issued cannot tempt me to eat today.

I realize now that we have been misinformed by Lt Ralph Moor about the Edo. They are fierce fighters and ready to die for their king. Admiral Rawson should have brought bigger landing parties. We are only a few men here alone in the middle of the jungle, surrounded on all sides by a terrifying enemy.

God keep me safe

Hugh Hardy

I don't know what normally happens after you've committed the first major crime of your life. After you've been reduced to rubble by the girl you love. But I certainly wasn't expecting champagne and canapés with the Imperial Horticultural Society's Spring Ball Organizing Committee.

So when Roland said, 'Look, Mi££ion, we've got to make a mini detour on the homebound journey,' I just nodded my handsome head (without its fake diamond earring) and said, 'Yo.' Not knowing it was going to be a problem.

'You see, Mummy will be furious if I don't show up. This is her first engagement in London for ages,' fussed Roland, 'and she'll start asking all sorts of difficult questions about where I've been.'

Where *we'd* been.

I thought of that alarm sounding into the night. I thought of those grey figures slipping beneath those huge trees and how they weren't going to give up. I clutched the door grip and pressed my nose against the window.

'I promise it won't take long,' said Roland.

Even then I didn't realize I'd actually have to get out of the taxi and make small talk with the Sword of the Warrior Kings shunted behind me in a tartan golf bag.

'OK,' I said, 'Manz a likkle tired, so you go on in, bruv, and do the family thing. We'll wait for you right here.' I was hoping to get a bit of time alone with Sapphire. And at least one of us needed to keep a lookout.

But there is nowhere to wait on a double red no-stopping line that runs unbroken from the West End to the City. We even had a hard time getting out of the taxi.

So Roland paid the driver off. Overpaid him actually. Told him he'd be recommending him for regular use by lords and ladies who ran spring balls. He asked him for his card and smiled in a self-assured upper-class way. The cabbie, who'd been giving us a few weird looks, nodded. 'I read ya, matey,' he said.

As soon as he'd driven off, Roland said, 'Did you find it?'

I looked up, puzzled. All around us, London was suspiciously quiet. If they'd followed us, where would they stop?

'The clue?' said Roland.

I shook my head. A taxi passed. And an ambulance. 'You'll have to check out the sword. There was nothing there, just an information card and a few old coins.'

Roland looked like he was about to dive head first into the golf bag. '*Not here!*' I said. Was he mad? I scanned the street again. I'd better watch out for the police too. That was a new complication I'd have to get used to.

Roland started fiddling with his tux collar. 'I'll have to introduce you formally. Mummy is home tonight and she'll want to know why you're, erm, staying over. I'd say you're school friends,' said Roland, 'but . . . ermm, you see, clearly, they don't take girls at my college . . .' He turned to Sapphire apologetically, as if that restriction was his own personal fault.

'OK, say you met me doing the Duke of Edinburgh's Award thingy or something,' said Sapphire.

An uneasy look passed over Roland's face.

'You have done the award, haven't you?'

'Well actually, now you come to ask . . .'

'Not even the Bronze?'

'Ummm . . .'

'God! You'd think at such a posh *boys'* school everyone would do it!' Sapphire exploded.

'I could say that you two were . . . well, Mummy knows Max already . . .'

Touchy subject. Before Sapphire put Roland right about her feelings for shallow, likkle, coin-ring me, I swiftly cut in. 'Look, crew,' I said, 'let's keep it real. Say Sapphire lives on the same street, OK? And you just invited her over. If your mum doesn't want us to stay, I'll volunteer to see her home. We'll all get down together and you can let us in round the back.'

'There's a problem with that too . . .' said Roland. 'You see, my dad owns the street . . .'

'THE WHOLE STREET?' snapped Sapphire.

Roland hung his head.

'Whatever,' I said. 'The next street.'

So that was it. We walked in through the Jacaranda Gate to the Orchid Garden of the Imperial

Horticultural Society: Roland Piggot Bluntstone, Sixth Heir to the Earl of Dorchester, whose dad owned an entire London Street; Maximillian Wolf, Warrior King of The B.L.A.C.K. A.R.M.Y., Bang Bang Gang General and Gangsta Kid Criminal; and Sapphire Issa-Hilcote, Keeper of the Sacrificial Dagger of Ancient Benin, and the most beautiful girl in Greater London. I imagined our entrance through those gates like the trailer for the movie. I stuck my one spare hand into my fawn trousers – sagged them as much as I could – undid the top button of the shirt collar, and walked the walk. Beside us to the south, the Thames slid by. A thousand winter stars twinkled in its ripples. To the right of us, a Ferrari roared off towards the West End. To the east, a flock of startled pigeons rose in one mass, swirling up and up as the camera eye followed them, until they became as small and white as stardust . . . Behind us, the golf bag bumped along. Ahead of us lay danger. The theme music swelled into a crescendo and—

'Oh Rolly Poly, darling!' sang a middle-aged female voice. 'I thought you were simply never going to get here!'

'Meet some friends, Mummy: Max you know, and Sapphire.'

'Oh, darling, how delightful of you to bring your

pals . . . What a sweet name . . . What a pretty girl . . .'

Her mobile rang.

'Belle, darling, just can't talk, Rolly has just arrived! And it's already getting to nine . . . I've simply got to . . . No you'll look sweet in the pink . . . Don't be silly . . .'

Roland rolled his eyes at us in apology. I felt that it needed some response. Something harsh and Kid Gangsta-ish to gee him up a bit. So I moved in close and said, 'Manz tired, u-get-me? Manz carrying around stolen stuff – so Man would appreciate a likkle love. Like, we understand the family thing, but . . . do I need to stress the rest?'

'Mi££ion, I'm sorry, I'm really, really awfully sorry. Believe me; I didn't want to see Mummy at this point. It won't take long. Just as soon as she's shown us all off. Just brace yourself. Pleeease?'

Sapphire looked uneasy. 'Roland,' she said, 'it's not a good idea being here. We need to get somewhere where we can examine that sword and search for the clue. What if that cab driver says something? It'd be too easy for the police to find us. We should go.'

'For real,' I said. 'The police could raid this place in their sleep.'

Roland's mouth sagged and his eyes popped.

'And the bikers,' continued Sapphire, 'what chance

would we stand?' She waved her arms at all the shadowy shrubs and the high walls, which hid the garden from the outside world.

Roland turned a colour somewhere between dishwater and yoghurt.

But there was nothing he could do. Lady Bluntstone shunted us towards a pavilion, tugged Roland inside and propelled Sapphire into a group of worthy-looking ladies. I lodged the golf bag by the umbrella stand and draped my jacket over it, before I too was catapulted into high society.

Lady Bluntstone showed us off all right. Flutes of champagne were thrust into our hands; queer little rolls of pastry stuff were crammed into our mouths with some ab-so-lute-lee disgustingly salty, red, little, tiny balls of fishy stuff on crackers.

'Meet Lord Spicer,' she said, steering the three of us toward a man of uncertain age, uncertain height and large sad eyes. 'Rolly's chums!' she said. 'He's got *so* many friends from *so* many places . . .'

'Hello,' said Roland.

'Pleased to meet you,' said Sapphire.

'He's just *so* popular!'

'Ab-so-lute-lee,' I finished.

Lord Spicer gave us a limp handshake, and muttered something about *lavatera arborea* and its uses as a temporary filler in perennial somethings, and smiled a wet smile.

This was terrible. This was such a big mistake. Everything from the marbled floor to the smell of polish, to the fluted pillars and chandeliery kind of lighting told me this was just the wrong place to be.

And then as if to prove it, the phone rang. The phone? My phone. My mobile phone. It read WITHHELD.

NO TURNING BACK

No. 52

Admiral Rawson to Admiralty. (Communicated by Admiralty, 16 February)

(Telegraphic.)   *Ologobo, 12 February 1897 (via Lagos 15 February).*

    WITH reference to my telegram of the 4th instant, I took expedition up Benin River in hired steamers 10th February, landed Warrigi 11th, marched to Ceri same day, attacked and occupied Ologbo 12th…

    Shall continue advance towards Benin from Ologbo directly I have established base there. Advance will be slow, owing to dense forest and absence of water.

(signed)   *R. MOOR*

I knew it was them after the first ringtone. A strange clammy sensation slid down my spine like a snake uncoiling. They knew I'd got the sword. They'd think we'd got the name of their spy in The B.L.A.C.K.

A.R.M.Y. Taliesin stupid Jones would have told them. Instinctively I checked Sapphire was nowhere near the exit. Roland's mother was introducing her to another Lord Somebody Or Other who seemed fascinated by the lemonade stain on her top. Certain that no one would follow me, I stepped outside.

I flipped open the phone. 'Yes,' I said, tight-lipped.

Outside, the night had grown much darker. No stars twinkled. No pigeons soared.

'It seems you're becoming a nuisance.'

An evil wind blew off the Thames. The snow scattered down from the trees. My breath froze on the air. 'Tough,' I said.

'And we don't like your attitude.'

'Good,' I said, 'it's not for sale.'

'If you bring us the dagger – tomorrow night, ten p.m., Market Lane car park, top storey, we'll overlook it.'

I smiled. What were they up to? I mean, did they think I was stupid?

'Be there.'

OK, I'd play along. 'What's in it for me?' I said.

'Your future.' His voice was deep like the kind of deep down a mineshaft.

'You'll have to offer more than that,' I said, making sure I was well concealed behind bushes – just in case.

'Warrior King, if you don't come, if you haven't got what we want – then you are going to go somewhere else.' I could tell he was trying his best to sound menacing. It worked.

'Like where?' I said, heart hammering.

A faint laugh.

'To a funeral.'

It was a cheap line, so I didn't ask the obvious question. I got told anyway.

'Yours.'

And just to rub it in – in case I was underestimating them – down the phone I heard the sound of gunshot, of a curious dull thump, of shouting, of screaming, of commands, of car horns. Then the sound of a police siren far away.

They'd taped Angelo's murder.

I started shivering. Vomit rose into my mouth.

His voice broke across the noise. 'A really hot funeral – a big bright cremation that could burn down a whole street . . .'

Then the line clicked dead.

Slowly I folded the lip down on the phone. Tomorrow night. Car park. Ten o'clock. I tried to breathe normally. I tried to mash out the sound of the screaming. I bent down behind the shrubs, pressing my hands over my ears.

Someone rushed right past. It was the tall Lord Whoever, who had been perving on Sapph. He stopped and peered around into the night almost as if he'd been sent out to call me in. He had a strange grey twist of hair that flopped over one eye from a middle-parting hairstyle, in what I suppose was meant to be a distinguished way. The rest of his hair was deep brown, almost black. I wondered vaguely if he'd dyed it, or if that was the way it was. Caught there in the front security light he looked thin, like a ragged fox on the run.

I didn't show myself. I was trembling. I scooped up snow and pressed it against my face. Then I stayed crouched up behind the bush thing, until he rushed on towards the exit. There was something hungry in that look of his that scared me almost as much as the phone call.

But there wasn't time to think about him. We had to get out. Fast. Maybe that call was another trick, a trickier trick than ever I could work out. Maybe they were going to surround the place and shoot us down by the gates . . . All I knew was: *get out and get out now*. It was the same feeling I'd got in the youth centre. GET OUT. Get back to Roland's, where everyone knew the score. Where Arnold and his bodyguards could hold the fort. Think about everything later.

So I raced back into the pavilion and didn't have to pretend much to look upset. Lady Bluntstone rose to the challenge like a Saviour of Nations. 'Take him home immediately, Rolly,' she commanded. 'He's obviously allergic to caviar. Give him a dose of your great-auntie's tonic, the rose water one in my bathroom, and put him straight to bed. Let your friend Sapphire stay over as well, in case she feels sick too . . . Is that OK?' (Nods at Sapphire.) 'Good. Ring her parents. We simply can't send anyone home ill!'

So I was rushed back to Roland's. When we got there, I told him and Sapphire everything. Right from the phone call to the weird Lord Whoever, who had hurried out.

Roland said, 'I don't think there is anything suspect about Lord Esterton. What you experienced is called displacement. You were scared after the phone call, so you transferred your fear on to him.' He continued: 'They did an experiment once – they made men cross a rope-bridge over a bottomless ravine. At the end of the bridge there was a girl. All of the men afterwards said they fell in love with her. The researchers had a hard time convincing the men it was just a rush of relief on making it to the end of the bridge – that is until they had them cross a normal bridge over the ravine with the same girl at the end . . . then they realized she was pretty ordinary, and—'

'Whatever,' I said, 'you're probably right. Next time Man'll ask the More Dread Crew to organize me a girl and we'll test your theory, but until then I'm telling you that lord guy was well dodgy.'

But Roland didn't look happy, and it wasn't because I doubted his theories. He stopped nervously babbling. He went quiet for a long time. He stared at the Persian carpet. Sapphire started examining the sword, searching all its little mouldings and decorations for any clue.

'You don't really think they'd burn down my house, do you?' he said at last.

Neither of us answered.

Sapphire stood up and wandered around, sighing and pulling at strands of her hair. Then suddenly she stopped and confronted us. 'I know you're not going to like this, but I think we should give the dagger back,' she said, 'and the sword too.' She let her arms fall helplessly to her sides, but her gaze didn't waver.

What? My jaw sagged. 'Are you nuts?' I mean, was she nuts?

'We've stolen the sword and there's absolutely nothing there that helps,' said Sapphire. 'It's all just getting worse.'

'But . . .' I started. Then shut my mouth. This was the girl who had called me two-dimensional, remember?

'And there's no point in trying to win against this gang. They've got guns. They've got spies and everything going for them. They're probably more of a huge organization than a gang anyway. They know who we are, where we are, what we do, probably everything we're saying right now is being relayed back to them. It's hopeless.' She put her hands on her hips and tried not to look like she was going to burst into tears.

'Mummy's sent Arnold and the guards home, too,' added Roland, hanging his head.

'Here,' said Sapphire. She dumped the Sword of Ewuare across my knees. 'Check it out. Nothing.'

It was true. There was nothing that was the slightest clue to anything – in, on, with, by, or under that beautifully decorated sword. No great revelation, no plan, no purpose. No name. The letter we'd so carefully deciphered had led us up a dangerous trail to nowhere.

'I'd like to keep trying, but how can you defend yourself against petrol bombs?' said Roland. His shoulders slumping. His fingers twitching.

I turned to him. 'We can't give it back,' I said. 'For a start we'd never leave that car park alive, and for next – I mean?'

I looked at both of them, searching their faces for some spark of hope.

'Rollz? Sapph?' I said. 'What about Angelo and Mogul?'

Nothing. Not even a half-hearted gesture.

Maybe once in what seemed like another lifetime, I'd been ready to hand that dagger over. But not now. I'd promised Angelo. I'd even promised Mogul King. And I'd changed. I wanted my promises to mean something. I didn't want to wriggle out of anything any more.

I wasn't like Roland and Sapphire, with homes to go back to, and houses that could burn down. I'd got no mum, no brother (no girlfriend,) so I didn't care. There was nobody to betray – except myself.

And that was what made the difference.

I was going to fight these people, not just for Angelo and Mogul, but for *me*. And that was when I first felt a weird pain in my chest. Something like hope and longing and other stupid stuff. Perhaps after all there were some things worth dying for. So I shook my head at Roland and Sapphire. 'No,' I said. 'Never.'

They both looked back at me.

'It's the only solution,' said Sapphire. 'I'm tired of living like this . . .' Her delicate chin wobbled. 'Scared all the time. I want to go home. I want to see my mum and . . . and . . .' she rushed out of the room and locked herself in the toilet.

'Mi££ion, it's not a game any more. This is my

parents' place and I can't put it at risk. Tell me something, anything, some other way we could solve this, and clearly I'll be there beside you all the way . . . but . . .'

'She's just upset,' I said. 'We're all tired. It'll be different in the morning.' All the old bits of comfort I'd ever heard spilt off my tongue. They fell flat on the carpet. I had no plan. Nothing.

Roland wasn't listening anyway. He was tugging at the tassels of a cushion.

I gave up. Sapphire didn't want me. Roland was worried to death. Everything was falling apart. Only one thing left to do, then. I stood up and put on my best, bravest, most cheerfulest smile. 'I'll go away,' I said. 'I'll be fine. You'll see. Man'll leave. Man'll find somewhere.' I looked longingly at the futon in the alcove like a drowning man taking his last glimpse of the shore. 'You won't have to worry any more.' I gazed around the room as if searching for some huge exit sign which read: *This Way To The Rest of Your Life*. 'Leave it to me.'

And outside the night was filled with the sighing wind. And traffic. And lorries hooting far away, and cars on the South Circular. And bikes.

Large BMW engines.

MORE ABOUT GARDENS

THIS IS THE CHRONICLE OF HUGH HARDY, BLUE COAT, GUNNER, ABOARD THE THESEUS, *IN THE YEAR OF OUR LORD EIGHTEEN HUNDRED AND NINETY-SEVEN.*

14 February 1897

We were sixty-two NCPF troops and twenty-nine Blue Jackets, alone against the Kingdom of Benin. And such as we were, we left Ologbo, that camp of sordid corpses and death, to set out against the unseen enemy. I prayed to God that I should not see so much killing and bloodshed again.

It was the most unnerving and fearful advance I could ever have imagined, far worse than will one day be written of by historians or survivors. We had to move in single file along a bush-cut path. The heat was intolerable, the undergrowth thick and dark and rotting. Sweat trickled endlessly into my eyes, blinding me. My uniform stuck to me, glued by my own sweat. One chap lost his pith helmet and collapsed with heatstroke after scarcely an hour. At any moment I feared an ambush, and with the thick impenetrability of the forest around us, and

*the devilish cunning of this soft-footed enemy, I feared my own
death at every footfall.*

*After four hours we encountered a scout who told us that the
enemy had cut parallel bush paths next to our own and were
set to ambush us before we reached the crossroads. And as if to
prove his words true, a volley of Dane guns shattered the
gloom. In the heat of the forest the gun smoke from the damp
banana leaves thickened around us like an evil fog, and the
fumes overcame us so that we staggered and ran and fired
volley after volley of the Maxim down the twisting paths until
we became exhausted and frenzied with fear.*

*After an hour we captured a camp at the crossroads. Three
soldiers were wounded. One had a foot crushed by the wheel of
a seven-pounder.*

*There at the crossroads camp the heat of the midday sun
was intolerable. We dug wells, but all were dry. A terrible thirst
overcame us and the water supplies finished. And so the rest of
the 14th we spent retracing that five-hour march, throats
parched and mouths dry, back through the bush, collecting
water in any container we could find; from the river eventually
at Ologbo again. Setting up portable boilers to sterilize the
creek waters, digging tanks, proofing them with canvas, and
pouring into them our pitiful tin cans full of water.*

*Those hours silently marching through that thick dark
forest, hemmed all about by fumes and death, terrified of new
attacks and deadly snakes, will live with me for ever.*

God bless us all and preserve us through to final victory.
Tomorrow we strike out for Benin City.

Hugh Hardy, Crossroads Camp, 15 February 1897

I didn't leave that night. Roland wouldn't let me, although the relief in his eyes told me I should really have insisted on going. But I didn't sleep well either. It wasn't that the comfy futon was less comfy, or that I'd really been allergic to the red salty stuff. It wasn't the bikers, or the phone call. It wasn't stealing the Warrior Kings' sword. It wasn't Sapphire and her spiteful comments. It wasn't even the thought of leaving Roland's in the morning and being alone out there, with nowhere to go.

No, it was Angelo.

He stalked into my dreams and seemed so real and alive that I couldn't believe he wasn't. It seemed that he stood there on the threshold of some other place, looking and looking, and all the times his eyes were asking, 'Will you let me down?' And behind him, the other place waited dark and open like a yawning mouth filled with shadows. And I wanted to rush to him and save him. But instead my legs grew into tree trunks and took root and I could not move.

I woke up shivering.

I got up and went to the kitchen to fix myself a hot

chocolate. I fixed Angelo one too and left it in the microwave, so he could heat it up if it got cold. I know. Don't say anything. I took mine to the window seat in the big bay at the front of the house. I sat curled up on tapestry cushions, staring out into the night below.

How had all this happened? How come one day I was bopping along OK and the next I was here on the run? Where was I going to go? My throat felt suddenly very tight. I sipped at the hot chocolate. I burnt my tongue.

The dagger. It had all started with the dagger.

And Mum.

What was it about Mum I'd thought of earlier? The dagger? I'd seen it in her study before she'd died. It'd been lying on her desk right beside her laptop, right beside the picture of Angelo and me on Chesil beach.

That was it.

So how had Mogul King got it? That was weird. Had I really remembered that right? Suddenly, I wished I knew where Sapphire had put that dagger. I wanted to pick it up. I wanted to examine it, to put it under a microscope. I wanted to enlarge every detail, until I could read it like a three metre high advert.

It all led back to those Benin Bronzes, didn't it?

What the hell had that professor said about that Punitive Expedition? About that prophecy and that curse? Where was that scrapbook? I totally needed to read it.

Outside, the street lights shed little pools of orange every fifty metres. An aeroplane passed somewhere far away. There was that same light on in the attic room opposite. Everything else was quiet. No cars went up and down the street, no wailing police siren, no late nightclubber staggering home.

It was too quiet.

'Just up town, innit, bruv,' I said to myself. 'In posh areas they get to enjoy a likkle peace.' But I wasn't convinced. It was unnatural. *OK*, I thought, *wait and see. Something will come down the road soon. When the next car passes, you can go back to bed.*

But no car passed, no night bus, no police patrol, no pedestrian. That's when I knew something was very wrong. You see, Roland's street is on a bus route.

When you know something is wrong, there is no point in kidding yourself. No point in going back to bed and pulling the duvet over your head. Not if you're a wanted criminal, anyway. It might be a stake-out. The police might have cordoned off the road for a dawn raid. That's if I was lucky. *The MD Crew might be planning a likkle dawn raid of their own.*

I'd better go and check.

I pulled on a pair of black tracksuit bottoms, a dark

fleece and my trainers. I pushed open the French windows at the back of the house on to Roland's little balcony. From there an iron spiral fire escape wound down into the grounds below.

The garden was fantastic. I'll fill you in at some future point about the steel sculpture, the fig tree, the ornamental lake and the black slate set in Cotswold stone, dusted with snow, sparkling in the moonlight. Right then it was fantastic in another way. It stretched the length of the street.

Yeah, I suppose Lady Bluntstone being a garden enthusiast and Lord Bluntstone a property magnate, they'd worked out a deal. Basically, the other houses had their own tidy little squares of lawn and patio, but nothing else. The end half of their gardens had been fenced off; so that when you went down to the bottom of Roland's you could walk through arches of trellis covered in rose and honeysuckle, follow a path of stepping stones, cross a bamboo bridge and emerge secretly fifteen houses later at the junction.

Which is exactly what I did.

Five minutes later, I punched in the door exit/entry code and I slid out of a brick arch. I closed a timbered door behind me. I pushed aside frosty ivy and peered out.

Nothing.

The shadows were quite deep against the wall. I dissolved into them. I crept towards the junction.

Nothing.

I waited. Traffic was moving on the South Circular. Soon enough headlights showed. A vehicle indicated as if it was going to turn into Roland's street, slowed and turned. Then it stopped. It backed out and carried on. Something had made that driver change his mind. From my position against the wall, I couldn't see what it was. I decided to cross the road. I decided to creep up behind the parked cars and get a better view.

Like a cat in the night, I slunk across the road. I stooped down. I crouched behind the cars. From there I edged forward until I could peep out from in front of the icy bumper grill of a Land Rover – straight down Roland's street.

I caught my breath at what I saw.

There was no police barricade, no *Road Closed* sign, no squad of BMW bikers, no flashy car with the barrel of an Uzi sticking out of the window. No, instead there was a yellow police incident board standing right in the middle of the street, which read:

There in the shadow of that Land Rover, a terrible chill swept over me. My knees started trembling. I felt ill. My stomach softened and slid into my legs. These guys were sick.

We were three miles away from Gervase Street. I was clenching my hands so tightly, my nails dug into the palms of my hands. First the tape recording. Now this. I held on to the side of the car. Tried to breathe. I wasn't going to leave it there.

I stumbled out from behind the Land Rover. I didn't

care any more whether anyone saw me or not. I grabbed the incident board. I dragged it back, right across the road. It clattered, and the sound of metal on tarmac rattled and screeched from house to garden to gutter and kerb. And I didn't care. I dragged that incident board as if it was a dead body, bouncing it over manhole covers and paving slabs. I think I shouted too. I think I said things I don't ever want to remember. I tried to throw it over a wall, but it was too awkward and too heavy, and I was shaking too much. Like a madman, I wrestled with it until I reached the high street. Then I left it standing there outside a fish and chip shop, and I leant against a wall, covering my face.

Eventually, I made it back to the brick archway into Lady Bluntstone's garden. I fumbled behind the stiff ivy and pushed the door open. I ran, tripping over the old vines and skidding on the slate and gravel. It wasn't until I was well over the bamboo bridge and could see the spiral staircase spidering upwards that I allowed myself to exhale properly.

I stumbled up the iron staircase, shaking – and not from the cold.

And as soon as got in I crawled on to the futon. I lay there, my face buried in a tapestry cushion.

THE STREETS OF LONDON

'One cannot hear a brother's cry and sit down beneath the palm tree.'
Ibo wisdom – Nigeria

I didn't sleep well. I tossed and turned. Why had they left the sign there? Why wouldn't they leave Angelo alone? Even dead he wasn't safe. I heard police sirens. I imagined motorbikes. I shivered beneath my duvet. They must have seen me. They'd come and get us. All Lord Bluntstone's priceless rugs and paintings would go up in smoke. I'm sure I heard fire engines. I think I cried. I can't remember. It didn't help anyway. And dragging that sign had made my bad hands hurt again. I lay on them and they ached.

And the next day I was depressed. I mooched around, not eating toast, not saying anything, while Roland and Sapphire stared into their empty coffee cups. Everyone was waiting for something to happen. Something like me leaving for ever. Where was I going to go? I wracked my brains for a plan. But there was only one place I wanted to be.

I wanted to go to a little cut-through called Gervase Street East, where the snow was stained red.

But I couldn't seem to leave. And so the morning passed. We didn't eat any lunch. The waiting carried on until I couldn't stand it any more. I had to go. That was all.

So as soon as I could bear it, I whispered to Roland, 'Manz going now, u-get-me?' He nodded and patted my shoulder rather awkwardly. I picked up the golf bag. I turned my face from them. I tried to swallow all those feelings tucked up where my bow-tie had been. 'Yo.' My voice squeaked a bit. 'The dagger?' I said.

'You gave it me,' said Sapphire.

I shrugged. Who cared about the dagger any more? If those guys caught me, they still wouldn't get it. Sick joke.

Sapphire didn't move.

'Give it back to them then,' I said. 'Whatever.' I could really just see her, dressed up as me, going to the top storey of that car park – all alone after dark. I don't think.

'I hate you,' she said. 'I hate you so much. You're just going to walk out on us, aren't you? Go on – walk out and save your own miserable skin.'

'Yep,' I said. 'And why not? Man likes his own skin. It's a nice fit.'

'You've got to take the dagger back!' she screamed. 'You can't just walk out on us!'

'It's me they're after,' I said, 'so just give me the dagger and I'll take the sword too. I'll walk out with both of the treasures and then you'll be safe. You can go on home to Mummy, get your Police Protection and forget about me.'

'I won't give it you,' she yelled. 'Unless you promise to go to the car park.'

'Have it your own way,' I said. 'I'll take the sword and I'm gone. I just hope the More Dread Crew won't bother you. You know, I'd do anything to save Roland's place – and you. But I won't give the dagger back. U-get-it?' I turned. She could make up her own mind what she was going to do about that.

She did nothing except stare at me in absolute surprise.

So I made the brotherhood fist. Once for Roland. Twice for Sapphire. I touched it to my chest and headed for the door – still expecting someone to do something. I guess I wanted one of them to rush after me and say, 'No! Don't go! Come back, all is forgiven!'

Nobody did.

They both just stood there and watched. Well,

Roland tried to give me a roll of bank notes. He succeeded.

I went out the back. I went down the spiral staircase. I went through the arched trellis and past the stone angel. I went across the bamboo Japanese bridge and I left. I didn't think about Sapphire or Roland. I didn't look back. I didn't look forward either. I didn't think about the chain of tomorrows stretching ahead. There was no need. I was probably never going to see them. I just had one place to go before I died. I was going to pay my respects to a patch of pavement where an incident board should have been standing and wasn't. I pulled my hoodie up. I put my 'pathetic' designer shades on. I slung the golf caddy across my back. I stuck my hands in my pocket. I kept my head down. The only time I looked up was when I paid for the bunch of flowers at the petrol station.

And that's when I saw the headlines.

ANCIENT TREASURE STOLEN
by T Jones

AS NEWS breaks of the theft of an antique military sword, stolen last night during a sixth form evening at St Theobald's College, the House of Lords is calling for stronger laws to protect our heritage.

'This is outrageous,' said a spokesperson at Whitehall. 'These foreigners just get into our country without the proper papers and think they can steal our British treasures. My grandfather went to St T's and he would roll over in his grave to hear of its desecration. Campaigns to repatriate spoliated items are nothing more than organized looting. Our ancestors fought honourably and died civilizing Africa and preserving curios that would by now have been lost to mankind.'

It appears that a Nigerian using a false name, gate-crashed the ancient school, through which twenty canonized saints have passed, and pilfered the item. 'We have always welcomed foreign students here, but after last night we may have to re-think our open door policy,' said Mr Lambrick, Headmaster. This theft comes at a time when Britain is divided over its role in returning contested items in many of its national museums and is investing heavily in Southern Nigeria, in a multi-million pound oil deal with the Nigerian Government.

Continued on page 8.

I was stunned. I didn't get it. I stood there bewildered. I read the article again. The newspaper made it almost sound as if the sword was English, military and a national treasure. How could they have got it so wrong?

That's when I saw the second article. It was a bit further down the page and only one paragraph long.

OUT OF THE FRYING PAN
INTO THE FIRE

IN THE early hours of this morning a fire broke out in a local fish and chip shop. It is not known yet whether the fire was accidental or one of the increasing number of attacks on businesses owned by members of the ethnic community. Fire-fighters were called to the scene by a passing motorist. Mr Conan Edgerton, spokesperson for Southwark Fire Containment Division, said, 'Unfortunately we got there too late. The place must have gone up like a bomb.'

I dragged my eyes away from the paper and picked up the flowers. How many fish and chip shops were there around here? I remembered the police sirens from last night. I remembered dragging that sign too. You may think I'm suspicious, but I started thinking that maybe the fire and the signboard were linked. You know: fire is to signboard like dog is to kennel. I hadn't been too happy to start with, and that newspaper did nothing to make me happier.

Depressed, I hid the flowers inside my jacket, hoping the stems wouldn't break. Then I headed back on to the streets.

It was still cold. The traffic slushed beside me. The snow on the pavement was dirty. There were a few people out. I avoided them. Even if I had to die soon, I wasn't going to make it easy for anyone. As I walked I thought about headlines. I thought about signboards and fish and chip shops. I thought about nice big bright cremations of whole streets. I thought about campaigns that tried to get museums to return looted items. I thought about multi-billion pound oil deals. I thought about why those guys wanted the dagger back, the Home Office and street gangs, and I thought about puzzles. Puzzles that I couldn't figure out.

And all the time I headed on towards Gervase Street East. Drawn on by that patch of pavement as if all the answers in the world lay buried there.

Outside the Marcus Garvey Centre the snow had been hosed away. The black stretch of pavement had iced over. I stood there looking down at the tarmac. Looking and looking. I don't know why I hadn't thought of it before, but suddenly I wondered what my auntie had done about a funeral. How was she? Were my little cousins missing us? Had she told anyone I'd never come home? Right now, were social workers booking appointments to see her about me? And had she ever been here to this patch of pavement where Angelo died?

The tarmac was pitted. The ice was thin and treacherous. In my head I tried to recreate what had happened: Sapphire had stood here. Taliesin was following us out of the youth centre. I'd stood over here. There was the wall. Maybe if I looked long enough, I'd see Angelo. If I concentrated I might see him. Just for a minute. Just at the edge of my vision. Maybe like in a movie, time would shift and he'd be standing there, reaching out to stop me, his face tilted to one side . . .

From inside my jacket I pulled out the flowers. I bent to tie them to the railings, at the front of the centre, where he'd stood. I tied them very carefully, taking time, because maybe when I turned round, he'd be there. Two of the flower heads had snapped off. The rest looked wilted. I swallowed, chewing at the inside of my cheek. The bunch looked very small and the flowers very cheap. I wished now I'd bought the roses. Those daisy things were gaudy. To make it worse, the cellophane around them was torn.

I trembled a bit, because if the flowers weren't right, Angelo wouldn't be there. I wanted so much to make it right. I fumbled and untied them. I couldn't see properly, because something kept getting in my eyes. I took off my dark glasses and put them in my pocket. I wiped at my eyes to get the dust or whatever it was out. Then I tried to straighten the flower stems, tease the petals into shape, like an old woman arranging a bouquet. Instead I broke off another bud.

I sat down on the tarmac. I spread them out. They looked more pitiful than ever. My nose was running. My hands were cold. In fact, I must have been very cold, because a shivering fit took hold of me. I couldn't knot the ribbon back around the railings at all.

I don't know how long I sat there, scrabbling at the

flowers, afraid to turn and see that stretch of hosed pavement. I don't know how long. At last I felt a hand on my shoulder. I was too miserable to care whose.

A voice said, 'You'd better come in, Maxi.'

TO BE OR NOT TO BE

'If you see a snake and do nothing, sooner or later it will destroy you.'
Munshi wisdom – Nigeria

Leon Nicholas Ziggy Braithwaite Brakespeare helped me up and took me into the centre. He sent his little shadow Denetia out and sat me down in the office. He pulled up a chair for himself. Then he just sat there. He didn't talk. He didn't try to wash anything away with sympathy, or explanations, or Coca Cola. I didn't talk either. At least not for a while. I somehow couldn't work out any reason for saying anything.

At last I said, 'What's the point?'

'What do you think it is?' he said.

'What is the point of being alive if you have to die – if everyone you care about has to die?'

'No point.'

'It's not fair,' I said, my voice cracking. 'It's not fair.'

'No, it's not fair.'

'It's not fair and now my life's wasted.'

'That's not true.'

'But there's no point.'

'It's up to you to give it a point,' Leon said.

'But there's no point,' I finished. 'You said so.'

'No, and yes. It's not death that matters. We all die. Life's a losing battle. And, yes again, that's not fair. But it's *how* you live. It's the courage with which you fight the battle. That's the point.'

'I'm right out of courage,' I said, trying to smile.

'Find a purpose,' he said. 'Find something. Something of significance.'

'It's all right for you,' I said, suddenly angry. 'You've got your politics and your change-the-world stuff.'

'It's not mine,' said Leon, 'it belongs to everyone. There's a world out there that needs fixing. I'm just one person with some glue.'

I smiled. This time it lifted the corners of my mouth. 'Should I go to the police?' I said.

'That depends on what you want.'

'I don't want to,' I said. 'It's complicated.' Suddenly I longed to tell Leon everything, but I was afraid. I sat there struggling with myself. It all seemed too late.

'There are others you can go to,' Leon said.

'Like?'

'How shall I put it?' He smiled. 'See, it's like school. In the classroom the teachers are in control.' (I didn't correct him.) 'They force the kids to sit still and read from books that don't interest them much. But in the corridors, the kids are in control. They've got their own kingdom.'

He was right about that.

Leon said, 'The world is the same. Only the streets are the corridors. You have a choice like Hamlet, "*To be or not to be . . .*".'

I looked up at him. He was getting round to his favourite topic. 'To be or not to be – what?'

'Maxi, we live in a system where many of us work hard for very little and die without having lived our dreams. It's been like that for a long time. It's because of the way the world works. It's the way governments run it. And many people vote for that, because they don't know any better. You see you can only govern people who choose to be governed. But just below the surface of this predictable nine-to-five world *another world could exist* – a world where people could chose to do the right things all by themselves! A world where people could live their dreams . . . And there would be no need for unfair systems, maybe no need for governments at all!'

I sat up a bit straighter and looked warily out of the window to see if I could spot any other world out there.

'Maxi, remember everything you do, every word you say, has a resonance now and for ever – even the things you choose not to do. So it's your choice to be part of the same old system, or to work towards that other world waiting out there, where everything wonderful is possible.'

I suddenly had this idea of everyday life – the traffic lights, the ticket machines, the zebra crossings, the *News at Six* – and all the time, there just around the corner, behind that door, another world waited. A wonderful world where all the laws made sense, where people laughed and worked hard and loved it. A world which ran counter to everything I knew.

'But just as there is another better world out there waiting, there is also another worse one. A world where evil will flourish if good men do nothing.'

'Was that what Mum believed?' I asked.

'Yes,' he said. 'The B.L.A.C.K. A.R.M.Y. doesn't want to break laws and destroy systems. No, we want to change them, make them fairer, put things that are wrong, right. We want to pave the way for that wonderful world waiting to happen. But we have another role as well. We must stop those that would make a worse world from getting their way. That is what we work for. That is why we campaign for things.'

'I've got one of the Benin treasures here,' I said, suddenly on fire with the idea that somehow magically I could change things for the better. I pulled the golf bag open. I took the sword out. I gave it to Leon. 'Have it,' I said. 'Give it back to Benin!'

Leon's eyes came out on stalks. He touched the sword so gently, as if it might melt away right in front of his eyes. He let out a long low gasp of air and weighed the sword on his hands like it was made of pure gold. Then he shook his head. 'No, Maxi, I can't take it. Things have to be put right, but they have *to be seen* to be right too. The Campaign is as much about changing the system as about getting the treasures back. But take the sword to Dreader Dread. He knows of its importance in our battle.'

'Who's he?' I said.

'Just a person like all of us,' said Leon, 'and a poet, a great poet, a visionary.'

'But I don't understand,' I said. 'What's he got to do with anything?'

'If you want to understand what is happening to you, if you want justice and help, if you want to be part of the great struggle for a better world – go to him.'

'Will he know why Angelo died?' I said. A rush of hope made my heart beat faster.

'He knows everything,' said Leon.

At that moment Denetia stuck her head around the door and gave me a lovely smile. 'Cuppa?' she asked.

Leon nodded. I just sat thinking of what it was that this Dreader Dread knew, that Leon couldn't or wouldn't tell me. 'Some things are hard to understand, Maxi,' Leon said gently. 'Everyone at The B.L.A.C.K. A.R.M.Y. only knows the things they have to. That is the only way we can protect ourselves.' He laughed as if he'd already said too much. 'Don't trust anyone too easily, don't trust anything. Things are never as they seem. Start by searching for the truth.' He pulled open a drawer in his desk and handed me a mobile phone. Something in my heart lurched. It was Angelo's.

'He dropped it,' Leon said.

That was a lie. Angelo didn't drop things. That phone had been in his zipped-up coat pocket.

'Search for the truth,' repeated Leon. 'Start with this phone. It has many of the answers you're seeking.' He put it on the table.

I grabbed it. I switched it on. I fumbled. KEYPAD LOCKED. UNLOCK. MENU. MESSAGES . . . TEXT MESSAGES. MULTIMEDIA MESSAGES. CHAT . . . SELECT. I pressed TEXT MESSAGES. I pressed INBOX. I saw a list of text titles and the first one read: I NEED 2 MEET U 2NITE. I pressed the open envelope icon MOGUL KING 078986665402 – I NEED 2 MEET U 2NITE THINGS NOT GOING WELL HOLLER ME @ ABOUT 4 I THINK THE GREY MEN HAVE WORKED OUT WE R ON 2 THEM – IT CUD TURN NASTY – WE MUST MEET UP. I pressed BACK and scrolled down to SENT MESSAGES. I saw:

MOGUL KING 078986665402

MOGUL KING 078986665402

MOGUL KING 078986665402

SAPPHIRE 07778543345

MOGUL KING 078986665402

MOGUL KING 078986665402

MOGUL KING 078986665402

I wasn't ready for any of it.

Denetia came in with the tea. She put it down and gave me a hug. 'I just do *feel so much* for you,' she said. I think Leon let her know it wasn't the right time.

I just sat there.

Mogul King?

I turned the phone off. I put it in my pocket. *Angelo? Trust no one. Leon's other worlds waiting out there?*

Angelo had been texting Mogul King.

Mogul King had been texting Angelo.

'Was Angelo part of it?' I said.

Leon nodded, a sad gentle fall of his head.

'And Mogul King?'

The pattern clicked together, everything falling wildly into place.

Mogul King and Angelo had been working together with Leon to stop this worse world, this More Dread Crew from . . .

From what?

Had Sapphire known? Did she know?

I didn't.

A whole conspiracy was going on. Everyone was in on it. (Everyone except me.) There'd been meetings and plans and everybody knew about everything. And nobody was surprised when Angelo had died. *And nobody had told me.*

I turned to Leon. My breath rattling behind my teeth. 'How will I find Dreader Dread?' I said, laughing in a high dry squeak.

'It will be hard for you. You weren't ready,' he said. 'You were so young and carefree and happy. We tried to protect you. We tried to let you stay in your little world. Especially after Richenda died. It was because we cared. We wanted to see you skipping about and believing in a better future, but we can protect you no longer, I think it is time you knew everything. I'm sorry. I'm so sorry. The world can be very cruel, Maxi. Believe me, if I could have—'

I cut him short. 'Where do I find this Dreader Dread?'

'Go to the creek's west side, number 93a, St Agnes House, Marlon Street. Say Brother Leon sent you.'

FEELING LIKE A BIG ZERO

THIS IS THE CHRONICLE OF HUGH HARDY, BLUE COAT,
GUNNER, ABOARD THE THESEUS, IN THE YEAR OF OUR
LORD EIGHTEEN HUNDRED AND NINETY-SEVEN.

15 February

We advanced on Agagi early on the morning of the 15th February 1897. We were issued with our last rations: two quarts of water for the White men, one for the carriers and Black troops.

Captain Hamilton has decided that this last advance on Benin is our only chance now of success, and indeed survival; for if we wait for further men at Crossroads Camp, it will destroy us. We could be delayed a fortnight if water must be trekked from Ologbo every day. Two weeks' setback will take us into the rainy season, and this is what we fear most terribly. For whilst water might be more abundant, the continuous tropical downpour will turn the paths into rivers and the jungle into a swamp. We will be marooned, beset by fevers from the malarial-infested slough of filthy water, and the Edo will find us unable to strike tinder to gunpowder. We all will perish.

Our advance on Agagi was slow. After two hours of interminable tramping through that unforgiving jungle we had only gone two miles. Word down the line said the rear had only just left Crossroads Camp.

At one-thirty, fighting began on our lead scouts. Parallel paths cut to either side of us, as we had encountered yesterday, were discovered and we started to run wildly in terror of another ambush. Captain Hamilton ordered us to take over both of the paths and drive the enemy forward with volley power and Maxim rounds. But today the Edo resistance was much tougher. One soldier was killed right in front of me with a bullet between his eyes. Maybe they have learned not to fear the dreadful noise of the seven-pounders. And, worryingly, the marks on the trees from yesterday showed us that our aim with the Maxim had been too high anyway. We must have missed many of those we could have killed. So instead we used rockets to scare the Edo, but I am beginning to doubt that they can ever be scared again of such a terrified bedraggled parched column of men as we are.

Thirst-driven and near to collapse, we found a recently abandoned war camp near Agagi. We searched for water but with no luck. All we found were abandoned clay pitchers which told us beyond doubt that the Edo brought water in from Benin. Captain Hamilton sent Captain Turner back with this *news, while the rest of us lay on the ground, our tongues blackened and swollen.*

16th February

In the dead of night, Captain Hamilton informed us that due to the water crisis and the fear that our carriers would desert us and leave us to thirst to death, there was to be a change of plan. We are to reduce our ranks from eight hundred men down to five hundred and sixty and use the 2nd Division as additional water carriers. A flying column of the five hundred and sixty will advance from Agagi tomorrow to take Benin City. I am to be one of them. God preserve me and let me see my Malvern hills again, for our number is so seriously reduced, I think that if it were known back in England that a mere five hundred and sixty men are to storm a dynasty that has lasted these one thousand years, they will be saying their prayers for us all night. Even the Charge of the Light Brigade had more men.

God help us.

Hugh Hardy, Gunner at Arms.

I left the Marcus Garvey Centre. I trailed the golf bag behind me. I tried to remember, 93a St Agnes House, Marlon Street. I didn't know what to think. I just kept repeating the address. I didn't know what Dreader Dread had to tell me. I didn't know if I wanted to hear it. Angelo had been texting Mogul King. That meant they knew each other. That evening, going to the youth club hadn't been a random thing. Why hadn't Angelo stopped and talked to Mogul, then? Why hadn't Angelo told me what was going on?

Why had I been left out?

His phone bounced around in my inside pocket. Every time I thought about it, a wave of nausea hit me. *Mogul King and Angelo knew each other*. Had secrets. Both of them working for The B.L.A.C.K. A.R.M.Y. Suddenly I hated Angelo with an unexpected searing pain. I wanted to punch him. I wanted to smash his face against a wall. I didn't want to know his stupid secrets. I wanted to scream and kick and rip his hair out.

Did I ever really know him?

I couldn't believe he hadn't told me.

You know, I left behind more than the youth centre that evening – like all my innocence. Ha ha. Angelo had joked: fools rush in where angels fear to tread! A great joke for those who knew what was going on. Good old Maxi. The total, complete, laugh-out-loud fool.

At the bus stop, waiting for the bus to take me to Dreader Dread, I smoked my first cigarette ever. I bought just one stick from a newsagent. I drew in three puffs and choked. I flicked the rest of it into the traffic. It crashed on the street and sprayed the air with a thousand sparking embers. I can still see it now, that dark street, that cigarette.

I'd thought I was so grown up.

And then I just stood there. You know if you tilt your chin up and look at the stars, your tears run down the back of your throat and nobody can tell you're crying.

I can remember how I stood there, lips tight, chest heaving, repeating, 'Trust no one. Believe nothing.'

And then my phone rang.

Without thinking, I picked it out of my pocket and flipped it open. 'Yes?' There was a slight click, a half-stifled sob, then a thin voice.

'Please help me.'

'Who is this?' I said.

'It's me.'

'Who?'

'Roland,' said Roland.

'If you want your cash back, I—'

'Mi££ion . . .'

I shook my head. This was all I needed.

'You've got to help us, Mi££ion.'

Something in my heart cut.

'It's Sapphire,' he sobbed. 'She's taken the dagger. She's gone to the car park.'

DRIVE BY

'A monkey does not leap into the same trap from which its sister was taken.'
Ibo wisdom – Nigeria

They don't have taxis in the far reaches of South London, but they do have minicabs. I jumped across the road to the nearest cab office, to the nearest cab, and grabbed the nearest cab driver. I said, 'Market Lane multi-storey car park as fast as possible.'

It took too long to get there. At every traffic light I thought of Sapphire's beautiful face. I cursed myself for leaving her. At every roundabout (of which, thank God there weren't many) I thought of that dense *phutt*. As every car held us up, I thought of that pause, that snort, that faint *click* . . .

If anyone tells you it is not possible to get so stressed out that you actually feel you are going to explode into a red mess of skin and tissue, they are wrong. All the way in that stupid cab I was a landmine about to blow. *Why had I left her to try and return that stupid dagger? It was my fault. My stupid, stupid, stupid fault. I should have seen it coming. That's why Angelo didn't trust me with all his secrets. Because I'm stupid.* Maybe there are some things worth dying for, but there was *nothing* worth risking Sapphire for. That cab went so slowly. A lifetime later we got there.

I catapulted out of the minicab behind the police station, smack in front of the multi-storey car park. I blessed Roland for giving me money. It was 10.10 exactly. I was so scared. My liver had turned to jelly. My brain was blobbing around like a lump of fungus. The minicab was an Opel. That's not important. I punched in Sapphire's mobile number. It was turned off. I wasn't sure which way to go in. The car entrance or the pedestrian exit into the market?

I chose the nearest. I raced across the parking lot and past the ticket machine. I sped round the entrance barrier and ducked under the high-vehicle bar. Then I hid the golf bag on the ground floor behind an ancient Citroën that looked like it had been abandoned for centuries. *Where was she?* The Citroën was near the pedestrian exit. That's not important either. Everywhere was dark and silent. I started hissing, '*Sapphire,*' into the long lines of parking spaces. I crept silently, searching every level. *Where the hell was she?* I peered under cars, fearing that I'd find her dead, slumped under an axle.

My heart was sticky against my ribs. Level one was clean. Level two was clean. I kept on hissing and hissing '*Sapphire, Sapphire,*' trying to make my voice sound like the sighing wind. My throat was dry. My chest tight. She was already up there, wasn't she? Beautiful Sapphire surrounded by that pack of deadly wolves.

I was afraid. My legs were shaking and my grey mushroom brain couldn't think of any clever plan to help rescue anyone. I nearly called the police. I didn't know what to do. I remembered Leon saying, '*Trust nothing, trust no one, search for the truth . . .*' So I searched my way up the levels. I peered with a fractured heart under every car. I thought of nothing but Sapphire alive and Sapphire surrounded by those wolves.

But wolves do not fear wolves, do they? Was I not a Wolf too? I tried to summon courage. I tried to call it to me. I tried to tell myself: *Leon said 'Life's a losing battle, but it's the courage with which you live it.'* I dragged that courage right out of my bones and blood and commanded it to stay right there with me.

And so I came up to level five and there was still no Sapphire. I could hear the purr of expensive engines. I could hear the echo of car coughs rattling through dark empty spaces. I could hear the throb of my blood, as it raced round my skull. I could smell the exhaust fumes, as they curled down to meet me.

And at last I emerged on to the top storey of Market Lane multi-storey car park. It was 10.17 p.m. It was a dark cold February night. I was scared out of my grey blobby brain cells. And there they were, parked in an oval of headlights, all shining their main beams into a central car-ringed arena. I couldn't read their number plates. They must have done something weird to them, because the light glittered back like it does on reflective safety coats. Nobody was out of any car. Nobody had lowered any tinted window.

And there was Sapphire, standing alone like a damsel about to be burned at the stake. There she stood in the middle of that dark empty space, sobbing and sobbing and holding out the dagger. I could hear her voice, faint and empty, like it had travelled over a great desert to reach me. 'Please, please, let us go . . .'

Please, please, please . . .

And my heart broke. I wanted to race into the centre of that ring of flashy cars and grab her and save her.

'Stay where you are.' A voice shouted out of a car window. A voice I recognized only too well. I jumped, because I thought he meant me.

Sapphire froze. I peeped around a bumper to see where the voice was coming from.

'Stay in the centre and put down the dagger.' That same voice. There he was, directly opposite, sitting in a dark expensive car. With my mouth dry and my blood still thumping in my ears, I skirted the parked cars. I doubled up. I stayed so near the floor a whole pride of lizards would have been impressed. At last I managed to manoeuvre myself behind the smooth Mercedes-Benz CLK DTM AMG.

As I crouched, I heard him say, 'Hold on.' Was he talking to someone else in the car? Or on a mobile?

I had to find a small chink in his huge ring-of-cars armour. So I lay on my belly. I inched under the chassis of that Mercedes right up to the very driver-side door of his car. He *was* talking on the phone to someone. In fact he must have had two phones, because now I could hear him pick up another call.

'Hello?' he said.

'Merlyn,' said a second voice, very faint. 'I wish to speak to a Mr Merlyn.' This voice was quite different from Mr More Dread Crew's voice. It was very husky and very deep and very African.

'Yes?'

Now that was Mr More Dread's voice. So Merlyn was Mr More Dread.

'Oh, this is Abiola Olusamilola speakin'. I've arrived.'

So Mr Abiola Olusamilola must be the voice on the other end of his phone!

So far so good, Million, I thought.

'Right, Mr Olusamilola, make your way to the top level of the town centre multi-storey car park – come alone and bring the money.'

'No problem. Five hundred thousand, used notes – that was the agreement, yes?'

Sapphire stood looking so small in the centre of that ring of lights. I wanted to race to her – to tell her I was there.

'Is it the very dagger? Has anyone tampered with it?'

This was getting interesting.

'Hold on.' There was a faint scuffling and then Merlyn's voice rang out. 'Verify for me that dagger. Bring it over.'

Sapphire jumped as if hit by a whiplash. She picked up the dagger. She started towards the car. I shifted back as fast as I could, right behind the front wheel. I wanted her to see me, but I was afraid she'd give me away. I tried not to think what part of me the wheels would squash first if he decided to back up. Not only that, the fumes under that car were starting to make me feel really sick. The heat of the engine was unbearable. But as I pressed my nose against the concrete floor, I remembered my Science teacher, Mr Eck, saying, 'There is always five centimetres of oxygen at ground level . . .'

The car door opened. Both sides. A foot landed centimetres from my nose. A pair of feet. Expensive leather shoes. On the passenger side another pair of shoes. I was still wracking my brains for a plan…

'You, whatever your name is. Show me the dagger. Stand back over there.' There was that tell-tale click of a gun. I stuck my head out from behind the wheel. I saw Sapphire holding up the dagger. She stepped back. The leather shoes stepped forward.

'Hold it up properly, you imbecile,' said Merlyn.

You know something? I didn't like the tone that boss man, Mr Merlyn More Dread Crew was taking. Bring it here. Put it down. Pick it up. Like she was a nothing – u-get-me? In fact I didn't like anything about him. I didn't like the car he drove (much) or the crew he hung out with.

The leather shoes had moved into full view now, plus trousers and jacket. And before I could suck my teeth, I got my first look at Merlyn. He was tall, clean-shaven and handsome! I thought I'd *feel* something, you know, something. This was the guy who'd killed my brother. But what I felt was surprise. *He was White*. I mean what kind of self-respecting South London gangsta crew had a White brother as its main man?

But that wasn't the only shock I got. Yep it wasn't just Mr Snappy Dresser Merlyn that made my jaw sag. No, it was someone else too. You will never guess who came round from the passenger side of the car, until I could see him standing there, lit up by the glare of a circle of head lights? Here's a clue. It was someone I'd seen just as recently as yesterday. Someone with a distinguished forelock of grey hair and a thin hungry look? Yep. You got it. Right beside Mr Merlyn of the More Dread Crew stood *Lord Esterton*, as fresh and real as a pile of dog muck. Boy, if I hadn't been on the floor already, you could have knocked me down with even an imaginary feather!

Luckily, I'm not the type to gasp and cry out 'YOU' in a loud voice, so I nipped my head back behind the wheel and held my breath. My brain was thinking fast. *Lord Esterton with the MD Crew? Lord Esterton with the MD Crew? Lord Esterton with the MD Crew? Oh Sapphire. Poor Sapphire. Oh poor, poor Sapphire.*

Merlyn waved Sapphire back. 'Good,' I heard Lord Esterton say. 'Let's go ahead with it. When that foreigner is two minutes clear of this place I'll have Special Branch pick him up with the dagger. Home Office gets it back and the oil deal goes ahead. We fix the Nigerian High Commission . . . and let's see how much sympathy this Olusamilola's coalition party and their demand for the return of the Bronzes and for a separate Biafra gets after he's caught red-handed!' He laughed. 'The whole affair can be put to jolly old bed! Things are looking up, Merlyn. Turning out better than we'd thought.' Lord Esterton punched numbers into his phone now and said, 'Special squad. Division five. Code: King Arthur. Surround central area from police station in a cordon around the car park. We have a red alert situation. Nobody is to slip through the cordon. Wait until I give the order.' Then he turned back to Merlyn. 'Olusamilola will be exposed. The Nigerian Government will be embarrassed. We can force them to act against those insurgents in the Niger Delta once the oil deal is through. Fantastic! We stop a major political disaster which could ruin us, and we solve the problem of the old dagger! Certie will be so relieved, that will stop him having a heart attack.'

My jaw dropped till it touched the concrete. *They were going to doublecross old Abiola Olusamilola.* Take his money and stitch him up!

'Put the dagger back on the floor, over there again,' said Merlyn, pointing at the spotlit arena. Sapphire stumbled back to the centre of the ring of cars, her head sunken, wiping her eyes. I mentally shoved all my feelings under a pretend bow-tie. I had to do something and I had to do it NOW! So I slid back under the front axle.

'What about her?' said Lord Esterton when she'd gone about ten metres away.

'We'll arrange something,' said Merlyn.

'Don't you think you're overstepping the mark a bit, old boy? Letting the mission get below the old skin? Saving an energy crisis is one thing, but we're not supposed to overdo the old killy billy! And she's very attractive you know . . .'

I wished then I could have stood up, taken a swing with a right fist at their ugly heads. But I couldn't. My arms wouldn't obey me. Instead, I scrambled backwards and inched out from under the car. Then I crept like a cat in the night towards the exit ramp.

No, I was not running away.

I'd thought of one desperate, solitary, hopeless idea.

God, how I wished I was smarter! Wished I had Angelo to think for me. Wished Roland was there to tell me what to do. Wished and hoped and prayed that my idea was going to work . . .

I got to ground floor level and slipped back into my spot behind the Citroën. There was the golf bag. I pulled it out. I stayed still, all nice and curled up, until I saw Abiola Olusamilola's car arrive. It was a black limo with the Nigerian green-and-white flag fluttering from a little pole on the front. I sprinted to the first turn with the golf bag flying behind me and waited. The limo had to stop and reverse to get round the curve.

Just when it was poised, unable to move freely, I stepped out of the shadow of a VW and appeared like a ghost at the driver's window. I rapped on it. 'By the Sword of Ewuare,' I hissed dramatically, drawing that ancient blade from the golf bag, 'you'd better listen to me.' I thought that should fetch him.

The window slid down three centimetres.

I didn't waste any time. 'You're being set up,' I said.

Silence.

'They'll take the money – five hundred K, isn't it? – then give you the dagger, but two minutes after you clear this building, you'll be nicked!'

'Why are you telling me this?' said the slow deep voice I'd heard on the phone.

'To tell you the truth, bruv,' I said trying to sound reasonable, 'this sword needs to go home, it's been rusting away over here for too long.' I looked at him to make sure he'd recognized the sword. I was in luck. His eyes, like Leon's, were sprouting out of his head. 'So I'll give it to you, if you'll help me free the girl.'

The window glass rolled down a bit more. 'What girl?'

'The one upstairs, the one that brought you the dagger, the one that your "friend", Merlyn, is going to kill.'

'I see,' said Abiola. 'It seems that the gods of my people are awake tonight.' He smiled and looked again at the sword and nodded as if he'd been expecting some divine intervention. 'They have sent me a dagger, and a sacrificial maiden, and you, a hero with a legendary sword to save us all!'

Maybe I'd been wrong. Maybe my one solitary idea was less than hopeless. 'Look, bruv,' I said, 'Man can't hang around to chat. If you want the deal, this is what to do: I get in the car with you. You drive up to the top level. You ram the nearest car out of the way. Drive straight through their circle. Stop. We snatch the girl and the dagger. Then you ram the car on the far side out of the way. Then we exit pronto on the exit ramp at the other end without any of this backing-up-to-get-round-corners business. By the way, is your car bulletproof?'

'This seems a fairly fierce way to treat my business associates,' said Abiola, raising two large and beautifully arched eyebrows, 'but if you think it will work I do not see why we should not, as you say, "give it a go".'

I was surprised. Surprised at myself. Surprised at him. He was such a cool kind of guy. Like for real. Over eighty grand's worth of company car and a teenager with a tall story! I liked him!

'Let's do it then,' I said.

'Yes indeed, my brave warrior, for in my country we say that even though we worship the head, the heart too must be listened to, for it calls us to the right path. So, Saviour of the Sword and the Dagger, and Hero of the Maiden – you have tugged at my heart strings in a most romantically fashion. Therefore, tonight I will believe in the unbelievable and do the undoable, because the gods of my people have always said that when the Sword of Ewuare is raised, it is wise to do what the Sword Bearer says, for he follows the path of the heart, and as we know—'

OK, he was a cool kind of longwinded guy.

'Whatever,' I said. 'Can we go then?' I mean we'd have time for all the spiritual stuff later. If there *was* a later. Meanwhile, Sapphire was up there scared and alone and in danger . . .

'I will ask you to help me too,' continued Abiola Olusamilola. 'For we have a saying in my country that the one who comes in the spirit of Ewuare will . . .'

I glanced over my shoulder and seriously wished that this new Nigerian brother would hurry up and finish whatever he'd got to say. Maybe he needed geeing up a bit. I waved the tip of the Sword of Ewuare near the open window space and said, 'Look, bruv, can we go – or can we go?'

He threw open the car door and I saw that everything about him matched his eyebrows. He was elegant. From his trimmed little beard, to his neat moustache, from his wide rimmed glasses, to his well-cut greying hair, from his gentlemanly cufflinks to the white handkerchief in his left breast pocket (with the monogram). Boy, he was absolutely spotless.

Woo!

I got in.

'Let us go and rescue the lady then,' he said, 'but after, be warned, young, dashing hero, I will ask a favour of you!'

'No prob,' I said.

'Then know that I will give you the priceless treasures of my ancestors to guard, and you will keep them again for me. Is this not sensible? So that when they stop me (for I believe with you that this Merlyn fellow is not to be trusted and I do not think I will get very far in a dented, bullet-holed limousine) the treasures will be safe?'

'But,' I said, 'bruv, I ain't got no place to hide nothing. How am I going to keep them safe?' And my heart sank because that dagger and that sword might have been priceless, but it looked like I couldn't seem to get rid of them.

He smiled with all his fine white teeth glittering in his fine dark face. 'You, I think, are a Jewel amongst Saviours, a Champion amongst Warriors. I have faith you will find a way.' And with that he pushed the automatic window button, the glass slid shut, the radio said, '*Fuel shortages threaten British businesses . . . Major companies teeter on the brink of ruin as Britain tries to negotiate new oil deals with Nigeria . . .*', his engine purred and the limo rolled on.

We took the turn to level two in three manoeuvres, and the turn to level three in four. I was beginning seriously to doubt if Abiola would be able to manage a smooth curve-in-one getaway, so I said, 'Might be a good idea, Mr Olusamilola, if you practised taking the ramp curves more efficiently. When we are on the way out, it might be important to do it quick.'

'Ah! Hero of the Evening,' he said, 'I see as ever, you defeat the lion before he has had time to scent you. Let me try and see if what you suggest can be done.'

He tried.

And failed.

I sucked my teeth and panic started to rise in my throat. *Sapphire was still up there . . .*

However, by the time we took the ninth floor curve, he was very nearly OK. Just one and a half turns(!). I crossed my fingers and tried to think of a stunning Plan B, just in case.

One more level to go.

The nose of the limo rolled out on to the top storey.

Abiola flipped his phone open. 'I'm here Mr Merlyn, but my car has got slight braking problem – please give me small space to stop with hand brake. My fitters – oh, they have cheated me. They have stolen my brake pads and put in some very inferior ones . . . probably made in Hong Kong . . .' The limo swung up the last ramp, took the curve in one (oh yay!) and hurtled towards the ring of purring cars parked on the top floor of the multi-storey car park.

I wound my window down. I held the door open. I was ready.

I heard Merlyn yell to his crew, 'Pull back! The limo's in trouble!' There was some hurried backing, but before anyone could begin to imagine what had hit them, we careered forward. We slammed into a classic Porsche, knocked a Jag sideways, and made it to the middle of the ring of cars.

I yanked my door wide. I jumped out. I picked up the dagger. I shoved it in my pocket. I grabbed Sapphire. She screamed. I pulled her towards me. She stopped screaming. I hugged her. I yelled, 'Jump in the back!' She screamed again. 'NOW!' She recognized me. She flung her arms around my neck. (That would have been nice in another life.) She hung on to me. I pulled her off (life, eh?). She screamed some more. I pushed. I shoved. I bundled her into the back of the limo like a sack of rice. Very nice, lovely, superior, tasty, beautiful, Basmati, finest quality rice. Then I jumped in the front. Yanked the front door shut. Punched the window button – and Abiola hit the gas.

By that time (of course) the MD Crew had woken up to the fact this wasn't a putrid brake problem. You could hear their thoughts dropping into their shaved white skulls. The next thing we heard was gunfire.

We rammed into the exit drive-well. Bullets smacked on the door panels. The back window cracked into a spiderweb of fissures. We took the level eight curve, level seven curve, level six, level five, all in one smooth, fluid series of turns. I laughed. Sapphire cried. The More Dread Crew fired. Abiola Olusamilola said, 'In my country we have a saying . . .' Nobody listened. And then, four curves later, the limo slid out on to the first floor of the car park with all of us, plus sword and dagger safely inside.

We stopped.

'No!' I yelled. 'Keep going!'

Abiola turned to me. 'Here, this is where you play your part, O champion! One good turn deserves another, eh? Keep the treasures well for me. Know that their return will delight a nation and fulfil an ancient prophecy. I will drop your princess as far away from here as I can, before the police catch me. I will personally make sure she is safe.'

'But where do I go?' I said. 'How will I get them back to you?'

'I give you my mobile phone number. That part is

very simple. It is the other parts that are hard.'

He reached across and gave me his private, gold-crested calling card. I stumbled out of the car, dragging the golf bag behind me.

'Max,' shrieked Sapphire. I turned to give her the thumbs up. She looked at me just like I'd always dreamed she would. 'Maxi, I'm so sorry . . .'

I blew her a kiss.

She smiled!

'You owe me,' I said. 'I'll take two chocolate bars and a—'

'Go quickly,' said Abiola.

'That all?' I picked up the golf bag.

'You and these treasures are not strangers,' Abiola said with a wise smile. 'They will be quite safe with you.' I saw him bow his head as if me holding the sword was something that needed the greatest respect. 'Yes indeed, for you have come in the spirit of Ewuare. But that is not all . . .'

I looked at him, hoping there wasn't going to be some next long thing.

And as I waited, chilly air whistled past. Engines on the floors above coughed and ground down towards us. Seconds hung in the air in slow motion.

'I must know your name,' Abiola said. 'For we have a saying in my country, "You may know a man by his deeds, but if you wish to know him better you must also know his clan."'

I laughed then. I mean was he mad? My name? Even likkle youth knew better than to give out their names to strangers. I mean, rescue missions aside, how well did I know this brother? I shook my head. 'Now you're taking liberties,' I said.

Headlights swung into the exit ramp.

'I must know,' he repeated. 'Please tell me your name!'

Hey! Those headlights were getting a bit bright. It was time I was moving.

'*Please? For I must know if you are the one?*' he said again.

The one what?

I didn't bother asking. Instead I just said, 'No, I'm not the one.'

'In my country . . .' he began.

Hi-ho, I thought. Whatever. I needed to be in the next place.

Fast.

So I gave in.

'I'm Warrior King,' I said. 'Warrior King of The B.L.A.C.K. A.R.M.Y.'

WARRIOR KING OF THE
B.L.A.C.K. A.R.M.Y.

*THIS IS THE CHRONICLE OF HUGH HARDY, BLUE COAT,
GUNNER, ABOARD THE THESEUS, IN THE YEAR OF OUR
LORD EIGHTEEN HUNDRED AND NINETY-SEVEN.*

17 February 1897

*In the cool of the morning, we of the flying column left Agagi.
We had five days' supply of bully beef and biscuit and three
days' supply of water. Within an hour, we were under attack
from both the front and rear guard. This time we were too
weak to fight much. Fear sapped our strength. For we were
sure that our deaths were lying in wait for us, out there in that
thick fermenting jungle. So we clung together grouped along
the path, some men walking backwards at the rear to guard
our retreat and some sideways to search the bush.*

*We found many small enemy camps abandoned with their
fires still burning, as if those heathen cannibals had raced
ahead to start the kitchens in which they would boil or roast us.
We saw them jump as we fired into the pots and ashes of their*

camps. And they ran, scattering their few pitiful possessions, escaping into the bush. There was no rest, no let up. We were under constant attack. We fired a rocket as we had done on the advance from Crossroads Camp to increase panic, but whether we were successful or not, I cannot tell, unless you count the two abandoned villages at Awako that we took.

Exhausted and as half crazed as savages ourselves, we camped in one of those villages at Awako. Three men were wounded, and their howls filled the night with gloom and terror. There was nowhere for us to sleep. The few huts were commandeered by our superiors, and our carriers were so over-laden with water and ammunition supplies that they had not been able to carry enough tents. We had to make a rough bivouac on blankets under canvas. And there we lay half dead, bitten by insects, filthy – for there was no water to wash off the blood and sweat of battle. Our carriers were dying. Those who tried to steal water were flogged and left raw and bleeding for the ants. Others tried to steal off into the rainforest to lick dew or drink water from leaves and holes in tree trunks, and were killed by the enemy or shot by our guards on their return as traitors and spies. Some of us younger ones are trying to put on good cheer and are betting on our beard growths. Admiral Rawson is not in good health. Moor looks fit and cheery as ever, as if he enjoys such death and despair.

No Christian soul could ever enjoy such privation and anguish.

Forgive us our trespasses, O Lord, and watch over us.
Hugh Hardy

Abiola's car took its last turn and disappeared out of the car park. Sapphire's beautiful little nose was pressed against the spiderweb of cracks on the back window. I think she was waving.

I heard the cars of the MD Crew rumble on the ramp. I caught one last glimpse of Sapphire's lovely face. I think she was blowing me a kiss. I didn't hang around to be sure. I scrambled across the car park, dragging the golf bag behind me. I flung myself behind an old van while the cars of the More Dread Crew flashed past. I stayed there trembling long after the sound of all those expensive engines died away. I prayed Sapphire would get back to Roland's safely. I crossed my fingers, touched wood and said 'backy blue bucky high' three times.

Yes, I know – but sometimes it works.

At last I moved. I couldn't see anyone. I stuck close to the wall. I made it to the exit stairwell. I dusted off my jeans. I struggled down the back stairs. One flight to street level. I got on to Station Road – but like on the night of January the sixteenth I knew something was wrong. Someone was following me. I heard their soft tread on the stairway behind. I felt a rush of icy air, as the interconnecting door to the level above blasted open. Someone was still in the car park. Someone had been left behind to double check. Of course. What was I going to do now?

Outside, I scoped the street. I listened. I tried to predict. Everywhere shivered with shadows. A cat howled somewhere. The moon slid behind a cloud. The orange glare of a streetlight glittered off the tarmac. I felt a bit sorry for myself. It's not a nice way to die, you know. All alone on an empty street.

I put the dagger into the side pocket of the golf bag. I removed Angelo's phone from my jacket and shoved it in too. Best to have all the precious things together. I lifted the bag, judged its weight. If I had to run, it would slow me down. I thought of trailing it after me. I thought of fenced-off road repairs. I thought of uneven pavements. All waiting to trip me up.

I hesitated. Should I leave Angelo's phone in the golf bag? If I had to abandon it, his phone would be lost. A strange jittering started inside my rib cage. There are different kinds of fear, you know. I thought about putting his phone back inside my pocket. Those unread text messages. But I didn't. I don't think I was ready to know the truth. I probably wasn't ever going to be ready. I was the fool, remember? The joker.

Still it wouldn't be a joke, hanging around until the

owner of those footsteps showed up. The police might be near, but I doubted they'd be rushing to *my* help. So, bag over shoulder, I set off at a lope down by the market.

Like a bullet from a gun, a hooded figure shot out from behind the steps to the leisure centre and started closing in on me at speed.

My heart started pounding. I broke into an all-over body sweat. Time for the chase scene. You know, the one when the hero flees through the deserted streets (shouldering a golf bag); cars scream after him, police vehicles collide with each other. I didn't have much time to work on the fine details. I figured we could do that later. If there *was* a later.

I raced down through the shadows. Doubled back by the traffic lights and out on to a lane. Dark pavement flashed under my feet and a chill wind bit into my lungs. My eyes watered. The caddy was heavy across my back. I couldn't seem to shake him off. He stuck like a wasp, determined to sting. I heard engines. BMW engines. I looked back. I realized there wasn't only one guy! There were three. And two of them were on motorbikes. You're right, I'd forgotten about those bikes, hadn't I?

I'd have to dump the golf bag.

It's hard to think clearly while you're wearing down

the rubber of your best-ever trainers, but I got one thought quite clear. *Escape.* Other thoughts came later, like: *How come the More Dread Crew are linked up with Lord Esterton? Does Sapphire love me now? And what the heck am I going to do with the golf bag?*

Actually, I pitched it over a garden wall. I heard it land with a curious tinkle of muffled metal on concrete. If I survived, I'd go back for it. If I didn't, someone was going to get a surprise on the putting green. I wondered if I'd broken Angelo's phone. I suddenly regretted not having read those messages. The bikers started catching up fast. One of them overtook me. I came to a full stop.

The bike coughed. The engine sounded familiar. A little misfire on the second piston. I thought about recommending him a good garage, but decided against it. Instead I switched from athlete to survival mode. *Don't show you're scared. Try to keep them talking. Work on Roland's theory. Try to make friends. They'll have a knife. The police will arrive soon. (Maybe.)*

'OK boys,' I said, 'forget the torture, whatever you want – I'm your man.' I smiled my most Winsome smile to date.

They didn't look impressed.

'You want my autograph? You want directions on how to get to London Bridge? No? You want a High Noon Tex-Mex Mighty Meaty Pepperoni Plus with free delivery? Are you sure? Let me guess, you want a holiday for two in sunny Benidorm . . .' I forgot Winsome and tried Best Mate.

Nothing doing.

Don't despair. Look around for any chance of escape. Keep light-hearted. It'll downscale the threat. How did Roland do it? I'm sure he was kind of funny . . .

'Look, guys, haven't we met before? All you needed to do was give me a likkle tinkle – Crazy Frog, Mosquito, even Nokia, I don't mind – but I hate to break my evening jog. Another five miles to go . . .'

Well, I'd asked for it. I got it. Right in the solar plexus. Then they threw me face down on the pavement and started searching me.

'OK,' I said, 'I . . .' But I couldn't engage them in any more small talk because my mouth was pressed against the tarmac.

They rolled me over. 'Tell you what . . .' I said. (Surely Lord Esterton's two minutes must be up by now? Why couldn't I hear police sirens?)

Panic.

Just keep going, I told my heart, *while you're beating I'm in there with a chance. You're not scared. This is not scary.*

'I gotta really great idea,' I said. 'You guys let me live and I'll see what I can do about your thing?'

It was an offer nobody could refuse. Wasn't it? I mean how was I going to give them anything if I was dead? They didn't answer. They threw Roland's money across the road. Laughed at my mobile. Removed my shoes and (ouch) ripped the air bubbles out . . .

That was too much.

'NAH!' I hollered.

I couldn't bear it. My new Nike Air Maxis (expensive, fashionable, black with subtle cream edging)!

I bounced up from that tarmac, jumping around in my designer socks.

'Look, YOU,' I said to the biker. 'Seriously, those cost ninety-five quid an' I got them at a knock-down price off the internet for only sixty-nine ninety-nine! And you just busted them!'

He stood there and stared through his stupid visor.

'MY TRAINERS! They cost me sixty-nine ninety-nine! DON'T YOU UNDERSTAND?'

I could tell I was wasting my time.

I'd have liked to have ended it right there. After all, firstly they didn't understand what a bargain those shoes had been. Secondly, they weren't any good at being friendly. And thirdly, respect for all living things – like expensive footwear – was a concept they weren't too familiar with – but then there was the little matter of that Mac 10 that Biker Bruv Two had just drawn out of his knee-length cycle boot.

'We want it,' said the biker. He shoved the gun closer.

I was too mad to be scared any more.

'OK,' I said. 'I get it. 'I'm not a donut, u-know.'

That might not have been the best response. It might have annoyed them. I was not to find out. Because suddenly the sound of those long-awaited police sirens rent the air from east to west. And before you could say 'It wasn't me', the first guy leapt up behind one of the others and they were gone. I guess they didn't want the police to find that mini machine gun. Either that or they wanted to catch McDonald's before it closed.

Know what you're thinking.

Some guys get all the luck, eh?

I picked myself up. I picked up my laughed-at, last year's mobile. I picked up my sad, torn, shredded Air Maxis, with the technological, super-absorbent cells and the ripped-out air bubbles.

I pulled them on. Heart breaking. I wondered why Roland's theory hadn't worked second time round. I mean you'd have thought there'd have been more common ground . . . And then I limped back down to that garden wall and picked out the golf bag. I couldn't go anywhere with it though. Even long-awaited police sirens come with their downside. I just dragged the golf bag fifty metres into a side street, removed Angelo's phone, and decided to dump the rest in a green plastic rubbish bin outside an estate. Just in case.

The police wouldn't find it there. Even if I got moved on. It'd be safe. After all, nobody went hunting for bargains in rubbish bins around there.

Before I sat down behind the bins to wait, I sent Abiola a text with directions on how to reclaim his Bronzes. Just in case, you know, those guys returned to finish me off. Before I pressed SEND though, I took out the sword for one last hold. I brandished it to the sky and took four pictures of it with my mobile. Then I stuffed it back in the golf bag and heaved the whole clanking lot into the bin.

Abiola sent me a text back almost immediately. MANY THNX WARRIOR KING BUT I AM TRUSTING YOU TO KEEP THE TREASURES AND BRING THEM TO ME AT MY EMBASSY. IT MAY BE HARD FOR ME TO VENTURE ABROAD AGAIN AFTER THE AMBASSADOR HAS SEEN THE LIMO. AT THE MOMENT HE IS TRYING TO DEAL WITH THE DIPLOMATIC EMBARRASSMENT CAUSED BY ME BEING ARRESTED. NEVER MIND, DON'T FORGET YOU ARE THE ONE TO FULFIL THE PROPHECY. I HAVE SENT WORD TO OBA OPELAMI WHO WILL ASK THE GODS TO GRANT YOU SUCCESS. IN MY COUNTRY WE HAVE A

SAYING THAT . . . SOME TEXT MISSING . . . WE WILL MEET AGAIN. ABIOLA.

Thanks, Abiola, I thought. The gods are really going to make a whole lot of difference. But I wondered about it. Was I really *The One*? Was *I* going to fulfil the ancient prophecy? If I was or could or did . . . maybe Sapphire might revise her opinion of me! You never know. After all I *had* rescued her, and I did look good in fawn trousers . . .

The thought of Sapphire smiling at my photo (worldwide) spurred me on. I remembered the words of the Enugu professor on that last horrible night at the youth centre, his Powerpoint show and the prophecies: '*One will come in the spirit of Ewuare and will call himself "the Warrior King", and he will overturn even you!*' To tell you the truth, I could have managed a little overturning right away.

So there I sat, behind those rubbish bins, on a freezing night in early March, thinking about overturning the world and wondering what the hell I was going to do.

I thought about phoning Roland.

I thought about phones.

I thought about Angelo's phone. Somewhere in the dark night, a bird hooted. What was it that I didn't want to know?

You see, when you've been insulted, mugged and had

your best-ever trainers shredded before your very eyes, there is no point in hanging on to Never Land, is there? I mean all those fashion accessories don't really add up to much, do they? When it comes down to it, like Leon says, it's the courage you face life with that counts. So I turned Angelo's phone on. I opened it up. I pressed the green button on the left-hand side and prayed to goodness it wasn't broken.

It was about time I faced the truth.

BEHIND THE RUBBISH BINS

'When the antelope is wounded by the arrow, it runs so fast its
suffering may not be noticed.'
Yoruba wisdom – Nigeria

INBOX

OPENING FOLDER

MOGUL KING
SELECT
GOT YR TXT. YES I KNEW YR MUM, SHE GAVE ME VITAL
INFORMATION BEFORE SHE DIED – YOU KNOW IT
WASN'T AN ACCIDENT DON'T YOU? MK

MOGUL KING
SELECT
SORRY 2 HEAR YR BROTHER, MAXI, IS NOT ADJUSTING
WELL. HIS PREFERENCE FOR LIVING IN A BIG DREAM
SCREEN REALITY MAY B A WAY 4 HIM 2 COPE. GIVE HIM
TIME. LET HIM LIVE IN HIS FANTASY WORLD – IT'S
NICER. MK

MOGUL KING

SELECT

WELL WE NEVER MET BEFORE BECAUSE WHEN YOU'RE
AS INFAMOUS AS ME, YOU LIVE A LONELY LIFE. IF YOU
GET TOO CLOSE TO ANYONE IT CAN BE USED AGAINST
YOU. I RESPECTED YOUR MUM BECAUSE SHE RESPECTED
MY SITUATION. I WISH WE COULD HAVE GOT CLOSER. I
RESPECTED HER WORK TOO. MK

SAPPHIRE

SELECT

SLEEP TIGHT BABES. C U SOON XXX. S

MOGUL KING

SELECT

CAN'T REALLY BLAME YR BRO. YOU SHOULD TRY TO
PROTECT HIM AS MUCH AS POSSIBLE FROM THE REAL
WORLD AND THE WORK OF THE B.L.A.C.K. A.R.M.Y.
THAT'S WHAT YR MOM DID, BECAUSE SHE KNEW HE
WASN'T READY 2 GROW UP. HE WAS THE LIABILITY OF
THE FAMILY. THE 1 EVERYONE WORRIED ABOUT. HE
MADE HER LAUGH, HE WAS SO IMMATURE, BUT IT
TROUBLED HER 2. ALL THAT PREOCCUPATION WITH HIS
IMAGE, AND ALL THAT WORSHIPPING 4 STREET
CULTURE. AND WE KNOW WHERE THAT LEADS TO.
DRUGS AND VIOLENCE. BELIEVE ME I KNOW. AND I
REGRET IT. THERE'S ALWAYS 1 IN EVERY FAMILY ISN'T

THERE? MY DIRTY BIZ CD WAS BASED ON HER RESEARCH. I HAD SUCH AN ADMIRATION FOR EVERYTHING YR MOM DID. CAN'T SLEEP AT NIGHT NOW, THINKING OF WHAT THE MEN IN GREY DID 2 HER. U KNOW WHAT SHE USED TO SAY? FOR EVIL TO FLOURISH IT ONLY TAKES A FEW GOOD MEN 2 DO NOTHING. WE WERE WORKING ON THAT. IT WAS THE PURPOSE OF THE ALBUM. AIN'T GOING 2 B 1 OF THOSE GUYS DOING NOTHING THAT'S 4 SURE. MK

MOGUL KING
SELECT
MD CREW WERE HERE. IT WAS SERIOUS. DON'T B SCARED. DEY DON'T KNOW BOUT U. DON'T TELL YO BRO, MAXI, IF HE MIGHT GET SCATTY, BUT TXT ME HIS NO IN CASE I HAVE 2 WARN HIM.

MOGUL KING
SELECT
THANX. I'VE SAVED MAXI UNDER WARRIOR KING (JOKES) WE CAN USE IT AS HIS CODE NAME IN CASE HE OPENS YR MESSAGES.

SAPPHIRE
SELECT
BABES U SEEN DIS? NEWS JUST BROKE OF A FIRE AT RAPPER ARTIST MILLION POUND MANSION. IS IT THE

234

GUY U TOLD ME OF?

SAPPHIRE
SELECT
HI BABES. U CUMING 2 X CENTRE 2NITE?
SENT 15:45:11

MOGUL KING
SELECT
MEET ME UR ENDS 2NITE. 6 PM. TAKE GR8 CARE DEM R
EV RE WHERE. MK
SENT 13:59:25

MOGUL KING
SELECT
YOU HAVE RECEIVED A CALL FROM THIS NUMBER
07898666540 AT 3:50:23 ON 19.01.05

Answer Phone
*Welcome to Orange answer phone. You have one new
message. To listen to your new messages press one.*
Angelo, it's me, Mogul – go back home – don't try to
meet me – they've staked out everywhere. I'll try to get
to the Marcus Garvey Centre. I've got to give the
dagger to Leon. For God's sake, be careful . . .

I sat there for a long while with my head in my hands.
I knew the rest of the story. I understood. Angelo had

never got that last voice mail on the night he died. We'd just walked right into it. I understood why I'd had to help Mogul. Of course I had to. Angelo was doubled up with asthma. He was Mum's friend. He was about to be killed. I understood why we'd carried on to the Marcus Garvey Centre. We'd been supposed to give the dagger to Leon. But Leon didn't even know he was supposed to get it. That was what Mogul had made me promise to do. He'd thought we'd got his message. But Angelo was killed before we'd had a chance to work that out. I understood how the More Dread Crew got my name and number. Why they called me Warrior King. They must have taken Mogul's phone from his pocket. I understood Leon's anxiety. I understood everything. Even the things I didn't want to understand.

Mum had been murdered.

And, for maybe the first time, I understood that everybody thought I was some kind of problem kid who was too juvenile, too much of a 'liability', too 'immature', too impressed by labels and street culture, too likely to be 'scatty' to be told the truth. That if Angelo hadn't been so worried about *me*, he might still be alive . . .

Mum had been murdered. And I'd never suspected. Had no idea. Hadn't got a clue what for, or by who. I mean where had my head been?

I thought about opening up the SENT box, but you know, there's only a certain amount of truth you can bear.

I'd read enough. I couldn't wait until all those police cars shut up. I didn't know where to go or what to do. I should have listened to Angelo back then at the youth centre. If I had, by now that dagger would have been with Leon instead of in a bloody rubbish bin. Angelo would still be alive. But I couldn't give it to Leon now anyway. I'd promised it to Abiola. It was part of my deal with him. So there was no way back. There never is, is there? Once you've set your foot on the road, that's it.

Feeling less like a hero than you can ever imagine, I called the only person who I could think of. I'd been meaning to ask if Sapphire got in safely anyway, but instead I said, 'Bruv, Manz had all his money lost and is stuck. Can I rely on back up? Just for tonight?'

'I'm coming in a cab right now, Million,' said Roland. 'I'm just so glad, so very, very, totally, glad . . . Sapphire's home . . . Look, stay where you are, I'll be there in ten!'

A MATTER OF HONOUR

At four-thirty a.m. we were issued with cocoa and biscuits. We marched out of Awako at six a.m. We Blue Jackets from Theseus under Captain Hamilton were in the lead, with Major Roche's Marine battalion following, then came the carrier column while the Blue Jackets under Captain Campbell brought up the rear. We killed two enemy Edo before we left, but by seven-thirty a.m. we were engaging greater numbers of Edo than we'd ever met before. Chief Petty Officer Ansell of St George was killed by a head bullet. We tried to bury him in a shallow grave by the wayside, for we have heard that these savages return and behead their victims and carry their skulls on sharpened sticks to mount on the stockades of their compounds. Many men were wounded.

At eleven a.m. we stumbled upon a mess of ghastly, grisly bodies, fresh human sacrifices left strewn on the path, men and women slaves, gagged, mutilated and dead. Whether this was to terrify us into abandoning our expedition or was meant to please their bloodthirsty gods, I cannot say. I pulled my stained clothes over my nose and tried not to breathe for fear of vomiting.

At 11.45 a.m. the column entered the wall and ditch system around Benin that was part of its defences. At noon we gained the innermost wall, fifteen foot high, with spiked sticks upon it. I shuddered as I looked upon those sticks, fancying that I could see my own head impaled there by the close of day ... We crossed a twenty-foot ditch on a rough causeway and took a gate defended by three riflemen and three old smooth-bore canons. The three riflemen and other defenders from behind the wall were driven off by the volley of our guns and we breached the stockade with a sixteen-pounder and a cotton mine. Exhausted, but with better fighting spirits than we had felt since we left Ceri, we stopped for a water and bully beef and biscuit break. And so we consumed the last of our supplies and drank the last of our water, beside a dead leper woman, gagged and pegged out on the grass, and near a goat – alive, but with its legs broken.

As soon as we were thus refreshed, we hastened to form a line of attack. With the city there in front of us and our strength returned a little, we fired two rocket shells over the stockade and into Benin City. They travelled through the air and fell into what we later learned was the Oba's compound.

I am too tired to write more and the light has gone.

JJH

I won't go into the smile that stretched across Roland's rosy face when he found me. Or the way he nearly choked and tried to give me a wad of fifty-pound notes. Or even how he said 'Mi££ion!' a million times, and did a little kind of upper-class jig on the pavements.

I won't go into how my eyes got itchy and how I gave him a shoulder punch and missed.

Roland is all right, you know.

Anyway, we retrieved the sword and the dagger and the golf bag from the dump bin and safely made it home to his. On the front doorstep Sapphire welcomed me with a hug (which I tried to make last as long as possible and will treasure to the end of my days). Roland herded us inside. He swung the door shut. Then he pounced on me and wrung my hand until my fingers ached (again). He steered me round the mansion with his arm draped over my shoulders, cheering out, 'I say!' Sapphire followed. Every now and then she danced in front of us, brushing dust from my coat and straightening my collar.

And all the time I felt a fraud.

I wasn't a hero. I was a stupid laugh-out-loud liability. And I'd somehow got these two nice people into trouble so deep it would drown them.

In fairness, I took the only best decision I could. 'Man really appreciates the love you've shown, bruv,' I said, bashing Rollz on his back, 'but Man meant what he said yesterday. It's me that is putting you both at risk. After tonight, I'm gonna get going.'

Roland's eyes grew wide. I think a sad, lost, lonely, look passed over his face.

'Nothing personal, but it ain't too safe to stay any longer. For any of us.' I grinned up at him, because this time I meant it. I wanted to save them. I wanted to get them back their safe lives, where they still had a chance at happiness.

He relaxed. 'Just what I was thinking, Mi££ion. I think the More Dread Crew will definitely come after you. But we probably shouldn't wait until tomorrow. They'll probably come tonight.'

'For real bruv,' I said, relieved that he could see how serious it was, sad that I wouldn't even have one night. But for once I wasn't thinking about myself. 'You're right. Man'll get going straightaway.' Hell, who cared what happened to me anyway?

'However, according to gang rules . . .'

'No, Rollz,' I said, 'you don't understand . . .'

'Well – we're a gang of our own now, aren't we? And *we* have to take gang rules seriously, even if they don't.' I held up my hand. I didn't know where he was coming from, but I could see that he didn't understand. Firstly, we were *not* a gang. Secondly, I didn't hold him to any sort of not-a-gang honour. Thirdly, we were not a *we* any more. I was releasing him. He had to stop right there. I was done with gangs. He had to nod his head and wish me luck, let me keep the money, accept he'd done his bit, accept it was time not to be in a gang any longer.

Perhaps strong personalities can be inherited, because suddenly a look worthy of Lady Bluntstone flashed across his soft face. 'What those guys did to Sapphire amounts to a Dis,' he announced as if he was already in the House of Lords. 'They assured you that if the dagger was returned . . .'

I had to put a stop to this nonsense.

'Yes, but—' I started. He needed to keep Sapphire right out of this. Enough was enough.

'And if our gang has been Dissed, then we have to revenge. I mean, forgive me for saying it, but I didn't make the rules.' Little spots of colour gleamed out from his rosy cheeks.

I was left with my mouth half open. I mean, how can you stand up to a future world leader? He was right again (as usual) – that is, in an ideal-gang-on-ideal-gang world. But I still tried to stop him. 'Bruv, I know you're into gangs – theoretically – but these people aren't like the gangs you know. In fact—'

'It's your decision, Mi££ion,' he said with that

Lord-Somebody-To-Be light in his eye. 'You accepted the multicoloured beads of a dying gang general. Clearly, you are the boss. It's your choice whether we are to mount a punitive expedition of our own, or not. But either we stand up to them and show them what's what, or, clearly, we might as well fall on our swords, right now!'

Well, that put me on the spot.

This was a judgement call. If I accepted the Dis, I'd lose my credibility. Roland would be terribly let down. (What does 'fall on your sword' actually mean?) If I revenged the Dis, we'd probably all end up dead.

I sighed as all my good intentions slid away. Because when it comes down to a matter of honour, there really is no choice. Is there?

'Man needs to stick 'em up then, innit?' I said.

Roland clapped me on the shoulder, as if I'd just suggested tiddlywinks.

Sapphire looked very worried. In fact she turned horribly pale. 'Sometimes, Maxi, I think you take this South London thing a bit too far. We don't have to be a gang. We don't have to revenge. All the revenging in the world won't bring Angelo back. We just have to get ourselves out of this mess and go home.'

Roland stood up. He drew himself to his full, short height and pronounced, 'That was yesterday's thinking,

Sapphire. Clearly, we cannot appease these villains, so logically we must take a new directive. And that directive will be, as our leader, MaxiMillion, suggests, a direct all-out attack. A throwing down of the metaphorical gauntlet. A duel to the death! An expedition must be dispatched for the punishment of the More Dread Crew for this outrage. And about time too! We can't let them get away with taking the biscuit any longer!'

DIRTY BUSINESS

At 1.20 p.m., after travelling unhindered down a new bush path, we entered the town. My heart was thudding and a new strange alertness made me somehow see everything in brighter colours, as if this afternoon should be my last, and it must impress upon me the details of every visible thing. The sun was strong. Everywhere shone in sharp relief. We had travelled a mile at the double, Red Coats and Blue Coats, and now we spilt out on to a broad avenue, our coats blazing against a green sward, and then heavy fighting began on both sides. The Edo fired on us from the safety of the trees and an embankment with buildings on the furthest side of the avenue. And before us a group of fifty or more terrible figures advanced upon us. An ancient cannon fired down on us, blasting us with nails and stones. Hamilton and Burrows manned the Maxims and searched and cleared round after round at our hidden enemy. Admiral Rawson took charge and we rallied to him, forming a loose square shielding the carriers in their column with the ammunition until we broke the force of the enemy.

Many of us lay wounded and, were it not for the

ministrations of Dr Roth, we should have died there on that green avenue. But he crawled to help us and led us wounded and bleeding to the shelter of a great silk-cotton tree where we were shielded. And there we lay shrieking and cursing. One of us suffered such agonies, he tried to pull Dr Roth's revolver and end himself there. Others were helping each other, tying up wounds and comforting the dying. I was detailed to this heap of wounded humanity and saw with my own eyes great bearded fellows holding each other as tenderly as mothers while they bled and suffered and died.

Ten of us died there in the dappled shade of that great tree.

We regrouped after the worst of the killing and set out in our formation, three sides of the square intact to the centre of the city. With frequent volleys of fire ahead and beside, we moved. I tied up my wounds and resumed arms in my company of Blue Coats and we moved half company at a time forward. The last stand of the Warrior Kings of Benin was outside the Oba's palace. They fired an old palace cannon full of shrapnel, but Admiral Rawson shouted, 'Now men, before they load again – charge!' and the bugler sounded the charge and we stormed straight into the last soldiers of the Oba and we took possession of the palace.

Praise be to the Lord of Hosts that has spared my soul.

Hugh Hardy, Gunner at Arms, Benin City, 1897

'Rollz,' I said, 'have you got the latest Mogul "Rapper"

King CD, the one with *Dirty Biz* on it?'

'Of course,' said Roland. 'Very interesting and quite different from his usual lyrics.'

'Put it on.'

'But Mi££ion,' said Rollz, 'I don't think this is the right occasion to start listening to music. Clearly we've got a campaign to plan, an offensive to launch, and we need to evacuate the premises to boot!'

'Put it on Rollz,' I said. 'I believe it may hold a clue to who the More Dread Crew are and what they're up to. And if we are going to mash them up, we need to know who they are, right?'

Roland shot to the music centre and ruffled through his CDs. Within two minutes the opening strains of *Dirty Biz* filled the room. Mogul King's voice rapped out:

> *See dem crewz up there in high places,*
> *Got dirty secrets, got shameful faces*
> *Using violence to cover their traces*
> *Some of them working for government bases*
> *For them it's just a clean-up operation*
> *The men in grey are saving the nation*

'Pause,' I said. 'What do you make of that?'

Rollz gulped. 'Well, clearly, it's about the government . . .'

'Do you mean *that* is supposed to be about the More

Dread Crew?' said Sapphire.

I didn't know. Mogul King had said on the texts: MY DIRTY BIZ CD WAS BASED ON HER RESEARCH. I HAD SUCH AN ADMIRATION FOR EVERYTHING YR MOM DID . . . IT WAS THE PURPOSE OF THE ALBUM.

'What has puzzled me,' said Sapphire, 'ever since I saw that Lord Esterton at the car park, is what he was doing there? I mean, with a South London gang?'

It was a good point. But I didn't have a good answer for it.

'Shall I play the next bit?' asked Roland.

'Yep,' I said.

> *But they'll send their men in to Ancient Benin,*
> *Burn our palaces with pleasure and loot all our treasure,*
> *And they'll say they can't return it after they burn it.*
> *Leaving our villages plundered and pillaged*

'Plundered and pillaged,' said Sapphire. 'That's what that creep Taliesin Jones is always saying.'

'You hear that!' I said. 'Ancient Benin! We are on to something!'

> *And now in our struggle to do the right thing*
> *We've stirred up panic in every government wing.*
> *They fear we may succeed and the Bronzes may be freed*
> *And only violence can ensure our silence . . .*

Cos the past is all history, done and dusted
And they don't want their new deals to get busted
Like all that oil in the Niger Delta
When the Edo people still ain't got no shelter
And if we raise our voices it will limit their choices
To get cheap petrol in their Rolls Royces

'This is serious!' said Roland.

Lord E and his crew knew what to do
In the House of Lords he exercised his vocal cords

'Lord Esterton!' gasped Roland. 'That's who he means! *Lord E and his crew.* He knew! Mogul King knew that Lord Esterton was in the More Dread Crew! That's why he was killed!'

Sapphire flicked the player off pause.

Certie is second when his collection was threatened
At the risk of causing strife he volunteered an ancient knife

'Who is Certie?'

'A knife?'

'The sacrificial knife?'

Sapphire laid it down on the polished walnut table. There was something about that dagger that still niggled away. Roland suddenly opened up his laptop, got up Google and typed in: *sacrificial knife Ancient*

Benin treasure. Three hundred and forty thousand nine hundred and eighty-seven sites popped up. But hey, we knew what we were looking for! The seventy-first one was a catalogue from the British Museum. Roland opened it. It said: *search by image, age, title or country of origin.* We typed in *image*, and two pages later, there it was – just like the Powerpoint pic of Mr Enugu Professor . . . Our dagger! All three of us pranced around like lunatics. Under it was written this entry:

Sacrificial poniard of Obas of Benin, probably used in the sixth century. Bronze, some diamond and stonework. Taken by the Punitive Expedition 1897 as part of seized assets to offset payment. Stored in the Museum of Mankind 1897 – 1998. Transferred to the basement storage facilities of the British Museum, Lot 2309, 1998. Viewing by appointment and permission only.

We clicked the *viewing* link.

Viewing for all artefacts stored at the museum is available subject to permission and regulations. Contact Chief Curator & Custodian, Sir Robert Terselas.

So it had lain undisturbed as part of the Foreign Office loot for over a hundred years . . . and now it was lying here on Rollz's posh table?

How come it wasn't still in box Lot 2309 under the British Museum?

Certie is second . . .

Sir Robert Terselas.

Sir T – not Certie!

Sir Robert Terselas, Chief Curator and Custodian of the British Museum!

Roland gasped and went pale.

Suddenly I remembered Mum had said something about that dagger . . .

'I know a bit about politics, enough to know this is all getting very scary,' said Roland. 'If *lords* are *using violence* and *working for government . . . For a clean-up operation . . . The men in grey . . .* then Mogul King was talking about the Home Office!'

'Then they aren't a real gang . . .' said Sapphire, 'they're just pretending to be one . . .'

Trust nothing. Trust no one. Nothing is as it seems. Hadn't Leon said that only this afternoon?

'Why would they, though?' I said.

'Oh my God!' said Roland. 'They're pretending to be a South London gang so they can infiltrate our areas, so they can blame everything on real gangs . . . They're giving proper gangs a bad name. This is terrible. Clearly, this is even worse than I ever imagined!'

By this time I was a bit lost again. Although I wasn't

too sure about the giving-gangs-a-bad-name thing. Most gangs I'd heard of managed to do that quite well on their own.

'What are we going to do?' whispered Sapphire.

'If they know we've guessed who they are,' said Roland, 'they'll stamp us out, just as if we were tiny ants, remove every piece of evidence like we never existed. Clearly, that's their job. Can't you imagine it – someone, somewhere, in some grey government office saying, "This Benin Bronze affair is causing the government acute embarrassment. If they prove their case it will open up a precedent for every Tom, Dick and Harry to reclaim every last scrap of Empire we've ever owned. And they'll probably demand apologies and money too. We'll look like idiots! Our heritage will go down the pan and our credibility with it. It can't be allowed to happen. Get on to the Home Office straightaway.'''

'That's why they killed Mogul King, isn't it?' said Sapphire. 'That's why they killed Angelo.'

I suppose it was a sign of the times that I didn't even stop to wonder if Roland had got that quite right. *Clearly* he was very upset about gangs getting the blame. But would the government really do that?

'And Mum,' I said, 'she was murdered too.'

Roland looked at me like he'd known that for a long

time. Then he paced around and continued. 'And can't you imagine another grey suit answering from the depths of his Chesterfield with a glass of brandy being gently warmed in his hand, "I agree old boy, and don't forget we've just clinched the oil deal with the Nigerian Government. They're as anxious as us to quash those separatist insurgents in the Delta. The last thing they want is for ancient history to disturb the fragile peace currently being imposed over the region. Although they are a bit sensitive about those Bronzes . . . They want that dagger thing for the Lagos Museum – why don't we just give it them and mop up the rest very quietly?"'

Frankly I couldn't imagine the depths of a Chesterfield or warm brandy, but then Roland was usually right.

Sapphire sank down on to the futon, her face in her hands.

And whether Roland was right or not, those guys at the car park hadn't been out collecting for charity.

'There's only one thing we can do,' I said. 'We've got no choice. We've got to expose them – and we've got to do it before they kill us too.'

'But how can we?' said Roland. 'Do you have any idea how powerful these people are? It's totally hopeless . . .'

'We'll think of something,' I said. 'Come to think of

it, you were on the right track earlier, bruv.'

'I was?' said Roland.

'Yeah, like you said! "A direct all-out attack!"' I stood up and punched the air as if to drive my point home. 'They don't want a Benin Bronze scandal? Boy, we'll give them one so big it'll make them rethink history! We'll break into the British Museum and swipe the lot! We'll get the whole damn nation chatting about it!'

'How are we going to do that?' said Sapphire.

'Easy,' I said. 'We're gonna stick 'em up, innit!'

SOUP SPOONS, SURPRISES
AND A CUNNING PLAN

'When the ants are on the move, it is unwise to cross their path.'
Yoruba wisdom – Nigeria

Roland beamed like he'd been awarded the Nobel Prize. Then gave me a look that would have made a spaniel despair.

Sapphire didn't say anything.

I paused with my Melt-Antarctica smile ready. 'We've got to do this, Sapph,' I said. 'Then we can all go home, eh?' The Bronzes could go home too. I owed that to Mum.

Mum.

Suddenly it came to me what she'd said. She'd picked up the dagger and run her finger over the diamond and said, 'This dagger will fix them all, it's full of surprises!' Then she winked at me and put it away in her desk.

Surprises. What had she meant? How had she got it?

Sapphire was still silent.

At last she spoke. 'OK,' she said, 'but it'll be very, very dangerous.'

Roland jumped up and started piling pullovers, T-shirts, tracksuit bottoms, soap, shampoo, shower gel and toothpaste into a large hold-all.

'What you up to, bruv?' I said.

'Packing of course, Mi££ion. You're absolutely right about staying here. It's absolutely not safe!'

'Will you be OK alone? Will you call out Arnold?' I asked.

'Have your parents gone away again?' said Sapphire.

'Oh crumbs, yes. Mummy only comes up for the night when it's her Spring Ball Committee, and Daddy is in Jinja – so I'm coming with you.'

'Jinja?' I said.

'Yes, you know, Uganda, source of the Nile, coalescing the East African support for carbon emissions.'

'Right,' I said, 'Man knows all about that.'

'So I think we should go to *Thaddeus*.'

'Thaddeus?'

'Yes, she's a bit primitive, but she's got all her essential bits.'

'Well, that's good,' I said. I mean had Roland flipped?

'So if you'll grab extra plates and cutlery and a few more towels, we'll be fine.'

'Roland,' said Sapphire quite kindly, 'Thaddeus is usually a boy's name, but anyway, even if she's a woman, it's very unkind to refer to any lady as "primitive" with "essential bits".'

'Oh *Thaddeus* isn't a lady,' said Roland, dashing around shovelling an alarm clock, laptop, torch, electric kettle, extension cable, mobile charger and washing-up liquid into the bag.

Sapphire was so shocked her beautiful mouth dropped wide open. 'Well we can't all have lords and ladies for relatives—' she began.

'*Thaddeus* is a boat,' said Roland. 'She's a super little converted ninety-two foot TBP tug with a twenty-two ton bollard pull, boasting eight berths and a hell of a noisy motor. She's moored up on C Band Wharf, Chelsea, and nobody's been aboard her for at least ten months. She's the next best thing to a cave in Afghanistan! We can hide up and hole out and nobody will ever find us. See – here're her keys!' Roland dangled a couple of Yale keys in front of us and skipped off to find more soup spoons and napkins.

'Yo!' I said. For the first time since I'd read Angelo's messages I was beginning to feel I could revisit my old immature, buffoon self . . .

Trust my man Rollz to have an answer for everything!

* * *

257

Two hours later, at exactly three a.m., we sat in the tiny galley of *Thaddeus*. I won't go into all the details of how we left Roland's, but you can be sure it involved the back garden and a Japanese bridge.

We were too tired, of course, to put together any serious Benin Bronze plan right then. Instead we sat huddled up and nibbled chocolate bars. Under us, the hull quivered with the slap of the river. Around us, the air whistled. *Thaddeus* was a very neat craft, but on that night she was cold. Very. Roland didn't want to fiddle around on deck trying to hook her up to the main grid. He also didn't want a light that hadn't been there for ten months to suddenly shine out from her starboard porthole. So we just sat there, wrapped round one flickering candle. We pulled out musty blankets from the sea chest. We cuddled ourselves inside them. We thought about tomorrow and how we would work on the fine details of the Great Plan. We thought about yesterday and all the things that had happened. We thought about today and the car park. And we stared into that candle flame as if in its blue centre we could see a better future.

And outside, the cold river ebbed down past Battersea, past Vauxhall and the green glass windows of the Home Office building, past the Houses of Parliament and past the chambers where the House of

Lords met and decided things. Things that affected us. Things we didn't have a clue about.

We kept completely hidden for a week. We did not go on board. We did not hook up the electricity. We turned off our mobiles. If the spooks were out to get us, we couldn't use any modern technology at all. We ate the supplies Roland had brought. We suffered. But as every day passed we felt safer. On Friday the sixth of March, disguised as best he could, Roland reconnoitred the British Museum. He took notes. He sketched a map of every place I'd need to pass through. And we made a plan.

This was it.

We'd steal back the remaining seven Ceremonial Treasures. Then we'd give them to Abiola to give back to Nigeria. That dealt with that part of the plan. Then came the clever twist. The loss of the Bronzes would be sensational. We'd be such high-profile criminals that we'd make the front page of every newspaper . . . and so would our true-life confessions! Haha! We could reveal the activities of the Home Office and the More Dread not-really-a Crew. And how they'd pretended to be one, and killed Mogul and Angelo, and how it was all a government clean-up, and how it was something to do with Nigerian oil, and we'd splash it in white-on-black, ten-centimetre high, bold caps across every breakfast table worldwide!

We figured quite reasonably that if the cat was out of the bag and the Bronzes were gone, there'd be no reason left for us to be silenced. I mean, this was a government operation, wasn't it? The More Dread Crew (or whatever their new code name would be) would have to regroup and sort out a Plan B or something. At least, that was our thinking.

There were a few problems with the plan of course. Like how to get our confessions on the front pages of every newspaper in the land without getting caught. And there was the matter of actually stealing the Bronzes. But apart from that, I thought it was pretty foolproof.

There was one other thing I didn't mention. We'd need help. You visit the Africa Room at the British Museum, and you'll see why. The plaques wouldn't be too hard to get. They were only nailed on to mounts – quite open to the public and quite pull-off-able, their only protection being a security alarm and camera. But getting the ivory chest mask would be difficult. That was locked in a cabinet with unbreakable plate glass, secured to the floor, and probably hot-wired to Jupiter too.

Impossible, you might say.

Well, that's where our plan got clever.

See, London is full of illegal workers who get the boringest jobs, cleaning and fetching anywhere they can. You show me one big building and I'll show you a dozen workers from all over the globe who know the place like the back of their hands.

Hey, even the crown jewels sometimes need a bit of a dust and polish up, and you can bet the Queen doesn't go down there herself to do it.

So I may be immature, two-dimensional and *scatty*, a constant worry to my family, and living in a total big screen dream reality, but I've got some mates in low places!

Low enough to open up a few doors from the inside.

I'd have to make them an offer they couldn't refuse. Roland worked on the nicer points. This is what he came up with: *TEMPORARY CONTRACT BETWEEN WARRIOR KING AND THE B.L.A.C.K. A.R.M.Y. AND THE UNDERSIGNED (LOW LIFES)*:

The agreed above person(s) and others such as are deemed necessary – but not exceeding five in total – will get half a million pounds (well, hey, let's make it attractive – after all you can be quite generous with large amounts you're never going to have to find!) *if and only after they have lent every assistance to help successfully steal and secure six Benin bronze plaques and one ivory chest mask from the British Museum.*

In the event of The B.L.A.C.K. A.R.M.Y. failing in its promise, the Government of Nigeria will back this contract. (I figured if Abiola was ready to pay half a million for the dagger, he'd stand the same for most of the rest . . .)

Signed:

Low Life 1 . . . .

Low Life 2 . . . .

Low Life 3 . . . .

Low Life 4 . . . .

Low Life 5 . . . .

Witnessed . . . .

I thought it was a pretty impressive piece of writing. I felt sure the low lifes would have every confidence in it. Roland was fussy though. He wanted to go to a branch of Oyez and get a proper legal form. Sapphire said that if you were doing something illegal, it really didn't matter because nobody could enforce it in a court of law anyway.

Sometimes being too smart isn't helpful.

Once that was done though, all we needed to do was hook up with the said low lifes.

So that was it. Someone was going to have to go silently into enemy territory and slip unarmed, back across the river into the Dirty South to a dodgy meeting place where known criminals gather. That someone was going to have to stay out of sight from any of the More

Dread Crew's prying eyes and, sticking quietly to the back streets, find enthusiastic rescuers for the Benin Bronzes. That someone was going to have to be totally sure the hired crooks were two hundred per cent trustworthy, plus completely experienced burglars, who were ready to work against impossible odds, and be so true and trusty that they would not betray us.

Now who that someone was going to be, naturally caused a lot of excitement aboard *Thaddeus*. We all competed for the privilege of not being the one to do the job. I mean the person would need courage and stamina, be an excellent negotiator, stealthy and brave all rolled into one. So logically I was the main candidate. My argument, however, was not that I was *not* any of those things, but that as I was *obviously* the best candidate for the job, I should give one of the others the chance to expand their skills. I mean even gangs have gotta have a staff development plan. You know what I mean?

I was overruled two to one.

Sometimes being in a gang of three sucks.

'We're counting on you, Mi££ion,' said Rollz.

'You really are the best person to do this,' said Sapphire. 'After all, you probably know masses of dodgy people anyway, and you'll be able to talk to them on their level.'

I may be slow, but there was something about that encouraging comment that wasn't encouraging.

So that was it.

So on our twelfth day of boarding *Thaddeus*, I set out in search of accomplices for the greatest and most daring Punitive Expedition to get the Benin Bronzes ever planned since 1897.

I think I may have mentioned somewhere before that I wasn't A* at planning. But I did work out one thing: that once I'd located the correct criminal, we'd better meet in a public place where it would be hard for said low life(s) to murder me. I also had another flash of genius and figured out we'd better meet somewhere where there was an English translation service (just in case foreign criminals were involved or I forgot how to speak English) – so the choice of course was obvious.

Everyone who's ever flirted with the thought of serious crime knows the exact place to go. The place you could only describe as *the* international criminals' employment agency. Its fame was legendary. And I'd always longed to go there!

Mr Smith's Dental Surgery.

Even though they didn't know it, those Benin Bronzes should have been smiling all over their metal faces. They were one brainwave nearer going home.

A VISIT TO THE DENTIST

'When we took stock of our conquest, we found many exceedingly beautiful
bronze plaques. All the walls and the timbered joists of the Oba's palace were
clad with them. We believe them to be of Portuguese make, as the
craftsmanship is singularly fine. I would have documented their positions, as
they seemed to relate the histories of the great deeds of long dead Obas, but alas
all were ripped quickly from their mountings, so those exploits are lost. The
palace altars were also furnished with impressive bronze heads and ivory
tusks, exquisitely worked. In one well we found forty-one tusks stowed for safe
keeping. Indeed there are many hundreds of pieces of booty now assembled in
the main compound. We have been photographing ourselves amongst them.'
Captain C. Campbell, C.B., of Theseus, recorded in ship's
Miscellaneous, 1897

So on the evening of Monday the twelfth of February, I
crossed back over the river and set out due south for the
open purple door of the dentist's waiting room. That's
Mr and Mrs Smith, Dentist and Orthodontist.

When I reached my destination postcode, I lingered.
I looked in shop windows. I spent a long time outside
the Sell Phone Shop on the high street. Sell Phone
shops, as all true dodgy guys know, are the correct places

to loiter when you are looking for a deal. My attention was momentarily glued to the latest Nokia update: *Yours for only a £15.00 surcharge, on Chat 200,* when I saw the shadow of a BMW slide across the darkened shop front. I heard its second piston misfire. I stiffened.

I turned. The only bike on the street was a police one. Weird? Or maybe not. Maybe I was just too jumpy. Then suddenly there was someone beside me. Much too close to be accidental. At first my heart skipped into my tonsils. Then I relaxed. There's a metal barrier between the Sell Phone shop and the street. The police biker could not have got to me that quick.

There was only one other person it could be. A citizen of the London criminal classes. I wrote in greasy letters in the dust of the shop window: *WE NEED TO CHAT AND NOT FOR JUST £200.* Then I gave him what I considered to be a knowing wink and sauntered on past the Underground, past a department store, and crossed over the road in front of a burger joint.

The police BMW rounded past me again. I'd ducked into a multiplex cinema. I stood in the front hall, pretending to look at the latest posters. I was pretty sure the police biker with the misfiring BMW hadn't see me. The dodgy guy who'd linked me at the Sell Phone shop turned into the cinema too. He was obviously a tout. His trainers had seen better days. He couldn't afford a haircut. Clearly, he needed business.

I pushed through the doors to the bar. There were a few people in there, sitting in leather chairs, chatting on about a book event in the local library. The tout followed. Outside it was raining. I heard the town hall clock tower chime half past.

When I was certain we hadn't been followed, I walked up to the tout and whispered, 'Mr Smith's waiting room. I want someone young and smart and into people-trafficking, but who's not above a little basic burglary, and has getaway wheels.' He nodded.

I left the cinema and crossed over in front of the town hall with my jacket pulled over my face. I wasn't taking any chances. I didn't peek out. That BMW biker might be a policeman, but that didn't make him safe, did it?

I paused outside the burger joint. I thought about getting one. I scanned the reflection of the street behind me. I saw my contact hurrying away through the rain. No bikes. I doubled back. Crossed the road. Up beside the town hall. Down beside the bank. Before you could fry an egg, I reached Mr Smith's Dental Surgery.

On the threshold of that open purple door I turned and paused . . . There was a brightly lit supermarket in the distance. Its neon signs flickering through the drizzle. It was tempting. The town hall clock tower stretched up into the sky. Grey clouds raced beside a kneeling stone cherub. But I wasn't the same old Maxi, was I? I wasn't *scatty* any more. I'd grown up. I'd left that happy fantasy world behind, hadn't I? I heard theme music winding through the traffic. I saw a rainbow arch into the morning. I imagined the credits rolling up the big dream screen . . . I flicked an eyebrow and raised my chin to its most handsomest angle.

Just for old time's sake.

If you've never been to Mr Smith's Dental Surgery, don't be too upset. It's just a converted front hall with a line of chairs. The paint is peeling off the woodwork, and the sliding doors to the rest of the building don't quite shut. But you're welcome there and you can wait – no questions asked[1] – no appointment necessary.

I did just that. Mrs Smith kindly asked me if it was urgent. I said no. She handed me a copy of *Woman's Weekly*. The three guys waiting beside me said nothing.

So I sat there, fascinated, wondering which dodgy deals were being worked on under the dentist's drill. Wondering if there was some kind of criminal protocol I didn't know about. If I was supposed to say a

---

[1] Like, 'How come your two front teeth are jammed into the back of your throat?' And, 'Yes, of course, to replace them in solid gold with inset diamonds would be quite easy . . .'

password or give a funny handshake . . .

And I waited.

After an hour and a half, during which time I popped out and scanned the street, just to check if my tout and low life(s) had found me and the biker hadn't, and twice Mrs Smith asked me if I'd *still* like to wait . . . I'd almost given up. In fact, I decided that I might even go for the root canal treatment to fill in the time, when through the door strode (well almost – given that it would be hard to stride anywhere in Mr Smith's Waiting Corridor) a pizza delivery kid with his crash helmet down and – from the smell of it – a garlic and herb medium-sized pizza in his left hand.

For a moment I held my breath. Was he one of the famed underworld criminals? Then he spoke. 'So here I am, O stranger of a thousand sparkling eyes, and descendent of the rotten seed of oysters.'

The three men beside me turned to look. *I* turned to look! I mean, faced with an opener like that, 'Wassup, rude-boy?' seemed an understatement.

Mrs Smith's eyebrows shot up about ten centimetres and she left the room (sorry, corridor) tutting. I guess you get used to weird language if you work at a dentist's.

'We have understood your message from the windows of Sell Phone and come to see for ourselves about the payment and the deal, for as the water lily blossoms in the desert, so too do we try to flourish on a bit of extra income.'

The old bloke on the last seat said, 'You can't flourish on anything these days.'

I gawped. I mean, what was this guy on? Or was this some new kind of underworld chat that had mysteriously bypassed me? For a split second I felt my confidence slithering away down the corridor. Then I stood up and sidled past the sliding doors and got near enough to the pizza kid to say, 'Manz got a likkle proposition, which I think you boys are gonna love.' The sound of drilling came from the surgery.

'Speak not with the forked tongue of many serpents, lest we cut it from your throat and feed it to Rottweilers.'

I stepped back, alarmed. The drilling continued. 'Forget about the forked tongue thing,' I said. 'I'm offering half a million in sterling, bruv, so if we're going to get serious, you've got to drop the attitude – u-get-me?' I thought that was just the right tone. You know, friendly but tough.

The pizza kid with the weird chat lines sniffed like I was foot powder. Mrs Smith popped her head back round the sliding surgery door. The drilling stopped. She looked the kid up and down with a professional glance. She said something to him in non-verbal hieroglyphics with her eyebrows knitted up, and I don't think she was asking about dental caries.

'OK,' he growled. His voice squeaking oddly at intervals.

That was much more like it.

'I want some Inside Help.' Everyone south of Nelson's Column must know what *Inside Help* meant.

'OK,' he said again.

Phew. 'I need it from your people inside the British Museum.' I liked the touch the word 'your' gave it. You know, I was giving respect without losing any.

'Simple,' he said, 'but . . . if you should fail to pay the agreed price, know that we will take pleasure in boiling the flesh from your splintered bones and leaving it in the wilderness to be trampled by foul warthogs.'

'Right,' I said. It didn't sound like the punchline to any joke, so I didn't laugh.

Mrs Smith popped her head back round the surgery door. This time she was definitely angry. 'It's all right, Walter, you can stop talking like that. For a start you sound silly, and secondly, it's not "foul warthogs" it's "the filth of swine" – try to get it right or I'll be phoning Auntie Krissie.'

I wasn't quite sure who exactly Auntie Krissie was. Where she figured in this. And why she was such a stickler about pig u-no. To tell you the truth, I was a bit out of my depth. Still, it was obvious that Walter was well known to the Smiths. So at least he was bona fide. I guess. Come to think of it, Mr and Mrs John Smith sounded oddly familiar too. Were they well known? I mean, had I met them somewhere before too?

'Well, we don't want to upset Auntie Krissie, do we?' I said.

Walter took off his crash helmet. Underneath all that flowery talk he was a kid of about seventeen with a handsome face and his hair done in pigtails. He scowled at me and said, 'You better deliver, punk, or Man'll mash you up.'

I can't say that Walter and I had the most comfortable relationship ever; I mean we weren't going to be best friends and play video games together. But before we left Mr Smith's, we'd struck a deal. It was the kind of deal you know is going to work. There was nothing warm and woolly about it. It was founded on that mysterious quality that all youth south of the river struggle for: RESPECT.

However, I've got to say – I'd shied a bit at the transport clause. I mean pizza delivery scooters that doubled for the Hot & Sour Noodle Shop during overtime hours weren't exactly what I'd had in mind for our getaway vehicles. Still, I wasn't going to be picky.

And, come to mention it here, I wasn't dead

impressed with Wally's 'experience' ratings either. I mean he claimed he'd organized quite a lot of workers (from destinations that could not for obvious reasons be named) into quite a lot of places (that for equally obvious reasons could not be mentioned either), and that was it.

But what could I do?

What with Sapphire and Roland waiting and BMWs sliding up and down the high street, I had to take whatever odds I could get.

So Walter signed our agreement, but only after he'd added a few graphic details under a new clause he'd invented, entitled: *What happens if the money is not delivered* . . .

I figured that was fair. I mean what was the point of arguing about whether your fingernails get pulled out before your toenails? Sapphire felt differently of course, but then she likes her fingernails.

Anyway it was miles too late, by the time she knew about it, for her to object. Because by then we'd put the plan into action, and I'd already started out for the Africa Room at the British Museum.

I SET OUT ON THE EXPEDITION

'There is no tree that cannot be felled by a small axe.'
West African saying

The day I set out on my mission was warm. Sunlight flashed off the Thames. Pigeons strutted on the deck. The morning held the promise of spring. I say 'promise' because maybe I wasn't going to live long enough to see any nice green buds on any nice green trees. The tide was high. The waves snatched at the gangplanks. I breathed in rivery air and wondered why I had to be the idiot who rescued the Benin Bronzes. I mean, why hadn't one of those heroes during the last century done it? It wasn't fair. In films, hero stuff was done by people who had special talents. Even Harry Potter could speak snakish. Although, come to think of it, snakish probably wouldn't have helped.

Anyway, beside me, traffic rolled on the inner ring road. Without any special powers, I scanned it as carefully as I could, watching every car to see if a BMW lurked in its blind spot.

My plan as usual was rubbish. I was going to attend a storytelling function in the Africa Room of the museum. There'd be lots of kids there. All probably way younger than me. Rollz didn't think that mattered. He said, 'Everyone will just think you're a bit babyish, that's all. Don't worry, Mi££ion – you'll look the part.'

Thanks.

During the storytelling function I was going to link up with Wally's Inside Help. They would 'help' me by getting me to hide in a straw horse on display in the Africa Gallery. Roland loved that part. He said, 'That's so *utterly* brilliant! Clearly it'll be just like the wooden horse of Troy!' (Whatever that was.) Anyway, once I was hidden inside this horse outfit, I didn't have a clue what I was supposed to do next. No doubt it had something to do with the supplies Sapphire had made up for me: chocolate bars, water, a tool kit (wire cutters, screwdrivers, a hammer – don't ask) and a Post-it note saying: *Don't forget the I'm-A-Three-Year-Old smile.*

As I closed the wooden gates of the wharf behind me, I switched to high alert. Letting Walter and the pizza delivery boys in on my quest had its disadvantages. I won't go into them. I'll leave you to imagine what some junior kid barely able to finish his spicy pepperoni might think up, if he knew half a million quid was on offer. So I scoped the street. One jogger: female with headphones. Plenty of cars. Two tramps slumped on a bench further up. One holding a can of Extra Special Brew. At least they looked like tramps, but then if you're a spy you've got to look like something, haven't you? I tried to memorize their footwear. I had a private theory that if spies had to follow on foot, they'd probably choose decent shoes.

Tramp A had on non-brand trainers. Tramp B – desert boots.

Walking fast, I headed for the nearest Underground. I wove through side streets. I stopped to check behind. No one. I chose a one-way lane, in case the two tramps had an accomplice in a car. As a precaution, to check out if I was being followed, I went into a greasy spoon café. I skulked in the window over a runny egg on toast. I saw two men pass. My heartbeat shot up. One had on desert boots!

Sweating, I pulled a stray newspaper over my face. I peeked out from behind it. Did they know about the houseboat? Who were they? No junior pizza delivery kid would dress up as a tramp. Those guys were old and White. I faced the other possibility. The More Dread Crew.

I wiped a piece of soggy bread round the plate. It wasn't appetizing, but I might not eat for a while. 'Mind if I borrow your ketchup?' said a voice from behind. I whirled round, ketchup in hand. Just an old woman. I tried to smile and mumble, 'Sure.' Someone else passed the window. I missed him. Sweat trickled down my neck. I wiped the palms of my hands on my jeans. The café wasn't the only thing that was greasy.

The woman behind me crunched her toast. I could hear the cooks in the kitchen clinking cutlery. I sat there, my heart thudding.

The woman behind me stopped crunching her toast. Outside the window, the guy with desert boots was back. That was enough. I pushed the rest of my breakfast away and left. I sprinted, dodging past people, dashing across red lights until I got to the tube station. I stopped. I looked behind me. There was no other racing figure, just a curious stillness. I checked for CCTV. I forced myself to calm down.

Inside the station, I leant up against a map of the Underground. What was I doing? *What the hell was I doing?*

Suddenly all my reasons seemed to evaporate. A full all-out attack? Front page headlines? Um, *hello*?

I should STOP right NOW.

But you know, I was caught on a wheel. And with each turn of the wheel, the spring at its centre tightened. There was no way to get off. There was no way to stop. The wheel would turn. The spring would twist. And unless I could somehow escape the More Dread Crew, one day I'd run out of time. I'd be just another sentence on another yellow incident board.

I bought a ticket from a scruffy guy who was recycling them along with copies of *The Big Issue*. I took a good look at his shoes. Then bunching up my muscles, without warning, I raced through the turnstile and down into the tunnels below.

There was no way anyone could have followed me. I disappeared like a five-pound note. I twisted round so many corners, even I got dizzy. And I didn't stand anywhere near the train tracks either.

The next train came. I darted on, just as the doors were closing. I sat tense on a chequered seat. I wondered what the rest of the day held. The tube stations flashed by. I kept my fingers crossed. I prayed Wally knew his stuff about Inside Help.

Knightsbridge. Hyde Park Corner. Green Park . . .

Then I saw it! Of course.

Inside Help!

Somebody had known all along where I went. Somebody had found us at the Marcus Garvey Centre. Somebody had known I was at Roland's. Somebody had tipped Taliesin off that we were at St Theobald's. What if the More Dread Crew were getting some Inside Help too? Somebody who we trusted? Somebody who knew what we did?

The name we were supposed to find with the sword! The spy Mogul King wrote about! The spy who was spying on *us*!

Of course.

I was walking right into a trap.

And there wasn't a damn thing I could do about it.

At Holborn I jumped out. Getting to the British Museum should have been easy. Signposts pointed to it from every street corner. But I didn't follow them. No, I darted through alleys, did U-turns and ducked into doorways. I was going to be smart.

No desert boots, no trainers, no decent shoes caught up. Just the reassuring tap of stiletto heels. Somehow I got to the museum. By the time I walked up the massive steps to the entrance, my back was sweaty. My legs ached. The sun was not its usual cheerful self. There was something phoney about its brightness.

Somebody was a traitor.

I looked up at the pigeons whirling high above London and said a silent farewell to the world I'd known.

THE GREAT CAUGHT

'I can practically get as much ivory as I like, but I can't get it carried away. I am too worried about other things to bother about loot . . . I have spent eight pounds on ivory besides two tusks that I have looted, and have also got a lot of little things to give people.'
Major Landon, Benin City, 1897

If you ever fancy doing a little robbery, don't choose the British Museum. Apart from the whole robbery bit, you have to get used to it. Not easy to do in a short space of time. You need a map and one of those routemaster sat nav things. You need stout walking boots and stamina. You need to know the difference between Palaeontology and Egyptology or you'll get lost. And you don't need to be followed by killers.

You see the British Museum is IMPRESSIVE. The Great Courtyard is so great it can swallow up Brixton Leisure Centre, Streatham Bowling Alley and Peckham Bus Station all in one – with the buses.

And that's before you even start looking for the galleries.

And then there is the ceiling of the Great Court. That is IMPRESSIVE x2. Acres of glass, set in diamonds in an immense geometric dome. I just stood there until my neck ached.

Still, I couldn't allow a few hundred metres of roofing to make me feel small, could I? So I sidled under those vast diamonds, skirting the edges of a circular structure, which rose in the centre of the Great Courtyard, until I found the café. I got myself a Coke and sat down on a stainless steel stool at the head of a stainless steel table, as far out of sight as I could, and pretended to look like an ordinary visitor. I sipped my drink. I cased the joint.

Step one. Through the jewelled roof I saw the Union Jack waving in a weird cartoonish way against a misty sky. The sun bounced off it and struck some of the triangles in the ceiling in a strange dappled light. OK, no CCTV up there.

Step two. The whole place reverberated in footsteps. Voices whined and whispered up, round the central stone thing to a splendid dome, where sunlight spilt in through a circle of gigantic glass petals. From there, strange echoes bounced back and boomed down. In fact the sound effects were dead spooky. Ancient cathedrals. Mad monks. I looked for microphone nozzles. OK, no sound surveillance up there.

Step three. I finished my drink and set off to see where the security guards were posted. I started with the toilets.

I've got to tell you that even the toilets in the British Museum are IMPRESSIVE. You go down this angled flight of stairs into a vast passageway that looks like it's been hollowed out of the Great Pyramid of Giza. (There's the smell though, which isn't quite so impressive.)

I washed my hands very thoroughly. I'd read somewhere that if you do that, you're less likely to leave your DNA all over the place. I pressed the tap with a red dot on it. I splashed water into a huge circular basin. Then I looked into the stainless steel mirror. I decided that even though I was growing out of fantasy it would be OK to cheat . . .

There he was: young Maxi, first junior criminal to ever successfully burgle the British Museum, a modern-day Robin Hood! I could hear the crowds cheering: 'Maxi-millian . . . Maxi-millian . . . Maxi-millian . . .' I could see the red petals falling . . . What we do in life has a resonance somewhere or other . . . I was going to make the world a better place . . .

Having settled that, I ruffled my hair. I pulled my clothes askew. And satisfied that I looked like someone who'd listen to fairy stories, I went up to the Great Court again. I went past the bookshop. I headed straight through a doorway to the Africa section. OK, no guards yet.

I stopped to look at a huge map with *You Are Here* arrowed in on it. I tried to work out where I was. All around me people surged past. Was one of them a spy? Had anyone followed me? Was someone behind one of those huge pillars . . . hidden amongst the bookshop stands?

My teeth clamped shut. My shoulders drew tight. If only we'd found that name with the sword. I sent Roland a text: I'M HERE. I THINK DER'S A MOLE IN DA BLACK ARMY — TRY THINK WHO?

I looked at the vast ceiling. I looked at the marbled floors. I really, really hoped I could do this. I'd prove I wasn't a liability. Maybe if I could get something right, Sapphire might hug me again, might change her mind about pathetic coin rings . . .

There was only one security man at the top of the stairs leading down to the Africa section. He was the first guard I'd seen. He was sort of hidden in an alcove. He looked bored. I went up to him. I'd read somewhere that professional criminals use local knowledge . . . I needed all the help I could get, so I got straight to the point. I said, 'Excuse me, sir, I am thinking up a movie in which a young lad steals some valuable art treasures in order to return them to their rightful owners – you know, the Elgin Marbles sort of thing . . .' He looked at me suspiciously. 'I wondered what sort of security you have here – I'd like to make the film as real as possible . . .' I tried Winsome and Hopeful together (usually a winning combination).

'Look, hop it,' he said. 'Everything's electronically covered. You'll have to rethink your movie. It is not possible to sneeze in this place.'

'Oh,' I said doing a passable version of Despondent and What-A-Sausage. 'So if there was a weak spot, where would it be?'

'Think I'm stupid?' He shook his head. 'Kid, even if I told you the only way in and out of this building that wasn't shut down automatically, you wouldn't be any wiser.'

Ha, I thought, *let's see if you still look so smug tomorrow.* But instead I sniffed, doing Double Hopeless with a dash of Given Up and said, 'Well it was kind of a cool idea. You see, I really wanted a scene in here. It's such a great place. How about a fire, where a likkle kid saves valuable fings?'

I pulled out my I'm-a-Three-Year-Old smile.

'Aah,' he said, 'that would be easier, because the alarms don't trigger the security gates to the fire escapes.

Hmm . . .' He paused. 'It would make a good movie actually.' He preened himself a little as if *he* was going to get the lead role. 'Want to go to Art school, do you?'

'Yep,' I lied. 'Royal College of Art.'

'Never had a camera crew in this wing before, although we've got *The Big Draw* on at the moment, they're doing a session, right now, down there,' he nodded at the stairs.

'Yep,' I chirped. 'I'm going to it and then to the storytelling.'

He patted me on the shoulder. 'You have fun, son,' he said. 'And give me a part if you ever make that film, eh?'

Tee hee.

He'd just told me the only sure-fire way into and out of the whole place!

So mentally chalking one up to me, I smiled my most pleasant You're-Such-A-Great-Guy-Probably-A-Movie-Star at him and darted down the stairs, under the words *Sainsbury African Galleries dedicated to Henry Moore OMCH*.

I took the steps three at a time down to the Benin treasures waiting to be liberated.

Just as planned, I was ahead of time. I found the exhibition piece I was looking for, a huge woven horselike creature made of densely twined straw. It was situated right at the entrance to the room where the

Benin Bronzes were; and had written beside it: *Masquerade Outfit. Vegetable Fibre Textile and Wood. Chewa People, Malawi, late Twentieth Century.*

Inside it, I could see there would be standing room for maybe two people, a bit like a pantomime horse. But before I followed up on Roland's master plan, I stepped past the fibre horse into the Sainsbury Gallery East. Into the room with the Benin Bronzes.

I had a date to keep.

A date with my Inside Help.

INSIDE. 'HELP!!!'

'We are not in the business of redressing history.'
Emloyee – British Museum

There they were, the fabulous Benin Bronzes. Each one suspended from the ceiling. Each one set on a white board. Each one about thirty centimetres square.

Wow.

Even a two-dimensional, shallow, *scatty* person like me had to hold up and stare. It was a good job I'd come early though (and not just because it gave me time to get used to the Bronzes). You see, I hadn't realized that there'd be more than six. A lot more. In fact forty-two more. The display was six high by eight long. A total of forty-eight of them gleamed in the artificial glare of the spotlights, the ancient bronze twinkling in burnished copper and brown. I looked at them and panicked. Which were the six Warrior Kings that I was supposed to steal? Which were the ceremonial treasures that the Enugu professor had shown us on his

Powerpoint that night at the youth centre?

Which were:

- the most famous of all – Ewuare the Great (the fiercest warrior and greatest magician the world had ever known)
- his son, Ozolua the Conqueror,
- Esigie, son of Ozolua and builder of empires,
- Oba Orhogbua, his son,
- and Ehengbuda, the Queller of Rebellions.

The bronze plaques of the six Warrior Kings who should always look down from the Oba's palace walls?

If I'd known at the time there were actually nine hundred plaques to choose from, all of which told the history of the Warrior Kings and their adventures, I might have double panicked. Luckily I didn't. Instead, another thought started to worry away at me. Even if I *could* identify the six, judging from the size of them, that was going to be a whole lot of heavy metal to trawl around.

I sat down on a fold-out blue chair intended for the kids in *The Big Draw*. I sent Rollz a text: DER'S 2 MANY PLAQUES HERE BRUV. HOW DO I NO WHICH ONES R DA 6? I sat there staring at them, waiting for his reply.

This is what he said: JUST LOOKED IT UP, IT'S THE ONES WIT 3 FIGURES IN THE CENTRE. 1 IS HOLDING A FLATTENED SWORD AND IS SUPPORTED BY DA OTHER 2.

ALL OTHER PLAQUES WITH 3 IN DEM WOT DON'T JOIN HANDS OR AV ANIMALS ENT IT. PS, I THINK IT MUST BE LEON. ROLLZ ROYCE

Leon!

Was he serious?

Somebody entered the gallery behind me, but I was too shocked to notice.

Leon?

But as I thought about it, it began to make horrible sense. After all, maybe Leon knew Mogul was bringing him the dagger. And I'd phoned him about the sword . . . I shook my head. Actually it did *not* make sense. Leon was the guy who talked about the better world. The one who had started up The B.L.A.C.K. A.R.M.Y. He may have had the opportunity, but what about a motive? Of course not, it couldn't be him. How can you betray yourself?

I was glad I was sitting down though. I gulped some air and tried to concentrate on the Bronzes. The shadowy figure that I hadn't quite noticed seemed to move across the gallery behind me. I saw his reflection on the glass cabinets to either side.

Shit. What was it I was looking for? Plaques with three figures in them. The centre one being the Oba in full costume. Suddenly it was easy. There were only seven, and one of those was on a horse. No animals, right?

Sorted.

I glanced nervously around. How could it be Leon? I looked at my watch, five minutes to rendezvous. I took stock of the treasures. The dagger. The sword. Six Obas on bronze plaques. That made eight. One more to get.

I still couldn't get it . . . *Leon*. All that Maxi-I'm-so-sorry-for-you stuff; I mean, where did that come from?

I'd better find the last treasure, the ivory chest mask of Queen Idia.

I looked up. A dark figure slid out from behind a display and hurried away. Christ, I was supposed to be keeping a lookout. Not sitting there worrying about Leon or counting up treasures like days left to Christmas. What if I'd been noticed?

I catapulted off the blue fold-out chair. I searched the Africa Galleries. No one. Whoever it was had disappeared. I returned to the Benin Bronze room. There were three stand-alone display cabinets. I darted behind the first one. From there I watched everyone. A mum with two kids, a man wandering around in a beard (bit dodgy), a small group of school children. Seemed OK.

Time was running out. I had to meet Wally's contact now. So, staying as hidden as I could, I started trying to locate the ninth treasure. I searched the cabinet I was behind. It had fancy costumes in it, like the one I was expecting my storyteller to wear. I wasn't quite sure what the ivory mask was going to look like, but I knew it couldn't be embroidered cloth.

I slid over to the second cabinet. The mum settled her kids on to the blue chairs. The dodgy-beard man was scribbling things into a pad. The school children were mucking about. The second cabinet displayed bronze Warrior King heads and Altars to the Hand, round metal hat-box things. I took a good look at them, particularly at the bronze heads, but tempted as I was to bust them out as well, I realized that they would *definitely* be too much to carry around. Still no ivory chest mask.

So I turned at last to the third cabinet. And there it was. *She* was. Just as if she'd been waiting for me right down the centuries.

The Ivory Queen. The face of Africa. Idia.

And labelled nice and big too: *Ivory Chest Mask of Ancient Benin.*

She was so beautiful. And so sad. No smile reached her lips. Her eyes were cast down, as if she was gazing at something just out of reach. Her hair was done in tiny circles. Her coronet was made up of ten faces. Her neck was enclosed with a tight woven collar. Too tight. I thought she might choke. I mean, if she was alive she might have choked . . .

She looked so like Sapphire, *I* choked.

I couldn't believe it. I loosened the zip on my hoodie. Same nose. Same sweet wide mouth. Same unbelievable almond-shaped eyes. And my heart raced as I realized she could be mine! In a way that Sapphire never had been! There was no Angelo to steal her from me! No obstacle that could separate us! (Apart from the plate glass cabinet.) And through that glass I could almost hear her saying, 'Take me home, please, Maxi . . . please . . .'

Do you believe in love at first sight? I can say without doubt it exists. Your knees knock together. You break out in a hot sweat. Your heart rises into your throat. You start to stammer, even when you've got nothing to say! That's how it was when I saw Queen Idia. ~~I didn't care about that shadowy watcher any more. I didn't care about anything! I just wanted to laugh and skip down hillsides and frolic in the waves on some exotic beach . . .~~ (OK, strike that through.) I mean Queen Idia may have been a lump of ivory carved four hundred years ago, but that is not the point! I don't have any prejudices against ivory folk! I wasn't fussed by the age difference! In fact the only impediment to our love affair (now that Sapphire didn't want me ever again) was that Queen Idia was dead and I wasn't[2].

---

[2] OK, Roland, I get your point about the girl-at-the-end-of-the-bridge effect.

A situation that might rapidly change.

A new boldness took hold of me. I straightened my shoulders and lifted up my chin. I'd got work to do. Rescue work!

I checked out the exits. Apart from the Sainsbury OMCH stairway in, there was only one handy-looking exit out. It was around the side of the plaque display. It looked hopeful. It had *West Lift – Great Court* written on it. But I feared it would lock down as soon as I triggered the alarm. I was not discouraged though. I was going to succeed. So I worked my way round the entire walls of the Sainsbury East Gallery – and on the far side I found it: the fire exit!

There it was, with the lovely message:

Emergency exit only – Push bar to open.

Now there was only the matter of the security system.

If you think that I had any subtle plan to avoid triggering it, you'd be mistaken. My plan was different. Very different. I sent Roland and Sapphire a text. WILL ESCAPE WITH BRONZES THRO DA FIRE EXIT. EAST SIDE. MAKE SURE U R DER WIT WALLY AN GETAWAY PLAN.

That done, I set about scanning the CCTV monitors. You see, in my very different plan, I reckoned that the alarms would definitely go off, and the police would definitely arrive. They'd just have to arrive very fast! Faster than it would take me to race up the fire escape and jump on the back of a pizza delivery scooter.

So that left me with only two problems: how to avoid being identified on CCTV so that the entire nation wouldn't get to admire my handsome face on *Crime Watch*, and lastly how to break into the display cabinet that imprisoned Idia. The first was easy. A black balaclava. The second (unbreakable plate glass, anchored to solid steel and concreted into the floor) was about to be solved by my Inside Help!

This was the plan.

At exactly noon, not long before the storytelling started, I was to stand beside Queen Idia and eat chocolate. This would identify me to the Inside Help. He/she would approach me and say, 'Please, eating is only allowed in the canteen areas unless you've ordered a wham bam pizza, prawn with chunky pineapple and four cheeses, from Perfect Pizza Paradise.' I'd say, 'I'm sorry I didn't know, but as the butterfly settles on the perfumed flower, I think I'd like the pizza anyway,' (don't blame me for the corny lines) and then touch the cabinet that was to be left unlocked.

Not the most inspired words, I know. That's because they came from not the most inspired mind. (I'll give you one guess.) In fact I doubted they'd make it past the first redraft when Hollywood greenlights the film, but simple enough to remember – you'd think . . . However, as I took up position, I started to get them jumbled up in my head. A fog descended and I couldn't think straight. Was it, 'I'm sorry, I won't do it again'? or 'I prefer the spicy beef with green pepper'?

So there I stood, nibbling at my chocolate and anxiously waiting. What if nobody showed? This was the key element to the plan. If the cabinet was not unlocked, there was no way I was going to be able to smash through that plate glass with my pathetic little hammer.

'Please,' said a thin voice with a foreign accent, 'please, eating is only allowed in canteen area.'

I whirled round to see a frail girl with wide eyes and a sad face.

'Or you can have a pizza,' she finished.

'I'm sorry,' I stuttered, 'I didn't know.'

She stood there waiting. Wrong words? I stood there too. I mean, was I really supposed to say all that stuff?

'You've got to touch it,' hissed the girl, 'or I won't know which to unlock.'

Of course. I laid my hand on the cabinet beside me – where my beautiful Idia lay.

The girl smiled a bit and said, 'I will do it.'

What was I supposed to say now? As far as I knew, there wasn't a script for any further conversation.

'Thanks,' I muttered.

She smiled again the kind of smile that isn't happy. For some reason I said, 'Will you get into a lot of trouble?'

She nodded. 'I will lose job. After tonight I will be taken to work elsewhere. I do not know where.'

'But they won't catch you or anything?' Suddenly I was worried about her. 'Here,' I said nervously, 'if this all works out, I'll try and help.' I don't know why I said that. It was idiotic. I could hardly help myself, but I carried on. I pulled a pen from my pocket. I scribbled on to the chocolate wrapper. 'Here're my numbers. Try and call – I'm Max.'

'I'm English name The Julia,' she said, her dark eyes staring at me. 'When storytelling starts, I put out *Do Not Disturb* at top of main stairs. I put *Cleaning In Progress* by door to East Gallery. When cleaning, I pause alarm to corridor. You can hide then. I give you two minutes, pause on alarm system is set to two minutes. Then I am straightening everything from outside, tidy up, removing signs and praying for you.' She bowed her head and moved softly away.

'Thanks,' I said.

'Good luck,' she whispered. 'Later, when I going, I get friend to set security right for you. You no worry. Everything OK.'

'Call me.'

She did not look up.

It was time for your Man MaxiMi££ion to concentrate on the next part of the plan. The Horse of Troy.

IN THE DARK

The story was awful. I couldn't have faced a whole thirty minutes of it anyway. So when I saw Julia put up the cleaning sign, I was thankful. You know, I didn't give a monkeys whether Anansi fooled the tortoise, the elephant or the President of the USA, as long as I could fool the staff of the British Museum.

My hands went slippery with sweat. And even though I saw the cleaning sign go up, I stayed glued to the chair. Julia looked straight at me and nodded. I was sure everybody saw. What should I do? I rose silently to my feet. I turned and shuffled out. The storyteller threw one quick annoyed glance after me.

It missed.

I got through the door, past *Cleaning In Progress*. Out of sight, I hoped. Only two minutes. Was I really going to get inside that thing? My pulse was racing. Maybe I was going to get a fever. I looked hysterically around. I wasn't ready for this.

One minute.

Julia was waiting, nodding frantically.

I'd better do it then.

Expecting the world to come to an end in one shrilling crash, I lifted the vegetable fibre pantomime horse off its stand and over me. Inside was dark and smelt of old baskets. I stepped back on to the stand. I pulled the outfit down tight. I heard Julia straighten the display. I felt her tug the horse over its mounting. I kept as still as I could.

'Go to left side small,' I heard her whisper. 'Masquerade vegetable outfit not like that before.'

I moved a nano step left.

'OK, you OK now,' she said.

I was not OK. I was about as far away from OK as Pluto, *and* I'd ended up in the rear end of the horse, but I didn't want to disappoint Julia, so I said nothing. Instead, I thought of my lovely Queen Idia, lying there so patiently, as trapped as me. If she could bear it, so could I. Hopefully.

I heard Julia sweep in front of me. I was chewing the side of my mouth. Maybe some strands of fibre had been knocked loose. I heard her move the cleaning sign.

I heard the bleep of the security alarm as it switched itself back on. I held my breath. No bells rang. I took just an incy gulp of air. It was brittle and harsh and full of dust. I felt a sneeze pressing on the inside bridge of my nose. I heard the kids from the storytelling not laughing. The sneeze descended towards my nostrils. I blinked my eyes in the darkness. I pinched the sneeze till it grew and exploded into the back of my throat. My legs turned to jelly.

Through a tiny square window in the weave, I peered out on to the display opposite. There staring back at me were a horrible collection of horrible masks. There was an evil red face set in a mane of feathers. There was a wooden devil head with one huge ram's horn curling from its crown. There was a pushed-in mask with a carved effigy standing where it should have had hair. And there was the severed head of a White man with a pig snout and cloth cap. None of them were smiling. My heart started missing beats. Regularly. My mouth grew dry. Worst of all, a long baboon mask that ended in the jaws of a crocodile pointed its teeth at me. I opened my mouth and pointed my teeth back. I didn't want it to think it was going to scare me stupid for the next five hours.

Five hours! Imagine sitting through five Maths lessons, or crossing London six times, or watching *Lord of the Rings* part one and two – at a sitting, without an ice cream break – and all of it standing up. I got cramp in my leg, cramp in my shoulder, cramp in my stomach, a crick in my neck, an itch on my back and a terrible thirst that kept my throat dry and my mouth tasting like the Sahara Desert. I couldn't reach my water bottle, because I couldn't bend down. I couldn't bend down because that horrible vegetable masquerade outfit wasn't made for benders. In fact I felt sorry for the people it was made for. I tried to imagine two of us in there, scampering up and down in the tropics. I nearly fainted at the thought.

The storytelling ended (I could tell by the sound of weak clapping), the kids left. A few of them said, 'Wow, look at that crocodile face,' on their way out. The others said, 'Mum, when can we go home?' to which there were various replies, like, 'Look, darling! Look at this super tin blanket – it's all made from bottle tops.' Through it all, I stood there motionless.

Then the voices got fewer and fewer. The lights dappled on the glass of the baboon face. Shadowy figures seemed to drift past and strange echoes whispered up the walls. Far away, a tape repeated and repeated a tribal cry. It shrilled out against endless drumming, as if now that the people had gone, Africa was waking . . . and feathered fronds were waving . . .

and red evil eyes were winking . . . and terrible baboon crocodile masks were stretching their jaws and licking their teeth . . .

At last doors slammed, footsteps faded, the lighting dimmed, and I was all alone in the British Museum after dark.

THE GREAT MUSEUM ROBBERY

'The tongue learns to live amongst the teeth.'
Calabar wisdom – Nigeria

Inside the straw horse, I held my breath in the dusty darkness. I longed to move. I sent Rollz and Sapph a text: AM REDY. ONCE I DISTURB DIS COSTUME DA ALRM WILL TRIGGA. I'LL TAKE UNDA 5 TO GT DA BRONZES N MASK. FLASH ME WEN U R IN POSITION.

I started worrying. Here I was in a sort of basement, down two flights of stairs, almost directly in the centre of the British Museum. On which street did the fire escape escape to? I sent Roland another text: CAN U FIGURE OUT WHERE TO W8? The fibre costume creaked a little as I held my mobile up to get a signal.

Thank God Roland was smart. Perhaps he was right about Leon. But then why hadn't Leon taken the sword when I'd offered it? That shadowy figure must have been following me. Did they know about Walter and the plan? If they did, why weren't they here now catching me? Was I going to run out of the fire escape straight into a waiting police unit? Maybe it was a good job I wasn't so good at planning, because if I wasn't exactly too sure where the exit was, they couldn't be either. Come to think of it, they didn't know I was going to use the fire exit. I breathed in dry air and felt a little better.

As I waited for Roland's reply, I calculated. Once out of the horse it wouldn't be so dark. Everywhere was lit by dim artificial lighting. That was good. At least I'd be able to see what I was doing. OK. Run to the cabinet, free Idia. Run to the plaques. Second row, third, fourth, fifth, sixth and last. Wrench them from the display. Third row, fifth only. Run to the fire escape. Push bar. Escape. No sweat.

I started sweating. My heart started to thud. My hands felt sticky. Don't imagine problems. Wait for text.

Nothing.

What if I get cramp? What if Julia couldn't unlock the display cabinet? Sweat was pouring off me.

Text message.

WE R IN POSITION. GO 4 IT MILLION.

I went.

I think I was so tense I overdid ripping off the masquerade vegetable horse thing. I think I might have damaged it a bit. I certainly heard a long tearing sound underneath the *bbbrrring* of the alarm. Sorry. That was a mistake. I didn't have time to stop and apply superglue. I raced to the cabinet display. I fumbled at the glass front. How did it open? I pushed the stainless steel strip on one side. Pulled at the other. My fingers, slippery with sweat, slid across the glass. I was leaving huge wet fingerprints everywhere. All that handwashing wasted. Mountains of DNA. Don't worry, I told myself, Julia didn't clean the display – there must be thousands of prints on it . . .

It didn't open.

Frustrated, I banged my fist on it. I succeeded in bruising my knuckles. Queen Idia looked up at me, unblinking. Silently I prayed to her: *Let it open . . . let it open . . .*

This was all taking too long. Time was running out. Minutes were flashing. I abandoned Queen Idia. Let me get the plaques. At least let me get the plaques. 'I'll come back,' I told her.

The panelled floor of Sainsbury East Gallery was smooth. I seemed to skate over it. The alarms crashed in my ears. As soon as I touched the plaques they doubled in crescendo.

Second row, third square – check it's got three figures. I tore it off. It buckled a bit and the nail that held it ripped through the thin metal. Oh God. Can't be helped. I ripped the next one off, trying to be more careful, and then the third, fourth, fifth, sixth. They came away easily, as if they'd been waiting for me.

The six bronze plaques were lighter than I'd imagined. Either that or adrenalin was giving me super strength. The security light started to flash. I stuffed the bronzes under one arm and materialized back beside Idia. This time with only one hand to spare, I fumbled again with the catches to her prison.

Open. For God's sake. I pushed. I pulled. I slid. I twisted. I shoved. I poked. I prodded. I pressed. I kicked. I swore. I . . . revolved! The glass front to the cabinet revolved out and back. Queen Idia. God bless you, Julia. The lovely Queen Idia. Good Julia. I put my hot, sweaty hand out and touched her.

She was as cool as marble and as smooth as powder.

Gently . . . ever so gently, I lifted her out. I raised her to my lips. I kissed her forehead through my balaclava, then I snuggled her down inside my hoodie – next to my heart.

I felt, rather than saw, her cast a glance at the two ivory armlets beside her in the cabinet. 'Whatever you want,' I said and picked them up too. I slid one over my left arm and the other my right. Then I turned and charged for the fire escape.

It was just like the guy had said. The doors flew open

and no burglar grille descended. Within a split second I was bounding up the steps – two, maybe three at a time. It was very dark. The fire escape twisted in places. I almost missed my footing. Maybe thieves have got a sixth sense, because on each occasion I hesitated just long enough to be sure. I didn't slip. I didn't fall. I didn't bash myself against the walls. Like a cat, I twisted and landed on my feet.

On I raced. On and up.

At last I came to the top. One fierce shove. The push bar gave. The exit doors smacked open. I tumbled out. Panting, sweating, heart wild and arms full, I plunged into the yellow glare of Central London.

PIZZA DELIVERY

'It is good to help even the intika [tiny black ants],
if they have shown you the way to the mango tree.'
Fulani wisdom – West Africa

My chest was so empty of air and my head so dizzy, that at first I thought they were police. There they were. One to my left. One to my right. One dead ahead.

Bikers.

I panicked. Then I saw Sapphire wave from a pillion seat. 'Get behind Walter,' she yelled.

Not bikers. *Scooterers.*

'Listen, O Thief of a Thousand Priceless Things, hurry up,' snarled Walter.

'Say please,' I said. I mean I might just have robbed the British Museum and maybe every policeman in the Greater London area would be giving his Sunday roast to catch me – but Man had to demand RESPECT.

'Please,' said Walter quite meekly, handing me a helmet.

Boy! How easy was that?

'Here, Mi££ion,' said a voice from behind the last scooter. I saw Roland lift up his helmet and throw me a rucksack. I stuffed the plaques inside, swung it over my back. I patted Walter through his leathers. 'I'm right behind ya, bruv,' I said, and swung up on to the makeshift pillion seat.

And we were away. Streets flashed past. Police sirens wailed. Traffic lights flicked from red to amber. The roar of the engine. The tug of the night air. The scooter sliced round corners, spun down side streets and I felt the mad, wild, crazy feeling of success and freedom and sudden rush of hope.

It didn't last long.

Walter screeched to a halt on Chelsea Embankment. 'The money?' he said.

I mean, fair enough. He *had* helped, but there was one more little matter I'd got to settle before I told him the bad news. 'Julia,' I said. 'What happens to Julia?'

Walter spat (seriously, that's a disgusting habit). 'Who is Julia?' he said. 'What is she?'

'Your Inside Help.'

'She is nothing, Warrior King of the Shining Half a Million Quid. She is forgotten already. If you think she's a problem I will arrange for her to be reunited with Buddha.'

'No!' I said. Maybe a little too quickly.

Walter laughed, 'You want to marry her?'

'Look, bruv,' I said. 'You sort Julia out with a well-paid job and a nice cosy likkle council flat for real – or there's no deal.'

It was a good job Walter still had his helmet on. I don't think any of us would have liked the look on his face.

'And furthermore,' I said, 'if you don't like it – go to the police.' I paused to allow the point to sink in. 'You let her give me a nice little buzz tomorrow night, to tell me she's feeling snug and happy – then you get your money, u-get-me?'

He didn't want to, but, hey! Too bad for him.

That's the way the deep pan stuffed crust crumbles – innit?

AB-SO-LUTE-LEE MADLY HAPPY EVERYTHING IS GOING TO WORK OUT AND I CAN GO BACK TO BEING MYSELF FOR EVER . . .

'When the elephant steps on a trap, he is not trapped.'
Hausa saying – Nigeria

Aboard *Thaddeus*, Sapphire and Roland wanted to know everything. So I told them. I showed them the Bronzes. I explained how I'd cleverly blended into the stonework, figured out the surveillance system, tricked the Head of Security into giving me a personal lecture on the finer points of fire *escapes* and agreed to play a part in my movie! I told them how Julia had been wowed over by my stunning good looks and had risked her life to help me. I'd just reached the part when, with no sweat at all, I'd brilliantly cracked the complicated mechanism for opening the display cabinets, when Sapphire shoved two fingers down her throat in a very unappreciative way.

Luckily, Roland was more admiring. 'Gosh! Mi££ion,' he said. 'Well done!'

'Nuffing to it, bruv,' I said. 'Dare say you could have done it too, if you were a likkle taller.'

'Do you really think so?' smiled Rollz, all big, round, shiny glasses.

'Definitely,' I said, 'if you was a likkle bigga and maybe a likkle more handsome . . .' Sapphire made puking noises in the corner seat and said, 'God! Pass me the bucket.' (You know something? That girl has got one serious attitude problem.)

Still, Rollz was lapping it up. He was smiling all over his pink face, looking like he'd won the lottery.

'Tomorrow,' I said, 'I'm going to take *all* the Bronzes to Abiola, then I'm going to sell our story to *all* the papers and then . . . I'm going to rename myself MaxiBi££ion!'

I won't record Sapphire's response to that.

'I'll start writing the front page article straightaway,' said Roland. 'We can show them the ivory bracelets so they'll know we aren't time-wasters. What shall we call the story? Clearly, it will have to be something eye-catching and – how about, "Two wrongs to put it right"?'

'Better send a text to Abiola then,' I said. HAVE ALL YR TREASURES ABOARD A LITTLE BOAT ON A BIG RIVER.

K? AM BRINGING DEM 2 U EARLY MORN. HOPE YR
AMBASSADOR HAS 4GIVEN YOU 4 DA LIMO. WK

'If only we could get just one tiny bit of evidence that
the More Dread Crew are linked to the government,'
sighed Sapphire. 'I mean, something that will stand up
in court. I know we can tell the nation our story – it may
save us, but the idea of them getting away scot free with
killing Angelo . . .'

I agreed, but you know, there was only so much you
could do. I mean we'd get those ceremonial treasures
home, we'd create such a scandal there'd have to be
some investigation of something. But most of all, we
could stop running. Sapphire could go home, go back to
school. Roland could have a future in the governments
of tomorrow. We could all get off that wheel of fortune
that was about to grind us under. Hey, we'd outwitted
them! We were winning! And as for Leon? I still wasn't
sure it was him. But if he *was* a mole, I'd go straight to
Dreader Dread. South London would take care of him.
Things were looking good. *So good*. All we had to do
was get through tonight and get through tomorrow . . .

Should be like eating ice cream!

You would have thought that, given my daring
adventures, I might have deserved a breather. The
Director of the Universe might have thought: *Poor old*

Billy, he needs to have a few hours' kip and a toasted ham'n'cheese before we worry him again. Ha ha. No sooner had I lain down in the aft cabin than my phone rang.

'We need to talk,' said an unfamiliar voice.

'Not now,' I groaned.

'This is Dreader Dread,' said the voice.

I was a bit surprised, because firstly it didn't sound like I'd imagined Dreader Dread. Secondly I'd just been thinking about him in relation to Leon, so it was a bit like telepathy. And thirdly it was late and I couldn't think how this talk could be so urgent . . .

'Richmond Park,' said Dreader, in a tone that could have kicked a door in. 'Take the Star and Garter Home Entrance, turn right to the mound. We'll be waiting.'

'But,' I sputtered.

'It's about your brother. It's important. This phone may be tapped. I'll just say it once. There's something you don't know. We had to fake his death. He wants to see you. You must come . . .' The phone went dead.

Angelo alive? Richmond Park in the middle of the night? Was I dreaming? How come Dreader Dread . . . ? *Angelo?* I'd have to take the *Thaddeus* push-bike. No trains go to Richmond Park. The Underground would shut down . . .

I couldn't believe it. My heart shot into my mouth.

My eyes started to water. A wild, crazy, happy feeling started somewhere under my ribs. I COULDN'T BELIEVE IT!!

I did a somersault out of the bed. I let out a series of wild whoops . . . I swallowed them. Didn't want to wake Roland and Sapphire. This was MY SURPRISE. Imagine their faces when they woke up to find me AND ANGELO sitting chatting in the galley . . .

The cabin seemed suddenly too small to contain me. I wanted to rush out, skip over the river, twirl in the lights of London, dance on the rooftops and shout to the stars: ANGELO IS ALIVE.

ANGELO IS ALIVE!!!

EVERYTHING CHANGES

'When you long for honey, you forget about the bees.'
West African saying

I made a number of very serious mistakes that night. I'll start with the worst ones. Firstly, I didn't wake Sapphire and Roland to let them know. So later they didn't know where I was or why I'd gone out. Secondly, I really hadn't listened to Dreader properly; if I had, I might have been prepared for what came next. Thirdly, I was just too flustered by the mention of Angelo, the desperate hope that he might still be alive . . . so I didn't check the number. Those mistakes almost cost me my life. And those were just the ones I made *before* I got on the push-bike and, with a bursting heart, pummelled the pedals in the direction of Richmond.

It was a dark, wet, foul night. The streets were treacherous. Icy rain soaked into every crinkle of skin. My hands slipped on the handlebars. My feet slipped on the pedals. I was tired and horribly stiff. I had to keep stopping to check my *A to Z* to see if I was going in the right direction. Page eighty-six became soggy and the ink started to blur. Every time a police car screamed past, the blood in my veins froze. The tarmac ahead of me was black, only the red reflection of street lights shimmered across it. They say London never sleeps. It's a lie. When it rains, London is as quiet as the grave.

As I pedalled alongside the river, determined to cross over at Kingston Upon Thames, I thought: *Maybe it's true. Maybe Angelo is alive!* I wanted it to be true so much. Even if I'd had to pedal to Land's End . . . Oh, how I imagined his smile, his eyes dancing as he told me everything . . . My heart soaring as I told him back all the things that had happened . . .

I soon realized that going by push-bike was another big mistake. I won't go into the obvious reasons (like you have to pedal). For me, the worst thing was that it wasn't fast enough. I tried to flick the pages of the *A to Z* searching for any shortcut over the river that would shrink the distance by ten miles. I failed. So I carried on slamming down the Kings Road until it became the New Kings Road and after that the Newer Still Kings Road, until it felt like I must be at the So Totally Brand New Kings Road it was still in its packaging. Then it curiously became Putney High Street. That's what roads do, especially in the *A to Z* – just when you think you might be getting somewhere they pull some random switch on you. Still at least I was over the river, even though by then page eighty-six had fallen out.

I won't tell you about Putney Hill. I won't tell you about the Kingston Road. I'll leave you to imagine the endless slippery tarmac and the night wind whistling through a sodden hoodie and an icy T-shirt. I tried to block out the pain in my legs and chest, and concentrate on the hope in my heart that made every cramp and chill shrink to the size of a pin prick.

Angelo, I was going to see Angelo! How Sapphire would smile and how much I didn't mind if she loved him more . . .

At last I entered Richmond Park by Robin Hood Gate. A wild wind whipped across the heath. Bracken tossed in a sea of shadows. Solitary oaks stretched fingers out towards me. If London was empty, Richmond Park was a black hole full of dark energy. Nothing moved except the wind and the heaving undergrowth. I saw a sign and in the flicker of my dying dynamo it read: *ENTRY FORBIDDEN – DEER CULLING IN PROGRESS.*

I cycled down beside Prince Charles's Spinney – my front wheel sheering through puddles, splashing my sodden feet. Past Gibbet Wood, my lips dry and shrivelled with cold. Damp night air stuck in my nose and my chest heaved with the effort. And all the time my mind was racing ahead to where I jumped off the bike and sprinted to hold Angelo . . . to where I pulled his head into a fake arm lock and punched his silly shoulder and headbutted his head and laughed and laughed and laughed and cried and laughed . . . There was the car park above Isabella Plantation. There was a light!

I cycled like a crazy kid straight towards it.

And there they were, parked in a tight ring with their tinted windows and headlights on.

The cars of the More Dread Crew.

FOOLED

I skidded crazily to a halt.

A shot rang out. My front tyre exploded. The handlebars jerked. My heart started falling. No Angelo. The back tyre exploded. I tasted fear.

Merlyn stepped out of his car and walked over to me. 'You really do need to learn never to underestimate me,' he said.

At that moment I don't think I really cared about Merlyn any more. He was nobody. A grey man in a grey suit doing a grey job. How sad is that? And, imagine, he was dressed up as a gangsta too. Like he was The Man or something.

Pathetic.

And I didn't care about dying out there in that wasteland either. In fact, I *wanted* to. I longed to cross over to that other place and find Angelo, wherever he was.

You see, it was Angelo who mattered. And Angelo was dead, when for a brief few hours I'd had him back – alive and my brother again. Angelo with his kind wise eyes and his quiet smile . . . Angelo walking beside me, hopping over manhole covers . . . Angelo there with me, joking with me . . . being with me . . .

Who cared about Merlyn?

It was just that I didn't want to die right then. I was not quite ready. I'd got to live until tomorrow to finish everything. So I wasn't going to let Merlyn win. So I said, 'I didn't underestimate you . . . I mean, I did. I mean please give me one more chance to really, really not underestimate you, to really, really respect you – all of you, even though Manz never met all of you . . .' My voice went at full throttle, but my brain was going even faster. Buy time. Look for a way out. Run where they can't follow.

I scanned the parking lot, trying to work out how many there were. And if I got a break, where could I run to? Meanwhile I chattered on. 'You see, I'd like to meet all of you, if you'd only give me the chance, the privilege – OK, the honour.' (Surely he must realize I was buying time?) 'Look, I RE-SPECT you in capitals, bruv. I respect the cars you drive, the pizzas you eat, the ground you tread on . . . Believe me, I respect you so much that I've given RESPECT a new meaning, a better, more posher meaning . . . Look, Man respects you, Man will never underestimate you again, u-get-me?'

There was nothing out there in the park but the wind and emptiness. Merlyn could hardly have chosen a more desolate place. Gibbet Wood was the nearest cover, but it didn't sound very tempting; further off there was Isabella Plantation . . .

Behind Merlyn a car door swung open and two men got out. One of them was carrying something in a long black sock.

What should I do? My bike was a twisted wreck. Angelo was dead. If I screamed, no one would come. The misty dawn would reveal my body, stiff and cold. The headlines would read: *TRAGIC ACCIDENT AS YOUTH STRAYS INTO DEER CULLING PROGRAMME*. Merlyn pulled out his mobile, punched a number. 'Olusamilola? We've got one of yours here. Your little Warrior King. Two million, or he ends up feeding the fish.'

I tried to scream out, 'Don't do it! I'm nowhere near the river! It's a trick! They're going to kill you too – or blame my death on you . . .' But Abiola must have agreed, because Merlyn added, 'We've got matters to attend to. We'll phone you the place.'

That gave me one lonely idea.

'You'll never get the dagger,' I said.

Merlyn spun round.

'It's on its way to the papers right now, along with all the evidence . . . We know who you are . . . We know you aren't gangstas . . . We know you work for the government . . . We know you take on any disguise to cover your tracks . . . Do you really want to go down for your job? . . . I mean, what do you really care?'

A sneer flashed across Merlyn's face and, just as quickly, was blanked out again. 'It's personal now,' he said. 'I never lose on an assignment.'

As he stepped forward, I bent down, lifted the buckled bike and swung it straight at him. Solid handlebars and twenty-four gears all clunking together and travelling at full speed is not something you'd want to take a header at.

I didn't wait to see if he fell or not. I just turned and ran. I jumped over a line of wooden pegs ringing the edge of the car park, across the only road. Down. Away. Over the wet grass. Anywhere. Through the dense bracken. Dodging. Weaving. Rolling. Until I reached the iron gate to Isabella Plantation.

Gunfire. Behind me, I heard shouting. 'I want him alive!' And as I swung under the rhododendrons, I caught a glimpse of grey men pouring down the hill towards me.

I floundered through shrubbery. Thorns ripped me.

Roots tripped me. Sodden leaves trapped me. I fell into ditches. Stumbled into ponds. Soaked my already soaking self. If I could only stop long enough to phone Abiola . . . Footsteps pounced behind me . . .

Down pathways I squelched. Hid breathless amongst bushes. Whimpered into trembling hands.

All for nothing. They found me.

They marched me back to the waiting cars.

Merlyn said, 'Where's the dagger and all the other stuff?'

I said, 'I'll never tell you.'

His face twisted as he tried not to let his fury show. He hissed in my face, his spit showering me: 'You've caused me a lot of trouble. Do you realize I've spent weeks trying to mop this up, when it could all have been done so easily? I have someone inside your bloody Campaign who could have got me the dagger back without a single shot being fired, but because of you and your bloody mother and her bloody boyfriend and your brother . . . No, a bullet is really too good for you.' He wiped away the blood that still trickled down the side of his head.

Someone inside the Campaign? Ready to give the dagger back? I nearly wanted to laugh. I mean if Merlyn had only just *not* shot Mogul, the dagger *would* have gone to Leon and then he *could* have got it back from the Campaign and then none of this . . . It wasn't smart to think like that. Think only: *Buy time. Try to tell Abiola. Warn Roland.*

'But now we really do have to be sure you haven't sent anything to the papers, don't we?' said Merlyn. 'That would mean more delays.' He suddenly sounded reasonable again, as if he was merely checking a shopping list. 'So now comes the unpleasant bit, Warrior King.' He sighed. 'We know you're located near the river in Chelsea – you see, we've intercepted two of your calls from there. So we'd like you to tell us the whole truth: where you stay, who you've told, what you've done . . . I'm afraid I can't leave any loose ends, not now. I've gone to considerable trouble to get you and so far you haven't been very helpful. Now we can do this the easy way or the hard way. What do you say?'

There was only one thing I wanted to say. So I did. 'Suck my dictionary.'

Merlyn opened his mobile and barked down the line: 'Olusamilola, meet us at Chelsea Embankment – and you better make it two and a half million.'

Then he turned to me. 'Wrong choice,' he said.

The last thing I saw was his face peering into mine – then the lights went out. Little sparklers of fire twisted before my eyes. I felt myself being punched and suffocated at the same time. Arms clamped mine. A ball of thick cloth was stuffed into my mouth. Somebody kicked the back of my knees. I fell heavily. My heart started going crazy. A blow crushed all the air out of my chest. Another crushed my stomach into my rib cage. I tried to cry out, but there was no air left and the thick heavy cloth sank into the back of my throat.

Somebody knelt on the small of my back. Somebody tied something tight around my neck. Somebody kicked me again and again in my stomach and kidneys. I started to vomit, but the rag stopped it. Vomit spewed up into my nose. I couldn't breathe. I blacked out.

I came to moments later. Somebody had yanked the gag out of my mouth. Merlyn was sticking his face back in mine. 'The truth?' he demanded.

Another blow, flat and heavy, crashed into my side. 'You give us the dagger and the other stolen items. You tell us where your friends are – and everything else. You understand?'

I tried to croak, 'Up you,' but instead I was sick – a long gentle flow of blood and bile.

'Maybe you're a little deaf?' suggested Merlyn. 'Do you think this boy is deaf? Maybe he needs his ears popping.'

I closed my eyes as the kick landed. After that, I wasn't quite sure what happened. I think I said something. I think I heard someone say, 'We don't want

him to die, until we're sure he's told us everything . . .'
I think I felt someone shaking me, saying, 'Are you
telling the truth? What boat? How did you do the
robbery? Are your accomplices on the boat? Is
everything on the boat? You must tell us everything.'
But I don't know if I answered. I just lay there in my
own blood and blackness.

'We're finished here,' said somebody. 'Put him in the
boot. Let's see if we can find the Warrior King's boat.' I
heard doors slamming and then waves of pain crashed
into me, and I struggled to surf them, and failed, and
sank, and then nothing.

ONE GOOD TURN
DESERVES ANOTHER

'After the python has eaten he should be careful not to sleep on the ant hill.'
West African saying

Each jolt of the Audi slammed into my body. I lay hands tied behind my back. Feet tied to my neck. Vomit-soaked rag taped into my mouth. Alone in the boot of Merlyn's car.

At first I thought only of myself. But as the agony broke in waves over me, I remembered other things. Sapphire. Roland. Queen Idia. Lady Piggot Bluntstone's luxury houseboat.

I lay in terror trying to move a finger, a foot, a knee, trying to explore my stomach with cautious thought waves. My chest was fire, my legs strangely numb and trembly. Everywhere throbbed and ached and spun, and I think I lost consciousness again.

The second time I came round, I didn't try to think. I kept my mouth shut and concentrated on breathing through my nose. I think one, or maybe five, of my ribs might have been broken, because each breath was like splinters of lightning radiating around me. I could see nothing. I couldn't move. The string was tight and the space in the boot small. I started to worry that I'd run out of air. I stopped breathing through my nose. I tried to open my mouth. I blacked out again.

I came to with a jolt. It snapped me awake. The car had stopped. Even in my wrecked state I was afraid of more pain. Afraid of the eventual black sock raised to my head, of the darkness waiting out there. How would it be? *Maximillian dragged from the car boot, sat on the quayside – one low dense noise, one toppling body*. A sweat colder than the soaking clothes that hung to me broke, and I started to shiver.

Poor Roland. Poor Sapphire. They would never know what had happened. Merlyn and his killers would storm the boat, find the dagger – and my two old friends? I didn't think they would survive. Hot tears stung and as they trickled down into the corners of my mouth, I realized my lips were large and bruised and bleeding. I prayed to gods I'd never believed in. If I ever got out, I'd change. I really would. I'd do all the things I should. I'd grow up. I'd stop pretending I was The Man. I'd never walk the gangsta walk again. I'd throw away the coin ring and the fake gold chain and the diamond earring. I'd throw away the multicoloured beads. I didn't want to belong to that violent world. I'd live the way Mum would have wanted. She'd be proud of me. Just one last chance . . .

The car stopped. I felt the front door open and then the shudder of it slam shut. Silence. Darkness. I twisted a little. Not much. Then I heard a soft tap above my head. Somebody was tapping the boot. I heard a sharp wrench. A tearing sound – almost as if someone was forcing the bumper back, twisting it. Not the bumper. The boot.

Slowly, the lid of the boot inched open. I tried to turn. I tried to call out. But only a thick mumble of moaning escaped from me.

'Sssh, Warrior King,' said a low heavy voice. 'You be quiet-o.'

I couldn't see anyone through the hood – only the faint flush of street light.

'Now listen,' continued the voice, 'I am going to untie you. You stay still. It's dark. I don't want to cut you.'

I tried nodding. It hurt.

'I am going to take off the gag, you don't speak – OK?'

I twitched a finger. It meant YES. I hoped whoever it was saw.

'Then I am going to lift you out of the car. It will hurt. You will not scream.'

I tried twitching everything.

'You will disappear. I think it best if you jump into the river. You can swim? That is the only way. We have only a short time. I do it now.'

I tried nodding again. Maybe it didn't hurt quite so bad.

'You bring to me the treasures when you can, but try before next weekend. I may not be allowed out of the High Commission again – since our first adventure I am under diplomatic arrest. They fly me home next Monday evening. I will appear before the Assembly of Chiefs at a court hearing. Let me take them the treasures, and they will see the way the gods have worked through me. I believe in you, Warrior King. You will bring the lost Benin Bronzes to me, because you know it is your destiny to do it. That is why you are called the Last Warrior King. Please, I am honoured to help you. That Merlyn is not as smart as he thinks, even now he is looking for me down by the Chelsea Bridge. In my country we have a saying about such people . . .'

As usual, Abiola had too much to say.

My hands were freed. I heard metal cutting cloth. The hood was ripped off. The tape yanked. All of it hurt. I didn't care. An arm helped me to uncurl. Two arms supported me out of the car boot. A jacket was wrapped around me. My tongue was too huge and bruised to say thank you, my throat too dry; instead I croaked and croaked. I think he understood.

'He is not far. You go now.'

I looked up. I saw the large, dark, round eyes of Abiola Olusamilola.

He smiled. 'One good turn deserves another, Warrior King.' Then he turned and disappeared.

I staggered to the river. When I reached the wall, I slumped against it. I sank to my knees. With swollen hands I felt for my mobile. Broken. The screen smashed. Curious black ink had bled across it. I couldn't phone Roland and Sapphire.

Suddenly I panicked. Where were Merlyn and his crew?

In terror, I strained into the gloom. The rough wall behind me. Mist rolling gently off the Thames. A car horn far away and an aeroplane overhead. Then I saw them down on the quayside. My heart leapt in fear – and hope. They were on the quay at the *wrong* end of Cheyne Walk. If I hurried, if I could creep fast behind the cover of the wall, if I could reach *Thaddeus* before them . . .

I didn't stop to think. I dragged my screaming body up into a sprinter's crouch. I spoke to it. I said:

Just do this for me, guys. Just let me warn Roland and Sapphire. I think they heard. My knees stopped trembling so much, and my ribs agreed to ache only at every other heartbeat.

Then I set off, dragging myself along the pavement, every centimetre a victory, every metre a celebration. Until, shaking with the effort, I reached the swing gates to Chelsea Marina West Side.

I'm not going to tell you how I whimpered over the walk planks and stumbled clumsily behind the stern of *Flowerpot Magnate* and *Lazy Boy*, how I peered down the wispy waters of the Thames to see if Merlyn had realized his mistake and was coming, how my eyes seemed to swim in and out of focus, how I had a strange feeling that somewhere deep inside I was haemorrhaging thick dark blood. But I made it. I made it to *Thaddeus*. I feebly thumped on the aft door. Sapphire came and opened it, and I said, 'Don't scream. Please don't scream. Wake Roland. Get the treasures, under my bed, left side, and don't ask anything. We must go, Sapphire. You must believe me. We must go because Merlyn and the More Dread Crew are coming . . .'

I don't remember much more. I know I crawled to the dinghy moored up at the back of *Thaddeus*. I think I dragged the life vests out of the emergency box. I think I clutched them and tumbled into the dinghy. I think.

I know Roland and Sapphire soon slid in beside me. Roland was cross. He started on at me. But then it seemed that a fire ball broke loose from somewhere, and there was the sound of shouting, and then a sudden sear of heat. But by then I was very far away and the misty sky was so much closer. It was sinking down all around me into a great white soft blanket. I felt safe and cold and then . . . nothing.

Here are some facts. The More Dread Crew pillaged *Thaddeus*. They found many tins of baked beans and one loaf of thick white sliced. They weren't happy about it. Maybe they don't like beans on toast. They didn't find the dagger or the treasures or us. They were extra unhappy about that. They sprinkled petrol around the cabins. They struck a match and *Thaddeus* went up. It took half an hour to burn and ten minutes to sink. The fire brigade came. They cut *Thaddeus* loose from her mooring. *Thaddeus* floated into the middle of the Thames before she sank. Roland said she put up a good fight.

I was glad about that.

As for me and Roland and Sapphire? Well we floated down the river to no particular destination. Just the three of us with an antique dagger, a ceremonial sword, six priceless bronze plaques, two ivory armlets and a legendary ivory mask of the most beautiful woman in the world (excepting Sapphire), and one murderous gang behind.

Part Three

REBEL WITH A CAUSE

MEANTIME IN GREENWICH

'The offing was barred by a black bank of clouds, and the tranquil waterway
leading to the uttermost ends of the earth flowed sombre under an overcast sky
– seemed to lead into the heart of an immense darkness.'
Heart of Darkness – Joseph Conrad

I wish I could tell you more about that boat ride. I wish
I could say we drifted past the Houses of Parliament,
down to the Tower of London, down to anchor in a safe
haven and were fetched ashore by smiling, kindly
people, who, before they covered us in silver blankets
and served us with mugs of sweet tea, told us what
heroes we were . . . That I woke up to find myself back
in my auntie's house, with Angelo in the bunk bed
below me, and a new March morning, with nothing but
Cartoon Network waiting downstairs . . .

Instead, I woke to the sound of Roland scraping the
dinghy in to dock on a shingle bed near Deptford
Creek. Everywhere was dark. He looked at me, his eyes
very large behind his lenses. 'Sorry, it all seems to have
gone a bit pear-shaped, Mi££ion.'

It was either very, very late or very, very early.

I tried to give him a nice, cheering smile. My lips cracked and I tasted blood. One of my front teeth was gone. I tried to adjust it. You know – nice, cheering, lopsided smile. I failed. From the expression on Roland's face, I wasn't looking my usual handsome self.

Sapphire was weeping in the dinghy beside me. I tried to reach out my hand to squeeze hers. I tried to turn my head to give her a cheerful grin too. I failed again.

'They're coming,' she sobbed. 'Listen Max, they're coming.'

I tried listening, I could hear birds. I think they were birds anyway, but maybe my ears weren't in any better shape than my other parts. I think I heard the throb of an outboard motor. I nodded (painfully) at Sapphire in an encouraging way. The water beneath the dinghy started to swell.

'Who?' I ventured.

'*Them*,' said Sapphire, and I knew from the way she said it, it wasn't St John's Ambulance.

'Time for Plan B,' I lisped.

Roland and Sapphire helped me out of the dinghy. I staggered to the shore. They helped me up the steps to the walkway near where the *Cutty Sark* was. I heard the wail of the motorboat then – and the screech as it cut a circle and turned back towards us.

Inside my poor battered head one tiny brain cell was trying to be useful. It asked: *Where do we go? How do we get away? How are we going to move about with fractured ribs?* It wasn't getting much help from my other brain cells, but I'm glad to say it kept on asking its sad little questions.

We struggled past the old market square. Each step seemed to jolt a thousand places that I didn't know I had. My mouth tasted of blood and I felt a sudden searing thirst. *Oh God*, I thought, *that's it, I'm bleeding internally*. Behind us, the motor engine cut and the hull of a very much larger boat scraped on to shingle. Then a cry of triumph. They'd found the dinghy.

I started to shiver.

'They're behind us – please try to hurry, Max.' Sapphire tugged at my arm. A spear of pain shot through me.

Roland was great. He stopped and turned round. 'You two go on ahead,' he said, balling his fists. 'I'll keep them back for as long as I can. I'll give you a headstart.' He clenched his teeth and for a second his round, rosy, chubby chin looked chiselled.

'Rollz,' I gasped, 'don't be silly.'

'Well . . . should we give them the treasures then?' he suggested.

'I think we're a bit past that,' I said. 'Merlyn isn't going to be satisfied until he gets me.' I didn't add *and you too* but that was the truth. Merlyn was now on a mission of his own. We all knew it.

It was then that my one, brave, lonely, little brain cell struck lucky.

Off Gonson Creekside, St Agnes House, 93a Marlon Street, SE8! The address I'd chanted into my brain that night Sapphire went to the car park, where Leon had told me to go . . .

The lyrics to his song 'The Streets of London' rang round my head like an echoing gunshot. (You may think I'm rambling. You may be right. But you try keeping your thoughts straight when you've just had your head kicked in.)

Wa gwan?
Wa gwan?
On the streets of London?
In the county's dungeon?
If we can't walk them
We better run them
Wa gwan?
Wa gwan?

You see those were the lines from Dreader Dread's album called *Street Poets & Visionaries*. And Dreader

Dread lived at *St Agnes House, 93a Marlon Street SE8!* *Greenwich.*

GREENWICH.

Get it?

That's where the Cutty Sark was!

Dreader Dread, you know, the one I'd been going to meet . . . The one who could tell me the truth about Angelo . . . The one who lived in Greenwich . . .

If we could only reach his place. He would help us. At least I hoped he would. My brave brain cell had a go at another thought, but didn't get any further. I tried to hiss the news to Sapphire. It came out more like a yelp. We must be pretty close. My heart started to beat in hope. We might just make it . . .

Where was my tattered *A to Z*? Somewhere in my pocket? I fumbled around in my jacket. I pulled out some papers. I started reading.

From: "Lyoness" <morgaine@hotmail.com>
To: "Merlyn Wizard" <whitewizard@homeoffice.gov.uk>
Subject: Operation King Arthur
Date: Fri, 05 March 12:59:35 +0100

Dear M,
All files ready to be corrupted on PC. Key evidence removed or contaminated. No little heads have popped up to be cut

off. I so feel for you having this matter drag on so.

All best

Morgana le Fay

That wasn't it. Come to think of it, this wasn't my jacket either. This was the one Abiola had taken out of the boot and wrapped round me. Hey, the boot of Merlyn's car! I looked at the next email.

From: Home Office <fcardew@homeoffice.fco.gov.uk>
To: "Merlyn Wizard" <whitewizard@homeoffice.gov.uk>
Subject: Operation King Arthur
Date: Mon, 08 March 14:09:15 +0100

Merlyn,

Speed this thing up. Get the Mordred agents working faster. Get the dagger IMMEDIATELY. Not one whisper is to hit the news. Successful oil negotiations with the petroleum team in Niger Delta are riding on this. The Nigerian Government are about to sign America and Britain the exclusive development rights to oil fields in Coalition Party, ENRP, territory in the Niger Delta, on Wednesday next. Further upsets and digging up ancient Benin history will enrage insurgents and blow the fragile stability in the region sky high. Especially as we have no intention at all of returning bronze artefacts. The whole thing is dynamite. Billions are involved. They've been promised the dagger SO GET IT. The

Nigerian Government is sticking its heels in with a 'no dagger – no deal' clause. Do I make myself clear? Then clean everything up. No more casualties. You've overstepped the mark on this assignment. Keeping the country up and running and secure is our brief, but deaths call for investigations. I HAVE made myself clear, haven't I? Cardew

No more casualties? Like I was really going to take out a pension fund on that! From the fury that I glimpsed behind Merlyn's sneer, I could just imagine the kind of clean up he planned for me.

And so the whole thing was about the price of oil. No wonder they wanted that dagger back! No dagger – no deal, eh? I shook my head. (Ouch.)

But revealing as Merlyn's coat pockets were, sadly there was no *A to Z*. I tried to remember Leon's advice: '. . . *go to the creek's west side*.' That would mean following the creek up into Greenwich, crossing over and then pushing south again. Not that far, if it was a sunny day and I had two good legs . . .

'We've got to hide him,' said Sapphire. 'He can't make it. Maybe tomorrow, if—'

'Got something here to show you both,' I said.

The sound of faint shouts broke through the night air.

'OK,' said Roland, 'we'll have to break into the

grounds of the Royal Naval College. I used to have some chums there and I know the place quite well.'

'Well, hurry!' hissed Sapphire. She pushed away the papers I was holding out. So I shoved them back in my pocket. I'd tell them later. If . . . Yes I know, don't say it.

We struggled left down something or other Walk, down by the *Cutty Sark*. I saw the ship's long shadow thrown out in two directions by two different street lights. I heard the shouts behind grow louder. I heard the echo of heavy boots on cobbled streets. 'I can't go any further,' I whispered and clutched out at Sapphire to steady myself.

'I've got another idea,' said Roland.

'For God's sake,' said Sapphire.

'On the deck of the *Cutty Sark*,' said Roland, 'they'll never find us.'

'We'll never get up there either,' said Sapphire.

I figured she was right. The *Cutty Sark* towered three metres or more high. Her roped riggings creaked in the wind. And she was set in a dry harbour too, that sunk around her like a moat.

'Oh yes we can,' said Roland. 'My chums showed me how the sailors do it – quite easy really.'

'You and your chums,' said Sapphire, 'will have to think again. Since that fire, security cameras will be all over this place.'

'Then on top of those workers' containers,' hissed Roland.

And his chums were right about the old heave-ho. Although I had to bite on my fist to stop myself sobbing in pain as Roland and Sapphire hauled me up.

And only just in time.

No sooner had we pressed ourselves flat on the containers' roof, than down the dock's edge came the More Dread Crew. They stopped beside the *Cutty Sark*. I tried to breathe slowly.

'Must be near here,' said one. 'Search round the other side.'

I heard footsteps fading away then looping back.

'We search the boat?' said the first one.

I stopped breathing altogether.

'That kid can't have climbed up there. Every bone in his body is probably broken.'

I heard another set of footsteps. 'I want the dagger,' said a voice I knew only too well. 'He's making a fool out of us – and it stops tonight.'

If you can nearly die twice in one day, I did then. For Merlyn said, 'He's here. I can smell him. Get up there on deck and check every centimetre of that boat, then search the surroundings. I'll notify the local police that this is a Striking Force swoop. The security won't record anything you do. So feel free to do anything when you get him. Just make sure he's conscious though when you hand him over. I'd personally like to clean everything up.'

OF SHIPS AND
SHOPPING TROLLEYS

'The leopard has spots because sometimes he wishes to hide.'
West African saying

Through the darkness I heard Sapphire catch her breath. I heard Roland not moving a muscle so loudly it was like an alarm clock. What were we going to do? I heard boots on pavement and hands grasping at the sides of the ship. I heard a voice say, 'You check up there. I'll check the quayside.' A beam of blue torchlight swept up the container beside me. My heart bulged out until it was the size of a pumpkin. I started sweating down my back. My blood was hammering so fast, I felt sure the whole thing would shake.

I heard a steel toecap scrape against the ship's side.

Footsteps returned from the direction of the river. A second boot banged against the hull. 'Nothing down by the water,' said a voice. 'D'you need a leg up? You'll be able to see on top of those workers' containers from there.'

Roland stiffened beside me.

I heard the crunch of boots land on the ship's deck. I prayed to Abiola's gods.

A breeze sighed down the Thames. A spot of rain splooshed on to my hand. I could almost feel the beam of his torch as it slid over the deck, as it searched behind the storage bays over the tarpaulins . . . up and down the meshed riggings . . . out through the night towards us . . .

I felt Sapphire suck in her breath. I dug my nails on to the iron beneath me. I clenched my teeth and sweated and prayed: *Please . . . please . . . please don't let him see us . . .*

'Nothing up here,' he said. 'Merlyn doesn't realize how hard he kicks. I told you that kid wouldn't be able to climb anywhere.' I heard him moving across the deck. 'Can't see much in this bloody mist either.'

I thanked the gods for the mist now rolling at speed off the Thames. I listened to his footsteps retreat. There were a couple of crunches as he sprang down. My breath came back. My legs started shivering. Sapphire moved very slightly. Roland jerked.

'And that means he can't have gone far either,' continued the voice, 'so I'm going to wait right here until he drags his sorry little arse out of wherever he's put it.'

We lay there long into the hours of the morning, the icy mist from the Thames working its way into every bruised and broken bone of my body. Sapphire tried to cuddle up to me. In a different life I would have been ready to go through it all again just to feel her silky breath on my face. Just to feel her arm around me. But I wasn't the Maxi I knew. I just lay there and shivered, and shivered, and explored my broken mouth with my tongue, and tried not to think of anything but staying alive and staying awake.

At last Roland ventured silently to the container's edge and peeped over. Dawn was slipping up the Thames along with the grey mist. A skyline appeared and the hum of traffic grew louder. The man or men below the hull of the ship stirred and became restless. One of them said, 'This isn't going to find him and it's not going to please Merlyn either.' The other grunted.

Then suddenly, as if that settled it, they left.

At least we thought they did.

We moved. We rubbed our frozen legs. We began a slow, painful descent. Everything from my jaw to my ankles seemed to have seized up. I could hardly crawl. After Roland and Sapphire had literally carried me down, I slumped in a heap on the street cobbles. I knew I was about to pass out. I tried to lift up my head, but even that was too much. Instead I mumbled into my chest, 'You lot go on. Leave me here.'

But Sapphire and Roland said something that I either couldn't hear or understand. And then a thicker sort of white haze seemed to roll up off the river and wrap itself around me and carry me up and out of the way of my own body, as it lay there shaking and tormented.

Apparently they got a shopping trolley. They put me in it and wheeled me round to Dreader Dread's, Off Gonson Creekside, St Agnes House, 93a Marlon Street. Apparently the two men looking for us saw them. But not until they'd crossed over the creek and were pushing southwards. Apparently it was quite dramatic, and there was a short chase in which I was rattled over driveways and bumped down tarmac at top speed with Sapphire shrieking. I'm sorry I missed that bit. I didn't know a thing about it. That is until I was tipped out of the trolley head first. Apparently I was not very appreciative of all their efforts and said some things best forgotten, as I catapulted through the main entrance of St Agnes House.

93A MARLON STREET

'When the ants unite they can kill the elephant.'
West African saying

Dreader Dread picked me up off the wall-to-wall vinyl tiles and carried me as easily as if I'd been a puppy into his tiny council flat. He put me down on a low divan and looked at me, shaking his head. I looked at him. Six and a half feet of red, gold and green. Not much taller than Nelson's Column. His huge crocheted hat squashed against the ceiling.

Roland looked around for a chair, found an upturned drum and sat down. Sapphire hovered. 'He needs a doctor,' she said.

'Then him come to the right place,' said Dreader Dread. 'I is a doctor.' He stretched out his arms, filling the whole the room. 'I is a doctor, a human helicopter . . .' And whirring his arms in circles and humming like a herd of giant bees, he buzzed down the corridor to what I later learnt was a small kitchen off the end of the hall. There he brewed up some dreadful concoction of leaves and herbs. He brought it right back, raised my head, held it firm and said, 'Drink it down! Don't worry; it's sugar free.'

'Helicopter?' said Sapphire.

'Flying,' said Dreader Dread.

The potion tasted bitter, but no sooner had I swallowed some than a warm glow spread out inside me.

Sapphire still looked puzzled. 'Flying?' she said.

'That's cheating,' said Dreader. 'You keep pinching my words.'

I handed the glass back to Dreader Dread.

'But he may have broken something,' said Sapphire. 'Shouldn't we call out a proper doctor?'

Dreader Dread laughed, a laugh that caught you joining in, even though you didn't know why. 'You don't like me medicine?' he said.

'But . . .' said Sapphire, looking worried.

'She means,' added Roland trying to step in, 'are you a qualified doctor, you know, with a degree? I mean . . .' He realized straightaway he'd made a mistake.

'Is it degrees you want?' said Dreader Dread. 'Don't worry, I *is* a barometer, a human thermometer!'

Sapphire opened her mouth, thought better and shut it.

'You'll see,' said Dreader Dread, 'me medicine is very vitalistic.'

And he went out to the kitchen to fetch me another cup.

'The guy's nuts,' said Sapphire.

Roland looked doubtful.

'Not nuts,' I whispered, 'a poet. He deals in words. Helicopter equals flying doctor. Qualifications mean degrees. Degrees mean a thermometer.' I sank back on to the cushions. Whatever stuff Dreader had put in that potion, it sure felt good. I looked up at the whirls on the dingy ceiling and felt happy.

'That's it!' said Dreader Dread when he returned. 'Now you got a smiley pon your face!'

'Oh Max,' said Sapphire, as I drained the cup. And a little worried wrinkle appeared between her eyes.

Dreader Dread laughed his delicious laugh again. I started to relax. All the pain drained away down a tiny plughole. I floated. I felt for the first time since Angelo had died a strange peacefulness. I heard Roland say, 'I'm awfully sorry, Mr Dread, I didn't mean to infer that you weren't . . . well . . . you know —' there was some throat clearing '— you see, there may be some unpleasantness . . . there're these people, called the More Dread Crew . . . and . . . well, they're not really a crew, and well . . . they may come here . . .'

At that, Dreader Dread laughed even louder. 'The More Dread Crew – here?' he said. 'You is full of funny jokes. Oh dear, I'd like to see that Merlyn Wizard here.'

I opened my eyes. He knew about Merlyn?

Sapphire looked worried. But when she saw my eyes were open, she put on a fake everything-is-completely-fine smile. I think she did that just for me. Because she wanted me to feel relaxed and happy. It worked! I felt happy, times a million. When the girl you love smiles for you, who cares if it's fake?

That's when the hammering on the door started.

Roland looked out the window. 'It's them,' he said.

More hammering.

'I knew it,' said Sapphire and bent her head into her hands. 'Poor Mr Dread, we've brought you nothing but trouble . . .'

I tried to drag myself up to sill level. I clutched at the window and pulled the net curtain back. Outside, the street was eerily quiet. Something was definitely very wrong. It might have been the shiny cars parked opposite. It might not. You can only be optimistic. I slumped back and looked again at the whirls on the ceiling. They didn't look quite so much fun any more.

Dreader Dread stood up. He tucked a stray lock back into his hat. He smiled. Then he left the room.

He walked down the tiny corridor and opened the front door.

All three of us listened to every word that followed.

'Why is you kicking down me door?' Dreader's voice sounded like silk over razor blades.

'I'm Police Inspector D. K. Carter,' said a voice. 'Would you mind if we came inside?'

'I haxed you a question,' said Dreader, 'and now *you* is hasking me one back.'

'Stand aside,' said a voice I recognized as Merlyn's.

'I can see you're in a charming mood, Mr Whirling Merlyn whose lips are curling,' said Dreader.

'Go back to your doggerel, Rasta. We've got business to take care of.'

'Not in my yard.'

If Merlyn's voice could have got any harder it would have turned to stone. 'Don't waste my time.' I heard him crack every one of his knuckles, and then some.

I struggled back to the sill. And gasped. It looked like Merlyn was going to bust in. Several of his men muscled forward. Sapphire's lovely face turned ashen. Roland stood up and moved across to defend her.

'I think you is forgetting something,' said Dreader.

Merlyn tried to shove past him.

I clutched the window ledge, suddenly dizzy.

'The search warrant.'

There was a hush. Like the calm before a storm.

'You never heard of that one before?'

'Ridiculous,' said Merlyn. 'You think *we* have to get a search warrant?' He kicked at the doorstep and shook down his shoulders, like he was going to punch something.

'I is haxing for a search warrant and you is not coming into my house without one,' said Dreader, very reasonably.

There was a silence that felt like thin ice. Then Merlyn said something that nobody wanted to hear. I struggled to keep my balance at the window.

'I excuse your language, but I'm not finished yet,' continued Dreader. He pulled out his mobile and rang a number. 'Aloysius? Get yourself down here, with your camera and a couple of youth from *South London Voice*. I got a front page article for you! It's that government official Mr Merlyn whose bin giving the Campaign such a lot of trouble. Looks like him finally gone batty.' He turned back to Merlyn. 'Still want to come in?' he enquired.

Merlyn snorted, but he did not reply. At last he muttered something like: 'This is insufferable! Trust some people's poet to try to threaten me with the press.' But he did stop and turn and walk back to his headlights. From there he yelled, 'You may think you've won this round, Rasta, but I've warned you before. Don't. Cross. Me. You've only got till Monday morning! If you put one foot outside your door, you won't be going around making any more random poems. Your name won't be Dreader Dread. You'll be getting a new one. DEADER DEAD!'

My head felt light. I sank back on to the cushions. The swirls on the ceiling seemed to move all on their own. I heard Dreader shut the front door, but Merlyn's voice carried on. 'So long, *dead man*. We'll be back, and then you and your poetry are going to be *posthumous* . . .'

You could definitely tell he was rather frustrated.

Dreader came back inside. All the sparkle gone from his eyes. He came across to me and put his hand on my mine. I tried to smile, but after you've lost a front tooth it's kind of hard. 'I'll do my best,' he said, 'but Merlyn has a point. We can't hold him out for ever.'

We all sat there stunned. The More Dread Crew knew where we were. It was Friday afternoon. The local courts would shut over the weekend. Could Merlyn go somewhere else and get a search warrant?

'Well,' said Dreader. 'It's true Merlyn has an obsession about us, and he'd like nothing more than to bust in here, but I think we have till Monday. See, he won't stick his neck out too far. He doesn't want anything too high profile. He's still just doing his job, remember – and in that kind of work, his bosses don't like unnecessary ripples or anything that will add up to a scandal. They'll write him off and he knows it. Even top MI6 agents are expendable. But we mustn't lose guard. There is more than one way to get into this house.' He stood up and pulled tight the grille gates across the window. He fastened the burglar bars behind the door. The letterbox was already nailed shut, but he tested it anyway.

So we had two and a half days of safety. And then what? I guess I knew how it would go. They'd bust in. The police would arrest us. We might never make it to the police station. An unforeseen accident. Maybe. Maybe they'd surround the house with snipers, claim we were terrorists, kill us all straightaway. Was that it?

Dreader sat there. Everything from his leatherless shoes to his huge natural fibre hat seemed shrunken. 'I've known the day will come,' he said. 'It was written like that, long before you and I were born.' His voice deepened and darkened. 'We don't have long now. We must eat and drink, and sit like the elders did around the fire. We must summon up courage and give libations to the forces of the universe, and then the Council of the Small will begin.'

THE COUNCIL OF THE SMALL

'But there is something that I must say to my people who stand on the warm threshold which leads into the palace of justice. In the process of gaining our rightful place we must not be guilty of wrongful deeds.'
I Have a Dream – Martin Luther King, Lincoln Memorial, 28 August 1963

So later, much later, when we were full to bursting with dairy-free omelettes, alfalfa salad and butternut squash, when we had settled down in front of a smokeless fuel fire with a goblet of fruit tea, Dreader said, 'You have been asking me questions, and now this is the time for answering. But first tell me what you know so far.'

So we did. We told him about the treasures and the terrors, and how the More Dread Crew weren't a crew, but were a Home Office squad. How they'd killed Mum and Mogul and Angelo, and how we'd run and hid and fought back. How we'd rescued the treasures, and how we planned on giving them back and selling our stories to the world. How we suspected a spy at the

B.L.A.C.K. A.R.M.Y. and how we thought it was Leon. How Abiola had helped us, but was in trouble himself for it, and how we'd come, at last, to him.

At first he didn't say anything, but his eyes grew sad. 'You have done well,' he said at last. And I noticed that he was much older than I'd first thought. There were threads of grey in his eyebrows. A tiny mesh of wrinkles creased his forehead. And his shoulders, although broad, were rounded.

'And so the time has come,' he said, as if he knew that such a time was bound to come, and he had been spent a lifetime warding it off.

Then he lit up a hookah pipe that hubbled and bubbled through a water filter, and the room smelt unexpectedly of flowers and spring and freshly-cut grass. In the flicker of firelight, a soft haze filtered into the spaces around us. Dreader smiled. Wisps of smoke curled into the air. The flames from the fire died down and all around us the shadows closed in. Then Dreader's voice seemed to change. The strong Jamaican accent gave way to a deep, soft tone that reminded me of something else, of times gone by, of great adventures and great deeds . . .

'Evil is a force, that is how you must see it. With every generation it rises, and every generation is given a chance to challenge it and beat it back. But evil never dies and it never sleeps. It only rests and grows strong and rises again.

'Now it is your turn to fight for the world you know – even for other, better worlds waiting to happen.'

I looked into the shadows that pressed close around us. I wanted to say: *But why us?*

Dreader spread his huge hands on his knees. 'The B.L.A.C.K. A.R.M.Y. has known for some time that there was a spy. Every time we have striven for human rights and justice . . . every time we struggled to support the liberation movements in Mozambique, Angola, Namibia . . . every time we championed the cause of Reparations to Africa, and tried to work within a framework of law and justice, we have been betrayed.'

We listened, spellbound by the quality of his voice. For it seemed to us that it conjured up the struggles of generations of lives in the dusty streets and open plains of Africa. I didn't really understand what those struggles were, but I understood the bow of his shoulder and the steadfast angle of his jaw.

Dreader put another scoop of environmentally-friendly coke on to the fire and stared into it. There was something so noble and so sad about him; I hung my head.

At last he spoke. 'If it is Leon, then I am truly sorry, for he is one of the greatest campaigners we've ever had, but I am not yet convinced of it. The men in grey specialize in ripping organisations apart from within, casting doubt and suspicion. Now, show me the emails you have found in Merlyn's coat pocket.'

We showed him. And he read them by the light of that fire. 'Ahh,' he said at last. 'See how they play their little games, calling themselves after heroes from history. Operation King Arthur, is it? Merlyn and Mordred and Morgana! Seems they have reached the M letter!'

I think I laughed at that. I mean, that we were merely in the queue of an alphabetical procession of government jobs.

'And so our old friend Merlyn has finally cracked, eh?' said Dreader. 'He has finally "overstepped the mark"; but beware, this will make him doubly dangerous. For long he has nursed his hatred of our movement, so we must be very careful now. He has no future left. He will not be renamed as Nelson in the next N mission. You see how power corrupts! Some government agencies, and some men in them, think they are above the Will of Jah. They believe they can do what they want and are not accountable to the world and us small ones in it.'

And I did see. I saw just how little chance we all stood of surviving. Roland looked really shocked.

'Was that why they didn't get a search warrant to get at us at my place?' he said. 'I mean, because my dad's a lord, and not really a small person . . . well, not that you are . . . I mean . . .'

'And I hear he's a very good lord too,' said Dreader. 'Helping us out in Uganda and searching for global peace. But yes, of course, Merlyn – like all bullies – will only persecute those who are smaller than him.'

Sapphire stayed quiet, her beautiful almond-shaped eyes staring into Dreader's face.

'So,' he continued, 'the rest is as we know: an oil deal, a missing dagger, a cover-up. But now I know what we can do!'

Dreader stood up at these words and cast his hands into the air, and it seemed then that the light from the fire lit up his face in a great tawny glow, and at his back the darkness retreated. At that moment, I imagined him speaking in verse, moved by some great spirit, shaking his locks like the mane of a wild lion. And I wished I could have seen him on one of his rare performances on the streets of London . . .

'The time has come,' he said, 'to force those who would embrace evil back into the shadows from where they came and, like all the forces of this world, wait for their time to come again. For this persecution of our small lives must not go unchallenged. The Bronzes must go home and the government must be exposed for the shameful part it has played. I like your idea of delivering the treasures to Abiola. I like your idea of involving the press. And I like it best because it is your own solution. Now, if you are strong enough to take the Bronzes across London to the Nigerian High Commission, I will help you. I will show you how we can trap these people and bring ruin on Merlyn, but the decision is yours. Yours alone. For there is yet another thing . . .'

I held my breath.

'One amongst you must bear the blame. For it is only in this way that we can really expose the deep-rooted evils of our society and change history. One of you, after the treasures have been returned, must give yourself up and stand trial.'

'But why?' cried Sapphire.

'Because,' said Dreader, 'good can never flourish by breaking the law. Those Bronzes you have carried here were stolen by you, but they in their turn were also stolen. We must make that point. We must change the law. That is what we have to do. So one of you must take on that role, must set a precedent in the courts of England and prove that we are right.'

'But that means risking prison!' cried Roland, as if the whole of his future was being washed down the plughole right in front of him.

'And what if we can't prove it?' said Sapphire.

'Prison or not, to fight evil means that you must be ready for anything,' said Dreader.

'Yes, Sapphire, think of the suffragettes,' said Roland.

'NO WAY!' said Sapphire. 'I AM NOT GOING TO PRISON.'

I sighed. My ribs ached. My head ached.

And I knew just who that person was going to be.

After that, we sat silent in the flickering glow of that firelight. The flames danced in blue and yellow and threw strange shadows over us. At our back the darkness waited. I don't know what the others were thinking, but I'd gone back to those golden days of childhood, where the world was a safe and wonderful place. A place in which I had a glorious future in an epic movie where I saved the people I loved from certain death, and the world from terrible destruction, where I was carried shoulder high . . . And here I was a broken thing, my family gone, sitting in a council flat in South London, contemplating prison.

'We're going to do it, of course,' I said.

And all three of them looked up, as if they'd been waiting for me to say it.

'We're going to fight all that injustice; fight for a better world.'

'Then we'll need a plan,' said Dreader.

'You'll want to see the treasures too, won't you?' said Sapphire.

'And clearly, you need to help us work out who's the Inside Help,' said Roland.

'And we'll have to let Abiola know we're coming,' I added.

'And we'll all need to get some sleep,' said Dreader.

And behind us the shadows darkened, and we shivered and drew a little nearer to the fire.

'Because I have a feeling that when Sunday morning comes, we will not sleep again until this fight is finally over.'

DEPTFORD CREEK

'Even an earthquake cannot stop marching ants.'
West African saying

Behind Marlon Street is a thin viaduct that leads across Deptford Creek. If someone was desperate enough, they could crawl across it and get down on the Greenwich side. From there, if that same someone was very resolute, they could glide down back streets, slide alongside walls, hide behind dustbins and duck into shop fronts until they emerged quite mysteriously outside Greenwich train station. Once successfully in the station, it would be easy enough to take the westbound train to Charing Cross. From there, of course, it is only one hop to Trafalgar Square and Northumberland Avenue . . . and the Nigerian High Commission.

I tested out the idea on Dreader.

'If that someone was a cool cat, and wanted to be really sure he would get clear away before bigger cats found him, he would arrange for a little diversion to happen just around the time he put his foot upon the viaduct,' said Dreader.

'If only he could,' I said.

'Lie down, Maxi, and rest,' said Sapphire. 'You're getting a bit delirious.'

'I think I know someone who could help,' said Dreader.

'I'd call my dad,' said Roland. 'Clearly, he could drum up something, but he's still in Jinja . . . and there's the problem of the houseboat that they don't yet know about . . .'

'Seems about time some of me poetry got some ratings,' said Dreader.

'We could report a bomb scare, perhaps?' said Sapphire.

'Or set fire to something,' suggested Roland. He winced. 'Or maybe not.'

'Seems about time me neighbours enjoyed a likkle street party,' said Dreader.

Even if Roland and Sapphire weren't listening, I was.

'It's nice to help out me local council,' said Dreader. 'They always need news about things happening in the area.'

'That's what we could do with,' said Sapphire, 'something happening right on this street, so we could get a chance to slip away, maybe even out the back and over that viaduct.'

Sometimes for all her plans of university, Sapphire is a bit slow.

'Nothing is likely to happen here!' said Roland.

Dreader frowned, but did not point out that maybe not *all* things *only* happened in up-market places. Instead, he smiled and said very politely, 'Did you know that Sunday is International Street Poetry in Deptford Day Night?'

'International *what*?' said Sapphire.

'Is it?' said Roland.

'Funny how things always seem to be happening right on me doorstep,' mused Dreader. 'I better phone up the council and tell them I'm willing to do a poetryathon for charity. That should get the party started.'

'I'm beginning to get an idea,' said Roland.

'Hey!' said Sapphire. 'What if we make our getaway while the street party is going on?'

Dreader clapped his hands. 'You is a human lightbulb,' he said.

Sapphire smiled. (I think she got that one.)

'And did you know that a poetryathon on International Street Poetry in Deptford Day Night always starts, in the evening, along with fireworks?' Dreader added.

'I didn't,' I said, 'but I'm sure glad. It seems like the perfect time for a desperate thief to get going on his desperate mission, wouldn't you say?'

This time both Sapphire and Roland got it. They nodded their heads as if they had just had that brainwave themselves.

'And did you know that a poetryathon always ends up in Trafalgar Square about the same time the Nigerian High Commission opens; after we have marched all night, of course, through our neighbourhoods, speaking in verse down through the high streets and low streets, housing estates and skateboard parks?'

'That would be a terrific diversion,' said Roland.

'That's it!' cried Sapphire. 'The Nigerian High Commission is really near Trafalgar Square! We could meet outside . . .'

'And all the press will be there too,' said Dreader, 'because (although I say it myself) I've got a large following of fans, and the press is always interested in celebrities.'

Roland and Sapphire looked so pleased. I guess it's nice to have brainwaves.

So that was the plan. We'd escape over the creek while the street party went on, and take the train to Charing Cross. Dreader would divert the nation and lead a march to the High Commission. We would spend the night in hiding by Trafalgar Square (Dreader said he had a contact near there who'd help us and did a nice line in jerk vegetables with rice and peas). Then we would meet up and complete our original idea of returning the treasures and exposing the More Dread Crew in front of the worldwide press!

Good morning Britain!

Boyakasha!

Later, when we were alone, I asked Dreader about Mum. Was she working for the Campaign all those times we'd stayed at Auntie Ellie's? Had Angelo been helping her? Had they both gone on missions? Did he think they were both two of the greatest campaigners as well? Had they ever mentioned me, said I'd helped even a little tiny bit? I hungered so much to hear him speak well of them, to bring them alive again.

He took my hand gently in his and patted it. 'Both of them loved you,' he said. 'For them you were a symbol of all that's best and needs protecting. It inspired them never to give up. They were brave and loyal,' he said. 'Both of them, caring people ready to do anything for those they loved and for those who are oppressed and suffer . . .' Then he looked deep into my eyes, and the dark centres of his looked like the sea under a stormy sky. 'But not better than you,' he said, 'for you have shown all of us how to be a true hero.'

And it was strange, but I felt a weird sensation in the back of my nose and eyes. And I had to tilt my chin up and smile quickly to stop my lips trembling.

And the dagger, I choked, how had she got it?

'From Sir Robert Terselas's office. She saw it there lying on his desk. She read the covering letter lying next to it. How it was to be used as a government sweetener. She took the letter and the dagger as evidence,' he said, 'evidence that all the government's and the museum's excuses to us, all their reasons for refusing our petitions to return the Bronzes, were trumped up and insubstantial.'

I bit my lip and couldn't speak. I had to keep flexing my fingers so that I could concentrate on something. And I found myself blinking very fast.

And on the day she'd died, had she gone on the boat with it? Had Mogul King been on the boat too? Was he really her boyfriend? Had others from the Marcus Garvey Centre gone as well?

Dreader looked sadly into my quivering face, held my fretful fingers gently between his great hands and listened.

Was that when she'd given the dagger to Mogul?

Had one of the others pushed her? Did she ever talk of me, say that I was growing up a little? That she thought I'd turn out OK?

I don't think he answered me, but his huge presence somehow helped to soften all the unspoken things that stayed tight inside my throat.

I can't say that by Sunday evening, I was anywhere near well enough to crawl over that narrow viaduct. My mouth was still horribly sore. My head spun when I sat up. Breathing was agony and my kidneys were in bad shape. But I had improved a little.

This was how it happened.

Dreader kept me horizontal all that first night and allowed nobody to touch me. He strapped up my ribs with long strips of thick bandages. I don't know if they helped, but they were warm and felt good. He took towels. He dipped them in boiling water. He pressed them on to my waist and back, then dipped them in icy water and pressed again. These treatments went on for hours. Then he gave me more herb potions and I fell into a deep dreamless oblivion.

By morning I could stumble to the loo, but only with the help of Roland on one side and Dreader on the other. Then started one full day of therapy.

'You can do anything if you set your mind to it,'

started Dreader. 'You can control your body and accelerate your healing.'

I longed to believe him, but every fibre of my body disagreed. I mean, I tried to visualize healing waves washing over my fractured ribs. I tried to submerge my bruised abdomen in curative bubble baths. I repeated mantras like, 'I am whole. I am filled with strength and energy.' Not.

By the time evening came, all I can say is, I could stand up. I only threw up if I tried to move.

Quite rightly, Sapphire was worried. 'I'm really sorry for ever doubting you, Mr Dreader,' she said. 'Max is really improving with your medicine, but I don't think he's ready yet. I mean he can't run, he can't climb. What if the More Dread Crew ambush us? He won't stand a chance.'

Dreader just looked at her. 'He'll do,' he said. 'He'll have to. You only have one chance to get to the High Commission. If you're there by daybreak, Mr Abiola can help you. If you fail, he will die anyway.'

Sapphire stamped. I was impressed by the way her foot hit the floor. I wish I'd had the strength to do it.

'Then Roland and I will go. We'll leave Max here,' she said.

'Leave him for Merlyn to find on Monday morning?' asked Dreader.

So evening came, and with it our last chance to sleep in a comfy bed. Our last chance to eat bean bake with roasted turnip and listen to Dreader's soft voice by the light of a smokeless fire.

I still look back on that evening as one of the happiest I've ever spent. Never mind my pain. Never mind anything. Maybe one day if I get out of here, I'll walk down Marlon Street and tap lightly on Dreader's door and ask him if, since the history of time, there's ever been an assistant street poet? And if the time has come for him to train up someone, someone who wants to do things that resonate now and for ever and likes herb tea . . .

But Sunday morning came, and Sunday afternoon, and Sunday evening, and with it came the fireworks and the police cordons and the television news crews who announced over their portable public address systems: *'Channel News is here at a council street in Deptford to cover an historic occasion when Dreader Dread, people's poet, is conducting an epic poetryathon in honour of his newly coined idea, "International Street Poetry in Deptford Day Night". He plans to march to Trafalgar Square in aid of a debt-free Africa. Dreader Dread is known to shake the nation when he appears to speak. Already, thousands are making their way to Deptford to listen to his poetry. At his last appearance, he recited one thousand lines of "The Streets of London". His theme today may be quite different. We can only say in his own words:*

> "Wa gwan? Wa gwan?
> across the nation
> to my local station
> crime and frustration
> consternation
> Wa gwan? Wa gwan?"

Sapphire started packing up everything she thought we might need: towels, carrots, flashlight, apples, raincoats, dry clothes, umbrella, parsnips . . . (?) Roland poured over maps of Charing Cross and Waterloo and examined every London Transport timetable he could get. I tried out the mobile Dreader had lent me, along with standing up straight and sitting down, trying to get up to speed. I figured I might need to.

And so as the moon climbed level with the rooftops of Marlon Street and every window bounced with silvery light, Dreader went to the front door. Gently, he opened it and stepped out. A cheer went up from the street. A fanfare of wild clapping resounded down to the river and back. The crowd went crazy. The cheering lasted for twenty minutes and drowned out every loudspeaker. Sapphire, Roland and I waited, our eyes manacled to his back. My heart started pumping way too fast. Then the crowds shuffled back, ready to be amazed.

We'd planned that at Dreader's first words, when the air was at its most tense, we'd leave by the back gate. It had a few advantages. The crowd would be transfixed, and any movement by Merlyn to follow us would be easily recognized. We might be able to gain a few minutes' headstart. Maybe long enough to reach the viaduct before Merlyn realized we'd gone. Then we had seven or eight minutes to get to Greenwich. Roland had found out that trains stopped at Greenwich Station twice every hour. They ran direct to Waterloo East and Charing Cross. If we timed it exactly, the train would be pulling out of the station as Merlyn arrived on the platform.

The disadvantages were obvious. The train might be late. Merlyn would know that the street poetryathon was a smokescreen. He'd be waiting somewhere else. I might never make it. Abiola might not have got my message. There'd be no one to meet us at Trafalgar Square. What would we do then? Where would we spend the night? How could we stay hidden until Dreader arrived?

Dreader started . . .

'My new rhyme is for all the peoples of this world who are never going to hear it. For all the youth who are

never going to read it. My brothers and sisters out there
– this is for you . . .

> *'The world is not a fair place*
> *Maybe it's better in outer space*
> *But when you come down to earth*
> *It all depends on your land of birth . . .'*

We turned and headed for the back door.

We closed it behind us. We slunk to the end of the
vegetable patch. We tiptoed through the garden gate
and out on to the tow path next to Deptford Creek. The
moon sailed high. The water rippled in a ghostly glow.
We turned right and headed into the west.

Then we were gone. As silently as shadows, we
disappeared round the bend in the path. We walked like
feathers towards the thin viaduct that spanned the creek
fifty metres away. We could do it. Behind us, a blaze of
fireworks burst out on the cold air. They exploded above
us like gunfire. Instinctively we ducked, as if from
unseen bullets.

Maybe right now the More Dread Crew was
watching those same rockets. But they wouldn't be for
long. Pretty soon they'd look around. They'd realize
we'd gone. I didn't want to be anywhere near Deptford
when they got over being amazed by Catherine wheels.

However, when I reached the start of the viaduct, my

heart sank. One look at the fifteen-centimetre wide concrete span, and I knew I couldn't do it.

'We'll have to balance,' said Sapphire, 'like on a beam.'

I looked at the slim arch straddling the creek. It rose in a gentle curve. Beneath it, the waves of Deptford Creek were choppy. The tide was on the turn and ebbing fast. The creek waters sinking by the minute.

'Doesn't look strong enough to hold us all,' I said. 'Better go one at a time.'

'And quickly,' said Roland.

I glanced behind us. There in the blur of fireworks, shadows seemed to merge and detach. They swam towards us through the gloom. I stared hard at those swimming shadows. 'Yep,' I said, 'they're coming.'

Sapphire went first. She seized the golf bag. 'Let me take that,' she said. She put one dainty foot upon the bridge. She opened her arms like a summer butterfly and stepped out. Effortlessly balanced. In a matter of seconds, she was over and beckoning to us.

'You,' said Roland.

I shook my head. I didn't tell Roland I couldn't do it. There was no use in two of us getting killed.

Roland wobbled. He stuck his feet out at weird angles. He sort of rolled. For a minute I thought he'd fall. I caught my breath so fast it jabbed a dagger of pain into my chest. Roland swayed and ducked and tottered. Sapphire hissed, 'Don't stand still, move forward.'

Roland seemed to clutch at the air in front of him and lurch forward. Then he scrabbled with his feet. Suddenly he was over.

Now me.

I glanced behind. They were definitely there. Two figures closing in. More materializing in the gloom. I glanced ahead. On a good day, with a fair wind behind me, I could have taken the whole creek in a broad jump. Maybe. Right now I could barely stand straight. I edged forwards.

'You can do it, Mi££ion,' said Roland.

'Get going,' I said. 'Don't stand there like mugs.' Probably, they thought I was thinking of their safety. In a way I was. But most of all, I didn't want them to see the way I wasn't going to get over that bridge. After all, Manz got his pride.

I looked at the rough concrete span. I looked at the river swilling below. If I'd been stronger, I could have waded. Probably. If I'd had longer, I could have walked to the footbridge half a mile back. If I'd been Superman, I could have flown. If I'd been Harry Potter, I could have put on my invisibility cloak.

Still it gave me a likkle idea. Even if my waist wasn't

working, my brain was. Invisibility cloak. Hide. Fool Merlyn. Double back.

It was my only chance. I waved Roland and Sapphire away. They hesitated. 'For God's sake move!' Roland hung back. 'Move! Look after the treasures. Wait for me for as long as you can, then get them to Trafalgar Square,' I hissed. 'Have faith.'

At that, Roland spun on his heel, grabbed Sapphire's arm and tugged her into the street opposite. I searched for somewhere to hide. Nowhere. No shadowy doorway. No large recycle bins. No spreading tree with handy branches. Just one open tow path. One impossible viaduct. One churning river.

River it was, then.

I sat slowly down on the creekside, held my ribs and my breath, and slid in. There were some maintenance rungs driven into the concrete – something a bit like steps. Loops of steel. I suppose they were there in case some poor idiot had to repair the viaduct. I clung on to them and lowered myself down. Right down, until my legs sank into the icy, muddy river. The rush of it pulled me off balance. I twisted.

A wave of pain crashed into me, yanking me away from the rungs. I grabbed at the steel, as it slithered from between my fingers. I heard them arrive. I heard somebody shout, 'They're getting away. Get round the other side of this river. Cut them off.'

Even if I could have grasped the rungs, I don't think I could have held on. Every twist was agony. I didn't try. I allowed the rungs to brush against my fingertips. I felt freezing water close over my chest. I took as large a breath as I could and let the current take me.

NEVER GIVE UP

'Everything we do has a resonance now and for ever,
even the things we choose not to do.'
Leon Nicholas Ziggy Braithwaite Brakespeare

Like laundry in a washing machine, I spun into the ebb
tide. Everywhere was thick and dark and deadly. The
fireworks exploding above were pinched out like a
candle. Water roared into my ears. My eyes stung. The
river just opened up and swallowed me. I don't think I
tried to breathe. I remember thinking: *So this is how it
all ends, how interesting.* Then I was slammed into
something so hard that even if I had managed to gasp a
little air, it would have been knocked right out. I can't
describe that degree of pain. I won't try. You'll have to
wait until you have three or more fractured ribs with
extensive internal bruising and you are flung at full
speed on to a concrete wall by a raging river.

I passed out.

Luckily not for long. If I'd been out any longer, I
would have drowned. Instead, I found myself washed up

on the concrete curve of the inlet, the receding waters of the Thames swilling around my neck, dragging me seaward. The More Dread Crew long gone.

This time I clung to the bank. There was no pain to fear. It couldn't get any worse. I heaved myself across the concrete, its rough surface rasping against me. The skin on my hands grating off. I was terrified of being swept around the corner out into the wide rushing Thames. I longed to find a set of slimy steps, a frayed rope, a crusted ring to hang to. I longed in vain.

At last, after an age of inching against the flood of the creek, I hit a rainwater gully. By climbing into it and wedging myself tight, I found that I could at last rest. Everything I had was trembling. I waited, trying not to cough. Trying not to shiver. Trying not to move a muscle until the pain subsided and my breathing became easier. *Think*, I told myself. *Think of what Dreader said. Mind over matter. You can do it. You can raise yourself up. You can walk out of this gutter to Greenwich Station. You can and you will.*

So I did.

It took a long time.

But I did it.

I was three hours late, but Roland and Sapphire had waited. They were so pleased to see me that I promised myself I would take the blame for them for everything we'd done together and everything to come. For ever.

We were so late, we'd missed the last regular train. We hung around the station, unsure what to do. Roland kept watch on the street. Sapphire scouted the platforms. I sat shivering behind a baguette stand. At last a late train came. There was an announcement that it had been delayed somewhere else and was going through to Waterloo East only. I think it was about one a.m. We weren't seen. At least, I didn't see anyone, but I was never going to underestimate the More Dread Crew *ever* again.

On board that train, Sapphire bought me a hot chocolate with whipped topping. That was the sweetest thing she'd ever done for me. Sadly, my teeth were chattering so much and my hands were so trembly, I spilt most of it. Roland tried to make me swap my clothes for an emergency tracksuit we'd borrowed off Dreader.

'Nah,' I said. 'Manz not feeling to change u-get-me?'

Roland looked very worried.

I tried smiling at him. If it was possible, he looked even more worried.

'You see, Million,' he said, 'all the bandages Dreader strapped around you will be sodden. Clearly, the last thing you need is cold wet bandages against fractured ribs. Fibrositis will set in and that will double the pain.'

The word 'pain' did it.

Gritting my teeth, I stumbled to the loo and dragged off my wet clothes, and very, v-e-r-y carefully unwound the miles of bandage, before getting into Dreader's red, green and gold tracksuit. It was nice and fleecy. I won't say any more.

By the time I'd got back to my seat, Sapphire had fetched more hot chocolate and was exchanging meaningful glances with Roland.

'We've been thinking,' Sapphire said.

'Don't,' I returned, 'it won't help.'

She straightened up a bit, like she was trying to look determined. 'You can't tell me to stop,' she said. 'We only let you go on pretending you're the boss because we want to. We don't have to.'

Ho! So that was it, was it? Now things were getting tough, my crew wanted to mutiny, eh? I timed the trembling and took a large slug of hot chocolate. It burnt my mouth.

'Please stop, Sapphire,' I said. 'Manz not feeling to get harsh on anyone – if you want out, there's the door. (Well, emergency exit).'

'You hateful, stupid, selfish, hateful, hateful, self-centred, self-everything . . . Oh God!'

Roland started to hush her. Sapphire sat down in one tremendous thump.

'*You*, Maximillian Wolf, are *not* the only one who wants to see Merlyn and his crew get it,' she said. 'You're not the *only* one who's suffering. Angelo was my friend too, my very, *very* bestest, *bestest* friend. My . . .' She started sobbing.

'Please,' I said again, my voice cracking.

'We just let you play boss because we're sorry for you,' added Sapphire.

Ouch.

'She didn't mean that, Mi££ion,' said Roland. 'She's upset. It's been very frightening for her. I mean, Angelo killed in front of her, having to leave home, and now you. Look at yourself, Mi££ion. She's worried. She's so worried that she doesn't know what she's saying.'

'When you didn't come, I thought you were dead,' sobbed Sapphire.

I stared at her. I mean, I'd never thought about it from that angle.

'Hey, babes,' I said.

'Just *don't*! Don't! Don't!' said Sapphire. 'Don't try to pretend you care. I'm not going to care about anyone ever again!'

I cast a puzzled look at Roland.

'Clearly, overwrought,' he whispered. And then we all sat there in silence while the train shuffled its way across London and out into the darkness of Southwark.

I didn't know what to say. I guessed whatever I said would probably be wrong. From the look on Sapphire's face, keeping shut was wrong too. So instead I closed my eyes and pretended to sleep.

At last I couldn't keep up the drama. 'OK, so tell me Sapphire, what have you been thinking?'

She turned a tired, sad, tearstained, fierce face on me. 'We were thinking that you're not well enough to do this. I was thinking we should take you to a hospital. Roland said his family have got a private Medicare insurance . . . He thinks we could get you treated on his healthcare plan – maybe as a visitor . . . That way, nobody would know, nobody would find you. You'd be safe . . . This train is stopping at Waterloo, you'll never be able to walk to Trafalgar Square. But St Thomas's hospital is near—'

I closed my eyes again. 'No,' I said in Dull Monotone. 'Dreader says I can do it. So I will.'

Sapphire stamped her foot. I knew she was going to say something spiteful about Dreader, about how he wasn't the only one with an opinion, how he was a stupid old man with a poetry problem – but my Dull Monotone stopped her dead.

I don't use it often. It has that effect.

I switched to Rueful. 'But nice try, Sapphire,' I said.

She sat down and burst into tears. 'Max,' she said, 'I

390

can't bear it. I just can't bear it. You don't know what it's like. I lost Angelo. I can't lose you too. I think I'll just give up. If you die, nothing – *nothing* – will mean anything, any more, ever again.'

HOPE!

On 26 March 1897 the Consul-General, Ralph Moor, initiator of the British Punitive Expedition that sacked Benin city and brought to an end the rule of the Warrior Kings, wrote to the Marquess of Salisbury.

Old Calabar

My Lord

I shall hold a court under Native Custom Law to bring the guilty persons, the kings and chiefs of Benin City, to justice and thereby conclude our punitive expedition.

I have, &c

Signed R Moor

If I hadn't lost a front tooth and been bent over in agony, I think I would have jumped up and done a cartwheel.

Sapphire cared!

She cared enough not to want me to die!

I know you'll probably think that's nothing. That nobody even wants to see a dog die, let alone a person. But this was Sapphire and she was talking about *MOI*!

I nearly asked her there and then if she'd like to go on a date – you know, after all this was over, and we were back in school . . . We could go to the movies . . . take in a burger . . . go shopping in Croydon Mall . . . but I didn't want to push my luck! Instead I hugged myself with my secret all tucked up inside. And felt warm and happy.

At least, warm and happy and in agony.

And I didn't lose guard. 'Somebody's got to keep a lookout then!' I said, full of a great desire to live for ever.

Roland took first watch. He positioned himself outside our carriage door and kept an eye on the corridors. At every station, he got off and scanned the platforms. Then he got back on again and went back to his position.

I sent Sapphire on a mission too. I figured she needed to do something to show me how much she cared(!). I figured I needed a chance to double up in pain and moan without breaking her heart. 'Painkillers,' I said. 'Paracetamol, aspirin, ibuprofen – I ain't fussy as long as you get a week's supply.'

And so, slowly, the train crawled its way closer to Waterloo. Sapphire got the pills and Roland thought he only saw four dodgy characters and a dodgy dog. A thin mist settled. It thickened as we neared the river. By the time we reached Bermondsey it had swirled in tight against the carriage windows. It was so thick that when you looked out, you just saw yourself looking in. I have to admit that half the time on that train, I wasn't really resting. I'd got my eyes closed all right, but actually I was thinking: *Sapphire loves me. Sapphire is going to hug me. Sapphire is going to stroke my hair and marry me.*

And I was trying not to think: *Sapphire has worried me, Sapphire thinks I'm going to die – that's why she's being nice.*

Was I really in such bad shape? Was I going to be able to get to the Nigerian High Commission? I shivered. The warm glow evaporated. I began to doubt. I wasn't ever going to take Sapphire to the movies, was I? Even if I survived the next twenty-four hours, I was going to end up in prison.

Roland noticed that I was upset. He came and sat next to me. 'It never was going to be easy, Mi££ion,' he said.

'Who wants easy, anyway?' I shot back, shivering.

'But I'll stick by you. If we can get the Bronzes to Abiola, and if you turn yourself in, I'll try to get you the best barrister I can. After all, let's look on the bright side, clearly you can't get much more than eight years.'

His cheerful comments didn't cheer me up. Instead I started trembling a little. He went back to guard duty.

I don't know if any of the MD Crew did get on that

train. If they did, Roland missed them. Anyway, it didn't make much difference. It was only a matter of time. They'd figure out where we were going. They'd choose their spot. They'd come . . . and when they did, I wasn't going to be ready.

I tried to prepare myself a little. I tried flexing my arm and failed. I imagined kicking and felt imagined pain. I opened a box of ibuprofen and swallowed four tabs. I was still feeling strangely cold, like my blood was thickening. I tried balling my fist. Zero. I tried arranging my face into an extra, super mean look. Nothing doing. Then we arrived at Waterloo East.

I stumbled off the train, dragging my broken, sorry self in red, gold and green across the marbled floor. I was beginning to feel very, *very* cold. My hands were trembling again and my head aching. I sank down on a bench, but Roland soon hauled me up.

'We can't hang around here, Mi££ion,' he said. 'We've missed Dreader's contact. We've got to find a safe place to hide.'

'Here, hold my arm,' said Sapphire.

I said nothing. I was starting to feel very strange.

'Max?' said Sapphire, her voice weird and harsh. 'Oh my God! Feel him, Roland! He's burning up!' She placed an icy hand on my cheek. 'He's running a fever.'

'Couldn't run anything right now, babes,' I said, but

I don't know if I really said it, because my voice felt far away. It felt so far away that I feared it would never be mine again. In fact, my legs suddenly felt like they weren't mine either. The mist was much, much closer. I slumped down on the floor, thinking: *I'll just rest a bit*.

And that was the last I knew.

HAPPY?

'The trial of Oba Overami and six chiefs took place in the Benin court-house in September 1897 before Sir Ralph Moor. Obadesagbon had already committed suicide rather than be humiliated . . . On the evening of the first day's trial, Obaiuwana cut his own throat. Uso and Obakhavbaye were sentenced to death and executed by firing squad the next day. Ugiagbe was pardoned because of his extreme youth. The Ologbosere, still at large, was condemned to death in his absence.'
Taken from *City of Blood Revisited* – Robert Home

When I came to, it was about four a.m. Everywhere was quiet. The doors at the side of the station were all closed. Sapphire was nowhere to be seen. My head was resting on the golf bag. From where I lay, I could hear strange echoes and the rumble of luggage trolleys.

Roland was there. 'Thank God you're OK, Mi££ion. We thought . . . Don't say anything. The More Dread Crew is here. Sapphire's gone to find their exact position.'

It was a lot colder than I remembered. I was still shivering.

'Here, have my jumper,' said Rollz.

That was kind of him, but his jumper had been knitted by Mrs Peel. It had yellow crocuses sprouting on a lime-green field. With horses in the background. Need I say more?

'I know,' said Roland sadly, 'but it's better than last Christmas's. That had a plate of spaghetti on the front and a knife and fork on the back. The spaghetti had long woollen noodles hanging off it.' He smiled a big round-faced smile at me.

'I understand,' I said, 'but cold or not, Man can't let his standards drop, u-get-me?'

I peered out from my hiding place behind more luggage trolleys. There was the front of the station. One of the gates was partially open. There was a train on the platform. No engines were running, no lights flashing. I tried to move. It wasn't nice. I flexed my toes and then my knees. It didn't get any nicer. Finally we crept (very slowly) on to the platform and hid again behind a series of thick pillars.

'I'm getting worried,' said Rollz.

'When did you first realize they were here?' I said.

'Sapphire's been gone too long.'

We waited. Where the hell was she?

We soon found out.

A man stepped out of the shadows. A tall thin man

with a foppish piece of grey-streaked hair that flopped over his forehead. Guess who! He seemed to be searching for a spot to get reception on his mobile. Just feet from us, he stopped. He raised his phone to his ear and said, 'There's been a delay. We've located the girl and we're just waiting for her to lead us to the others.'

'Oh Jesus,' I groaned.

Roland muttered, 'What are we going to do now?'

There were a number of things we could do, I suppose . . . dance an Irish jig . . . try doing a perfect headstand . . . So I put on a cheerful grin and winked. 'Looks like Man will have to get vexed then,' I said. 'I was hoping to avoid it, but sometime people push you too far, don't they?'

Roland looked at me like I'd finally flipped.

'Give me the dagger, then get out your phone,' I said. 'Pick up the golf bag and get ready to run.'

Roland stayed there, staring at me.

'Come on,' I said.

In a daze, Roland gave me the dagger. I shoved it in the pocket of the red, green and gold tracksuit. He needn't have looked so scared – I'm not violent and it was far too blunt to use.

'Now the phone – get it out,' I continued. 'You don't want to miss this. Come on, Rollz! Put it on video record!'

'We can't phone the police. You know what Dreader told us . . .'

'Roland, just humour me, because you care, because I'm about to die. Whatever. But I'll save you and Sapphire. You see, I'm going to go out with a bang. Well, a slap actually. Then you just run for it. But I want it on digital. This'll be the best phone-videoed happy-slap ever captured on a Sony Ericsson.'

Roland continued staring.

'Have it your own way,' I said, 'but you'll regret it.'

And I stood up. I scrunched myself into a running position. Lord Esterton whirled round. The windows of the train looked like they were all focused on me. I broke the pain barrier with my take off. I staggered straight at him, the flat of my hand wide open. He raised his eyebrows like he'd never heard about happy-slapping before. My hand made contact with his cheekbone. Like a cricket ball shot for six, his head snapped back. His legs shot forward. He landed with a *whump* on the platform. I stumbled on my ribs, hurting like hell. 'RUN!' I yelled. I dragged myself forward, praying that Sapphire and Roland had heard me. Praying they'd take advantage of the last chance I could give them. The half-open gate swam towards me. The pain in my chest stabbed me. I thought of Lord Esterton grovelling around on the floor. That would have made me smile, if my face hadn't been so swollen. I wanted to turn and point and laugh out loud. Impossible. Then I heard Sapphire's voice beside me. I HEARD SAPPHIRE'S VOICE!

'I'm here, Max. I'll help you.' That was nice. But she should save herself. That was the whole point. Still, I reached for her hand. I really hoped she'd seen that slap.

I hoped Roland had got it on camera.

I hoped I wouldn't have to run much further.

Sapphire took my hand. (SAPPHIRE TOOK MY HAND!!!!!) She helped me. I heard Roland say from somewhere to my left, 'Mi££ion, you nearly gave me a heart attack. Clearly, you must be delirious.'

Sapphire held me up.

We couldn't make it to the exit, so we stopped, turned sharp right and climbed down behind the train on to the tracks.

Sapphire kissed my cheek. (!!!!!&#**XX!!)

Sapphire said, 'Oh Max, keep going . . . please keep going . . . I need you alive . . . please don't die . . . I need you so much . . .'

MWAHAHAHAHAHA!

With Sapphire to live for, I was *not* going to *ever* die.

I struggled to keep my footing on the sleepers.

Roland said, 'Left! Keep left.'

We kept left.
In fact, I was going to live for ever.
Hopefully.

WATERLOO EAST TO
CHARING CROSS

Outside Waterloo East on the northbound tracks, the morning mist cloaked the line in eerie silence. Long rust-red lines, worn smooth-black, spidered away in all directions. They crisscrossed in the gloom like the strands of a giant web. We ran forward along them, balancing on the steel rails, towards the river, towards Abiola and Northumberland Ave. At least, Sapphire and Roland ran. I squealed and moaned and stumbled.

Behind us, Waterloo East Station rose in thick shadow, its platforms ready to spit out Merlyn and his Crew. 'Come on, we've got to lose them,' I shouted. But even as I spoke I saw a shape detach itself from the murk behind. It hesitated on the platform edge like a great bloodhound.

I staggered forward. My heart beating. My legs complaining. I glanced behind again and saw the shape had become a man. A man who was flipping open his mobile and barking orders into it. I reached down to steady myself on an icy girder. I tried not to hyperventilate. Too much fresh air might finish me off.

Sapphire hesitated. In the distance a dog wailed. She looked very frightened. But she needn't have, because the touch of that frosty metal rail had suddenly jogged my one brain cell back into action.

I had the beginnings of a mad, bad, crazy plan.

Firstly, Merlyn wasn't the only one who could use a mobile. So as I stumbled forward, I got out my phone too. I called up Walter. I won't repeat everything he said. I'll spare you the bits about goats' droppings and the livers of lizards.

'Walter,' I said, 'Manz in a tight spot.'

Apart from shouting, 'Wot time do you fripping call this?' and something else quite unmentionable, he actually listened.

'If you could meet me at Nigeria House, Northumberland Ave, in about half an hour, Man could sort out your back payments, u-get-me?'

(Well, I know that was stretching the truth a bit, but I only said 'sort out'.)

A bird cawed. A faint shuddering began underfoot. Sapphire turned a horrid cold pale.

Walter's reply was quite civil. 'Worm that crawls beneath the heel of my shoe, if you're fripping bullshitting, I'll grind you into grime and delight in scattering your lungs and bits of stomach tissue to the four winds.'

'OK,' I said. 'But bring your back-up boyz and pizzas. Some other crew are after your bills.' Sapphire paused, half waiting for me to keep pace. Roland was in front, almost disappearing into the mist.

'Listen, you better not let those next brothers get my notes,' Walter said.

He might have said more, but I figured the thought of losing his money had made him run out of adjectives. I helped him out. 'Man is going to try to stay alive, just so Man can give you your money – after that, Man is all yours to feed to the ducks in the pond, u-get-me?' Then I hung up. I mean, I'm a nice guy. I wanted him to save some of his insults for when he found out just exactly how much he wasn't getting.

OK, first stage of Maxi's little plan.

Stage two coming up.

Still staggering forward, I got Abiola's answer phone.

'*You have reached the voice mail of the suspended Second Secretary of State, Abiola Olusamilola, at the Nigerian High Commission. Please leave your message after the tone. If you wish to re-record your message at any time, press the hash key . . .*'

'Abiola,' I said, 'this is Warrior King. We're on our way. Open up your embassy right now and have a few security guards, five hundred thousand pounds and a bulletproof jacket ready. There may be trouble.' I hung up.

That was as far as my plan went.

Walter and the pizza boys, with Dreader, a crowd of thousands and Abiola on my team. Merlyn and the more Dread (or was that Mordred?) Crew on the other. (I did have a wild idea that it could all end up in a custard-pie kind of pizza fight. But that is because I am still an immature teenager.) Anyway, extra pizzas can never be a bad thing, can they? After all, when we were through, those left alive were still going to need to eat.

Like I said, it was only the *beginnings* of a plan.

Roland adjusted the golf bag on his shoulder. He turned back towards us and shouted, 'We can't go this way, Mi££ion!'

'No choice.' I pointed through the mist at Merlyn. As we looked, he snapped his phone shut. He seemed to be debating whether or not to get down on to the tracks too. Behind him, dark shapes were already gathering along shadowy platforms.

Roland got my point.

We pushed forward. In front of us lay Hungerford Bridge, the railway crossing over the Thames. There the tracks merged. They pressed themselves close together and ran one over the other. Beyond that was Charing Cross and our destination. Going that way would be quickest. Quickest but riskiest. High-speed trains might compete with us for the narrow space on the bridge. But if we left the rails and tried to find our way by road, the police might get us. Merlyn was bound to have updated them.

There really was no choice was there?

The shaking underfoot was getting a bit more serious, especially when you stood on the rails. Typical, I thought, it'd be just our luck to get struck by an earthquake too.

'Go back,' yelled Roland. He was frantically waving his arms around.

Was he crazy?

'Maxi,' hissed Sapphire. 'Get off the line. Come this side with Rollz and me.'

In the distance, I heard the rumble of an intercity express. I skidded to a turn. From the south-east a haze of lights tinted the mist sulphur-yellow. I saw Sapphire and Roland hauling themselves up on to a different line. Merlyn was drawing back. A train lurched into view round a long curve.

'Mi££ion!' yelled Roland.

Then, like a great snake uncoiling itself, the intercity express thundered down at us.

'Maxi!' shrieked Sapphire again.

I tried to stay relaxed. It looked scary, but the train was bound to stop at Waterloo East – wasn't it? 'We got to . . .' I said, trying to haul myself to their side of the tracks '. . . get over the river.'

Roland and Sapphire turned, eyes fixed on me.

'. . . That's where Abiola is, down there . . .' I tried to stay focused on where we had to get to. I tried telling them again. But the rush of air from the approaching train hit me like a slap in the face. It whipped my words away.

'. . . Just below. That's his street . . . I've phoned him we're coming . . .'

Through the pounding air, Roland and Sapphire continued to stare.

I wasn't sure why the thought of the bridge had got them so tongue-tied. I pointed into the vapour, down the lines, to where the giant girders spanned the Thames. It looked quite pretty actually. The tracks gleamed like silver in the early morning and behind them glimpses of water sparkled far beneath. Roland and Sapphire just kept on staring at me, like those kicks to my head had sent me nuts or something.

Too late, I saw the danger.

Down the shuddering tracks squealed the carriages of the intercity express. The entire length of the rail under me shuddered like jelly. I started shuddering like jelly. My heart wobbled from my ribs to my stomach.

The train was going straight through to Charing Cross! It wasn't going to stop!

Sweat broke out down my back. *What should I do?* I had to get out of the way. I couldn't work out which of the tracks it would switch to. *Which way should I jump?* I froze in terror, like a rabbit on a motorway. Time seemed to stretch. Seconds sang through the cold air like bullets and exploded around me. *Which way?* I sent up a prayer to all the gods of Ancient Benin. 'Please,' I said, 'please give your likkle Warrior King one more chance to get your treasures home.'

Suddenly I could move.

I jumped.

I let the gods choose.

I rolled sideways. A searing pain shot right from my bad shoulder across my bad chest into my bad leg. And the train was there. Centimetres away were grinding wheels. Screeching metal. Searing heat. Right where I'd been. I lay there, gawping. Lighted windows and streaming mist flew past. I struggled to my knees. I clasped my hands together. 'Thank you!' I screamed. 'God bless all you gods!'

'Roland, Sapphire! It missed me!' I yelled, trying to project my voice through the passing train. But my words were swallowed in the scream and tear of metal on metal.

The train passed.

'I'm OK!' I shouted. 'I'm sorry. I didn't figure it wasn't stopping. Let's get going before another one comes. I've promised Abiola's gods . . .'

Roland looked terrible. He sank down on to the tracks, clutching at his sides. All the rosy had gone from his cheeks. His glasses were set at a weird angle and his hair was sticking everywhere.

Sapphire just stood there like a lovely ghost, her beautiful face deathly pale.

NEARLY THERE

'You are not prepared to accept the position which
I offered you and you are not fit for it. The alternative is that you are to be
removed from this country for good and you will never come back.'
Sir Ralph Moor's final judgement on Oba Overami, Benin City, 1897

About five metres to either side of Hungerford Bridge, two modern footbridges span the River Thames. They're kind of fancy and painted white. I think they work by suspension. They have slanting uprights all the way along, anyway, which look a bit like sailing masts with rigging bits. At intervals, the hanging footpaths are anchored to the main bridge by white metal poles.

Of course, there was no hope that once we were on the old railway bridge we could get down on to them. I suppose people aren't really encouraged to take shortcuts across electrocuted rail tracks, just to save time getting down on to footpaths, are they?

But one feature about them was really interesting. You see, on the far side of the river, the west side footbridge descended directly on to Northumberland Ave.

Abiola's street!

So as I rolled clear of the five-thirty a.m. from somewhere or other, inside my head, my one trusty, lonely brain cell started making the middle bit of its mad bad plan.

Time for action.

The train passed. I stood up. The fog cleared. I dusted myself down. Roland and Sapphire suddenly moved, as if released from some binding spell. Almost weeping with joy, they ran towards me. I had no time to capitalize on that and ask Sapphire on a date, because Merlyn stood up too and jumped down on to the track. In the distance I heard police sirens. So with one arm over Roland's shoulder and one over Sapphire's, we raced towards the river. OK, three-legged sort of very painfully raced.

Merlyn was not far behind. And not far behind him were the More Dread Crew. I couldn't keep a close eye on them all, as it's hard to turn your head when you are being supported on both shoulders. Also I had to keep my eyes on the tracks, so I didn't trip and pull the others down with me. And I think I was really too scared. My heart was beating so fast that I felt sick. In fact I was so scared, the fear sort of seemed to numb all the pain in my chest. I was trying so hard not to think: *What will we do if he's got a gun? Where will we jump to if another train catches us on the bridge?*

The tracks merged. We clung together. I took my arm off Sapphire's shoulder. 'We're nearly there, babes,' I said. 'Look.' I pointed at the river. 'See, we're nearly there.'

And we were.

There it was, Hungerford Bridge, a large, blackened, brick and steel, railway crossing. Thick iron girders crisscrossed like railings down its length. The gaps between them were about a third of a metre wide. Wide enough, anyway, for a boy of fourteen who hadn't been eating right to slip through. On either side of the old bridge, the footbridges ran. They were supported by white poles which fanned out like the bones in a sparrow's wing. Sadly, the west side footbridge was miles too far away to jump down on to.

Bang went the middle part of my plan.

We stepped carefully on to the bridge itself. The rails were at their narrowest here. A third rail slightly different in colour ran close to the inside track. Roland yelled, 'Watch you don't touch it. It's seven hundred and fifty volts.'

Below us, the river was already rippling with the morning tide. 'Maxi, how can we get on to the avenue at the other end?' said Sapphire. 'The footbridges are miles away and that's a twelve-metre drop, down there.'

It was a good question.

'Not quite sure yet, babes,' I said.

I manoeuvred (carefully) away from the thick electrified rail and peered out to the west side, through the ironwork. I could see space. And no nice safety net.

Yep, you're right – I'd been kind of hoping we could sort of jump on to the footbridge a bit like Spider-man, without the web factor. I know. Don't say it.

Still it had only been a plan. No need to despair.

I yanked Sapphire along the rails after me. Roland seemed to have given up being cautious. He charged ahead without even a bleat. Behind us, the More Dread Crew came to the end of the bridge and waited. I guess they were hoping the 5.55 a.m. from Strood would finish the job off for them. Either that or they had some other plan.

I looked behind, trying to work out which. Hungerford Bridge is longer than you think. Merlyn and his crew were fast becoming shadowy figures in the mist. I think I saw a gun. I think I saw the early-morning sunlight dance off the black metal. But there was no early-morning sun, so I might have been mistaken.

Once more, I felt the tracks beneath me shake. I heard rumbling in the distance. I was already going as fast as I could. I was holding the others up. Without me, they might still stand a chance . . .

I looked through the bars again. There were a number of smooth steel girders, then brickwork and below that the river. So what do you do when there is no way back, no way forward, no way down?

And certain death racing straight towards you?

Just a few metres ahead, one white pole arched from the footbridge across four metres of empty air and anchored itself to the steel bastion of the bridge.

It would have to do.

My one reckless brain cell was making a comeback.

'I'm going across it,' I said to Roland. 'You've been a great sidekick, bruv. Man'll understand if you don't want to take the last drop – bit further on is Charing Cross Station. If you hurry, you'll make it. Don't argue.' I took the golf bag from him and slung it on to my shoulder. 'You'll have to run though – but you're a gangsta now, so I trust you.' I tried to punch him playfully on the arm.

'Mi££ion,' said Roland, 'I've made a terrible mistake.'

'Forget it, bruv,' I said, 'we all make mistakes. Even the late great Tupac Shakur made a mistake.'

'He did?' said Roland.

'Sure,' I said, 'but out of RESPECT we don't mention it.'

'I thought I wanted to be in a gang . . .' gasped Roland, 'but clearly, I don't think I'm actually cut out for it . . .'

'Look, Rollz,' I said, 'that's not a mistake. You been the best sidekick any gangsta could ever have.'

'Have I?' said Roland.

'You have,' I said. 'And now I'll tell you a secret. I gave up being a gangsta when I was in Merlyn's boot. So the gang is dissolved. Look . . .' I unhooked Mogul's multicoloured beads from around my wrist and let them drop through the girders into the river below. 'Now just flash your upper-class identity at the police when you get to Charing Cross and meet me outside Nigeria House as soon as you can.'

I turned to Sapphire. Her beautiful face white beneath its olive glow. Her large dark eyes full of despair. 'Love-u, babes,' I said. 'Take care.' And (taking a risk bigger than falling into the river) I blew her a kiss. She didn't move. I thought about it, and I just couldn't resist the moment. After all, if I was about to die . . . 'Would you go on a date with me?' I said. 'I mean . . . after all this . . . when Man gets back into some decent clothes?'

Then get this!

Sapphire fell into my arms. She nestled her beautiful head against my shoulder. She gulped (I think they were meant to be words). She heaved. She shuddered. She superglued herself to me and held on to me with all the force of vacuum packing.

'Max . . .' she sobbed.

I wriggled a bit. Don't get me wrong, this could have been the most fantastic moment of my life, it was just that . . .

'Maxi,' she said again.

'Oi, Sapphire,' I said, 'Man likes the love you're showing, but you're leaning right on Manz fractured ribs.'

She let go (thank God). 'I'm sorry,' she sobbed, 'I'm so scared, I don't want to lose you . . .'

'Ssshhh,' I said, 'take more than idiots like them to stop the Last of the Warrior Kings.'

For once she didn't roll her eyes, or snort, or say, 'Gimme-a-break.'

So I shot her a Devilishly Handsome, tooth-challenged smile, and for a brief moment heard the theme tune swell wistfully into the morning, saw the hero's handsome profile bend down to kiss the girl he loved, felt the audience reach for their tissues, knew the whole world was holding its breath . . . when I was interrupted by Rollz. 'We better be going!' he yelped.

'Ab-so-lute-lee!' I said.

I hugged Sapphire one last time and whispered,

'Either way, babes, after this you get to go home.'

Then I slid out between the girders. I let myself down, hanging on to the bridge with my fingertips. I balanced for an instant feeling for the top of the steel support pillar with my toes. My ribs and shoulders couldn't take it. I let go. On my way down I tried to steady myself, to land without twisting an ankle.

Four and a half metres from the footbridge, with the impetus of my fall knocking me off balance, I struggled to gain a foothold. Like a tightrope walker, I stepped out on to that slim white pole. I slung the golf bag horizontal to act as a balance. And for a moment, I swear, I really heard music. Wild crazy drumming winding like a theme tune towards me. For a moment, the purple lights of the London Eye lit a halo around me. The bells of Big Ben struck six a.m. And if there hadn't been a thick mist, early-morning commuters would have been amazed to see a teenage boy standing there. Ten metres above the river. All alone, swaying over the rushing Thames, as it seemed to reach up and bash the air around him.

RULES OF SURVIVAL:
TAKE OUT YOUR RIVAL

'I appeal to the Almighty and the Spirits of the departed Obas of Benin, my
fathers, to judge between me . . . and the British troops, in search of their own
liberty and benefit. Oh, Benin, merciless and wicked, farewell!'
Oba Overami's final lament on leaving the city, trussed and accompanied
by sixty NCPF troops to board the *Ivy* and go into exile for ever.
15 September 1897

You'll want to know what Merlyn did, won't you?

Sapphire told me later that he fled back from the
bridge as the train approached. From there he started to
find another way across. He soon reappeared on the
South Bank next to the footbridge. Yes, the same
footbridge I was trying to get to, as I stood on the white
anchor pole poised like a circus acrobat. Still it gave me
a little time-window – in which I bit my lip. The tilt of
the golf bag started to dislodge the treasures. I could
feel them shifting towards its open neck. I tried hard
not to think of the airy gap between me and the ripples
below. I tried not to imagine beautiful Queen Idia

plunging downwards. I tried to lift the golf bag a little. It threw me dangerously off balance. Gently putting all my weight on my right leg, I shifted my left leg forward. The treasures slid a little further down the bag. If I could get three good steps, maybe four, I could kind of lunge the rest of the way and sort of grab the railing of the footbridge. At least, I hoped I could.

However, taking any kind of step, good or bad, was tricky. In fact I couldn't do it. I had to sort of slippy along, shuffling with my left leg stuck out in front. Every time I shuffled, the treasures shuffled too. I could feel at least one of them balanced loosely by the neck of the bag.

Somehow I made it to halfway.

That's when I lost nerve. *What was I doing?* I hadn't been able to cross that viaduct over Deptford Creek. How in hell was I doing this? I froze. I couldn't move. I remembered Sapphire's advice: '*Keep going. It's easier,*' but I couldn't. My heart was thudding against my ribs. I had to sit down. Terrified, I lowered myself until I straddled the pole like a kid on a crossbar. I thought: *Don't look down. Ten metres below you is the icy Thames.* Sweat broke out all down my back. I began to sway wildly. I clutched at the pole. The pain in my ribs and stomach was back. I tried to ease myself along, pulling myself with both hands. I balanced the golf bag across my knees. I pulled again and shuffled a couple more metres.

With still a gap the size of a doorway left to go, I lunged. Only one hand found the supports on the footbridge. The golf bag tilted. Something rolled out of it. Something turned in the air and sparkled through the mist as it dropped. There was only the faintest splash as one of the priceless ivory bracelets from the treasures of Ancient Benin sank beneath the waters of the Thames.

Oh God!

I lunged again and this time grabbed the railings at the bottom of the footbridge with both hands. I yanked the golf bag back upright. Gasping with the effort, I still had to hoist myself through the bars and up on to the footbridge. Not easy with a bag full of dangling priceless treasures.

At first I couldn't quite get a grip and felt myself for one awful minute teetering on the brink of toppling backwards. The sound of a screeching train raced past. I smelt carbon and dust and dry air. I prayed Roland and Sapphire made it. A police siren wailed from much closer. A helicopter whirred overhead. And then in the quiet that followed, I heard another sound. Far, far away in the distance, bouncing in waves over the river . . . the sound of drumming. At first I thought I was dreaming, but as I balanced I heard it again.

Panlogo drums.

Dreader Dread and the poetryathon!

A rush of hope swept through me. Dreader had told me I could do it. Sapphire didn't want me to die. Angelo and Mum were depending on me finishing up family business. Abiola had got the go-ahead from the gods. Africa was waiting . . . I tightened my grip. In horrible agony, I flexed my shoulder, swung my leg up, and hauling the golf bag, slithered through the railings of Charing Cross west side suspension footbridge.

No time to congratulate myself. The suspension footpath was already shaking under the combined weight of Merlyn and his crew. I staggered upright and set out for Nigeria House. Down the footpath I raced (OK, hobbled). Two little old ladies walking their dogs stood there looking at me in shock. I smiled (OK, grimaced). The golf bag wobbled behind me. I saw the first ray of sunshine break through the mist. I made it to the steps on to Northumberland Ave.

Down the stairway I rushed and out on to a wide walkway. I ducked between the stairs and the overhead railway bridge. Then raced on to the avenue.

Behind me Merlyn followed.

And so did his shadows.

In desperation, I jumped into the street in front of a taxi. I waved my hands and yelled: 'Hey, you! Help!' I was thinking: *Stop the taxi. Get inside. Get to the High Commission. Escape from the More Dread Crew.*

Brakes screeched. A light went on in the window of a flat high up on maybe the seventh floor of a grand terrace of houses. The taxi's wingmirror clipped my outstretched hand. Agony spiralled into my shoulder. *Oh God*, I thought, *this is just like that night, so long ago with Angelo* . . . I prayed that taxi driver would help me. I screamed, 'Nigeria House,' at him. He pulled to the side, did a three-point turn, and sped off in the opposite direction.

So I ran.

I held the golf bag strap away from my injured shoulder. Merlyn clattered down the steps from the suspension bridge and ran too. I think he was shouting something. Behind him, the mist swirled up from the Thames and, from the sound of footfalls, I knew the others were sprinting too.

Damp shimmered on the tarmac. Mega doses of adrenalin flooded into my legs. My heart banged. My shoulder felt like it had burst open. I didn't know if I could take it. My breath came like a loose exhaust. The light went off in the tall house. I made it a third of the way up Northumberland Ave. I heard the doors to The Conan Doyle creak open. I saw a worried face peek out. Then I heard the doors slam shut.

By some miracle, just as I felt there was no hope left, I looked left and I was there.

Nigeria House.

I struggled over. The double wooden doors were locked fast and on them was pasted: *For Visa Section use door on the side lane*, with an arrow beneath. No Abiola. I tried to take that in. I saw Merlyn and the others racing up the avenue. I pounded on the doors. Nobody came.

Nobody except Merlyn and four hooded others.

I looked around for something to fight them with. I picked an empty bottle off the tarmac. I threw it at them, wishing it were a hand grenade. It crashed on the street and sprayed the air with a thousand sparking splinters. I can still see it now, that wet street, that broken bottle.

It was no use. They raced towards me, past the theatre on the corner, down the centre of the road, and then they were there too. Right behind me, driving me back against the locked doors.

How I hammered on those doors. 'Open up! Let me in!' I screamed. 'Abiola! Abiola!' I tried to ruffle in my pocket for my phone. I prayed he was up and awake. I prayed he would answer it. I prayed he stayed in Nigeria House and not in some residence in St John's Wood. 'Abiola!' I screamed.

No reply.

Instead, I heard the steady laugh of Merlyn and the others ripple out behind me. I turned. I forced the golf bag into a space at my back. 'I'll never let you take them,' I said.

'I don't see why not,' said Merlyn. 'You were never a match for me. Now just hand the treasures over like a good little warrior.'

'Over my dead body,' I yelled back and began again to beat on the closed doors.

'Easily arranged,' said Merlyn, and he indicated with one hand to one of the others. Forward stepped a hooded figure and in his hand was something in a long black sock. He raised it.

'You'll never get away with it,' I screamed, 'I've told everybody about you, about *Code: King Arthur*, about the Home Office, about the oil deal!'

'Whatever,' said Merlyn. 'As far as you're concerned, this is where I win and you lose . . . Take him out.'

The man with the long black sock stepped closer and placed the muzzle of the sock against my head.

I screamed and kicked at him, but Merlyn stepped forward and twisted my bad shoulder, so I just shuddered in agony. Everything became blurred. The world tilted. It seemed like I was watching a telly that was laced with sleet and arrows. Lightning flashes of silver pain raced up and under my skull, and into my spine, and down to my knees, which gave way and I crumbled to the floor.

As I lay there squirming, another hooded figure stepped forward. In one swift movement he pulled off his hood. There was no mistaking the bulk and beard of Sir Robert Terselas. 'I want the bloody dagger back first,' he said. 'I want to have it in my hand before you kill him. He may have hidden it somewhere, and I can't live under this kind of bloody pressure any more. Where is it, boy? Where is the bloody dagger your bloody mother stole from my office?'

'Never,' I said again, but my voice caught in my throat and I don't think he heard me.

In that split second when my life hung like a cobweb about to snap, we all heard two things. First, the wail of police sirens, as they screamed around Trafalgar Square. At that, all the More Dread Crew, as quickly as you could say, 'me too,' pulled off their hoodies. And, you know, that was something to see. Because underneath they were all in grey business suits, perfectly pressed and dry cleaned, all looking like they'd just stopped out of interest on their way to Whitehall. Did I say all? No, one short fat hooded figure didn't remove anything. Instead he whipped out a large Nikon camera and started taking photos of all the others. I was struggling for air anyway and my heart was jumping around like a fish out of water, but that took my breath away altogether.

Taliesin Jones!

I could not mistake that shape, even if he'd clothed it in a sari.

What the heck did he think he was doing?

Sir Robert Terselas started to go very pale, his breathing seemed to grow short and he gasped out, 'Hey, what are you bloody doing? We don't want our identities known . . .'

Taliesin zoomed in with a close-up right on Sir Robert's large, hairy, surprised face. 'Pillage and Plunder! Never trust a journalist, dude! They just can't resist a breaking news story!'

If I hadn't been staring into the sock-covered barrel of a gun, I might have laughed. Talk about undercover journalism!

Still, Merlyn and Sir Robert weren't laughing. With a flick of his wrist, Merlyn ordered the guy who was standing over me to turn his sock on Taliesin. 'Give me the camera,' he said.

That was when the other noise stopped the police cars in full wail. The drums of Dreader Dread and the poetryathon march burst into Trafalgar Square. And with one voice like a twenty-one gun salute, we heard the crowd chanting out the refrain:

We don't want no exploitation
of Third World situations
All we want is governments performing
To find a cure to global warming

MAY THE BLADE FIND
THE TRUE HEART

'A cruel man usually dies a cruel death.'
Yoruba wisdom – Nigeria

Down from the end of Northumberland Avenue streamed an assortment of poetic people. All of them were clapping along to the rhythm of the panlogo drums and chanting to the refrain of Dreader Dread's latest poetic message. In front and behind and beside them were large BMW motorbikes, astride which were policemen in full uniform. And, you know, I swear I could hear one of those large cylinders misfire on the second piston.

Sir Robert began to grow breathless. Beads of sweat stood out on his pasty, fat, wrinkled brow. 'Give me the bloody dagger, boy,' he pleaded.

I struggled to my feet. I banged again on the doors of Nigeria House. A police bike screamed up from the riverside and tried to hold back the march. Taliesin's camera flashed faster than a disco light.

'Bloody hell! The dagger,' breathed Sir Terselas.

And then the miracle happened! The doors of Nigeria House swung open and there, in full embroidered dress that swept from the delicately patterned hat on his neatly combed head, to his elegantly shod heels, stood the suspended Second Secretary of State, Mr Abiola Olusamilola!

'Ahh, Warrior King,' he said. 'Sorry for African timing. In my country we have a saying that even though the tortoise moves slowly he is never too late for—'

'Abiola!' I screamed and half crawled, half stumbled towards him, pushing the golf bag through the door.

'NO!' commanded an imperative voice.

And over my wrecked shoulder I saw Lord Esterton step forward. 'I'd like to observe, sir, that in that bag are stolen items, which I, empowering myself with a citizen's arrest, demand that you yield – both the boy and it – so that the stolen items can be returned to the Crown of England, and he can face trial.'

'Ahh! Stolen items . . . Oh yes, of course.' Abiola opened the neck of the golf bag and peered inside. He straightened up with a broad smile across his handsome face. 'Yes indeed they are *very* stolen items.'

'So I demand that you surrender them to me!' said Lord Esterton.

'Ahhh, that is the bit, I don't quite get you,' said Abiola, 'but never mind, in my country we have a saying that the chicken cannot always tell the difference between a worm and a snake . . .'

'HAND THEM BACK!' shouted Lord Esterton.

'But you said they were stolen,' said Abiola, 'and I'd like to remind you, sir, from whom they were stolen!'

'What on earth do you mean, fellow?' shouted Lord Esterton, going quite pink in the face. Sir Terselas sighed and clutched at his shoulder. Merlyn stood there with his hand in his pocket on what looked like a gun.

Abiola smiled, showing all his beautiful perfectly straight teeth. 'They were stolen from Nigeria,' said Abiola, smiling into Taliesin's camera. 'Looted by the British in 1897, but thanks to this plucky fellow, our Warrior King, they have now been returned.'

'POLICE!' shouted Lord Esterton. 'Get over here. This person is trying to hold on to stolen goods.'

The rider from the misfiring BMW bike stepped off his machine, leant it on its bike stand and strode over. 'Now,' he said. 'Let *me* take the disputed items and . . .'

Behind Abiola materialized three massive figures. All of them not much larger that Mohammed Ali. All of them with shoulders that could lift an aircraft. And all of them not smiling.

'*Ki lo de? Ki lon sèlé? Oga sir?*' said one of them.

(What is the trouble here, Mr Big Boss Man?)

'*Ó látì ló bà bàbà bá bè ĕ,*' said another.

(Do you want us to send someone to see the ancestors?)

'*Óbó ó lè tòtó si kiniwon!*' said the third.

(A monkey should not spit at a lion!)

And from their tone, none of us needed the translations.

Lord Esterton seemed to shake with rage. He straightened up and, pushing me aside (ouch), stepped forward over the threshold of Nigeria House. He put his hand on the golf bag and attempted to snatch it from Abiola's grasp. The policeman followed him. That's when the big bouncer guy Number One looked a bit peeved. With one hand he lifted up the policeman. With the other, Lord Esterton. He looked at Abiola, waiting for an instruction.

'I am arresting you for obstructing a police officer . . .' began the policeman as he dangled in mid-air.

'Ah! But you see,' said Abiola, 'you can't arrest anyone inside this building. If you didn't know, all of Nigeria House is diplomatic territory. You are now, technically speaking, inside Nigeria, so you see, you will quite understand, that your powers of arrest are not very strong here!'

'Arrrggghhh,' snarled Lord Esterton.

And you know I could really see his frustration. Tee hee.

'Wh-wh-what . . .' choked the police, ex-BMW biker, as his collar tightened under his chin.

But neither of them said a thing after they had hit the tarmac of Northumberland Avenue three metres away.

Still, Abiola's words had given my brain cell an idea. As quick as I could, I dragged myself over the threshold of Nigeria House. Good thinking, huh? *Let them try and arrest me now*, I thought.

And that was when Dreader Dread and the poetryathon march broke through the police cordon and arrived outside Nigeria House. There was a drum roll of panlogo, an answering roll of djembe, a further roll of the huge master drum of the Igbo, a chant of talking drums and then super dead silence. Even the choking squeals of Lord Esterton and the rapid breathing of Sir Terselas stopped.

And Dreader spoke: 'There is a time for everything . . . and today the time has come for the people of London to speak up for the people of Britain . . . and for their voices to be heard across the waters to the south; and across the City to the east; and over the Queen's palaces to the north; and past the highways to the west; so that everyone who loves democracy shall hear, and have his own mind upon it. Gathered around this door are the true hearts of England, ready to chant down Babylon. For here,' he waved his hand quite explicitly at Merlyn and Sir Terselas and the sprawled Lord Esterton, 'here are three members of a government department who have taken the law into their own hands and feel that it's OK to use whatever means they like to achieve their ends. Here they are, agents appointed by your vote and paid for from your taxes, on a mission today to silence our voices when we ask for justice and accountability. Now I hax you, DO WE WANT THAT?'

And the crowd answered in the chorus that they had chanted all the way from Deptford High Street.

'We don't want any intimidation
We want a just and honourable nation.'

And the drums rolled, and the people cheered, and the police cars arrived, and Taliesin produced a microphone and a tape recorder.

Dreader held up his hand. Silence fell. 'Before I go back to my little flat, I want to thank the people of Britain.' He turned to the More Dread Crew. 'You have your answer, Merlyn. The times have changed,' he said, quite sadly as if he too understood the ebb and flow of power. 'Now is not your time.' And he turned again to the crowd. 'Today we can be happy,' he said, 'for today we have defeated tyranny with poetry!'

A cheer went up that echoed from Trafalgar Square to Whitehall, and down the river past Big Ben and out into every suburb of London.

And when the cheer died away, I saw Sapphire and Roland standing beside Dreader with Leon and Denetia . . . and they were clapping and weeping and smiling all at once.

And then Abiola stepped forward (making sure he didn't cross the threshold of Nigeria House), and said: 'Ahh, so many big thank yous to the great people of Great Britain for restoring to me the treasures of my motherland . . . for we have a saying in my country that it is not the scar marks of the father that makes a man worthy of his clan. So today I will like to make all of you good poetry people of Britain, honorary Nigerians! You are all very worthy and very welcome in my country: Visa Section next door on the right.

'Now I have a Thank You, a Sorry and a request for the brave Warrior King, who has returned these wonders to my people. He has in his possession a sacred African dagger that always finds the true heart – and with it, it carries a secret message that will reveal to you how true all of your hearts are. So with the permission of the people of Britain, may I ask him to give it to me?'

There were cheers and whistles and a resounding, 'YES!' which went up from all the singing, rapping, chanting, placard-waving crowd.

Sir Terselas clutched at his chest and went kind of blue around the mouth. The bike-riding policeman tried to crawl away behind a garbage drum. Merlyn had a look of pure poison on his face.

The crowd continued cheering. I pulled the dagger out from inside my red, green and gold tracksuit. (I mean – my big moment and a red, gold and green tracksuit?) Merlyn took a step nearer. He pulled out his gun.

And a shot rang out.

It sang through the cold air and hit Nigeria House about five paces away from me.

'NO!' shouted Abiola. Sapphire screamed. Taliesin took more photos.

'Don't move,' I shrieked at them.

'I warned you, once before, never to underestimate me,' hissed Merlyn.

'But—' I said.

'I never lose,' he snarled. 'Step out of the Nigerian High Commission and place the dagger on the pavement.'

I opened my mouth, then closed it again. I found my voice somewhere at the root of my throat. 'OK. Hey, forget the gun. I'm coming.'

But instead of stepping out of Nigeria House, I turned and held the dagger out to Abiola. I was tired, you see, tired of being afraid of Merlyn and his threats. My job was done. Abiola was wearing that bulletproof vest, Home Office cover-ups were chanted down, Sapphire needed to go home, Roland had resigned himself to being gangless, and I had a terrible longing to see Angelo again – yes, to join him wherever he was . . .

But before I could give it to Abiola, Merlyn sprang forward, his hand closing on my bad shoulder. 'Oh no!' he said. 'This isn't about anything except me winning now . . .'

I tried to shake his hand off. I tripped and stumbled down the step to Nigeria House, *over the threshold and out on to the pavement*. Merlyn tightened his grip. He pulled me into the street.

The crowd realized something was going on. There was a short scuffle. I saw police marksmen jump into place. Merlyn hissed, 'Give me the dagger. You've run out of time.'

Denetia broke free from the crowd and ran to help me. 'Pass the dagger to me, Maxi,' she said. 'I'll give it to Abiola.'

I saw her white earnest face, her little thin mouth and tried to stretch out my hand towards her. Merlyn's grip seemed to ease a bit. I could almost make it.

'Quick, Maxi,' she urged. 'Let me help. You're hurt. I so feel for you.'

So feel for me? There was something about that phrase that jarred. I hesitated. I heard Roland shouting something. Denetia grabbed my wrist and started tugging on the dagger.

That's what had been written on that email I'd found in Merlyn's jacket, wasn't it? *I so feel for you.*

I heard Roland yelling again. This time the words were clear. '*Inside Help!*'

Yes, helpful little Denetia Cowan. Who exactly was she helping? Suddenly the pieces of the puzzle slotted together. Denetia Cowan. Wasn't it a Lieutenant Cowan who had donated Ewuare's sword to St Theobald's? Was that a coincidence? Or a great-grandfather? Or the name we were supposed to find? All those helpful little phone calls. All that access to Leon's work . . .

Not Leon, but *Denetia*!

She'd been aboard that boat, on the Black History tour when Mum had fallen in. Had Mum found her out? Had Mum confronted her? Had she crept up behind Mum and pushed?

I was probably never going to know. But she was definitely never going to get that dagger.

'Maxi!' she said. 'I've got it! You can let go now!'

'Oh!' I said. 'OK.' And as Merlyn relaxed his grip, when he thought I was about to give the dagger to Denetia, I twisted my arm free. I smacked Denetia down on the tarmac. I struggled back towards Abiola.

Merlyn bounded past me. Caught my shoulders. I saw his face: deadly. But beyond him I saw the morning sun glint off the barrel of a police sniper.

There was a click, then a pause. I looked around, strangely calm. Somehow it was like déjà vu. A few raindrops splashed on my face.

That pause. That snort. That faint click. The sun shone. The rain fell. A rainbow arched over South London. I held the dagger out to Abiola. If the sniper was going to kill me, he better do it now.

Merlyn leapt and pushed me sideways. He grabbed the dagger. I staggered and fell.

He stood in front of me. Blocking everything.

A shot rang out.

There was no terrible scream. Just a curious dull *thumph*. In slow motion I saw. Merlyn lying across the threshold of Nigeria House.

I got up.

I looked at the dagger, clutched tightly in his hand.

Then without any kind of feeling, I wrenched it from his fingers and threw it to Abiola.

The crowd fell silent again. And there was the sound of shouting, of screaming, of commands, of car horns. Then the sound of an ambulance siren far away.

THE SECRET OF THE DAGGER

Sir Ralph Moor, formerly British High Commissioner for Southern Nigeria,
committed suicide at his London home during the night of 13–14 September
1909. He drank potassium cyanide. He was forty-nine years old. He died
thirteen years to the day from his brief but fateful meeting with James Phillips,
which prompted the ill-fated Phillips Expedition and massacre near Benin,
which led to the subsequent Punitive Expedition and the opening up for trade
of the Niger Delta. Sir Ralph Moor died almost twelve years to the day from
the exile of Oba Overami and the death of Captain Turner.
Adapted from *Cities of Blood Revisited* – Robert Home

In the hush that followed, the crowd parted around the double wooden doors to Nigeria House. The ambulance men arrived and, with one look at Merlyn, loaded him on a stretcher, covered his face with a blanket and carried him off. They picked up Lord Esterton too, but he was still squealing.

As for Denetia, well she seemed to have disappeared, along with all the rest of the More Dread Crew. Only Sir Robert Terselas stood there, too weak and ill to move, leaning his bulk up against the door jamb.

Abiola took the dagger. He turned it gently in him hand. He read the note pasted on to it, so many years ago: *Handle with Care.*

'A clue,' he said, 'even at the end, the noble Oba Overami wished everything to be understood. You see this handle was once used to conceal poison; in case the sacrificial victim should not die quickly, the poison would end his suffering.' Abiola twisted the carved ivory handle and pressed on the huge diamond. The end flipped open. 'You see,' he said, 'it opens out, and inside is a surprise.'

From inside, he drew a shred of yellowed rolled parchment. As he held it up, I thought of Mum: '*This dagger is full of surprises . . .*'

Abiola uncurled the shred of parchment. He read.

This pledge is drawn up by RALPH MOOR, spokesperson for the Niger Coast Protectorate, on behalf of Her Majesty's Government, and should stand for ever as a token of goodwill between the people of Benin and their descendents and the citizens of Great Britain. Therefore I, as your new King, pledge to restore to you OBA OVERAMI and as many of your chiefs as will serve you well and obey my leadership. I pledge to rebuild your palaces. And restore to you all your treasures in Her Majesty's name. In return you,

OBA OVERAMI must surrender entirely and accompany us with two of your chiefs to an appointed place where you will be schooled in British Ways to befit you for your position on your return.

Let God be my judge.

Signed   *R MOOR*

So that was it! That was the reason why this blunt buckled ancient dagger had caused so much trouble. The British Government had promised to rebuild all the palaces and *return all the treasures*! And it had never happened. Just like Oba Overami's return from exile had never happened! That was why the Nigerian Government had asked for the dagger back. All along they'd known that if they got the dagger back, inside it was the evidence to make a compelling case to ask for the rest! No wonder they'd said, 'No dagger – no deal!' And the British Government, *so* desperate for the oil, just *had* to have that dagger . . . and Mum, my lovely mum had taken it . . .

Abiola must have known that note was there all along, and that was why he'd been prepared to spend half a million on it. Mum must have found it and used it to threaten Sir Terselas. Sir Terselas must have kept that a secret – hoping to destroy it at some point, to protect his collection. And the Home Office must have realized how dangerously close they were to having their oil deals wrecked by a lost dagger.

I smiled. Funny, wasn't it? One hundred years later. Same stuff. Different day.

As Abiola folded the parchment back into the dagger's handle, a wail went up from Sir Terselas. He plucked with fevered fingers at his chest and shoulder and shuddered to his knees. '*No*,' he breathed. '*No, nobody knew about it . . . I just wanted to hold that dagger for one last minute . . . to remove that paper . . . the Bronzes are ours . . . are mine . . . They cannot be returned . . . My life's work . . . I was entrusted . . . I have preserved them for the world . . . without me they will be lost . . . museums recognize no arbitrary boundaries of space or time . . .*' Then he reeled forward and crashed to the tarmac.

Abiola waved the crowd back, indicated to let the ambulance crew through again.

'Although there is no hope for him,' he said quietly to me, 'for in my country just as we know that the blade will always find the true heart, so will it expose the false one. I think you will find his heart was very false, little Warrior King!'

I believed it. Just about as false as Ralph Moor's had been when he'd promised things he knew he was never going to deliver, and destroyed for ever the culture of the people of Benin. I suppose Oba Overami must have feared he'd be sent into exile for good and his treasures never returned, that was why he'd hidden the pledge in the dagger. Those gods of the Edo sure worked in mysterious ways! Still one thing was for certain, that little scrap of paper was going to be very useful to Nigeria, The B.L.A.C.K. A.R.M.Y. and the Return the Benin Bronzes to Benin Campaign!

And that was it really.

Well, mostly it.

Walter showed up of course. One minute we were back in Ancient Benin thinking about Oba Overami, and the next there he was, as promised, leaning elegantly up against his scooter. Behind him, the entire staff of Perfect Pizza Paradise. His scootercycle leathers were spotless and his crash helmet was delicately balanced on his hip. His handsome face was set like a sculpture from some ancient temple, only a tiny muscle above his left eyebrow twitched. Behind him on his scooter sat Julia.

As I called him over, she looked up. She'd been crying. I felt bad.

'So, eater of pigs, you've decided to pay up?' said Wally.

'Cat got your tongue?' I said. 'Can't think up any new insults?'

Wally dragged Julia over. Then he slapped down a key, a council tenancy agreement and a brand new rent paying-in book to the Borough Council. He smiled. Sort of. Then added a blue carbon copy of an employment agency job form to the pile, and a British National Insurance card with a number on it. 'So, Warrior King who has no kingdom and whose words are as light as the dust on a sunbeam. The half a mill for the girl.' He grabbed Julia and shoved her towards me. He pressed the paperwork into her hand. 'And listen up, PUNK, you better deliver. You better deliver here and now, or you gonna see some madness.'

'Woo, bruv,' I said, 'don't be like that – you've got to show RESPECT! Man has the money. You didn't expect it to be in Manz pocket did you?' And with every creaky cracked bone of my body, I really hoped he didn't think I'd just have the money to give him right there and then . . .

Wally's shoulders twitched just a little bit, his smooth cheeks looked a tiny bit smoother. It wasn't much to go on, but I felt he was going to be reasonable.

'Well, where is it?' he said.

'You're going to like this,' I said. 'You're going to LOVE it. Man gave its safe-keeping a whole lot of thought. Man said to Manzelf – Man did – *Where can I keep Wally's money so that it'll be really safe?* You see, bruv,

Man don't want you to think Man doesn't appreciate all the love you've shown. Long live the vegetable supreme and herb and garlic mushroom special, innit?'

Wally shook his pigtail in an unappreciative way, but before I could bluff any further Abiola helped me out. Sort of.

'Half a million for a beautiful lady is an insult,' he said. 'In my country we will give ten hectares of the most verdant farmland and a herd of twenty fat cows for such a beauty, as well as nowadays an oil field and all the petrol it can produce – once we have won our rights to it! But if Warrior King wishes for such a lady, I will gladly purchase her for him. For I owe him my country's gratitude and my heartfelt apologies for the trials and tribulations that such a champion . . .' He held out a super little black briefcase.

I nodded my head, hoping like hell Sapphire hadn't heard.

And that's when the police finally broke through the crowd and surrounded me.

Wally took the money dead quick and scarpered. Julia gave me a grateful look and whispered, 'No visa for work permit in passport yet.' She nodded meaningfully at the police van and melted back into the crowd.

I just stood there, bracing myself for the handcuffs.

A MORE SHINING WORLD

Never again will we stand
On the threshold of a new age.
We that are here now are touched
In some mysterious way
With the ability to change
And make the future.
Those who wake to the wonder
Of this magic moment
Who wake to the possibilities
Of this changed conjunction,
Are the chosen ones who have chosen
To act, to free the future, to open it up,
To consign prejudices to the past,
To open the magic casement
Of the human spirit
On to a more shining world.
'A More Shining World', *Mental Flight*, Ben Okri

You know the rest. I gave myself up. I didn't even moan.
You see I'm doing this the way Dreader and Leon want.
I'm going to try and change the world. Make it a better
place for everyone. So here's what you need to know. I

never kissed Queen Idia goodbye, but I figured she'd forgive me because she was going home. I never told on Sapphire and Roland. Even now I'm not telling. I mean, you didn't really think I'd give you real names and real addresses did you? No way. Roland and Sapphire deserve to go home, to get on with their lives now.

I heard Sapphire got an offer from her best choice sixth form centre just last week. She's only got to make five A* to C grades. She'll do it. And Roland did his A levels two years early, so he's just starting at Cambridge. As for me I'm getting my education in the University of Life – HMP Hereford, Juvenile Detention Centre & Young Offenders Training Institute. I've finished my first six months, and it looks like they'll keep a place open for me for a long time.

I still can't make out if that sniper's bullet was meant for me or Merlyn. There never was an investigation, you see. I mean, thinking cynically, the Home Office might have preferred Merlyn dead after all. You've got to admit it, he'd become a bit of a rogue element. So it's highly possible *he* might have underestimated *them*. As for Lord Esterton, he did a runner. Apparently there've been sightings in South America . . . The British Museum trustees denounced Sir Terselas and said, 'He was not acting on Museum instructions.' And those bad apples in the Home Office themselves? Well the exposure over the Benin Affair hit them pretty hard, and a few resignations were called for. Mostly it got blamed on Merlyn – and he was conveniently dead, wasn't he?

You'll be glad to hear Abiola took the Bronzes home. The Nigerian Government forgave him, even promoted him. He's the Ambassador to Egypt now. I hear he has a swimming pool at his residence. He sends me *very* long letters and has a guest room permanently ready for me – for the future.

Leon and The B.L.A.C.K. A.R.M.Y. are doing OK too. They're very hopeful about The Campaign now, although apart from those nine treasures the rest are still right where they've always been in vaults below the British Museum. But we'll see, won't we? We'll see how long they stay there after the Nigerian Government and Dreader join forces and get going.

Oh and by the way, the Oba in Benin was so pleased about the return of the treasures, he commissioned a new set of Bronzes to be modelled and cast and hung in the new palace entrance in Benin City. Guess which Warrior King's adventures they tell?

Like I always said, I'm THE MAN!

So here I am, checking through this affidavit. Roland got me an excellent barrister, Sir Conrad Beaumont QC (no less!). He's here too. He's been fixing up this statement, adding little literary touches cos he thinks of himself as A Man of The Arts and he says sometimes my wording is a bit rough. He's been adding little touches of history too, to make our point, I mean, to prove we've got a case. The only thing is, he keeps trying to make me change my plea. He says he can get me off really lightly if I plead guilty. That's why it's taken so long. But that's not what this is about, is it? I keep telling him you can't change the world that way. You can only do it when justice is *seen* to be done. Anyway after I've signed this, they'll take me back to my nice likkle correctional facility. Hopefully by next spring the case will come to trial. I don't know how it will go. I doubt there's ever been a defence like mine before. I doubt my barrister, for all his talk, will really be able to sum it up. But I'm here, so I'll have a shot at summing it up for you. Here goes:

'Ahem!

'Your honour, ladies and gentlemen, members of the jury. I'm in your hands. I don't have a defence. I did it. I rescued those treasures and I sent them back to Benin, but there is something I want you to think about.

'Can you call it a crime if I returned back what was stolen in the first place? And I'd like to point out that I never blasted anybody to death or exiled the Queen when I was doing it. (Just a point.) So I think before the Queen puts me on trial, she's got to prove those treasures were hers to begin with. U-get-me?

'Well, I know you won't go out there and make any hasty decisions. But please consider the consequences while you're making up your minds.

'*Scenario One.*

'You acquit me. I jump around. I throw my hands in the air. I do cartwheels. I thank you. I rush off and buy Sapphire a box of chocolates and go on that date. And call up my man Rollz.

'After that, I sell my story to the press (not Taliesin). The world has to know. I'd like to keep the money, but that wouldn't be right, so I'll give it all to any of Dreader's charities. But the best thing is, by making that decision, you'll have changed the world a little bit. Made it a better place. You'll have set a precedent and maybe other people can get some of their stuff back too. You'll have sent out a very clear message that the time has come for us to repair the crimes of the past. That'd be nice, wouldn't it? The streets of South London will become safer, people will be less angry and everybody will have another chance to start loving their neighbourhoods and being on good terms with the universe.

'As for me? I got a film to make. I got a career as a

street poet to start. And I got somewhere to go too.

'Don't forget I got Abiola, and Oba Opelami and a whole kingdom to enjoy!

'*Scenario Two.*

'You convict me. I don't jump up and down, I don't throw my hands in the air. I don't do cartwheels. I don't ever see Sapphire again. No cute smiles. No more hugs. No date at the Mall taking in a burger and a movie . . . Nor Roland. They can't afford to have contact with me. They need to be out there, untouched, ready for Round Two of changing the world.

'Dreader's charities won't get any money. Nobody will get a thing back.

'And as for me?

'I spend a long time behind bars until I'm old and past doing anything with my life.

'I never make that film.

'Nothing I do resonates again.

'You see, we are all in your hands. You are the jury. You have the power to change everything. The power to make the world a more shining place. You have the power to keep it the same.'

'Use it.

'You choose.'

Signed .... *Max Wolf* ....

453

WRITER'S NOTE &
A LITTLE BACKGROUND

The Warrior Kings were a race of Obas (a title for a great man, ruler and chief) of the Ancient City Kingdom of Benin in Nigeria. Legend has it that the first of these (as opposed to the last), Oba Ewuare, AD 1440, known as Ewuare the Great, had to defeat many rivals to become King, and had to entirely rebuild Benin City when he did so. During his reign, he captured two hundred towns, constructed roads and walled his kingdom. He was believed to have had great magical powers and to have slain leopards with his bare hands.

Oba Ewuare, it is said, could send a hundred thousand warriors to fight for him a day. His armies were as huge as his influence. He established an hereditary line of kings along with many royal ceremonies and traditions. Chiefly he loved the arts, and under him and the five Warrior Kings that followed him, Benin developed the most advanced culture. It became the most important kingdom in all of West Africa. It was famed for its ivory carving, wood carving and fine bronze work. And for every battle, triumph and adventure the Warrior Kings had, bronze plaques were created to be showcased on the palace walls, as an illustration, a record and an applause for their deeds.

All this, of course, came to an end when in 1897 The British Punitive Expedition sacked the city and looted its treasures.

This story seeks in some ways to continue the narrative of the Warrior Kings. It was inspired by a visit to the Africa Room of the British Museum. Whilst I stood there gazing at the ivory queen Idia, a dodgy looking man with a beard hissed the word 'spoliation' at me. He gave me a package, which was in fact nothing more than a rolled newspaper with an article about an ancient piece of wood that had been 'repatriated' to Australia or New Zealand, I think. I confess, I was confused – I didn't even know what the word 'spoliation' meant!

I soon found out, for already the beginnings of a story had started . . . a package . . . a stranger . . . spoliated items . . . the Benin Bronzes . . . a new Warrior

King . . . and how the Bronzes might find their own way to get 'repatriated' . . .

In my search for the truth about the British Punitive Expedition I turned to many sources which I would like to acknowledge: the ARM website, which celebrates the work and campaigns of the late Bernie Grant, was of great help (and the genesis for The B.L.A.C.K A.R.M.Y.); *Cities of Blood Revisited*, by Robert Home, a text I managed to bid for over the internet, became my constant companion, along with some Parliamentary Papers from 1897 entitled, *Papers relating to the Massacre of British Officials near Benin, and the consequent Punitive Expedition*. All the historical accounts that I enclosed in the chapter headings and the Chronicle of Hugh Hardy are learned from these sources, although Hugh Hardy never existed, luckily for him.

All the other characters never existed as well. If there is such a person in such a post as Custodian and Curator of the British Museum, you can be sure they are nothing like Sir Robert Terselas; nor indeed do Merlyn and Lord Esterton bear any resemblance whatsoever to any government person or official.

However some of the characters were inspired by

people I know, and for this I'd like to thank Spider, Crow, Spin and Bucky and their crew in South London who taught me how to talk the chat and walk the limp. As well as them (man dem), my gratitude goes to Minty for all her in-depth knowledge of gangs; to Sakky and Joy for their critiques; to Angela Robson for all her support; to Andy and Phyllis Sternberg for rescuing me by lending me that laptop, six hours before I was due to fly to West Africa (!); to Robert Oyedepo for his great and speedy translations to Yoruba and to my writing friends, Susie, Caroline, Ruth and Josie. Also a big thank you to my agent, Anne Dewe, and my editor, Beverley Birch, whose feedback has made this story what it is. Many thanks.

I wrote *The Last of the Warrior Kings* as a tribute to one of the greatest dynasties of West Africa, and a lament for its demise. The text contains more than just a story. Hopefully it raises a concern about the current scramble for oil in the Bight of Benin and the kind of lengths governments may go to over it. A scramble that echoes other past scrambles over Africa. It argues a case for the repatriation of the Benin Bronzes. Because (for any of you that are interested in viewing them), they are still there in the Africa Gallery of the British Museum, protected by an act of Parliament from ever seeing their homeland again. And whilst the case for their repatriation is complex, I have hoped to show that the moral rights of it are simple. So that should such a trial as Max's ever come before a High Court in London, and should you, who are reading this, ever be called upon for jury service on it, I sincerely hope after due deliberation you would be able to return a verdict of 'Not Guilty'.

Sarah Mussi
Brixton, London